LEAGUE OF ELDER

Sands of the Solar Empire

THE BELMONT SAGA

Ren Garcia

Loconeal Publishing

Amherst, OH

SANDS OF THE SOLAR EMPIRE

Copyright © 2012 by Ren Garcia
Cover Art by © 2012 by Carol Phillips
Interior Image Art by © 2012 by Carol Phillips
Interior Image Art by © 2012 by Eve Ventrue
Title Page Art by © 2012 by Fantasio
Edited by Barbara Taft Verducci

Loconeal books may be ordered through booksellers or by contacting:
www.loconeal.com
216-772-8380

Loconeal Publishing can bring authors to your live event. Contact Loconeal Publishing at 216-772-8380.

Published by Loconeal Publishing, LLC
Printed in the United States of America

First Loconeal Publishing edition: August 2012

Visit our website: www.loconeal.com

ISBN 978-0-9850817-6-8 (Trade Paperback)

Also by Ren Garcia

The League of Elder Series:
Sygillis of Metatron
The Hazards of the Old Ones

The Temple of the Exploding Head Trilogy:
The Dead Held Hands
The Machine
The Temple of the Exploding Head

The Belmont Saga:
Sands of the Solar Empire
Against the Druries (forthcoming)

For more on The League of Elder, please visit:
www.theleagueofelder.com

www.loconeal.com

TABLE OF CONTENTS

Prologue:

Part 1—The Admiral's Pleasure

Part 2—All That Resists Him

Part 3—The Demon That Came For His Soul

LIST OF ILLUSTRATIONS

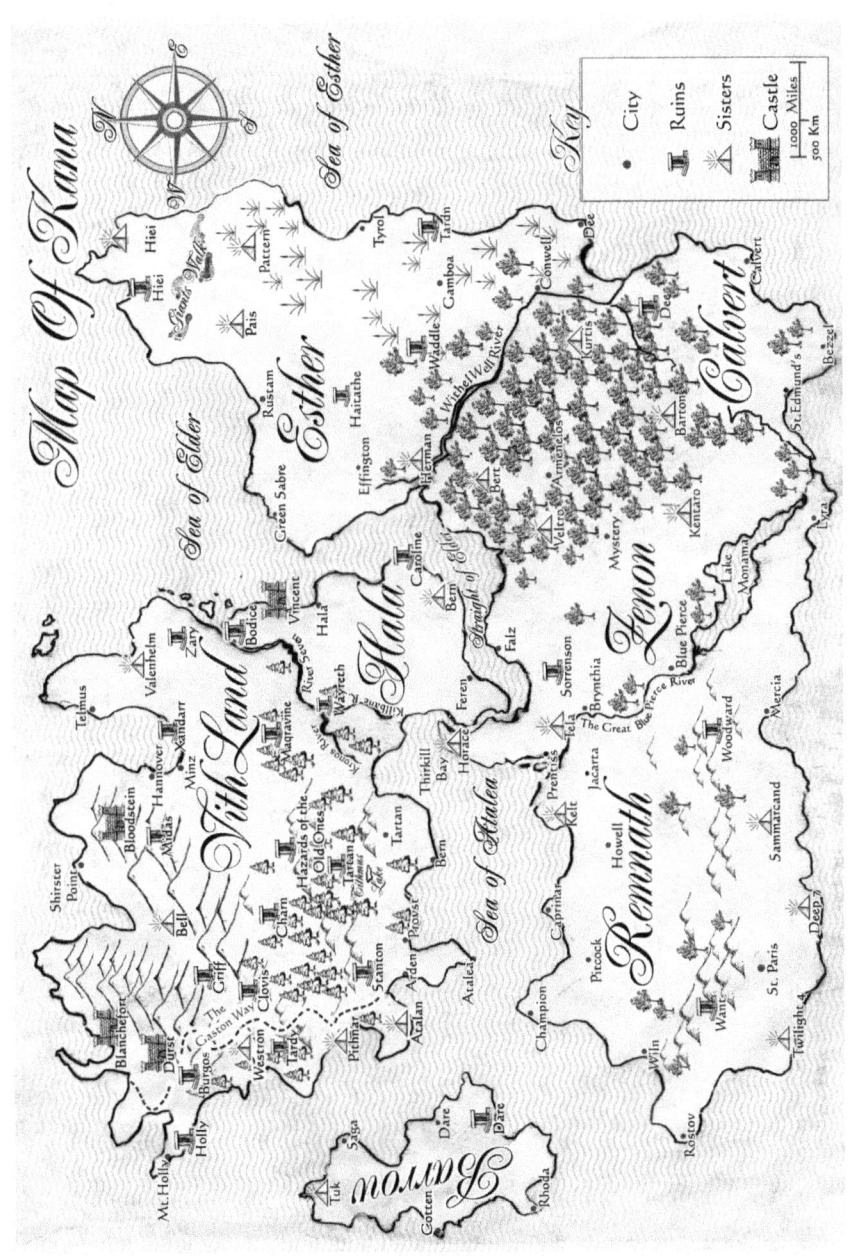

MAP OF KANA

MAP OF TYROL

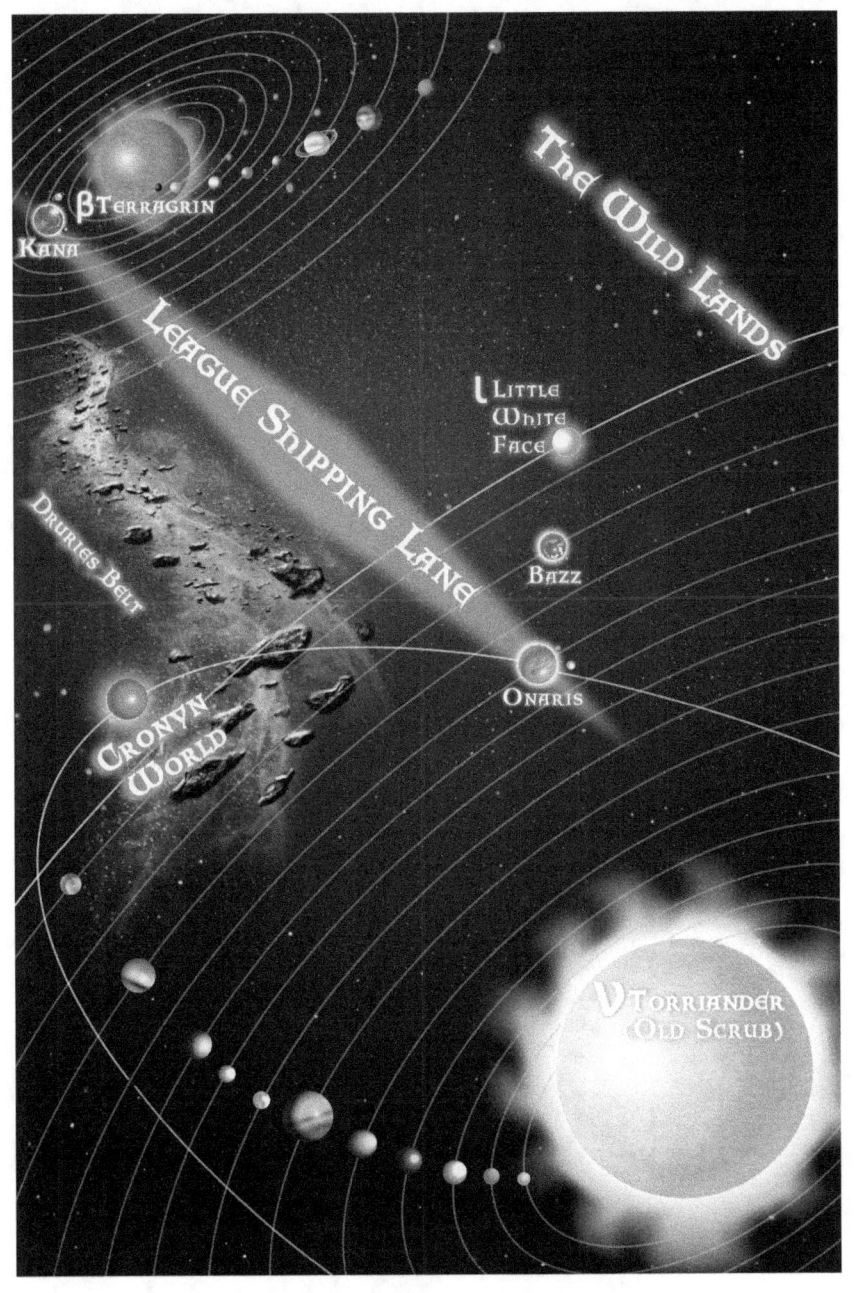

Map of Kana
and Onaris/Bazz

Prologue

I—The *Seeker*

The Admiralty of the 3rd Fleet had a rare situation on their hands—what to do with the *Seeker*.

Officially designated Main Fleet Vessel 4562, she was a forty year old *Straylight*-class warbird hailing from the old glory days of the League/Xaphan conflict, when fighting the Xaphans was honorable and romantic. The *Seeker's* current captain, Lord Gona of St. Paris, was suddenly retiring to the rolling hills of Remnath—his hastily penned resignation mentioned something about taking up wine-making at his sprawling estate—and her captain's chair, therefore, was open.

Captain Gona wasn't the only prominent officer leaving the *Seeker* in a hurry. The engineer informed the 3rd Fleet Admiralty that he too was stepping down at once. He gave them no particular reason. He quickly Appointed to another ship and was gone.

The same with the boatswain. Even the cook, a Chef Parsley, stepped aside, put his boots on the ground and opened a restaurant in Saga.

Finally, the *Seeker's* crew began filtering away, hooking onto other vessels as fast as they could get them, like rats scurrying away from a burning building.

Such a mass exodus from a once-great ship never looked good out in the public. Officers, cooks, and crew normally didn't flee from a prominent warbird like the *Seeker*, a veteran of Mirendra, a veteran of Two-Pitch Nebula—there must be some scandalous reason as to why, and the Admiralty, knowing how the gossip-mill could easily begin to turn, kept the matter quiet.

Very quickly, the *Seeker* was an abandoned hulk, running lonely in the low polar orbit assigned to her.

Lord Milos of Probert, the Fleet's chief engineer, was flown aboard the ship to give her a good sounding; perhaps the reason why everybody wanted to leave would make itself plainly known in short order. Perhaps there was some insidious gas present aboard the ship addling the crew's wits, or some undetected radiation causing the problem. Certainly Probert would get to the bottom of it.

He assessed the status and condition of the *Seeker* with his usual terse and blunt authority.

Significant wear metal fatigue in J's 27 through 45—the "neck" of the ship. Most, if not all, of the structural components, including custom-crafted parts and linkages, shall need replacing in dry dock. Cause: age of the ship.

Stellar mach coils 1, 2, 3, 4, 5, 6 and 7 are tach'ed out and require replacing, as standard Fleet maintenance procedures demand. As before, additional time in dry dock shall be required to perform the engine refit.

Battle Shot batteries 2 through 14, starboard-side and 10 through 17, port side, badly overdue for replacement, both through wear of use and a lack of suitable ordinance to arm them. As the Seeker does not have the capacity for a thermoplant powerful enough to make use of modern Sar-Beam weaponry, the batteries will need to be replaced and refitted by hand with a team of master armorers custom assembling each unit. Assessment: Possible, but ruinously expensive.

Probert discovered no odd gases or radiations aboard the *Seeker*, just an old, lonely ship whose grocery list of urgent needs was long and costly.

A final note on Lord Probert's report was interesting, though rather out-of-character for the renowned Fleet engineer who normally stuck to cold, stark facts and calculated data. He said the *Seeker* had a strange "feel" to it as he prowled the decks, and it wasn't due to gas or radiation.

Ship's haunted, he said in so many words. In interviewing Captain Gona, the engineer, the boatswain and the cook, the Admiralty got a similar story— the ship was beset by moaning demons and bad dreams. And all of them agreed they would never set foot aboard again.

So, there the Admirals were with a decrepit forty year old warbird that needed a large amount of expensive refitting to keep space-worthy, and, apparently, required an exorcism as well—just think of the scandal *that* would make.

Scuttle her, melt the *Seeker* down, and recast her as something useful; that seemed the clear course of action. However, this created a problem for the Admiralty because the *Seeker* was a fairly well-known and well-thought-of ship. Though having fallen into obscurity as of late, she had fought a great deal of battles with the Xaphans over the years and come through unvanquished, with the famed Captain Davage in command and his fighting countess, Sygillis of Blanchefort, sitting at his side. Also, the Sisterhood of Light, a highly influential sect the Fleet was always attempting to please, was very fond of the *Seeker* due to their past association with it.

"How is the *Seeker*," the Sisterhood often asked when they visited the Fleet. It was, quite probably, the only ship in the active Fleet they knew by name, and it was those casual but frequent inquires that help put a shield over the old ship that no other vessel could enjoy.

The Admiralty couldn't simply scuttle the *Seeker* and end her life—they would never hear the end of it: from the Fleet Captaincy, from the Sisters and from others as well. If things got too unpleasant, the Admiralty could simply retire the *Seeker*, and berth her in a lavish park somewhere—the only issue being that such a distinction was normally reserved for ships scuttled as a result of war. In this case, there wasn't anything wrong with the *Seeker* that a little time and love—and vast sums of money—wouldn't fix. The "haunted" aspect was clearly rubbish.

So, what to do with the *Seeker?*

In a virtual no-win situation, the Admiralty decided to raise the captain's chair of the *Seeker* to an open debate one last time, Free Boot style as sometimes was done; in doing so, they could have time to grease up the Sisterhood and any others who had a fondness for the *Seeker*—let them know, at a measured pace, that the famed ship was getting too old and dangerous to keep in service.

That way, she could slowly fade away, and those who loved her could accept it as what must be. The great days of the *Seeker* were clearly well behind her.

So, using the vague and contentious Free Boot system, the *Seeker's* chair was put up on the blocks. Anybody wanting the chair could simply present themselves and prove their merits. That person had to have a good sponsor, connections, a grand House behind them and, best of all, the willing coin to repair her. The pickings, however, might prove to be slim. Most of the young hopefuls coming up through the ranks of the Fleet and League Society wanted the captain's chair of newer ships, either right off the blocks awaiting a christening, or fairly new, just needing a coat of paint.

The Admiralty knew that few would want a once great warbird with only a few years of service left that needed an expensive dry docking and was rumored to be haunted.

So, who was it to be? Who would come and save the *Seeker,* with all the aches and pains and ghosts that come with her?

II—The Appointment

The day of days had arrived. Paymaster Stenstrom, Lord of Belmont-South Tyrol, was to face Appointment as captain of the old Main Fleet Vessel, *Seeker*.

He sat in a small holding room at the Main Fleet complex in Armenelos. The room smelled of fine food; a lavish breakfast had been brought in earlier by the Fleet orderlies.

A big breakfast served to an appointment candidate was tradition, for once he or she stepped out onto the red velvet and pooled light of the Admiralty floor, one could expect to be there all day and not have the opportunity to eat again until late evening. A hearty breakfast was meant to sustain the candidate for that prolonged period of time. Stenstrom, so far, had only picked at the plate of eggs and bacon, hashed potatoes, airy pancakes and ham set before him. He'd spread a bit of marmalade on a slice of toasted bread and ate it, but that was all so far.

Stenstrom wasn't alone in the holding room; he had esteemed company. Captain Davage, the Lord of Blanchefort, was his sponsor for this Appointment and was to offer the opening remarks on the floor. Davage was the *Seeker's* original and most famous captain, a fighting captain from the north and the scourge of the Xaphan hoards. He sat at the table regal in his Fleet uniform, blue-haired with his longish locks tied back in a tail, Vith-style. His glinting CARG sat saddled at his waist.

Stenstrom paced the room like a beast.

"One thing you need to know, Bel, is that the Admiralty floor is rung out. I'm certain you share telepathy with select people—I do. I share a deep telepathy with my countess, sometimes with my first officer, but that's all, for I've always believed that one's mind should be private. I don't even share telepathy with my children; however, the Admiralty floor is designed to pierce your mind. You shall hear many voices in your head. Sometimes it can be difficult to know when one is speaking, or simply thinking, so be ready for that. It can be overwhelming. Keep your stray thoughts in a bag, as they say, for the Admirals shall hear them."

Davage took a drink of his coffee. "You need to sit down and eat your breakfast. You've a long day ahead of you." Davage's easy manner and soothing voice helped calm Stenstrom. He was a good friend.

"I know, Dav," Stenstrom replied. "I'm simply ready to get out there and begin. I've been waiting for this day for a long time."

Davage smiled. "Do the thing with your hands, again. Come on, let's see it."

Stenstrom laughed and raised his hands, showing them, palms forward, to Davage. "Are you ready?"

Davage nodded.

In a quick movement, Stenstrom waved his hands. Where a moment earlier they were empty, now there were several brightly colored balls held between his fingers. He waved his hands again, and the balls vanished, replaced by a small golden locket. Davage clapped. "By Creation, how do you do that, Bel?"

Stenstrom chuckled. "Just one of the many skills my mother taught me. I'm certain you could Sight me and find out for yourself how I do it."

"I could, I could," Davage said. "But that would kill the fun, I think, ruin the mystery. I suppose I really don't want to know."

Stenstrom opened the locket he'd produced out of thin air and gazed at the picture within. He set it down on the table next to his plate and began eating.

Davage took another sip of coffee. "What do you have there, Bel? he asked.

Stenstrom blushed. "Oh, it's a picture of Lilly, a Lady of Gamboa."

Davage leaned forward. "May I?"

Stenstrom slid the locket to him and Davage took a look. "My, what a very beautiful young lady—most striking. Is she your betrothed?"

"Yes and no. She's a good friend, I suppose. She painted this portrait herself—she's a fine artist. I think painted pictures have more life for me than a holo or vid. She painted this picture just for me—there's a bit of her soul in it, I think."

Davage smiled. "A sentiment I share, though I have no hand-painted lockets of my countess—Syg can't paint. So, she's just a good friend then, this Lilly of Gamboa?"

Stenstrom began eating his eggs. "We fell in love several years ago; it was my mother's doing. She arranged for us to meet, and, oddly enough, it worked out, though I usually resisted my mother's attempts to pair me up with somebody. I asked for her hand, but, she, being a heady lady, didn't offer hers in return. Instead, she offered a compromise. She noted how young we both are, how we have seen little of the League around us. She offered five years—five years for both of us to explore and see what's out there, free of strings or entanglements. If, at the end of five years, we still love each other, then we will present ourselves to the League and be wed."

"I see," Davage said. "What a wise lady she is. And what are your thoughts?"

"We've a year to go. I've been around, obviously. I went to school in Bern and became a Paymaster, sailing the heavens, mostly with you, but I've not yet met her equal, and I doubt I will. I'm ready for Lilly. I wish she were here with me, this very day."

"And how does she feel?"

Stenstrom thought a moment. "I really don't know, I've not heard from her in some time; my letters go unanswered, my coms and vids unopened. Perhaps she's moved on, though I continue to have hope." He noted his attire. "Lilly helped me pick out my 'fighting' uniform here: my shirt, boots, pants, and this coat that I love so much."

Davage finished his coffee. "Yes, that coat…" he said, eyeing it hanging over the chair. "If I may offer a bit of sound advice, I would use the time given to you as best you can. You have five years—use it, let your heart soar. The last thing you will want is to look back some day and say 'I had five years, and I wasted it.' That will simply lead to regret."

An old fashioned clock hanging near the door chimed.

Davage stood and approached the seated Stenstrom. "Ah, it's almost time. You finish your breakfast and listen carefully to what I have to say. Despite what you might soon be hearing upon the floor, this Appointment is decided. It's done. You, Bel, shall be the next bonded captain of the *Seeker*. This debate is simply a reason for the Admirals to put on their uniforms and their hose and throw their weight around. An Appointment, especially an Appointment to the Captain's seat of a Main Fleet Vessel, is something they live for. An Appointment to a boatswain's chair or an engineer's chair is one thing—those are skilled, highly technical positions requiring a great deal of documentable craft and experience, and involves material that the Admirals have little or no knowledge of. Those are fairly cut and dry. A Free Boot Captain's chair, well now, that's an entirely different beast. *Anybody* can debate to a Captain's chair in such a situation, and, therefore, the Admirals are given leave to pick apart a candidate and discard them as they wish. However, despite their bluster, there are certain guidelines which they follow to a point, and, if you meet those guidelines, they are going to Appoint you, no matter how ugly the proceedings get. I know their guidelines, and you meet them all."

Stenstrom swallowed his eggs. "What are they?"

"Oh, the usual Society nonsense mostly. See, in theory, any man or woman may present themselves as a candidate to a Free Boot Captain's chair. In reality, only a select few may be successfully Appointed. First, a candidate needs a suitable sponsor. I am your sponsor, and proudly so, so that's that. Next, they look at your pedigree—who are you, where you come from— that's important to them. If you come from some seedy Calvert line, or worse, then that's a big black mark. Fear not; your pedigree is firm. You are the next Lord of Belmont-South Tyrol, a fine-standing Zenon House, and the Admiralty simply loves Zenons—loves them. Secondly, your mother, Lady Jubilee, is of the House of Tyrol, a wondrous Esther line."

Stenstrom stopped eating. "Dav, the Sisters had secretly investigated my mother and her House of Tyrol on suspicion of sorcery, black magic and demon-summoning several times in the recent past prior to her death. And, she was under Wirguild for nearly ninety years prior to that."

"Yes, Elders, rest her soul. Well, the Sisters, as far as I'm aware, did not issue any public edicts, condemnations, or statements on that matter regarding your mother; therefore, I wouldn't give tongue to it on the debating floor if I were you. So, as I said, your pedigree is confirmed. Again, anything other than Calvert and the like and you're fine. Next, the Admirals look at familiar standing."

"And that is?"

"If the Admirals are to be given any credit, they do give hard work, accomplishment and seniority its proper due. Fleet crewmen who work their way up the chain are often rewarded—look at me. I started as a junior helmsman of a barely space-worthy *Webber*-ship, and look where I ended up. The Admiralty appreciates such things. Now, you do not have any direct familiar standing; however, you have an abundance of indirect. Your father, Lord Stenstrom the Older, has been the captain of the *Caroline* for nineteen appointments—he's a beloved Fleet captain, any Admiral would say so, and, you, as his son, inherit a good deal of that positive will automatically. That alone is enough to check off on the Admiral's familiar standing point."

"I wish my father could be here today."

"No family members allowed, unfortunately."

"What about my service as a Fleet Paymaster?"

"That, Bel, is a negative. Don't get me wrong. A Paymaster is a well-regarded occupation. However, I can't think of any Paymasters currently in command of a Fleet vessel, warbird or otherwise. Paymasters generally aren't associated with the command chair. They are thought of as little men, sitting in a stuffy office somewhere, counting beans, observing transactions, and cutting checks. And, to that point, the Admiralty is going to want to know why you became a Fleet Paymaster and not an active crewman or officer."

Stenstrom put his fork down and smiled. "Shall I tell them why, Dav?"

"The truth, absolutely not! The truth, if I recall correctly, involves some sort of black magic ritual, robed, oiled females, and a heated knife plunged in your heart under a blood moon. That does not need to be spoken of on the debating floor. For the love of the Elders, think up a tawdry, mundane lie and stick to it. Don't dwell on it in your thoughts either, for the Admirals shall hear them on the floor. Make your lie and your thoughts as boring as possible so that the point will be forgotten and moved on from for lack of interest. So, discounting the Paymaster connection, your father's status shall grant you more than enough familiar standing to make the Admiral's list. There's one final category that the Admirals look at with high regard."

"And that is?"

"Money, Bel. The Admirals always cater to Lords and Ladies who can offer up a brick of pledged cash."

"I've got one hundred thousand Belmont sesterces to offer up, and quite a bit more in reserve."

"Yes," Davage replied. "Enough said."

The clock began chiming steadily. Davage looked up. "It's near time. Come, let's get you ready."

Stenstrom stood up from the table and wiped his lips. Davage approached and looked him over. "Let me straighten your shirt." He busily began fussing with his frilly white shirt and complicated buttons.

"Now, there are a few more things before we head out. As captain of a Main Fleet Vessel, you're going to have to keep a few rules in mind. I'll tell you what they are, and they might sound a bit contradictory, but hear me out. One, a warbird captain, as you are about to become, *never* takes an order from an admiral who is not within one hundred thousand stellar miles of his position."

"Never?"

"Never. One of the reasons the Fleet has been so successful over the years is because we follow the principles given to us by the Elders. And the Elders never said anything about taking orders from a far-flung Admiral on the other side of League space who has no idea what your situation is. There are a handful of fighting Admirals out there, Admiral Carfax coming closest to my mind, and in war-situations you have to listen to them. However, discounting those select situations, it's the captain, sitting there in the heat of battle that makes the decisions and calls the shots. Waiting for an Admiral to make a decision for you will get you and your crew killed. You know the man who replaced me on the *Seeker's* chair?"

"Captain Gona of St. Paris?"

"Yes, Captain Gona. He's gone off, retiring. He's going to ferment grapes and make wine at his Remnath home I hear tell, hence the *Seeker's* empty chair. Good for him. I am certain there are plenty of people who love Captain Gona; unfortunately, none of them may be counted as Fleet captains."

"Why?"

"Because he was considered a bore, an Admiral's man. He listened to the Admirals, took their advice, and played taxi to them. He ferried them around the League and sat at their beck and call."

"Is that bad?"

Davage picked up Stenstrom's pistols, two old-fashioned lock-style pistols with well-worn wooden stocks and handed them to him. Stenstrom slid them into either side of his green sash, the stocks jutting out.

"It's terrible," Davage said continuing. "Captain Gona took a proud warbird like the *Seeker*, my *Seeker*, and turned her into a lowly carrier pigeon, hauling freight and serving as Admiral Pax's personal chariot. As captain, you're going to be seeing a lot of tags and callouts for Admirals wanting this and Admirals wanting that—do not fall for any of it. Admiral Pax is notorious for doing so. He'll send a blunt call out: 'I want the *Seeker* to pick me up and take me to Planet X over here.' He'll make it sound quite important. He'll even issue threats and posts warnings on what would happen should the *Seeker* not show up. You must take steps to ignore his bravado. There are two questions you have to ask yourself when considering ferrying an Admiral: One—does the Admiral have a sufficient amount of breathable air available to him? Two—does the Admiral have a quantity of untainted food and potable water to sustain him? If the answer to both of those questions is 'Yes,' then let the Admiral sit on his doffed-out ass and await the arrival of a scout ship as he is supposed to. Scout ships have to follow the Admiral's orders; you do not. You've got a Main Fleet warbird, and you're sitting on it. That makes you immune to an Admiral's orders unless he's within one hundred thousand stellar miles of your position, and do not forget that; therefore, it is often wise to know an Admiral's itinerary when he's out in the League and avoid those places where he'll be at all costs. If you let the Admiralty in, if you play nurse-maid to them too often, you are done as a warbird captain. You will belong to them. You have to stand up and be blunt and rather merciless in your rebuff."

Stenstrom laughed. "I see. I'll remember that. What's the second rule?"

Davage picked up Stenstrom's heavy green coat. "When in the Fleet HQ, you have to respect the Admiralty. You have to bite your tongue, play their game, and abide by their rules. Here we are in the Fleet—here we have to play nice. I sound pretty rotten towards the Admirals, and, given some of the things they do, they deserve it, but truth be told, they've got a hard job. For many, they are the face of the Fleet to the League. They have to maintain relations, secure monies, which is an endless task, maintain the ships, and find the best people to fill the chairs when they come open. Here, you have to give them their due." Davage looked at Stenstrom's coat. "This coat you wear is not playing nice. The Admirals will pick up on it and give you no peace."

Stenstrom put his coat on. It was a beautiful coat: dark hunter green, silver and gold embroidery, and the letters HRN standing out in silver on the collar. Stenstrom took his locket and placed it in a pocket inside the coat's breast. "Lilly picked this coat out for me. We were in Minz when she found it. I like it," he said. "It makes me feel close to her."

"I advise you wear something else. Something … less inflammatory."

"As you said, I have to stand up to the Admirals. I shall do so with my coat. It's just a coat." He put on his huge triangle hat and adjusted it.

"Yes, just a coat. And it'll be just a piece of rotten fruit that comes raining down on you and your HRN coat. The Admirals pay for the right to throw things down onto the debating floor. It's a traditional way of making a fervent point—this coat will give them their monies' worth, I fear."

Davage then took the black, silk mask Stenstrom was wearing and straightened it. Stenstrom's blue eyes sparkled through the holes. Davage shook his head. "You know, the first time I saw you wearing a mask, I honestly didn't know what to think. I recall having you clapped in irons and I thought 'Who in Creation is this fellow?'"

"Just something I have to endure. I promised my mother I'd never endanger myself—she tended to be a worry-wart. This mask protects me from all things she conjured at me before she died. Elders, rest her soul."

"She sent demons at you with the thought of keeping you safe?"

"Yes."

"And you're certain you cannot take it off, if only for a few hours?"

"If I do, the Admirals shall get to watch me die upon their floor. Remove my mask and the charms within, and I die."

Davage clapped him on the shoulder. "So be it. Just be ready to be rather inconvenienced this afternoon."

The clock stopped, and the door opened. An adjutant stood in the doorway. "Sirs, the gallery is assembled. The Admiralty awaits."

Davage turned to the adjutant. "Thank you, we're coming."

Side by side, they left the room and began the short walk to the Admiralty floor. Stenstrom, fully decked out, could see the red carpeting and pools of circular light ahead. He could see the elevated gallery, dark, full of indistinct movement.

"Oh, Lt. Kilos wanted me to relay you a message, Bel," Davage said. "I believe she said she wants you to: 'Knock 'em dead'. She also wanted me to give you a little love tap across the jaw for her, but I think we can dispense with that for now. She, like Syg and me, is very proud of you."

Stenstrom laughed.

Davage spoke again as they walked. "You know, Bel, the *Seeker's* over forty years old—that's pretty veteran for a Main Fleet Vessel that's seen a lot of action—most warbirds cycle into the smelter long before that, and, I must say, I put her through my fair share of hell. But, no matter what, she always came through, always found the strength to get me, and Syg, and my crew home. Lord Milos of Probert, the designer of the *Seeker* and a good friend of mine, has always scoffed at the notion that these huge birds, these great ships he designed, have a soul, that we in the Fleet Captaincy are too sentimental assigning a great machine with feelings and a soul. Lord Probert is wrong, Bel; the *Seeker* has a soul and a heart to match. Captain Gona took away much of the honor she'd acquired, took away part of her soul. Give it back to her, Bel—she deserves it. Make her into a great warbird again, and she'll never let you down."

*   *   *   *   *

As Davage had predicted, the Admiralty floor rang out with thought. Voices filled Stenstrom's head, turning the whole place into a surreal, noisy dream.

I'm hungry.

Did you see that beautiful woman in the lobby?

Do my leggings make me look fat?

Who's this fellow we're looking at today?

Down on the red carpet in a pool of sterile light, he sat in the ornate chair as the Appointment began. Lord Davage stood and made his opening remarks.

That's Captain Davage down there. Oh, look at him …

Did he say Paymaster, the Appointee is a Paymaster?

He's a Paymaster…

Paymaster?

Who's his mother, again?

Oh, he's a handsome fellow, do you see?

What's he wearing? Is that a mask, or a trick of the light?

Stenstrom watched Davage as he easily commanded the floor. His lovely

Fleet uniform, his collar speckled with gold stars and ivy, his blue Vith hair tied in a bow as they did it in the north, his heavy CARG at his side. Stenstrom didn't have the Sight like Davage did. Under the lights high overhead, he couldn't see much in the crowd. He just knew there were a lot of people up there, rustling around, raining their thoughts down on him.

Lord Davage disarmed the Admirals to a large extent. He spoke rather eloquently, describing Lord Stenstrom's upbringing and pedigree in the House of Belmont-South Tyrol, his mother's status as a lady of Tyrol, and, most importantly, his father's legendary status as captain of the *Caroline*, for over nineteen appointments. That was a bedrock list of endorsements.

I played golf with Captain Stenstrom last week. ...or did I? Who was that?

Are Tyrols of Esther or Barrow stock?

He's wearing mask, look there... I'm going to pay for a bushel of fruit. I'm going to hit him in the face. Miss, Miss—two bushels here, cabbage if possible. Ah!

The Admirals muttered to themselves—very impressive. Lord Davage spoke well, as always, and brought up a number of excellent points.

And then there was money, which always impressed the Admiralty. Lords and Ladies with ready cash were always looked upon with regard. The Fleet, mighty and graceful, was fueled primarily by privately donated monies. New ships, new research, new appointments, were all paid for privately, and the lord or lady who could offer up a healthy sum was always a welcome sight. Again, the Admiralty was impressed and de-fanged.

He's got how much??

Belmont sesterces? How do those exchange into Grenville solaris? Wow!

We can renovate the eastern Fleet wing with that.

With Davage having thoroughly greased the Admirals, the remaining part of the Appointment should be a breeze, what with pedigree, familial connections, a stately mother, a legendary father and tons of ready cash, Lord Stenstrom should be an easy shoe-in.

But then, Lord Davage had to sit down, and Lord Stenstrom himself stood and took the floor to be interviewed. That's when the fireworks began.

Lord Stenstrom was a commandingly tall figure. He towered over the tall Lord Blanchefort. He certainly looked the part.

Look how tall.

He's a bean pole.

Is that a uniform he's wearing? Paymasters aren't supposed to wear uniforms.

From somewhere in the gallery, an Admiral spoke, or did he?

"Lord Belmont," came the voice. "How long have you been a Fleet Paymaster?"

Stenstrom cleared his throat. "Three years, good sir. I was trained in Bern."

"And where did you receive your tenure for admission into the IBBAANA Brotherhood?"

Stenstrom considered his response. "Calvert."

"Calvert, I see. And, aboard what ships did you serve?"

"The *Sandwich*, sir, a frigate, followed by the *New Faith*."

The gallery rustled.

"And, you have not been involved, as a crewman or an officer, in either the Stellar Fleet or Marines?"

"No, great sir."

But, he's wearing a uniform.

It's a lovely uniform.

"Lord Belmont," the Admiral continued, "you stand before us wishing to assume the captain's chair of a Main Fleet Vessel, a warbird, yet you have created a career for yourself as a Paymaster. We wish to know why this is the case."

Tell a tawdry lie, Davage had said. Stenstrom thought a bit of truth would be better.

"My late mother, fearing for my father's safety through his years of service in the Fleet, wished me to practice a more sedate career. I became a Paymaster. I honored her request."

"Your mother?"

"Yes sir. One should honor their mother."

The thoughts rolled in.

I hate my mother.

Perhaps he's a grand Nancy-Boy.

Oh stop it—he appears to be a good boy.

"A fine sentiment. And, of course, Paymasters are an honored addition to our spaceward ships. But, what good can cash-shucking, and coin rumbling do you in asserting your merits as a ship's captain?"

"I commanded the *New Faith* for a time during the Kestral Affair, with glowing after commentary from Captain Davage."

Stenstrom stepped forward—the HRN on his collar glinted in the light.

Hold up—what is that?

HRN??

What is 'that' doing on the Admiralty floor?

The gallery was beginning to froth. "Good Lord Belmont, what, pray, are you wearing?"

"Pardon?"

"Your coat? Where did you get that coat?"

Stenstrom looked at his sleeves. "I purchased it on the open market. I fail to see what relevance my coat his in this matter."

"That coat, sir, is the costume of the Hoban Royal Navy. Perhaps you've heard of them."

Miss, I'll have a bushel here. Fruit, make it rotten!

He's wearing a Hoban Royal Navy coat?

Fruit! Give me fruit to throw!!

Stenstrom was starting to feel he should have listened to Davage. "I have heard of them, after a fashion. I am not overly versed in their exploits. I simply liked the coat, so I bought it."

The Admiral spoke again. "Allow me to fill you in, sir. The Hoban Royal Navy was a far-flung assemblage of drunken yachtsmen who thought to take it upon themselves to post the defense of Hoban, in hopes of polishing their prestige and supplanting the Fleet in the region. That coat you're wearing is one of many such costumes they chose to wear. A question, sir, know you the rank of the coat you're wearing?"

"I'm afraid I do not. Again, I am not well-versed in the organization."

"Grand Plantain, sir. You are wearing the coat of a Grand Plantain—the ranks of the Hoban Royal Navy were designated in fruits. Yet another 'good idea' those fellows had."

Grand Plantain?

He's a big banana, haha!

Look at the banana!

I am going to cast a fruit at him, to make him feel at home. Ya!

An apple came down from the gallery and landed nearby.

Stenstrom found himself becoming rather annoyed. His tongue began to wag. "Your pardon, Admirals, a plantain is most decidedly *not* a banana."

So, he's a chef as well as a lily-livered accountant, is he?

Here, Paymaster, file this rotten orange in an appropriate place!

A smelly orange came down and whizzed over Stenstrom's head. Captain Davage sat there quietly and drank a coffee, nonplussed.

"Your late mother, Lady Jubilee, may her soul rest at peace, was a lady of Tyrol—that has been previously established," the Admiral said.

"Yes, and what of it?"

"House Tyrol has established roots and ties with the House of Croatoa. House Croatoa is prominent with the current governing body of Hoban. It is that body that formulated the Hoban Royal Navy and unleashed it upon space."

"Irrelevant, sir. Again, neither I, nor my departed mother, have ties to the Hoban Royal Navy—I simply liked the coat."

The Admiral who had been speaking continued. "Regardless, sir, you come before us, a green-fisted clerk wearing the trappings of a clown, and, I must know, for I can bear it no longer, why in Creation are you wearing a mask?"

The rest of the gallery began barking.

"Are you scarred?"

"Are you monstrous?"

"Remove your mask, banana-boy!"

"Give us your coat, so we may burn it!"

"I'll wager you are hideous!"

"How may we take you seriously, sir?" an Admiral from the gallery spoke. "Attired in a fool's coat, and that stupendous mask? Why wear you such a thing?"

By this point in the interrogation, Stenstrom was feeling good and salty. "Because I choose to. Because a great personal hero of mine, Lord Terrance of Walther, wore a mask."

"Lord Terrance of Walther was mad, a vigilant and censured by the Sisterhood for his bravado. You choose such a man as your inspiration?"

"I do. The Sisters were incorrect in their assessment. What tea-drinking female or insipid bed-wetter serves as your inspiration, sir?"

"Hooah!" the Admirals cried in reproach. "Hooah!"

The proceedings had degenerated into a name-calling and humiliation fest—not an uncommon thing during a contentious appointment.

Stenstrom removed his hat and pulled his mask off. There he was, a handsome, blue-eyed, black-haired Lord of Belmont. Mixed into his hair were slight wisps of silver—a gift from his mother's Tyrol stock.

He began to feel the familiar tug on his soul and quickly put the mask back on. He was enraged. "Standing here, I feel myself as a twelve-point buck upon the path!" he shouted into the crowd.

"Were you a twelve-point buck, at least you would have some use!" an Admiral yelled back.

Another outraged Admiral spoke up. "The Lord Belmont must think us sorry or half-witted to ever contemplate him sitting upon the *Seeker's* chair."

"Do not speak of me as if I am dead, sir!" he replied. "I am not dead—I stand before you. I am alive, sir. I'm alive!"

The gallery again stirred. "That... has yet to be determined. You have no experience, and apparently no sense."

"Again, I commanded the *New Faith* during the Kestral Affair and am proud to say I did well."

"You used your Hoban Royal Navy coat to keep the Captain's seat warm, whilst he defended his ship from a cowardly, implacable enemy!"

"Ah," Stenstrom cried. "Cowardly... a true buzz-word here in the Admiralty."

Oh dear ... Davage sat there and shook his head.

Get me a bushel!

Somebody threw a head of cabbage down and got Stenstrom in the shoulder.

Huzzah—right in the face! A fine cabbage cast!

Stenstrom picked it up and started to throw it back into the gallery. A small adjutant ran up to him and held out a collection basket.

Stenstrom got out his money purse and put the whole thing into the collection basket.

He's throwing!

Stenstrom threw the cabbage back into the gallery. Soon the adjutant returned with a basket full of vegetables. Grabbing two hand's worth, Stenstrom started throwing in earnest.

I'm hit! Ah me, I'm hit!

By thunder, he'll be a pair of tongs short of a salad when I'm finished with him.

Gah!—I just hit Admiral Veng in the back of the head. Apologies, Admiral!

The gallery howled and returned the favor.

          ✹   ✹   ✹   ✹   ✹

Lord Davage sat there and sighed. What was the point of all of this—the appointment was decided and this sorry carnival was simply a side-oddity.

A lemon came down; he ducked.

Davage stood, kicking his chair away with force where it toppled over. "ENOUGH!" he shouted, his Vith voice filling the gallery. The cascade of fruits and vegetables from the stands stopped. Stenstrom stood there with two fistfuls of cabbage, ready to let them loose. "What, may I ask, is the point of all of this? You know, as well as I, that this Appointment is decided. You, Admirals, have opened the *Seeker's* chair Free boot style and have invited an open appointment. Lord Belmont, despite his Hoban Royal Navy coat, is well-suited to take the chair, and he meets all of your criteria. Additionally I am personally vouching for his skill and his pending success. I gave him my ship in a time of great need, and I felt perfectly at ease doing so. You have no other willing to take the time and spend the coin to sit upon the *Seeker's* chair. Let us see reason here and set to the hard work ahead."

There was a bit of muttering, but the food-throwing stopped, and the rest of the Appointment passed with much less drama.

Let him have the chair, and pay his coin. See if he keeps it.

We can make things rather difficult for him ...

Welcome to the Fleet ... Captain Stenstrom ... for as long as that lasts.

Several hours later, Stenstrom sent a Com home to his father. He'd been Appointed as captain of the *Seeker*.

III—An Open Letter from the Fiend of Calvert to the Mad Lord of Walther

Published February 32, 003119ax—Synthnet (St. Edmunds)

I am he who was known as the Fiend of Calvert. I trawled the streets and wharfs there, shutting the eyes of drunks and fallen men. As rats are occasionally cleaned from the sewers and other places of refuse, I cleaned the Calvert streets of Elder scum.

I should be praised. I should be given a key to the city.

Instead, I was grievously wounded by the coward who calls himself the Mad Lord of Walther. He fell upon me from behind, applied a harassing wound, and then chased me cross the rooftops, laughing throughout the entire ordeal. Though pained, I managed to escape and had to spend a significant amount of time convalescing after the injury he so cowardly inflicted upon me.

Meanwhile, the filth in Calvert festers and grows afresh. Without the cat to keep the mice thinned, they overrun.

I have read your memoirs, Mad Lord. A fanciful bit of fiction, I must say. You claim that I am a lady, that you saw me as a woman in gray. I can assure you, sir, I am no woman. Would a woman be capable of doing what I have done?

If you would care to prove that YOU are no woman, sir, I challenge you to meet me in Calvert, and we may settle our dispute once and for all. Fail to meet me, and I might choose to call on Calvert afresh and resume my art at long last, as there are many throats there needing cutting.

This time you shall not catch me unawares.

Signed

??????????, the Fiend of Calvert

IV—Twins

The heart of the League consists mostly of two planets: Kana and Onaris. There are many more League worlds that have been added over the years, but Kana and Onaris are the principles, the bastions of the League—like two great rocks facing each other on a vast beach. Other rocks might someday be washed up or eroded into view, but these two were the originals, and all others came later.

They are, in the cosmic scheme of things, neighbors in space—twins almost. To a fast Fleet ship, traveling the distance from Kana to Onaris can, depending on the time of the year, take less than a day, perhaps a little more if the ship is in no hurry. Slower ships, like Fleet merchant-men, frigates, and private vessels might make the trip in two days, perhaps three if they were particularly slow.

Moving through the patrolled lanes between the two planets is like nothing—hardly a thought went into it. It was a boring trip, a maudlin one at that. Modern vessels, even the unsightly rusty ones, could move at colossal speed, luxurious in safety and all the comforts of home.

Kana and Onaris: two great rocks facing each other on a celestial beach, awash in the surf and bound together by cosmic sand.

Consider this: take away those modern ships, take away that speed and technology, and suddenly the small space between the two planets widens into a dark gulf full of the foreboding and the unknown—the grains of sand on the beach separating the two rocks now insurmountable and endless.

Kana is the third planet in the Beta Terragrin system, orbiting an energetic G class star, warm and yellow.

.2 light years away is Onaris, the tenth planet in the Nu Torriander system, its star a larger A-class globe the Browns called "Ole Scrub" with an outlying class-2 dwarf star companion not far away. Orbiting two slots down from Onaris is Bazz, a terraformed newcomer. Being so far from Ole Scrub, Bazz had pretty tough winters, but it was baked hard in the summer from the dwarf star they called "Lil' White-Face." As summers and winters on Bazz depended on planetary positioning rather than rotational tilt, the whole planet was in winter or in summer at once. An extreme place, lots of misfits went to Bazz—the frontier. Lots of people with things to hide went to Bazz in the old EX days before the Xaphans left.

Kana and Onaris: .2 light years apart. That is quite a lot of empty space between the two, space that isn't really all that empty. The League engineers have charts and maps detailing the mundane stellar bodies lying between

Kana and Onaris: nebulas, comets, asteroid fields, clouds of frozen methane and the like. However, most League charts center on the shipping lanes, the direct path ships use to make the journey from Kana to Onaris and back. Go off the shipping lanes and one enters the wild lands—the unknown where the small spaces truly become huge and engulfing. None other than local daredevils and old hermits riding the frontier past Druries Belt truly knew what was there, and nobody else really cared. What difference did it make? Here and there—gone in a blink and a surge of speed.

The "sands" of the Solar Empire, forever vast and unknown, stepped over with speedy ships moving entirely too fast to see what was there.

PART 1

THE ADMIRAL'S

PLEASURE

STENSTROM, LORD OF
BELMONT-SOUTH TYROL

1

—The Old Dream—

The day before he was to take command of his vessel, Stenstrom returned to his ancestral manor south of Tyrol. His father was there and so were many of his twenty-nine sisters. They sat in the great dining room his mother once loved and toasted to him and his success. After dinner he briefly went out to the hill and stood in front of his mother's gravestone.

After all this time, he still missed her.

That evening he sat in his father's study with his two favorite sisters, Lyra and Virginia. His father had been a Fleet Captain on the warbird *Caroline* for decades, and Stenstrom listened to his advice.

His father, giddy with excitement, thoroughly briefed his son on what to expect in the days ahead.

"You have an old ship to nurse back to fighting health. She's a good ship, a strong ship. I expect the next few months shall be rather sedate as you settle into command and oversee the *Seeker's* refits. Be certain to take an active role in the refits—do not allow some Admiral or Fleet engineer to run the whole thing un-tempered—assert your command as captain from day one. Put your nose into places where it might not belong. Do not be afraid to ruffle feathers and stand tip-to-tip with those prima-donnas. Next, you shall need to recruit an engineer and a boatswain. Again, do not allow the Admiralty to select one for you—be bold, be aggressive. Go out and make your pitch to those you feel you can trust. If you wish it, I have a list of names that I think would make fine additions, if I may say so. Take them as you wish."

"Thank you, Father."

Stenstrom the Older stood and poured four glasses of fine brandy. "Here's some of the good stuff. To my son, Lord Stenstrom, captain of the *Seeker*."

"To Bel, my favorite brother!" Lyra said.

"I hope you'll let me come aboard and cook for you and your crew sometime, Bel," Virginia said

Stenstrom laughed. "My mouth is already watering."

They clinked their glasses and drank. "Ah," Stenstrom the Older said, knocking it back. "Also, though your mother protested and inconvenienced you as only she could, I am certain she would have been so proud of you today, as I am. Your mother loved you very much, and as you know, that love carried with it a bit of an ordeal. Your mother could be overbearing, but she never meant anything not in your best interest. All in all—I think it made you a better man, better ready to lead."

Stenstrom stood there and remembered his departed mother. "Elders, rest her soul." The four of them were quiet for a moment.

He truly wished his mother could be here to see what he'd become.

That night he slept in his boyhood bedroom. He had a troubling dream that night—one of those select dreams that reoccurs periodically throughout one's life. This was a dream he first had as a little boy, and it never failed to come back to him before momentous occasions, like this one.

He dreamed of himself as a little boy, barely ten years old. He was playing in a vast sand pit behind his family manor along with Lyra and Virginia. Under the warm sun of the afternoon, his black-haired sister Lyra played in the sand along with him. Virginia sat nearby stuffing her face with something from the kitchens, watching them play. Virginia, with her mottled head of silver/black hair, was not near as tomboyish as Lyra was.

Laughing, he and Lyra wrestled in the sand. Lyra was several years older than he was, and much bigger. She got him in a headlock and then threw him to the other side of the sand pit. He could remember the feeling of flying through the air, a brief look at the sky as he fell into the unbroken sand. The puffy clouds. And he always recalled seeing stars out on the horizon in a squarish constellation, even though it was broad daylight.

His dream was always the same: the sand, his sisters, the wrestling. He hit the sand, and then, as always, the dream became cloudy.

There was a great clamor. Something hidden in the sand jumped out with terrifying speed.

There was a SNAP!

In his dream, he could see his two sisters standing there, Lyra in the sand with him and Virginia nearby. They were both staring at him. Virginia dropped the thing she was eating; it plopped into the sand. Her mouth was full of food, but she didn't chew.

Lyra then turned and ran. "Momma, Momma!" she screamed. Virginia just stood there open-mouthed.

As always, the last thing he could remember at the end of the dream was Lyra returning to the play area, leading Mother by her hand.

"Bel? BEL!" his mother screamed. "BEL!"

And that was all he could ever remember. That was the end of the dream. Whenever he had that old dream, it stayed with him all day long, just on the outskirts of his thoughts, lingering.

He sighed and tried to put the dream out of his head. He dressed, said goodbye to his father and sisters, and headed south to begin his new life as Fleet captain.

2

—St. Porter's Day—

S tenstrom arrived at the sprawling Fleet headquarters in the Zenon city of Armenelos bright and early to perform a series of perfunctory duties and take command of his ship. It had been a month since his contentious appointment with the Admiralty. His mentor Lord Davage had long taken his leave and returned to his ship and his loving countess.

He had an appointment with Admiral Derlith, of the 3rd Fleet. He expected it to be a formality, for that's all it should be; after that, he could be introduced to his ship: the *Seeker*. As he walked through the massive marble corridors framed with statuary under towering rotundas and lush botanicals, he was surprised how largely empty the complex was—he'd certainly expected it to be much more bustling. In the broad common areas, many of the little shops and eateries were closed, vendor stalls were covered with tarps, and the cantinas were also not open.

Ah! It was St. Porter's day, of course! Stenstrom had completely forgotten. St. Porter's day was a special holiday celebrated throughout the League. It was a day to express good will to one's fellows and make new friends. It was said a friend or new love made on St. Porter's Day was a friend or love for life.

With a quick movement of his hand, he produced his small golden locket. He opened it, and there was Lilly's radiant face painted in genius strokes, fresh and reassuring.

Fatefully, he had also met her on St. Porter's Day, four years ago.

He gave Lilly-in-the-locket one last smile, and put her back into his coat. Today was going to be amazing. This was his day at last.

Stenstrom took a moment and found a free terminal and sent a com home to Tyrol. There, he greeted his father and his sister Lyra and wished them good fortune, as was customary on St. Porter's Day. They were all smiles and wanted to know how things were progressing.

"Hasn't really started yet," he replied. "I just got here." He wrapped up the communication, sat a moment, and then sent a Com to Lilly in far away Gamboa. He wanted to see her. He wanted to tell her he loved her, at the very least he hoped for a hearty "good luck" from her.

He waited, not expecting the Com to be answered; Lilly hadn't been responding to any of his Coms lately.

The Com connected, he was elated. "Lilly!' he cried, "it is I, Stenstrom."

The image at the far end of the Com was hazy and indistinct, full of rattling and odd sounds. He thought he saw a point of light, like a lantern light appear in the distance and then the Com broke. The screen went black.

He thought to re-send the Com, but checked his time-piece and thought better of it.

Admiral Derlith awaited. He stood and continued on his way through the near empty complex to the environs of the 3rd Fleet in the back quarter of the building.

He felt confident. Good things were supposed to happen on St. Porter's day.

The area was set up as a series of small structures and landscaped courtyards mixed in with thick greenery from the Great Armenelos Forest which wasn't far away. It was so quiet today he could almost hear the trees growing and sopping up moisture. Stenstrom made his way through the maze of walks and passages and finally found the heavy oak door emblazoned with a brass sign reading: ADMIRAL DERLITH.

Stenstrom knocked loudly on the door with the meaty part of his fist.

After a few moments, the door swung open. A meek, small-shouldered fellow stood there. He was decked out like a Fleet adjutant, the personal assistant of a higher ranking officer. He wore an elaborate dark blue coat embroidered with silver stitching and a relentlessly frilly white shirt underneath. He wore dark blue knee britches, with white leggings and a buckled pair of black shoes. His hat was large and plumed.

He was a mousy fellow, short of stature and sloped of shoulder. His costume looked rather large on him as well. His hair was a bright banana blonde under his large blue hat.

"Are you Paymaster Stenstrom?" he asked quietly.

"I am. I have an appointment to see Admiral Derlith."

The small man swung the door wide and gestured for him to enter. "Yes, thank you, sir. Right this way."

The man led him through several courtyards and then into a small but lavishly furnished office. Inside, an iron-haired man in an admiral's uniform sat behind a desk. He gave Stenstrom a quick glance and didn't stand or stop what he was doing.

"Sit down," he said in a terse voice.

Stenstrom sat down and waited. The admiral was busy doing something at his desk; what it was Stenstrom really couldn't tell. He appeared to be speaking to somebody, his voice muffled by a directed Com cone.

Stenstrom could make out a few words, though he tried not to eavesdrop. *"Yes, he's here now. It's all arranged."*

The adjutant came in a moment later with a coffee service on a silver tray. Leaning over the table, his face close to the cups, he made the admiral a coffee and set it on his desk.

The admiral took a drink. "Josephus," he said. "This is cold."

"Beg your pardon, Admiral," he said and quickly left with the pot.

Without looking at Stenstrom, the Admiral spoke. "You have secured appointment to the captain's chair of the Main Fleet Vessel *Seeker*. You pledged, at the time of your appointment, one hundred thousand Belmont sesterces to be used to fund the refitting of the vessel, as it is in need in several key areas, per Fleet regulations. We have received your pledge, and all is well in that regard. At the present time, your appointment status is marked: Provisional. As you may be aware, there are a number of pre-conditions that must be met for that appointment to be validated and made permanent, or 'Bonded' as we say in the Fleet. They are as follows: One, you must board your vessel no later than 22 bells standard today—failure to do so shall revoke your appointment. Two, your first mission must be at the pleasure of the Admiralty—in this case, my pleasure as the *Seeker* is my ship. You will undertake a mission that I shall give to you, and you must complete it; otherwise, again, your appointment shall be revoked, and you will not be Bonded."

Stenstrom knew all of that. He had, at that time, nine bells to board the *Seeker*, and then the mission, the "Admiral's Pleasure" as it was known, was usually some tawdry, perfunctory exercise that was more tedious than challenging.

"I see," he said. "Thank you. And what is the nature of my mission?"

Josephus, the tiny adjutant, returned and prepared another cup of coffee for the Admiral from a steaming hot pot. He took it and casually began sipping. "Why can't you ever give me coffee like this the first time around, Josephus? This is more like it."

"I am sorry, Admiral," he said. "Paymaster, may I offer you a cup?"

Stenstrom smiled at him. "Thank you, I'm fine."

The Admiral finished his cup. "Your mission, Lord Belmont, shall be the following: In Warehouse 87 at the far end of the Fleet complex is a crate of fine, six-year-old Remnath brandy fermented at my very own home in the hills of Remnath. My House is known for its fine grape brandy. You are to take the brandy to a grand ball that is to be thrown by Admiral Pax at Fleet annex Teflegar-Martin II on the planet Bazz. The brandy is to be served to the Admiralty after the main feast has been enjoyed. The ball shall take place on September 32nd—that will give you twelve days to deliver the cargo."

"Twelve days to go to Bazz? Is that all, sir?" Stenstrom asked. A trip to Bazz, at a leisurely rate, should take no more than two.

"Yes, that is all. Recall, your appointment is at peril. You now have less than eight and a half bells to formally board the *Seeker*, and you have twelve days to deliver the goods to Bazz."

Admiral Derlith then returned to whatever it was he was doing. Without a further word the meeting was over.

Stenstrom stood and took his leave. On his way out, he passed Josephus, who was busy preparing a snack for the Admiral. He appeared to be having issues seeing what he was doing.

"Is there anything else I can do for you, Paymaster?" he asked looking up from his work, a mustard-loaded spreading knife perched in his small hand.

"No, I'm fine. Thank you, and Happy Porter's Day to you, my friend."

Josephus lit up. "And to you, sir. Good luck and safe journey."

Stenstrom tipped his hat, then made to leave.

"Sir?" Josephus said, calling out to him.

Stenstrom turned. The adjutant appeared to want to say something but had second thoughts. "Again, good luck, and be bold."

Stenstrom smiled. "I shall do so, sir. Thank you."

He left the courtyard and made his way through the vast complex to the warehouses at the far end—it was a good, brisk walk that took about thirty minutes. As before, he met few people along the way.

He got to the correct warehouse—Number 87—and tried the door.

It was locked. A sign posted on the door read:

CLOSED FOR ST. PORTER'S DAY. WILL RE-OPEN STANDARD HOURS 9/21.

Hmmmm.

Stenstrom stood there and thought. This could be a bit tougher than he first imagined. With the place virtually deserted for the holiday, how was he to secure, load and transport his cargo to the *Seeker*? Another problem immediately entered his mind—how was he going to get to the *Seeker* in the first place? He was no pilot. He needed somebody to fly him there, and the pickings here at Fleet appeared to be slim at best. There literally was nobody around to fly him up.

The enormity of the problem hit him fully.

Admiral Derlith …

He spun about in frustration. He'd paid his money. Now Admiral Derlith was going to see to it that he failed his appointment by plunking him square in the middle of a paid holiday. The man was apparently quite sly.

He could, should things get ugly, call up to the *Seeker* and have them send a ripcar down for him, but that would be embarrassing. He hoped the situation wouldn't come to that.

Stenstrom took his hat off and wiped his brow. He supposed he could simply send a Com to his father, or to his mentor and sponsor, Lord Davage, and they would sort everything out. One or two heated Coms to the Admiralty, and this puerile attempt to drum him off the *Seeker's* chair before he'd even had a chance to sit upon it would be quashed—cold.

But, should he do that, he would be partially validating the Admiral's low opinion of him. They had set obstacles before him, and now it was time to conquer them unassisted.

So be it. The loins were about to be girded.

3

—TYROL SORCERY—

He tried the warehouse door—again, it was locked. So, thusly inconvenienced and all alone by design, he determined that he was given lease to use any method necessary to accomplish his goal.

So, what was he to do? Unlike his father and Captain Davage, he had no Gifts of the Mind, the fantastic abilities people from the north and from Zenon could do; his mother's Tyrol stock had suppressed it in him. Neither he nor his twenty-nine sisters could perform the Gifts of the Mind.

But, that didn't mean he was helpless here. Far from it. He pushed up the sleeves of his coat and made ready. It was time to make good use of the skills his mother had taught him.

He could, drawing upon his training as a sorcerer, take command of this situation in any number of ways. For the simple task of opening the door to the warehouse, naught but a bit of slight-of-hand should suffice.

He produced, as if by conjuration, an elaborate set of manual and magnetic lock picks. He'd fully inherited his mother's dexterous hands, and his skill at producing hand-held items out of thin air was impressive. Mother had trained him well.

The lock to the warehouse was a simple manual type. Since nobody was around, there was no need to be sly about it. He selected a Raven's Tooth manual pick, inserted it, and tested around a bit, his trained fingers feeling the internal landscape of the lock through the shaft of the pick.

Voices. People approached.

Stenstrom ceased his work and stepped away.

Two Marines came into the area and stopped near the entrance to the warehouse. "This the door?" one Marine asked.

"Yep."

"I don't see anybody, do you?"

The other Marine looked around. "Nope."

Stenstrom was standing right there not ten feet away—yet another one of the skills that Mother had taught him—to melt into the shadows and be unseen. Stenstrom was adept at it. He leaned against the warehouse and waited for them to leave.

One of the Marines tried the door. "Locked up tight. What are we doing here again?"

"Got a report of a suspicious person snooping about."

"I don't see anybody. Let's to the canteen and set to it. It's St. Porter's Day for Creation's sake."

The other Marine looked around again and adjusted his cap. "All right, I'm satisfied. Let's log our report and be off."

Stenstrom stifled a yawn as the second Marine pulled his communicator. "Base," he said.

"Go ahead," came a reply.

"Base, A-1, investigating report of an unauthorized person skulking about Fleet Warehouse 87. We have investigated and have determined there are no unauthorized persons about. We are quitting the area."

"Negative," came the reply. "Accomplish standard Fret scan."

The two Marines winced. One of them got out a small device with a fold-down screen. He adjusted the screen and pressed buttons. "Well, go on!" he said to the other Marine. "Start spraying!"

The other Marine produced a small gray can from his coat and started moving about the face of the warehouse, spraying a thick, hanging mist from the can. He came within a few feet of Stenstrom, getting him in the face with the spray—it smelled like peaches.

The Marine holding the device waved it around. "I'm not detecting any hint of use of Gifts here. No Wafting, no Cloaks. I see a fading bit of heat near the door, but that's all. Probably just someone stopping by forgetting it's the holiday."

"May we please be off then?" the Marine holding the can asked.

"Base, A1," the first Marine said, putting his device away. "Fret scan complete—no activity detected. We are retiring from the area."

"Acknowledged." With that, the Marine put his communicator back into his coat, and the both of them walked away.

A moment later, Stenstrom returned to the door and continued his work. He slid the pick back in and, with a satisfying "click", the door opened. It was easy. Mother would be proud. He plunged inside.

Within was a vast warehouse. It was quite dark and Stenstrom could see the blinking lights of motion sensors placed at regular intervals. Again, falling upon his skills, he walked into the interior of the warehouse, his smooth, shadow movements not triggering the sensors.

He quickly produced a yellow Holystone. He gave it a shake, and it began to glow in his hand. Holding it up, he could see well enough to make his way about. Unlike many warehouses he'd seen before, which were dusty, cobwebbed places, this one was clean and tidy, full of knick-knacks and trinkets. He found several partitioned areas which were labeled with what, he guessed, were the names of various admirals: Pax, Scy, Garth, Riddle, and finally Derlith. This warehouse must be where the admirals stash their booty. Rummaging through the Derlith area, Stenstrom found a large crate labeled: BAZZ. Struggling, he pulled it out of its place. He found a pry bar and opened the crate. Inside, cushioned in a nest of soft straw were twelve black bottles of brandy, sealed with wax and labeled with a black covering.

Satisfied, he put the lid back on the crate. Testing the crate's weight, he discovered it was too heavy to lift and carry. He looked around.

At the far wall was a float lift.

Making his way through the dark warehouse, he found the float lift was off and locked down.

Out came the lock picks again; this time a magnetic Sarah's Rage pick did the trick, and the float came to life. Fiddling around with the controls, Stenstrom brought it under heel. After a bit of doing, he managed to get the crate on the lift and, floating on air, dragged it out of the warehouse and back down the hall.

One obstacle down.

PRIVATE TAARA DE LA ANDERSON,
110TH MARINES

4

—PRIVATE TAARA—

Following the signs, he then made his way to the ship park, which consisted of a control desk, a large hangar, and an open-air yard, twinkling with running lights. He needed a transport or ripcar to take him up to the *Seeker*. By this point, he was down to about six bells. A slow ripcar could get to the *Seeker* in about ten minutes.

As he feared, the ship park was virtually empty—the control desk sat unattended. Outside in the yard, crickets chirped.

Nearby, a lonely Marine girl, decked out in her fine red coat, stood guard in front of the bust of a stern-faced admiral mounted on a fluted column. The Marine had short black hair that was tucked up into her cap. She had a pair of sickle-like strands of hair that hung down across her face, almost meeting at her chin, sort of like hanging side-burns. Slung across her shoulder was a strummer, a large, mostly ceremonial rifle that the Marines used in large, important places such as Fleet HQ. It was an impressive-looking weapon that had virtually no firepower—it was just for show. Holstered at her waist was the real thing—a jutting, black SK pistol that had a large enough caliber to knock down a brick wall.

Hanging around her neck was a sign on a string. The sign read "MOM" in a harsh, hand-written scrawl.

She saw Stenstrom and burst into a smile. "Hi!" she said in an energetic voice. She then stiffened and adjusted her posture. "I mean, good evening, sir," she said in a much more formal tone, eyeballing his coat and hat.

"Hello," he replied. "I need immediate uplift to the *Seeker*. I was told I may request a transport in this area."

"Nobody's here, sir," she said, doggedly standing next to the sour-faced marble bust. "Everybody's gone home for the holiday, I think. I'm really sorry—they'll be back first thing at six bells. If you want to get some rest in the meantime, you can go to billeting, as I think they're pretty empty today."

Stenstrom looked at her standing there by the bust. "What are you doing?" he asked.

"Me? I'm guarding the statue of Admiral Pax here."

"You're guarding a bust?"

"No, I'm guarding the statue," she said, pointing at it. "That's what they said. After I messed up the surprise inspection and got everybody in trouble, they said: 'Guard Admiral Pax with your life until we come to fetch you.' So, here I am."

Stenstrom gazed at the sign hanging around her neck. "What's that sign?"

She blushed. "Oh, I sort of forgot about that. It means 'Maiden of Misery'—that's what my unit calls me, since I mess things up all the time. I have to wear it all day today."

"That's not very nice."

She shrugged.

He looked around, seeing no one other than her. "Well, 'Mom', you're sure there isn't anyone who can help me?"

"Nope, I mean yep. Nobody until six bells."

Stenstrom winced. Six bells was no good. Six bells was eight bells past his deadline. With nothing else to do, he determined to return to the Admiral's area and demand an extension, as he was clearly being set up to fail in a big way.

As the Marine guard stared at him, he considered his options. The last recourse he had was to do something considered rather embarrassing. He would have to call up to the _Seeker_ and have them send a ripcar down. It was a humbling thing to have to ask his new charge for a lift, but he, by this point, truly didn't care. He needed to be on that ship. Let Derlith and his lot have their laugh; it made no difference to him.

The Marine looked at him carefully, puzzled by his coat. "What sort of uniform is that?" she asked. I thought you were an admiral at first, but that's not an admiral's uniform. Now that I look on it, I don't know what it is. What's HRN mean?"

"It's a long story, he said."

"Is that a mask you're wearing? I can't really see clearly from over here, but it looks like you're wearing a small mask—like a robber."

Stenstrom shook his head. "I'm not a robber, though I rather feel like one at the moment."

She leaned up against the bust and adjusted her sign. "Hey, mister, may I trouble you for a moment? I can't leave my post until I'm relieved, and I'm terribly hungry. They've left me out here all bloody day. Could I possibly ask you to go and get me something from the cafeteria?"

"Are you allowed to eat while on guard duty?"

She thought a moment. "Well, sure. I mean I'm not in some elite guard unit, and I'm not exactly guarding some rare treasure either—I'm stuck here guarding an ugly stone face when I should be at the bars celebrating the holiday. I don't think anybody would be going out with me anyway though. My barracks is pretty sore at me right now." The lettering on the sign she was wearing glinted in the light.

"I'm in a bit of a rush ... I'm sorry, I don't know your name."

"Taara. Private Taara de la Anderson. I'm from Bazz—ever been to Bazz?"

Bazz... If only.

"No, no I haven't. Well, Private Taara, I am in a rush and I don't think

I've the time. I'm sorry."

She nodded and looked a bit deflated. The stern carved face of Admiral Pax stared over her shoulder.

Stenstrom began pulling the crate away, and looked back. He saw the poor girl standing there lonely and hungry in her red Marine uniform and her sign hanging at her neck. He supposed a bit of good fellowship couldn't hurt. It might even create some good karma for him. It was St. Porter's Day after all.

"Stand fast, Private Taara, and I'll be right back with something for you."

She lit up. "Wow, thank you, sir! I really appreciate it!"

"Watch my crate, will you?" he called.

"I will, and thanks again!"

Stenstrom walked down the hallway to a small nearby cafeteria. The place was mostly empty, and most of the usual hot items served weren't being offered—only a modest skeleton crew was present. Stenstrom selected a turkey sandwich and a side of bagged Kelsos. He didn't know what she drank, and, as she looked fairly young, he picked her out a can of red Gasol.

Poor kid, he thought as he gathered her food; from Bazz, she said— probably impoverished, probably had no choice but be a Marine. Probably one of those common types who roll through their lives hardly making a mark on anyone or anything.

Quickly, he returned to the ship park and gave Private Taara her meal.

"Thank you so much, sir," she said, unwrapping her sandwich.

"I wasn't sure what you liked, so I did my best."

"Hey," she said smiling, "as I always say: 'just eat, man—just eat.'" She took off her large strummer and held it out. "Could you hold this for a moment?"

Stenstrom snickered and took it—not really a spit-n-polish Marine, was she? Private Taara then seated herself beneath Admiral Pax's chin. "Please," she said, "what's your name, mister?"

"Paymaster Stenstrom, Lord of Belmont. I am the newly appointed commander of the *Seeker*."

"I wish I was from a neat Kanan House with all those fancy titles, but I'm just a kid from Bazz."

"Well, 'kid from Bazz,' have you had a moment to speak to your family today for the holiday?"

"I have—thanks! You're such a nice fellow. I am very pleased, sir, and, again, thank you for your kindness!"

Stenstrom looked at her. She had the sort of face that one didn't give much regard to at first—she was cute, nothing more. But, the longer one stared at her, the better looking she got. She was actually extremely attractive, in a tom-boyish sort of way.

"Well, I'm off to contact the *Seeker*. I suppose I'll have to ask them for a ripcar to be sent down." He tipped his hat and prepared to collect his crate.

Taara took a drink from her Gasol and suddenly had a thought. "Did you say the ship you're wanting to contact is the *Seeker*, sir?"

"I did."

She thought a moment, took a look around to see if anybody was coming, then made her way to the control desk and opened a terminal. "I thought I heard the *Seeker* is abandoned. Yes, it says right here that the *Seeker* was half-scuttled last week and is in terminal."

"In terminal? What does that mean?"

"I think it means she's in a decaying orbit." Taara looked proud. "You pick up a few things being posted here. Yes, and take a look—Fleetcom says a reclamation team has been dispatched for two days hence to board and correct her orbit—I guess they're pretty concerned about it. She was then scheduled to make berth in dry-dock 186 for a partial refit."

Stenstrom was getting angry. "And who ordered the *Seeker* half-scuttled? Let me guess ... Admiral Derlith, yes?"

Taara toyed about with her terminal. "Yep, Admiral Derlith. That's what it says right here. So, I guess the *Seeker* is abandoned right now. I guess there's nobody up there to send a ripcar down for you."

Stenstrom drew one of his pistols in a froth. He held it for a moment then slid it back into his sash.

"I'm really sorry," she said.

He shook his head. "Well, Private, I suppose there's a sign around my neck as well, just can't see it as easily."

She appeared sympathetic. "I know how that feels. Listen, for what it's worth, when my shift ends, I'll get you a drink at the canteen—might make you feel better. Would you like that?"

He sighed. "Thanks. If you could please watch my crate," he said, his voice shaking. "I shall be back. I've a few words to say to Admiral Derlith." Stenstrom stormed away.

"Happy Porter's Day!" Taara called to him as he left. "My offer still stands if you change your mind!"

"And to you," he replied. Though this was turning into a real gut-grinder of a day, Private Taara's cheerful demeanor made him feel a bit better.

LT. JOSEPHUS, LORD OF A-RAM

5

—A-Ram—

S tenstrom made his way back to Admiral Derlith's complex. It was getting late in the evening, and the sky was fading to early starlight.

When he got to the door, he banged on it hard.

After a time, the small, blonde-headed adjutant opened the door. He was wearing white gloves and holding a tarnished sponge that stank of silver polish. "Paymaster Stenstrom, well met, sir," he said.

"Where is Admiral Derlith? I must see him."

"Admiral Derlith has left the complex for the weekend."

Stenstrom pushed his way into the anti-chamber. The adjutant had been polishing a silver tea set; the room smelled of the labor. He had the holo-terminal on his desk opened up and was reading several postings in overly-large text, as if he had trouble seeing normal-sized text.

Stenstrom was in a good lather. "You may tell that scoundrel that he has not heard the last of Stenstrom, Lord of Belmont. I shall be back! I shall reappoint to the *Seeker*'s chair, and next time he'll not have a convenient holiday and a half-scuttled ship to foil my appointment!"

The adjutant stood there, his holo-terminal spinning around him. Stenstrom took a glance at the large-printed wording. It said:

AN OPEN LETTER FROM THE FIEND OF CALVERT

"The Fiend of Calvert?" Stenstrom asked, forgetting his anger for the moment.

The adjutant smiled. "Oh, it's a hobby of mine. I remember as a boy I was really scared of the Fiend of Calvert, as he terrorized the streets. I've made it my interest to collect as much information on his crimes as possible and see if I can determine his identity. I've all sorts of theories and what not. He was never caught."

"I heard he was dead."

"No, no," he said shaking his head. "The Fiend of Calvert is not dead."

The adjutant took off his gloves and cleaned his hands with a cloth. "I'm sorry about this situation," he said. "Sir, is there anything I might help you with?"

Stenstrom looked at the small, slope-shouldered fellow. "I have five bells to board the *Seeker*. As this place is currently a holiday-riddled tomb and the *Seeker* is abandoned, I have no way to board her in time. Then, after that impossible task is completed, I am to deliver a crate of cheaply-made brandy to Bazz, twelve days hence. Again, as the *Seeker* is half taken apart, I don't see her going anywhere in under a month."

Stenstrom removed his hat. "I'm sorry. I didn't mean to fill your ear." He could see himself reflected in the surface of the shiny tea set, wearing his mask and his HRN coat. The Marine girl Taara was right: he did look like a masked robber. "You do good work, sir," he said. "Again, I'm sorry to barge in here and trouble you."

The adjutant appeared sympathetic. "I heard the Admiral speaking to his peers regarding a 'fine deception' he had just accomplished. He—he was feeling rather proud of himself."

Stenstrom lightly clapped him on the shoulder. "Perhaps Admiral Derlith is the Fiend of Calvert, ever thought of that? Well, let him have his fun for the moment; again, I'll be back and hell shall be coming with me."

Stenstrom turned to leave.

"Sir?" the adjutant said, switching off the holo-terminal. "I can get you to the *Seeker*. I can fly."

Stenstrom gave him the once-over. A rather small fellow, no taller than 5'4, slight of build, and that bright head of blonde hair—rather ridiculous. But who was he to judge; he was wearing a mask and a Hoban Royal Navy coat. "You can fly, sir?"

"I can. Been flying all my life. I never could pass the Fleet or Marine standards for flight school because I have a fair amount of myopia, which isn't correctible by surgery, and my body is of a type that rejects Bio-plants. So, here I am, polishing silver, making coffee, and reading old press releases about the Fiend of Calvert. Stuck here on the ground when I belong in the air."

"Can you see properly to fly then?"

The adjutant reached into his coat and pulled out a thick set of glasses. "I can with these. With these I can see as well as anybody. The Admiral doesn't let me wear them when he's around. He says they're too ugly."

Stenstrom smiled. "You'll do. Come with me."

Smiling, the adjutant put his glasses on and followed Stenstrom at a brisk pace out of the area.

"Your name is Josephus, is that correct?" Stenstrom asked on the hoof.

"Yes, but I hate that name, and the Admiral knows it. I am Josephus, Lord of A-Ram. Please, just call me A-Ram. Have you ever heard of the House of A-Ram? It's a Calvert House."

"Sorry, no. I haven't. Well, A-Ram, good to know you. I am Stenstrom, Lord of Belmont-South Tyrol. Just call me Bel."

He held his hand out, and they shook hands. It seems he'd made a friend—perhaps the day wasn't a total loss.

Before long, they arrived back at the ship park. Private Taara had finished her meal and was glad to see him. "You're back!" she said in her happy voice, still standing by the bust.

"I am, and I've found a pilot. I would like to requisition a transport for immediate passage to the *Seeker*."

Taara looked around. "Oh, okay ... Where's the pilot?"

"I'm the pilot," A-Ram said.

Taara giggled. "I'm sorry, sir. It's just that you're dressed like an Admiral's adjutant."

"He was an adjutant this morning, but, as of this moment, he's a pilot," Stenstrom said. "He's been promoted."

Taara looked at him. "Aren't you the adjutant who's always getting yelled at by that gray-haired Admiral?"

A-Ram approached Taara. "I'm still an officer, Private, and perhaps a small bit of decorum might ..." He stopped in mid-sentence. "Do I know you?" he asked, giving her a full appraisal. "You seem familiar to me."

Taara shrugged. "I don't think so. Do you hang out at the Marine cantina? Oh! Do you go to the fights every weekend?"

"No, I do not go to the fights."

"Then, I'm not sure where you've seen me—I'm big into the fights."

Taara smiled and gave A-Ram a tap on one of his slight shoulders. "Bet I could beat you at arm-wrestling. What's your name?"

"A-Ram, and you could not," he replied, taking note of the sign hanging around her neck.

Stenstrom stepped in. "And I'll wager I could beat the both of you at once. A contest for another time. Private Taara, we need to get to the *Seeker* as quickly as possible and need to req out a ship."

Taara was a bit saddened. "Sir, I would love to help you, but I can't req you out a ship—I'm just a guard. And, I'm not supposed to do or touch anything other than guard this statue right now."

Stenstrom walked around the desk. Behind was the entrance to the main hangar where dozens of transports were kept.

He tried the door—it was locked.

"Sir, that's not going to help you," Taara called to him.

Out came the lock picks and soon Stenstrom had the door wide open.

He stepped in. The hangar was empty.

"That's what I was trying to tell you. All the transports have been sent to Provst for a cleaning. They're due to be back at six bells."

Again, Stenstrom drew his pistol in frustration.

"I'm sorry," Taara said.

They looked around. "I see a group of sub-orbitals over there, parked on the lawn," A-Ram remarked. "We don't need to req those; all we have to do is sign for one."

Taara saw the line of sharp blue sub-orbitals parked on the green. "You ...want to use a sub-orbital to mount a ship in orbit? Sub-orbitals aren't supposed to go into orbit, hence the name, right? Isn't that dangerous?"

"Only if you don't know what you're doing."

She thought about that remark for a moment. "Oh, okay."

They signed for sub-orbital 10 and quickly began loading the crate onto it.

As they did, a second Marine arrived, and Private Taara handed the fellow her strummer. She then made her way over to them. "Well, I've been relieved—the guy's statue will just have to get along fine without me now. I just wanted to say good luck, before I head back to my barracks. And, I really enjoyed meeting you two today—you seem like good guys to me. If you two weren't in such a rush, I'd invite you down to the canteen with me to hang out."

"We'll take a pass on that, Private. Perhaps next time."

Stenstrom shook her hand as he climbed in. She gave A-Ram another shove. "You're not getting out of the arm-wrestling thing, little guy. We'll do it when you get back."

"Umm, certainly," A-Ram said, climbing in.

She turned, thought it over for a second, and then turned back. "Listen, I know enough to understand that what you're about to do is very dangerous. Additionally, the *Seeker* is in a bad terminal and is currently uninhabited. How are you going to open the bay doors?"

"I suppose we'll just figure that out when we get to it," Stenstrom said, strapping in.

Taara appeared conflicted. "Listen, I'm off for the next few days. No doubt you two will need a hand if you do get aboard, and I'd like to come along. I've never been aboard a fighting starship before. It sounds like fun, and I've got nothing better to do. Of course, I'll bet you two an ale in the canteen that we'll get no higher than fifty thousand feet before we up and turn around."

A-Ram popped his thick glasses back on. "That's a sure bet," he said looking rather bug-eyed.

Taara smiled and tossed her "MOM" sign aside. She readied to enter the craft. "Oh, wait!" she said. She ran back to the desk and disappeared into the hangar—she and the Marine guard exchanging a few disparaging words as she did so, the guard pointing at the discarded sign. A few moments later, she re-appeared carrying three small devices. She exchanged more angry words with the Marine and then offered him some sort of obscene Bazz hand gesture. She popped into the back couch and buckled up. With that, A-Ram sealed the hatches and smoothly lifted the small ship up and away from the Fleet complex.

"What do you have there?" Stenstrom asked Taara.

"Aquanaughts," she said. "So we can breathe … just in case I lose my bet."

Moving fast, A-Ram climbed in a southerly direction, heading for the south pole, the sub-orbital moving effortlessly under his control. "I know how Fleetcom likes to orbit starships. Those listed as half-scuttled are assigned a low polar orbit in Zone A. The *Seeker* should be tucked nice and neat in one of them."

They climbed high above the clouds and the sub-orbital's engines, starving for air, began to rev to red.

"Look!" A-Ram cried. "There it is."

Stenstrom and Taara looked up. High overhead they saw a bright, fast moving star, heading from south to north. It appeared on the horizon, streaked past them, and then disappeared to the north. "She's really moving. I'd also say she's about twenty thousand feet above us still. We'll have to pick up some speed, close the vents, and pray we have enough momentum to reach the ship. We're only going to have one chance at this."

"See, I told you it would be tough sledding in a sub-orbital. They weren't kidding around when they named them," Taara said.

A-Ram punished the struggling sub-orbital, clawing for altitude.

Overhead, the star of the *Seeker* got ever brighter as the sub-orbital closed the distance. Through the windscreen, which was rapidly frosting up, they could just begin to see detail through the brightness, like looking at a distant planet through a telescope. Also, the *Seeker* appeared to be slowing down as it rose and fell—the sub-orbital steadily picking up and matching speed.

"It's really getting cold in here," Taara said as she rubbed her sleeves. She passed out the Aquanaughts, and they put them in their mouths, Taara helping A-Ram with his.

Sucking on his Aquanaught, A-Ram pulled a lever and shut the outside vents. He also enabled a green counter reader: 60:00. "All right, it's now or never," he said with a muffled voice. "I think I've got the trajectory and speed figured out. Bel, I'm going to release the timer. When the counter reads zero, I'm going to pull up hard. We should slide right in behind the *Seeker* where we can try to open a bay with the grapplers and get in."

He watched the now huge star of the *Seeker* disappear beyond the horizon, and then he released the timer. It began counting down.

The gauges spun, the engines, starving for air, all red-lined and sputtered.

"Zero, A-Ram!" Stenstrom said. "Pull it!"

He pulled back hard, and the sub-orbital lurched up. They felt the sickening release as gravity fell away, and the pale blue sky faded to black.

In front of them, the huge mass of the *Seeker* came hurtling into view. It was tumbling in its orbit, spiraling slowly from wingtip to wingtip.

"See, look at it roll," Taara said through her Aquanaught. "Its orbit is terminal. I think it got clipped by an old weather sat a few days ago and busted open a thruster."

The great ship looked like a bird shot dead on the wing. All of its lights were off, and the massive forward sensor was quiet.

Stenstrom gazed at it with wonder. Rolling, tumbling, in desperate shape—that was still his ship.

His ship.

"I don't think we can do this with the *Seeker* rolling like that. We won't be able to dock," A-Ram said.

"Can we start heading down, then?" Taara asked, clutching her coat. "It's freezing in here, and these Aquanaughts will only last a few more minutes."

Stenstrom looked at the ship. "Look there," he said. "Look to that large window in the aft tower section—that's the main mess I think. The way the ship's rolling, that window, centrally located near the pivot point, is hardly moving."

"And so?" A-Ram said.

"So, just crash us through it. Once we're inside, the blast shutters should close, or I'll seal the breech myself and send the bill for its repair to Admiral Derlith."

"Seal it? With what?" A-Ram asked.

"Holystones. You'll see. So, go ahead, A-Ram, just plow into it."

Taara shivered. "You guys can let me back down any time now."

A-Ram pushed his glasses back and punched it. He maneuvered past the rolling wings and made a bead for the large mess hall window spinning ahead like the center of a tire—not taking his eyes off it.

With a bang, the engines went out for want of air. They drifted ahead.

A-Ram pointed the nose at the spinning window as his controls, designed for atmospheric use, gave way.

CRASH!!

The sub-orbital plowed through the large window, smashed through the debris of chairs and tables within the mess, and slammed into the far wall, partially going through it. The decompression instantly began pulling the furniture out of the mess, and even began tugging on the sub-orbital.

The cracked hatch of the suborbital flew off and was sucked out into space.

A-Ram, though he was strapped in, was so slight of frame that he was pulled through his straps and out toward the window. "Where's the shutters?" he gasped.

Stenstrom caught and held him fast by the wrist. He flapped up and down in the suction.

Taara leaned forward and grabbed onto A-Ram's arm as well. His aquanaught was sucked out of his mouth and out the window. He screamed in pain.

"Taara, you got him?" Stenstrom roared.

"I got him!"

"I'm going to let go and seal the breach! You ready?"

"I'm ready!"

Stenstrom let go, waved his hands, and three lime green balls appeared between his fingers. They were instantly sucked away, past A-Ram, toward the blown out window. The balls hit the window frame and burst into what looked like a huge spider web. The window, now partially blocked, lost a fair bit of suction. A-Ram fell to the floor with a thud.

Stenstrom surged out of the wrecked sub-orbital and, standing, he produced several more lime green Holystones and threw them at the window. Before long, the breach was covered.

The ship, somewhat belatedly, reacted to the depressurization and the blast shutters closed with a clang behind the webbing.

He stood A-Ram up. "You all right? Is everyone all right?"

A bit shaky, A-Ram nodded, and Taara bounced out of the craft, clearly fine. They looked around and noted the damage. The mess was a mess. The suborbital was done—this flight into low orbit would be its last. Stenstrom and Taara pulled the cargo of brandy out of the wreck of the sub-orbital and looked it over. Inside, several of the bottles were cracked.

A-Ram, who had managed to hold onto his hat, rummaged through the crate. "Looks to be we've got nine bottles left. Bel, did the Admiral say how many bottles you were to bring to Bazz?"

"I don't recall him mentioning a specific number. He just said get the brandy there."

A-Ram arranged the bottles on the floor in neat rows. "Well then, that's in our favor. Since he was mum on that point, all we really need is one bottle."

There was no power in the ship. The Grav Pack was still functioning—it worked on a redundant, solar-powered system so it was usually the only thing working on a stripped-out ship, besides the emergency shutters and a tad bit of convection heat to keep the miles of pipes from bursting. Using the chronometer on the sub-orbital, Stenstrom made a recording and beamed it to Admiral Derlith's holomail.

He had boarded the *Seeker* with minutes to spare.

✳   ✳   ✳   ✳   ✳

They made their way to a nearby Ripcar Bay that was clear. Taara disappeared and returned some time later with a few bagged snacks and cans of flat Gasol. "This was all I could find." Sitting Indian-style, they ate in the dark, softly lit by a few Holystones and using the Admiral's brandy crate as a makeshift table.

"This is kind of cool," Taara said, "sitting here in the dark with two handsome fellows." Taara, apparently a bubbly person, raised her can of warm Gasol. "To Stenstrom, Lord of Belmont-South … whatever. Here's to your first day of command."

A-Ram smiled and raised his can. "I concur."

Stenstrom laughed and clicked his can with theirs, making his Gasol fizz. "And here's to good friends. As they say, a friend made on St. Porter's Day is a friend indeed."

As they sat there in the dark eating their unappealing meal, a bond was formed between these three people: Stenstrom, A-Ram and Taara. As Stenstrom said, a friend made on St. Porter's Day was a friend for life.

Such a thought could never have been truer.

6

—The MOLLY—

So now that they were aboard the *Seeker*—what was next? The ship, with the exception of working gravity, was dead and only had a few days left before its decaying orbit became critical and then entered the atmosphere as a flaming ball of wreckage.

"A reclamation team is coming in from Planet Fall, Bel," A-Ram said. "I recall seeing the order on the Admiral's desk. Either tomorrow or the next day—everything's in a bit of limbo due to the holiday. If they enter the ship, by Fleet rule, all appointments are cancelled. You cannot be bonded as captain if they board."

"Then we need to be out of here prior to their arrival."

"'Scuse me," Taara said. "The ship's dead. Her engines were removed and hauled out for scrap—I saw it on the roster a few days ago."

The three of them were trying to pry one of the central corridor hatchway doors open with a pole-like strut they had salvaged from the sub-orbital. They were hoping to reach the bridge. There, they could assess the situation and, with luck, right the ship. The door stubbornly held shut—they strained and sweated.

"Your boy, A-Ram, Admiral Derlith, had this episode planned out well. Bloody holidays! All I have to do is get a stinking crate of brandy to Bazz for an Admiral's party—but look—the *Seeker's* not going anywhere." Stenstrom wiped his brow. "And I'll wager that brandy is gut-wrenchingly bad, as well."

"I've heard the Admiral produces a very fine brandy," A-Ram replied.

Taara had her Marine coat off and was straining on the pole, her little hands gripped on hard. "Why drink brandy when a good honey ale is available?" She let go of the pole and stared at the unmovable door. "Elder's Balls, this thing is a pain. Well, why not use our heads here. You boarded the *Seeker*, so that part's taken care of. Why not just hire a ship to transport the brandy to Bazz? Heck, a slow stumblebum transport out of Armenelos would have it there in three or four days, and you've got twelve."

The hatch gave a metallic groan. They strained harder.

"No," A-Ram said, sweating on the pole. "Won't work—the Admiral's got us covered. By order, the *Seeker* has to deliver the goods. And, having a devious mind, he even wrote in verbiage stating that the *Seeker* in particular has to deliver it. Not a model of the *Seeker* sitting on another ship, and not another ship named *Seeker*—this one, and under its own power, no towing or barging." A-Ram released the pole, flexed his aching fingers, and tried again.

"The Admiral appears dead set against me commanding this ship. He welcomed my money with a smile, but, for the rest of it, I'm on the quits." Stenstrom said.

A-Ram let go of the pole. "That coat you wear really got to him. The Admiralty hates the Hoban Royal Navy. May I ask, why did you wear it to your appointment?"

Stenstrom looked down at his coat. "Because I like it. Because Lilly picked it out for me."

"Who's Lilly?" Taara asked.

"A dear friend of mine. My sponsor, Lord Davage, asked that I not wear it—apparently sensing the Admiral's hatred for the group."

"You shouldn't have worn it?" Taara asked.

Stenstrom thought a moment. "I suppose not. I guess I wanted to get their attention, to make a splash. I didn't give them their due, and look where I am."

He looked around. "All of this is my fault."

A-Ram continued on the pole. "I ... don't know if it was just the coat. One of the Admiral's hangers-on seems to have a firm agenda against you."

Stenstrom let go of the pole. "Against me?"

"Yes, I'm not sure who has it in for you or why, but your name's been kicked around quite a bit of late."

Taara clapped him in the shoulder. "Ah, don't worry about that stuff. Things will work out, you'll see. Put a bold face on it." She grabbed the pole and began straining again.

The hatch groaned. "Oh ... oh, I think we've got it!" Taara cried.

The hatch gave and opened with a clank. Beyond was a dark expanse of corridor stretching off into the distance. They all huffed and puffed; the effort to get the hatch open had been considerable.

A-Ram peered into the dark. "Bel, I thought the ship was abandoned."

"It is," Stenstrom said trying to pull the pole from its place—it was rooted fast.

"Well, I know I saw somebody standing there in the dark, just now."

"What?" Taara said looking through the hatch. "I don't see anybody."

Stenstrom, holding the pole, stepped through. "I agree. There is nobody here but the three of us."

"No, no, I'm certain I saw someone."

"I don't see anybody," Taara said, squinting.

They all went through into the dark beyond—the air was heavy and stale. A-Ram appeared apprehensive.

"We're going to have to take a good hard look at life support," Stenstrom said. "The air's already getting a little bad."

He waved his hand producing three yellow Holystones. He shook them and they lit up in a yellowish glow. He then handed one each to Taara and A-Ram. "These are cool," Taara said holding hers in her palm. "You're just full of surprises."

A-Ram shook his Holystone and held it up. He gasped.

"Did you see that?"

"See what?"

"I saw someone moving into the dark. I saw the hint of a passing cloak and a bend of the knee."

Stenstrom stepped forward. "Hello? Anyone there?"

No answer.

"Where did you see it?" Stenstrom asked.

"Just there," A-Ram said pointing.

Taara stepped out into the dark, waving her Holystone around, her long, black sideburns jangling about her head. "I don't see anybody."

Stenstrom joined her, seeing nothing. "I think your imagination is getting to you, A-Ram. There is nobody here."

A-Ram laughed and felt silly. "Certainly. You're right. Sorry."

They made their way down the section, their heels clicking on floor boards.

"Hey, Bel, what's that?" A-Ram asked, pointing.

Lying on the floor in the center of the corridor was a small white envelope. A-Ram stepped up to it and shined his Holystone illuminating a black flowing script written across its face in an elegant hand. "This letter is addressed to me," he stated.

"To you?"

"Yes."

"That's not possible. Did you know anybody aboard the *Seeker* from the previous crew?"

"Not that I can think of."

Stenstrom approached and leaned over the letter. It read:

to: STENSTROM, LORD OF BELMONT-SOUTH TYROL

"A-Ram," he said flatly, "this letter is addressed to me, not you."

"No, it's addressed to me, Bel I can read, you know."

Stenstrom waved his hand and produced a small chest. He opened the lid, popped the letter in and shut it.

"What are you doing," A-Ram asked.

"I'm putting this letter away for safe keeping. We need to focus on getting to the bridge for the time being." He waved his hands and the chest with the letter resting within, vanished. "We're all tired and possibly a bit oxygen-deprived from our trip up. We'll examine it in further detail later when time allows."

Not far down the corridor, another hatch emerged in the dim yellow light. Apparently all of the hatches were sealed. They groaned with the prospect of having to grapple open another one.

"The bridge is several levels up and probably twelve hundred feet away from us with about fifty hatches in between. We'll never get there like this. We need power," A-Ram said. "I'm dreading the prospect of manually opening another one."

"You know anything about *Straylight* ships?" Stenstrom asked.

"A little bit," A-Ram said.

"Not a thing," Taara said. "I'm just a grunt."

They approached the next hatch. Stenstrom tested it and it held fast. He sighed in frustration. "Let's have that pole and put our backs into it."

From behind them, toward the aft of the ship, came a distinct groan.

"What was that?" Taara asked.

"Just the ship, the superstructure torquing about," Stenstrom said.

"Ok," she replied. "Didn't sound like metal to me though. Sounded like a person."

"Don't be silly."

They turned back to the locked hatch, and Stenstrom fished the pole into the base. As he strained on the pole, he heard the distinct sound of rapid footsteps approaching, thumping on metal.

Bump . . . Bump . . . Bump . . . Bump . . .

"Who's running?" he asked. A-Ram stood there rather ashen, and Taara drew her SK.

"Gods," A-Ram said, "I've heard footsteps like that before when I was a boy. It was the Fiend of Calvert running across my rooftop."

"I heard something that time, but I don't see anything," Taara replied.

"It's the Fiend. He's on the ship with us. Perhaps he's the one who left me the letter?"

"Oh please, A-Ram—listen to yourself," Stenstrom reproached. "There is nobody other than us on this ship."

Stenstrom held his glowing holystone up to see. "See? Nothing, there's nothing. Just our imaginations. Come on, let's get this hatch open."

A-Ram crowded in near Stenstrom and grabbed the pole, tugging on it.

As they began to work on the hatch, a new sound emerged. It was a harsh sound, a grating of metal on metal culminating in an abrupt SNAP! SNAP!

Stenstrom released the pole and stood upright. He was most familiar with the sound.

SNAP! SNAP!

Just like from his old dream. The sound moved up and down his spine, unsettling him.

"Do you hear that?" he asked.

"Yeah," Taara replied. "Sounds creepy. So what are we going to do? And, you're right about the air, Bel; it's already going foul."

Stenstrom stood there listening.

"Bel?"

He pulled himself from his thoughts. "I'm sorry. We must to the bridge. I suppose we'll figure something out from there."

A-Ram released the pole. "I think it's time to play seriously." He unbuttoned his white shirt and reached in. A moment later he pulled out a gold necklace that he'd been wearing and showed it to them. "Here—I think this might help."

"What's that?" Taara asked.

A-Ram was holding a gold necklace with a charm in the shape of a freshwater fish dangling off it.

"Is that a guppy?" Taara asked.

"What are we looking at here, A-Ram?" Stenstrom asked.

"This, Bel, is the MOLLY. It's the LosCapricos weapon of my House. Do you know what it does?"

"No."

"It allows one to do things one wouldn't ordinarily be able to do, and to know things one shouldn't know."

Taara looked at it with interest. "What? The fish does that? You're pulling my leg."

"No—I'm serious. With the MOLLY, I can do and know all sorts of things."

Stenstrom was skeptical. "Sounds too good to be true. Have you ever used it to discover the identity of the Fiend of Calvert?"

He laughed. "No—it doesn't work too well on abstract things like that— it's great for technical matters and physical feats. It does have a few pretty severe drawbacks, however."

"And they are?"

A-Ram blushed. "Well, for one thing, you have to register with the Sisterhood before you use it—they keep a close eye on such things. Also— and I've never witnessed this myself— they say if you use the MOLLY too much, there are repercussions. I'm told that a demon will come for your soul."

"A demon? Is that true?"

"Again, I've not seen it myself. I've never used it for much other than small things." A-Ram laughed. "I used it to win an eating contest once, and that's about it."

Taara laughed. "Did you register with the Sisters for that?"

"Sure did."

Stenstrom pulled one of his pistols out of his sash. "Fate works wonders on St. Porter's Day, A-Ram. Remember this?" he said.

Stenstrom's weapon looked like an ancient lock-style pistol. It had a smooth iron barrel with a worn walnut stock inlaid with gothic golden lines. "This is the NTH, the LosCapricos weapon of my family," he said.

"Looks old," Taara said.

"It is old. Though it doesn't look like much, the NTH can kill anything with one shot—people, ghosts, robots, monsters, unsubstantial entities, and demons as well. I've used it to kill demons before, lots of times."

"You've fought demons?" Taara said.

"Sure have. My mother used to like to summon demons at me all the time. I've killed a lot of demons with these. Believe me, these things work. You do not want to get shot with an NTH."

"Why would your mom do that?" Taara asked.

"Because she was a Tyrol and a sorceress. Sorceresses don't play around."

A-Ram studied the pistol. "So, I take it your thought is for me to use the

MOLLY with abandon, and then when the demon comes to take my soul, you'll shoot it dead with this pistol."

"Sounds like a good plan to me. I'll shoot the demon dead, and I'll shoot the Fiend too if he shows."

He looked dubious. "I don't know."

Taara laughed. "Well, heck, I'll do it! I'm not scared. Bel here will look out for me, right? Give me that thing!"

A-Ram shook his head and handed her the MOLLY. She quickly put it on and stuffed it under her shirt.

"So, how does it work?"

A-Ram puzzled for a moment. "Well, it's hard to explain. You just do what it is you want to do. It's like moving your arm—how do you explain how to move your arm—you just do it. But, what about the Sisters? They'll get mad if we use it and not register first."

"Well," Stenstrom said. "Seeing as how there don't appear to be any Sisters around, and our Com facilities are probably working as well as life support right now how about we'll let them know first thing once we're on Bazz? I'm certain they won't mind."

A-Ram was dubious and, after a bout of inner turmoil, nodded. "Yes, yes, I imagine that will be fine."

"All right," Taara said. She turned to Stenstrom. "You got me, Bel?"

He raised his NTH and cocked the ancient-looking hammer. "I'm ready."

Taara took a deep breath and pulled her Marine cap off. She was deceptively good-looking: short black hair, fine brown eyes, her long black sideburns.

"What are these pieces of hair you're wearing?" A-Ram asked regarding her sideburns. "Is that common on Bazz?"

Taara appeared lost in thought. "What? These are Mollocks. They mean I'm not married. Men on Bazz like to know where they stand when approaching a woman they don't know. Want to get married, A-Ram? If so, I'll cut them off and give them to you. That's how we do it."

A-Ram giggled.

Taara, wearing the MOLLY, looked around the darkened corridor.

"Anything happening?" Stenstrom asked.

Taara pointed to the hatch. "Well, the first thing we need to do is check up on life support, then get the ship out of this list. The wingtip roll isn't serious. It's the nose-down list she's in that's troubling. We have approximately thirty-two, point six-four hours until she begins entering the atmosphere. Worse, we have approximately nineteen, point six two-eight hours before the Fleet reclamation team arrives from Planet Fall to recover the vessel—the scouting vessel *Demophalon John* is en route and under orders. Their boarding the ship will instantly cost Bel his appointment per Fleet rule—that is the main thing."

Stenstrom smiled. "Pretty impressive, Taara. How are you knowing all that?"

"No clue—I just do. Cool, isn't it?" She suddenly pointed at Stenstrom.

"Someone very dear to you is on that ship."

"What?" Stenstrom asked.

Taara blinked. "What'd I say?"

"You said someone very dear to me is on the scouting ship that's coming for us."

"I did?"

"Yes. I don't think I know anybody on the *Demophalon John*."

"I don't remember saying that."

A-Ram chuckled. "That's the MOLLY playing tricks on you. Happens sometimes. So then," he said, "how are we going to get the *Seeker* out of its terminal orbit?"

Taara walked down the corridor. "We're going to go three sections forward to access point J-91. We shall then enter J-91 and crawl five hundred feet forward until we arrive at engineering carbuncle 2. Once there, we will shunt eleven percent of the grav-pack's stored solar power to the outboard wing thrusters where we will stop the lateral roll. Using the same technique, we will then thrust the nose upward and climb to one-hundred seventy-four thousand feet where we will enter a standard D-Zone parking orbit right down the middle, and, thus, the crisis shall be averted. That's what the reclamation team is planning to do."

Taara shook her head and smiled. "Wow! Who just said that?"

"You did. What about life support?" A-Ram asked.

"We can check its levels, but there's not much we can do to get it going without engine power."

Stenstrom tossed her short black hair. "A-Ram, when should we expect our supernatural visit from the demon?" he asked, his NTH pistol at the ready.

"After she's done."

They walked to the next hatch, and A-Ram and Stenstrom started pulling on it again with the pole.

"No, no, fellas, look . . ." Taara casually approached a side panel, opened it, and pulled a small lever. The hatch opened easily. "See, it's easy if you know what to do."

"That would have been nice to know a while ago," Stenstrom said discarding the pole with a clank.

They made their way forward two more sections and found access point J-91. Taara pulled the cover off and slid into the small space, using her fingers to pull herself ahead.

She abruptly came back out. "You guys hear a fire? I hear fire—cracking, popping."

"I don't hear anything," Stenstrom said. "Do you, A-Ram?"

"No."

Taara shrugged it off and re-entered the access point. Shaking a fresh Holystone, Stenstrom followed, with A-Ram last. Looking at the bottoms of Taara's boots and the holstered muzzle of her SK, he crawled along after her, ready to use his NTH should a demon pop up. The noise the rolling ship was making was pronounced in the tube. Stenstrom could hear a steady "buuuuuuurrrrrrrrr" as the ship creaked relentlessly.

But then, he thought he heard the sound change. Suddenly the creaking became:

"bbbbeeeeellllllmmmmmoooonnnnnnnnnttttttttttttttttttt ..."

And that wasn't all. Stenstrom thought he could hear the sounds of people talking beyond, footsteps, a distant pounding, and, most disturbingly, a slight laugh.

"Shhh," he said. "You hear laughing, A-Ram?"

"No."

Stenstrom was relieved. "Good. I must be hearing things."

"I hear screaming," A-Ram said.

Sometime later, they crawled to Engineering Carbuncle 2. Stenstrom had spent a fair amount of time on starships, but he had never seen anything like it to this point. It was a cluster of ducts, cable trunks, connectors, and valves—it was like looking at a partially dissected elbow-joint, with all sorts of systems running here and there. Taara was already busy unplugging thick cables from an open access point.

"What do you have here?" he asked her.

"These are the power cables for the grav pack. Solar energy comes in, and is stored in the central grid, where it's then distributed throughout the ship via these cables. Right now, Section 84 in the rear of the ship is without gravity as I've unplugged it. I'm going to take this power and run it over here to the outboard thrusters." She blinked and smiled. "Boy—I'm probably really MOLLYing this all up—better not go anywhere with those pistols, Bel, since I'll probably have a whole slew of demons after me before long."

A-Ram came into the carbuncle. "That was horrible," he said, his leggings grimy from the crawl. "There is somebody back there; I know it."

Taara pulled the cable and plugged it into a connector hidden by a mass of wires. "There," she said. "The wing thrusters should now have power—not much, as the grav-pack doesn't store a whole lot of juice, but it should be just enough to ease us out of the roll."

Stenstrom gave her a pat on the shoulder. "Great work, Taara. So, what's next?"

"Next, we have to make our way to the bridge and give the wheel a yank. That should do it."

"What about life support?" A-Ram asked.

"According to these gauges, it's not bad. The ship isn't generating any fresh air, but a craft this size, fully pressurized, will have enough air to last the three of us quite awhile. It might not smell all that great, but it'll do."

A-Ram looked around. "Let's get started—and let none of us get separated until the issue with the demon—and the Fiend— has been resolved. And I don't think it's as easy to kill off a demon as you think it is, Bel. They can be pretty clever, so I'm told."

They made their way from the carbuncle to the main corridor. Opening the hatches one by one, they made the long trip into the frontal section of the ship. They opened a lift door and, using a set of service rungs, began climbing.

"How far up is it?" Stenstrom asked.

"Four decks," Taara replied.

In the drafty, dark lift shaft, they heard more noise, a groan coming up from below. "Did you hear that?" Stenstrom asked, pulling his NTH.

They heard, in the distance, a thin voice saying: "...*Taara... Taara...*"

"Oh, that's creepy," she remarked.

Stenstrom felt very concerned for her. "Taara, I shouldn't have let you do this. I should have done it."

"Why—I'm not scared. I wanted to do it. Besides, you'll protect me, should I need it, right? Let 'em groan all they want."

Stenstrom was impressed by her courage.

They continued climbing a few more decks and then opened the door to the bridge.

The Bridge.

Stenstrom had a quick flash in his head. The white-shirted crewmen manning their posts; the bustle, the excitement. Countess Sygillis of Blanchefort in her elegant gown sitting in the command chair (shoeless as always, no doubt), and Captain Davage prowling behind ever ready to grab the helm. He could hear the voices, the shouted orders. He savored the thought.

Wait!

One of his Holystones designed to detect danger was rattling in his HRN pocket. Something was waiting for them on the bridge. "You two wait here a moment, I want to check the bridge and make certain it's safe. There might be some floor boards missing or dangling cables still carrying a charge. Give me a moment."

Taara and A-Ram waited in the lift shaft as Stenstrom stepped into the bridge. It was incredibly dark. Even with his Holystone he could see very little, it was like a wall of darkness inhabited the bridge.

"How's it look?" Taara asked from the shaft.

"Just a moment."

He checked his HRN to see which Holystone was rattling. It was his Astral Plane detector, and that gave him great pause, for he'd had a number of encounters with the Astral Plane throughout his life and none of them had been pleasant. He reached into his HRN and pulled out several blue Holystones which could block the Astral Plane and close any doors which might be open. He threw them into the dark and they scattered.

Their effect was immediate. The wall of blackness pulled back. The Astral Plane played havoc on one's perceptions, he saw all sorts of things as the blue Holystones began to work. He saw sprays of color and momentary glimpses of the bridge. He thought he saw the floor studded with cruel, jaw-like metal traps designed to capture large animals. There was a vortex of movement and the doorway to the Astral Plane shut. His detector went quiet. After another moment, the bridge seemed to be clear. It was dark, but his Holystone lit it up in soft yellow light. He carefully stepped out, looking for traps.

"Are we good, Bel?" Taara asked.

He trudged about, not finding anything. The blue Holystone worked. He'd have to add a few more protections later to further secure the bridge. "Yes, I think so. Come on in."

They stepped in. Save for the yellowish light from their Holystones, the bridge was in pitch dark. Detail emerged as they walked in. The sensing positions were covered with tarps, the navigator's chair was missing entirely, and the Ops panel was removed. The Missive's station was still intact. Braided wire and bits of wall material lay about on the floor. The emergency lights, long since drained, lurked in the corners.

Someone had trapped the bridge.

Hints of movement. A-Ram was certain he'd seen somebody.

Stenstrom waved his Holystone—his thoughts dark. Who could have done this?

The helm wheel emerged from the gloom. It was turning slightly, moving with the ship's roll. Seeing it reminded him of his mentor, Captain Davage, and his Countess and of Lt. Kilos. This bridge was their place, full of their memory, and he pushed the dark thoughts from his head. The bridge was theirs. It was now safe.

He walked up to the helm and gently touched its worn surface. "Captain Davage once held this in his hand," he said with awe. "The wonders he once worked with this wheel."

A-Ram approached it. He looked at the wheel—eager. "May I?" he asked.

Stenstrom stepped back, and A-Ram planted his feet.

"My whole life, I've always wanted to hold one of these for real—it was a dream I had."

Stenstrom bowed. "Dream no more, A-Ram. Do your thing; the helm is yours."

He smiled and put his hands on the wheel. He took a deep breath. "What are your orders, Captain?"

Stenstrom blushed. "Taara, which way are we rolling?"

"To the starboard," she said, rooting around near the vacant Ops station. "Three quarter's roll per minute."

"Very well, roll three-quarters to port and ease us out."

"Aye, sir. Rolling three quarters to port," he said.

He turned the wheel, fought with it for a moment, and then eased the roll to a stop. "That was a lot harder than I thought it would be. There's a ton of resistance."

"The ship's not working right now, silly," Taara said. "Get a working ship, and it'll move like glass."

With A-Ram standing behind the wheel, Stenstrom and Taara surveyed the bridge.

"Well, the Ops panels are gone, along with Navigation. The Missive's station appears fine, and the sensing arrays appear to still be here, as they are rather obsolete, and it looks like the plumbing's out in Captain's Office—I mean—your office, Bel."

"Looks like we'll have a long walk to use the bathroom for now. What else do we have?"

Taara flopped down into the Missive's chair. "That's it—ship's pretty much dead. The gas-compression engines are still here, but without the SM coils to power them, they're not much use. At least it's quiet in here, and the air's not too stale yet."

"Do we have Com at all?"

"No way."

Stenstrom shook his head. "Well, here we are. It's not much at present, but it'll have to do until we get to Bazz. We have the whole ship to spread out in, but I advise we stay together until I can kill the demon coming for Taara's soul."

"Thanks," Taara said.

"Don't forget about the Fiend, Bel," A-Ram added.

"How could I forget? Taara, you can have my office to sleep in until we get matters sorted out."

"I'm not some tea-drinker from Kana, Bel. I don't need a room to myself. I can handle the two of you."

He laughed. "Fine then. So, let's to it. Let's get the ship out of this list."

LT. GWENDOLYN, LADY OF PRENTISS

7

—LT. GWENDOLYN—

The *Seeker* was now in a high Zone D parking orbit, safely pulled away from the slow, rolling dive it had found itself in. The demon that was supposedly coming for Taara's soul still hadn't shown, and Stenstrom wished for it to come so they could get its killing over with.

Since arresting the decaying orbit, they had managed to get a little power to the bridge by denying gravitational service to some of the rear areas of the ship. They now had dim lights, partial forward and ventral sensing, and port and starboard roll. They also had a feeble stream of stale air pushing in at 1/24th life support from a ventilator.

They also got the backup com system running.

It wasn't long before a message came chattering in.

Appearing dimly in the flickering Holo-cone was a stern-looking woman dressed in a lady's Fleet Tremblar uniform. From what Stenstrom could see, she was a rugged woman with dark brown hair tightly pulled back under her large triangle hat. She had a strong chin and a big forehead with either gray or green eyes. Very attractive, in a husky, solid sort of way. Behind her, crewmen bustled about. She stood with polished grace and had a long rapier-like weapon hanging at her side.

She spoke, her voice slightly garbled from the low power of the com.

"Are you Paymaster Stenstrom, Lord of Belmont?"

Stenstrom, unlike the famous Captain Davage who preceded him, liked the captain's chair, so he dramatically sat down in a flutter of his HRN coat and cleared his throat. "Aye, I am. Belmont-South Tyrol to be precise. Well met. And you are?"

"Lt. Gwendolyn, Lady of Prentiss, commanding officer of the scouting ship *Demophalon John*. What is your situation, sir? Fleetcom is very worried about you."

Stenstrom looked around and leaned forward. "Are they? Half-scuttled, that is our situation, as well they should know."

"What is the status of your life support, please?"

Stenstrom took a deep breath. "A little stale, but not bad."

Lt. Gwendolyn tried to look around, but apparently could see little through the poor connection. "Paymaster, my Hospitaler has a few important questions for you, if you would be so kind."

A female Hospitaler, wearing the usual black and silver uniform of a Samaritan, pushed her way into the Holo-cone. She, like the captain, was a solid-looking lady with blond hair twisted into a number of long, sinuous braids decorated with beads. Her silver helmet, winged in the usual fashion, sat askew on her head. "Paymaster Stenstrom, well met. I am Morgan-Jeterix of the Ephysians, Lady of Thompson, Grand Order of Hospitalers. Might I say I had the honor of serving with your father for a time—truly a goodly and honorable man."

"Thank you, ma'am," Stenstrom replied.

Lt. Gwendolyn appeared impatient. "Please get on with it, Morgan," she said.

Morgan shot her a look. "I wish to ask you a few questions, as, without proper life support, you can quickly become addled with brain asphyxia and not even know it. I want to assess your current medical situation."

"Very well, please ask your questions," Stenstrom said.

"What year were you born, sir?"

"03192ax," Stenstrom quickly replied.

"What is your birth date?"

"December 17th."

Morgan noted a few things down on a pad. "Are you feeling out of sorts at all?"

"No, not really."

"Are you ..."

Gwendolyn pushed her way back into the screen. "Thank you, Morgan. As you can see, the Paymaster appears, for the moment, to be fine." She turned to him. "I am relieved to see that you are unharmed. I also see that you managed to get your half-scuttled ship out of its terminal orbit and park at standard altitude for dry-docking, an impressive accomplishment considering the state of your vessel. Please be advised that we shall rendezvous with you in approximately seven hours. At that time, myself and my team shall board the ship and safe-tow it to Dry Dock 186 to begin its repairs."

"The repairs that I am paying for, yes?"

"I am not aware of such things, sir. To continue, at that time we shall rescue you and your people and take you back down to Fleet."

Stenstrom smiled. "Good Lt., if I may..."

"That's *captain*, if you please," she corrected. "I am the commanding officer of this vessel and I insist proper protocol be observed."

"Yes, thank you. As you can see, Captain, we here on the *Seeker* are in weather shape and have no need of rescue. We are a warbird on the wing. I have been recently appointed to the chair of the *Seeker* and have been tasked to go at speed to Bazz on the orders of Admiral Derlith. I intend to fulfill that mission."

Lt. Gwendolyn sighed. She put her hand on the hilt of her sword. "Paymaster, I appreciate your position, and am sorry that my presence aboard the ship shall cause your appointment to be rendered void. However, your safety, and that of those with you, is currently my responsibility, and I intend to deliver you and anybody else present on the *Seeker*, to the shore immediately. Am I clear, sir? I hate to be blunt and the bearer of bad news, but there it is. If it is any consolation to you, sir, I shall be glad to make a recommendation to the Admiralty regarding your inventiveness and tenacity in this matter. It is certainly to be commended."

"Thank you," Stenstrom said. "The Admiralty certainly has a keen eye for such things, do they not? And, please, allow me to be clear to you as well, Captain. I have a mission to accomplish, for my chair's sake, and I shall carry it out. You needn't hurry to our position, as we shall not be here upon your arrival."

Gwendolyn approached the Holo-Cone, filling it up. It was hard to judge how big she was, but she looked to be rather tall and solidly built. Stenstrom mused that, if she smiled, she would most probably be very attractive—but her face was set in a stern frown. "According to my logs, you have two unauthorized persons aboard your vessel. She snapped her fingers, and someone handed her a report. She looked at it. "Where is Fleet Adjutant Lt. Josephus, Lord of A-Ram?"

"Here, ma'am," A-Ram piped from behind the helm.

Gwendolyn glanced at him. "I know you, sir, do I not? Yes, yes of course, I've seen you in Admiral Derlith's office. Well met. Sir, you are considered absent from your duties—which is a serious charge. The Admiral is very concerned about you and is willing to forget this matter, but I must have you to his side with all speed."

"Lord A-Ram no longer is in the employ of Admiral Derlith, and he is no longer an Adjutant," Stenstrom said. "I have duly appropriated him, as is my right as ship's commander. Lord A-Ram is now my Master Helmsman."

"What?" Captain Gwendolyn said, shocked.

"I have appointed Lord A-Ram as my Master Helmsman."

"Paymaster, he is an adjutant—an assistant, a helper, and, if my memory is clear, he can barely see two feet in front of his face. Lord A-Ram, I do not mean to belittle you, but ..."

"Then why do so?" Stenstrom said, jumping in. "He had the skill and the raw nerve to fly me in a sub-orbital onto a dead ship in space. You claim he can't see—perhaps it is you and everybody else at Fleet who cannot see, for there was an unnoticed treasure in your midst the whole time, and I have stolen him away and given him his due at long last."

Gwendolyn sighed. "I am not certain what relevance that has in this conversation, Paymaster. Lord A-Ram shall be returned to the Admiral's office."

"Yes, where he may get a badly sore elbow polishing the Admiral's silver. By hook or by crook, Captain, I shall have a crew," Stenstrom replied. "Admiral Derlith has made no other choice possible. This man was wasted in that office and routinely humiliated by an arrogant Admiral. Here he is a Master Helmsman and greatly appreciated."

Gwendolyn shot him an increasingly dirty look. "I see. And where is

Private Taara de la Anderson, of the 110th Marines?"

Taara stepped forward and nodded. "That's me."

Gwendolyn turned to her. "You, Private, are officially AWOL from your barracks. I am compelled to inform you that I must take you into custody at once. Adjutant Josephus, will you please take Private Taara to the brig and await my arrival. Is that understood?"

"The brig currently has no gravity, ma'am," Taara chirped.

"Then select a suitable quarters and take her there. Once inside, she is not to emerge until I arrive."

Shrugging, A-Ram began moving in Taara's direction.

Stenstrom got a tad annoyed himself. A-Ram showed every sign of cracking and giving in to Lt. Gwendolyn. A-Ram was used to following orders without much question, and Stenstrom had to intervene. "Stand fast, A-Ram. Let's show a bit of style here, yes?" He turned back to Gwendolyn. "Perhaps you've cotton in your ears, Captain, or that tight bun you've imprisoned your hair in has restricted the blood flow to your brain," he said. "Lord A-Ram is under my command, not yours; therefore, stop issuing him orders."

A-Ram resumed his position behind the helm, dwarfed by it. He looked like he wished to be elsewhere.

Gwendolyn's eyes flashed.

"And," Stenstrom continued, "you will be happy to note that I have appointed Private Taara as my first officer, again as is my right. The *Seeker* has a long tradition of Marines serving as first officer: Lt. Kilos of the 12th Marines, and Lt. Verlin of the 53rd have served this ship proudly, and I wish to carry on said tradition. I am sorry for the confusion. If Admiral Derlith had left me a ship not in pieces, I would have Commed down the required communication hours ago. Perhaps you could do it for me, since you appear to have command of a nice, working scouting ship."

Gwendolyn was shocked. "A ... *private* ... as a first officer? Paymaster, such a thing is not done ..."

"It is now, and Private Taara shall serve me and this ship well."

She shook her head. "Paymaster, I am sorry, I am overriding your appointment. Adjutant Josephus, please take Private Taara into custody, immediately."

Again, A-Ram began moving from behind the helm.

"A-Ram, stand fast and buckle up! Captain, you are not issuing me or my crew orders, and you've naught but the temerity to attempt to do so."

Gwendolyn became rather perturbed. "Paymaster, when I board your vessel and take command, you and I are going to have a short but rather vigorous talk in the gym regarding seniority and proper etiquette, and I warn you, sir, I am a champion boxer."

"I can tell, the heavyweight division, yes?" Stenstrom said—Gwendolyn's mouth dropped open in shock at the slap. Taara and Morgan, on the screen, laughed.

Stenstrom stood and approached the Holo-cone. He was standing nose to nose with Lt. Gwendolyn. "Captain, it appears we are both victims of circumstance here—there's no need for us to work against each other. Please, allow me to complete my mission, and then I shall gladly allow you to board the ship and complete yours."

"I have my orders, sir—and you have yours. I order you to remain on station and await my arrival, where I, and my team, shall board the ship post haste. At that time, I shall relieve you of your command, take Private Taara into custody, and return Adjutant Josephus to the Fleet. Then, I shall escort you to the gym where I shall gladly relieve you of your teeth. Take your pick—boxing, wrestling, sambo, or a good old-fashioned, bare-knuckle fight—it's up to you!"

"Captain, I will remind you that you are in command of a scouting ship. I am sitting on a Main Fleet warbird, such as it is, and, therefore, your orders are nullified. And, by the by, should you choose to take a swing at me, be it known that I shall swing back with the utmost vigor. Lady or not, girl or not, I shall put you on the floor."

"My orders come from Admiral Derlith!"

"As do mine!"

Gwendolyn took her hat off, and her dark brown hair spilled out. "You have seven hours, Paymaster. If you are not where you are supposed to be when I come for you, then it's war between us, sir, and it will be a war that you shall lose in earnest!"

"Very well—then it is war. You have thrown down the gauntlet, and I am picking it up and slapping your punch-riddled face with it. If only to cause you the maximum level of annoyance, I am going to Bazz. Stenstrom out!"

Gwendolyn looked like she was about to explode when the screen went off.

A-Ram shook his head.

"That was cool, Bel!" Taara cried. "You really know how to tweak a person off. She looked really, really pissed." Taara gave him a shove. "Am I really your first officer?"

"If you want it."

Taara gave him a grand hug.

A-Ram was skeptical. "That was a fine show of bravado Bel, but the fact remains we're stuck here in orbit. We've no drive engines and are dead in our tracks. Likewise, you're going to be finding yourself in quite a fistfight once Captain Gwendolyn boards the ship," he said.

"Am I?"

"Oh, yes. She's one of Admiral Derlith's favorites—his niece I think. And yes, she was the Fleet's boxing champion in her weight class four years running, ladies division—and it wasn't the heavyweight class either. She's also really good at wrestling and sambo, for what that's worth. She has a fast right hook and a mean streak to match, so I'm told."

"What else?"

"That's about all I know. She was often in attendance in the Admiral's office. She was always quite nice to me—but then again I never slapped her in the face right in front of her crew, either."

"Oh, you're too kind, A-Ram. I'm certain she'll get over it."

"If you're going to fight, I want to be there to watch," Taara said.

Stenstrom walked to the back of the bridge. "Taara, I'm not going to beat up a helpless woman."

"She didn't look helpless to me. I'll bet she could take you—heck I'll bet I could take you too! You never want to fight a girl from Bazz."

Stenstrom ignored her. "So, if only to avoid an embarrassing session of fisticuffs in the gym, we have seven hours to not be here. What are our options? How are we going to do this?"

"We can't use power from the grav packs, Bel," Taara said, still all MOLLYed up. "That won't break us out of orbit—we won't be able to generate the altitude or the velocity. We have gas compression engines but no coils to run them—and they don't function in space anyway. We have no motive power, plain and simple."

Stenstrom tapped his chin and thought. "I was thinking, with the *Seeker* abandoned and mostly stripped, she's carrying much less weight then she normally would, and, therefore, the amount of thrust required to drive her will be greatly reduced."

"We would need a 770 coil, at least," Taara said, impressed by her own knowledge that she shouldn't have.

"If memory serves, a 770 coil is pretty big. All I'm talking is enough thrust to get us away from Kana and on our way to Bazz."

They sat silent for a moment.

"A standard T-60 transport has a fair amount of thrust. If you have five or six of those clamped onto the hull, that would limp us out of orbit I should think," A-Ram added.

Taara suddenly seemed inspired. She went to the Fore Sensing station and peered into the viewer. "We have a slow tap into Fleetcom's database. Let me just fiddle about with his here for a sec ... and, there we go!"

"What are you looking up?" Stenstrom asked.

"I had a thought. Yes, look here—Dry Dock 275. I recall the clerks at the hangar talking about an old tach-Scout ship that's currently docked there for a refit, so I looked it up. Here it is, the *Westminster,* an old *Belleraphon*-class scouting vessel."

"Go on, Taara, what are your thoughts?"

"I'm thinking we up-thrust out of this polar orbit and synch-up with Dry Dock 275. I think, if we reroute enough power, we'll just be able to reach Dry Dock altitude. And, better yet, the *Westminster* will just fit into Ripcar Bay 5. We'll put her in there, clamp her down nice and snug, then we'll just drop containment and fire her engines. That should get us out of here in a hurry."

"Ripcar Bay 5?" A-Ram said. "That's a forward-facing bay. We'll be flying backwards."

"So?" Taara replied. "There will be issues, of course. Our Line of Thrust will be well above our center of gravity, so we'll be a bit unstable and will want to drift. We can course correct as needed."

Stenstrom smiled. "And, I would imagine that there is a minimal crew up there on Dry Dock 275, what with the holiday and all."

A-Ram shuffled his feet. "I don't like this, Bel. We're talking about stealing a Fleet vessel."

"Oh, come on, A-Ram—I prefer the term *commandeering*. We're talking about *commandeering* a Fleet vessel."

"The Fleet is going to rain all over us," A-Ram replied.

"Are they? The Admirals make the rules down there in Armenelos, but let them enforce them up here in space. The Fleet Captaincy, should they get wind of this, is going to be pretty sore—not at us, but at the Admiralty. I can drop names with the best of them—my father, Captain Davage, and more. Captain Davage told me himself—a Fleet captain is expected to be bold and tenacious, and that's exactly how we're conducting ourselves in carrying out our mission. Taara, how much altitude do we need?"

"Dry Dock 275 is in the second shell of Zone B, about another fifteen thousand feet straight up. Good thing too—if she were in the third or fourth shells, we wouldn't be able to generate the velocity to reach her."

A-Ram sulked behind the wheel. "We're going to get into trouble."

"Look, we get into trouble—I'll buy our way out of it. Money talks, A-Ram, never forget that. I can buy Barr and mouthpieces that'll have the Fleet's head spinning. Besides, we're going to bring the *Westminster* back nice and neat after we've delivered our bloody brandy to Bazz. No harm done, so, with that in mind, let's make ready to up-thrust and do this."

8

—THE *WESTMINSTER*—

Slowly, the *Seeker* ascended several thousand feet. If the various sensors and automated equipment on the bridge had been functioning, they would have been hearing all sorts of claxons and buoys complaining about proximity violations and the like. However, the *Seeker's* bridge was blissfully quiet.

Soon, on the jumpy holo-cone, the rib-cage of Dry Dock 275 appeared in the distance. It was mostly empty; the only ship within was the tiny, bullet-shaped hull of the *Westminster*.

Carefully, A-Ram slid the *Seeker* to the aft docking collar, and the three of them made their slow way out of the ship.

The clean, fresh air of the Dry Dock was a real treat after the stale, smelly air they'd been breathing. They were met by a single Marine and an angry yardmaster.

"Didn't you get my Com? You're in the wrong Dry Dock! The *Seeker's* scheduled to make berth in Dry Dock 186 a few days hence. You need to get your tub out of here now!"

"Actually sir—I'm sorry—what is your name?" Stenstrom said.

"Senior Yardmaster Piro."

"I see. Well, Senior Yardmaster Piro, we're not staying, obviously. We're just here to pick up the *Westminster*—her presence is required on Bazz for a few days, then we'll have her right back just like we found her."

Piro was dumbfounded. "You're taking the *Westminster*? First I've heard of it. The *Westminster* is scheduled, after her refit, to go to Tantan and serve the Fleet office there. I'm going to get some confirmation. Sgt. Laval, would you mind so much?"

The Marine drew his SK and pointed it at them.

"I'd get your hands up in plain sight and keep them there, if I were you, right now," Piro said walking into his office.

Stenstrom smiled and raised his hands. "Oh, indeed." He glanced at A-Ram and Taara. "Come on, you two, get your hands up. Let's all be friends, shall we?"

A-Ram and Taara raised their hands. The Marine reached out and took Taara's SK. He then pulled Stenstrom's NTH pistols and set them aside. "I'm sorry about this," he said. "I'm certain it's just a mix up. Happens all the time."

"Yes, just a mix up. Sgt., you forgot something," Stenstrom said.

"Sir?" the Marine responded.

Stenstrom waved his fingers and a pink Holystone appeared in his hand. "Holystone," he said. "I always carry a bunch."

"Thank you, sir," the Marine replied. He reached up and took the stone. He instantly fell into a rather stupefied state. He toppled over, and Stenstrom caught him and eased him down. "Pink Holystone works every time. You'll have a nice little dream, Sgt., then you'll be just fine."

Taara put her hands down and walked into the Yardmaster's office.

There was a struggle from within.

Somebody hit the floor with a crash.

Stenstrom and A-Ram came in. Taara was dragging the Yardmaster's unconscious body away from his chair. "Taara, was knocking this man out really necessary?"

"Yes, Bel, it was. He's fine—he'll just have to live with the notion that he got knocked out by a girl is all. I'm certain that's not a tidbit he'll be sharing with his friends any time soon."

Stenstrom produced another pink Holystone and stuck it in Piro's hand.

They then scoured the Dry Dock, looking for anything they might have a use for. They found several crates of insta-meals which they loaded onto the *Westminster*, along with a few boxes of bottled water, four pressure suits with ten hours of air each, three portable generators, two Holo-terms, a Macon air condenser, a Havelock mag system, along with yards of cabling, and some hand-tooling, should it be needed.

They then piled into the *Westminster* and A-Ram fired it up. The transport was rather bullet-shaped with a fairly spacious cargo area and pilot's seat.

A-Ram strapped himself into the pilot's chair and pressed buttons on the organ-like panels in front of him. "Oh, after the sub-orbital and the *Seeker's* dead helm, this is like flying a dream," he raved as he pulled away from the dock.

Taara was amazed. "How do you know how to do all of this stuff—got another MOLLY on you somewhere?"

"No," he laughed. "Lots and lots of un-logged time in the simulators. I'm up on all these old ships. I used to go in them every day, and escape out the front hatch when somebody came in. I would have gotten into loads of trouble if they caught me in there."

They had the foresight to pre-open the doors to Ripcar bay 5, and A-Ram carefully slid the *Westminster* in—it was a tight fit. They then donned their newly acquired pressure suits and went out. They hard docked the *Westminster's* landing skids and bolted her down as tightly as they could. Taara, still using the MOLLY with abandon, ran a controller cable from the central node of the transport to a junction nearby. "This way," she explained over the suit's Com, "we'll have control over the ship from the bridge and not have to have somebody actually in the *Westminster* doing the flying." It took awhile, bumbling around in her pressure suit, but she finally got it set up. Taara also connected several power cables to the *Westminster's* generators and shunted the power, allowing the *Seeker* to make use of it.

Their tasks done, they gathered their booty from the Dry Dock and collected it in a cargo net. They then did a short space walk to the adjacent Ripcar bay where they manually entered.

"Well," Taara said getting out of her pressure suit, her short black hair a mess. "That Dry Dock was like a big old grocery store, wasn't it? Look at all this stuff we just stole. This is great!"

"We're going to need to be getting out of here post haste. The pinkies should be wearing off on those two shortly," Stenstrom said.

"You're just pissing people off left and right today, aren't you, Bel?" she added.

They returned to the bridge and set up two of the generators—it took awhile hoisting them up the empty lift shaft with ropes until Taara had the bright idea to cut the gravity in the area, allowing the heavy equipment to float up—that was some inspired stuff. The lights came on and the whole place seemed a tad cheerier. They also set up the Macon, and it began producing fresh, clean air.

A-Ram took the helm, and Stenstrom ordered the *Seeker* backed out of the Dry Dock. The Westminster fired, and off they went.

9

—Stop the *Seeker*—

Aboard the *Demophalon John*, Lt. Gwendolyn walked through the small corridors of the ship and headed to her quarters. Her crew, though efficient and polite, gave her plenty of space as she prowled the halls. Nobody said anything to her as she passed by either; they sunk into the walls, trying to be quiet and unnoticed.

Yesterday was St. Porter's Day. She would have forgotten all together, but she heard several of her crew wishing each other well.

Nobody gave her the "Happy Porter's Day" greeting.

Nobody wanted to get on her bad side or risk provoking the Grizzly Bear, the Snapping Turtle, the Angry Mountain; that's what they called her—she'd heard all the various names whispered in the mess and in the corridors.

Her crew, in short, was quite terrified of Lt. Gwendolyn, Lady of Prentiss.

Not only was she mean as a snake and pugnacious to boot, she had the connections in the Admiralty to really make things unpleasant for a poor junior officer or crewman—there were all sorts of rotten duties and crap postings just awaiting such an unfortunate soul.

The closest thing she had to a friend was Morgan-Jeterix, the ship's Hospitaler, and why not? Being a Hospitaler, Morgan was immune to the captain's fits of temper and threats of detail or demotion. And, though the crew had never seen such a thing, Morgan-Jeterix could probably out-fight Lt. Gwendolyn if push came to shove—nobody could fight like a Hospitaler.

Clearly, nobody really liked Lt. Gwendolyn much.

She wondered why sometimes. Sure, she demanded a lot from her crew. Sure, she went by the book. Sure, she could have a hot temper, and sometimes she went off at the mouth, but many captains did, and they had the love of the crew. Why didn't she? Why didn't she have a friend aboard? Why did she eat her meals alone and spend all of her free time in her quarters?

She opened the door to her small cabin and stepped in. She removed her hat and let her long, coffee-brown hair down out of its confining bun. She took off her gun belt and hung it from a peg, her family FEDULA, long and rapier-like, glinting in the soft light. Her feet were killing her; she pulled off her over-sized Falloon boots and took a seat. She'd had a long day.

She looked around. Being the captain of a *Tekel*-class scout ship, her quarters were the largest on the ship, yet they were rather small, just big enough for a table, a bathroom and a small bed; still, they were quite luxurious compared to what everybody else got bunked-in together. She didn't need a whole lot of room though. Her quarters were shockingly sterile and devoid of personal mementos and decorations.

A cold room for a well-known cold person.

She liked many of the ancient card games that were once played, and was quite good at them. She had several hand-made, hand-painted decks that were worth quite a bit of money. They were her most prized and sentimental possessions beyond her FEDULA, given to her by her grandfather.

She knew by heart dozens of games, but, mostly, she played solitary ones. Nobody wanted to sit down and play a hand of cards with the Grizzly Bear.

Might get eaten . . .

She took out one of her decks and sat down at the table, shuffling the cards around. She dealt eight cards for herself, and eight for a person across the table who wasn't there.

Her lonely thoughts began to spin.

Paymaster Stenstrom, Lord of Belmont ...

She understood how the Paymaster felt. Her mission, on the orders of Admiral Derlith himself, will cost him his chair. He had rubbed the Admiralty the wrong way during his Appointment, and they were going to make him suffer for it. He wouldn't be the first person they cheated out of a captain's chair.

Stenstrom, Lord of Belmont. That was a name she heard from time to time, growing up in the House of Prentiss. When her aunt, a thin, unsmiling woman, came for a visit, she would sit in the parlor and talk with venom about someone named Stenstrom, Lord of Belmont, and his mother—a woman whom her aunt hated above all others.

The words her aunt spoke were ugly and cold, driven by a confined, animal-like fury, all directed at some woman from Tyrol and her son.

And then, many times, her aunt called out for her in a callow voice: "Gwendolyn!"

She didn't want to go into her presence. She was frightened of her aunt, but was drawn, and couldn't help herself.

"Gwendolyn! Come here!" Sometimes she heard that voice in her nightmares:

Gwendolyn!!

Many times, she was stopped half-way by her uncle, Derlith. "Come on, Gwen, let's go outside and get some air," or "Let's put the gloves on and go a round or two—show me what you got." Many times, her uncle saved her having to go before her aunt.

Occasionally, he wasn't there to help her, and she had to go in and see her aunt. She never remembered what happened after that—it was blacked out in her mind.

So, there he was, Paymaster Stenstrom, a man with enemies all over the place. She wondered if he was aware of all the various people who hated him from afar.

Gwendolyn didn't hate him. As a girl, she had harbored a vague curiosity about the fellow: what he was like, how he looked, what he had done to deserve her aunt's considerable scorn. She was certain he was only a year or two older than she was—he was just a little boy as her aunt spewed her venom—what could he possibly have done?

No, she didn't hate him at all ...

But, she had her orders to take him into custody. Unlike the commander of a warbird like the *Seeker,* a scout-ship captain had to follow orders from the Admiralty. She had no choice.

She was under orders, but that didn't mean she had to like them.

She had the whole thing pictured out in her head. After she'd accomplished her mission, she had planned to take Paymaster Stenstrom into a quiet cafeteria at Fleet—there was one in the western wing of the complex that she favored—sit him down at a quiet table, and explain. He would, no doubt, be rather surly, perhaps pouting and nostalgic. She imagined herself being unusually patient and accommodating, listening to Lord Belmont cry in his beer. Since he'd been personally sponsored by the great Captain Davage, then he must be of good quality; he had to be. She planned to stick up for him, to come charging to his rescue and offer him help. She'd read Davage's report regarding Lord Stenstrom's performance during the Kestral Affair. He did very well, very well indeed, so, apparently, he was cut from command cloth. Surely some ship out there in the whole of the Fleet could use such a fellow, and she planned to help him in any way she could.

She wondered how her aunt would react to such a display—probably not well, though Gwendolyn frankly didn't care what her aunt thought. She was no longer a frightened child, and this was none of her aunt's business.

She imagined herself with all sorts of questions, sitting there in the cafeteria with him. A drab cafeteria in the middle of Fleet could hardly been considered a romantic place, but, in her practical and undecorated mind, it might as well have been a garden full of roses. Just she and Paymaster Stenstrom, sitting with their trays, absorbed in discovering each other.

Her questions were many. So, why a Paymaster? Why didn't he simply join the Fleet? He wears a Hoban Royal Navy coat—so he must have some hankering for it, some longing. Why did he choose such an odd route?

And, why the mask? Was he simply an eccentric lord from Belmont. Was he scarred, or was there some other reason for wearing it?

Why?

She wondered what he looked like without it—just like one of those cleverly wrapped presents she used to get on Nether Day, one that was obscured just enough to keep her from knowing what it was—to whet one's appetite to get it unwrapped and find out what was underneath.

Her fantasy continued. As the lunch went on, she had planned to tell him that she would do what she could to help him re-appoint to another ship. She wanted to make amends. And he would see reason and accept, warmly shaking her hand, and then she would get out her decks, push their trays aside, and they'd play cards. They'd play for hours, both of them laughing and talking with abandon, the cards going *fnap ... fnap* on the tabletop.

In her mind, she had Paymaster Stenstrom, Lord of Belmont—the man in the mask and the HRN coat—penciled in as a friend, perhaps more. Surely he, like her, was a misfit too.

But then, of course, the Grizzly Bear struck.

He annoyed her during their initial meeting—worse, he infuriated her.

Yes, I can see that—heavyweight division ...

What a cruel thing to say—in front of her crew. Morgan laughed—everybody laughed. And, of course, she saw red and went off at the mouth. What had she expected from him—her mission was to remove him of his brand new command. The idyllic and fanciful lunch shared in the Fleet cafeteria that she had hoped for began to seem more and more impossible.

Now, after her performance earlier, she'd committed herself to getting into a brawl with him, and all the good will she'd built up in her mind was temporarily forgotten. She had been furious. If she could have, she would have fought him right there and then. There's that temper again, and the willingness to attempt bodily harm upon another.

Getting into a fight with Paymaster Stenstrom, whether the man could properly defend himself or not—it hadn't mattered to her. Maybe her crew was right to be afraid of her after all.

✳ ✳ ✳ ✳ ✳

She was a Prentiss, a long-standing noble family from Zenon, their holdings not too terribly far from the ancestral Belmont holdings in the more southern city of Brynthia, if she wasn't mistaken. Unlike other Zenon Girls, who tended to be quite petite, ladies from Prentiss were large in stature—not fat or overweight, just broad-shouldered, tall and dense. Gwendolyn had six sisters, all like her, but, of all of them, she was the biggest and probably had the most vile temper and the sharpest tongue. Her tongue, in fact, had knocked her right out of the prolific Zenon social scene that her sisters participated so readily in. Though not very old, she was already considered a spinster; most of the eligible lords, looking to find a lady, denounced Gwendolyn of Prentiss as not worth the trouble, and they conducted their search in less volatile pastures. Such fiery ladies were often known as "Black Widows" in League society. Vith ladies were often labeled Black Widows, and sometimes Barrows and Calverts, but almost never Zenons. Sometimes Black Widows were a commodity—interested gentlemen occasionally finding them alluring and irresistible, like hunting for a dangerous animal that could lash out and bite. Yet, in her case, her stature and undeniably volcanic nature kept the brave at bay.

Fortunately for her, getting married wasn't foremost on her mind. She wanted to educate herself and become something other than the trophy wife on display in a grand sitting room other Zenon Girls dreamed of being. She saw the League around her and wanted to participate, to make her mark and leave an impression. She went to school in Arden, earning an **Ev** degree as an engineer of stellar mechanics—the only Zenon Girl in her class. She did, in fact, have a solid head on her shoulders.

She was also a favorite of one of her uncles on her mother's side, Lord Derlith of Cone, an Admiral in the Stellar Fleet—the younger brother of the mean old aunt she and her sisters were so afraid of. He always thought Gwendolyn had a good head and a stout heart, top among her sisters, though she clearly needed to work on her manners and her social skills. Like most of the Cones, her uncle had the sort of domineering personality that put a stopper on her temper—squelched it before it could top off and really come to a boil. And he genuinely appeared to be fond of his niece. He was patient with her, guiding her throughout her formative years. As an outlet for her energy and to help teach her discipline and respect, he introduced her to contact sports, which wasn't a pursuit proper Zenon Girls usually chose to indulge in, but Gwendolyn was certainly not a standard Zenon Girl. She took up boxing at first, and had an immediate talent for it. Her size and density were a big help. Soon, she began branching out—taking up wrestling and sambo as well. Such "vulgar" sports weren't in big demand on Kana, so her uncle took her to Onaris every year to compete, and she won a number of tournaments there over time.

He helped her gain admission to the Fleet and guided her quickly through the ranks, Gwendolyn eventually becoming the commanding officer of a scouting ship under his direct command, though engineering appeared to be her true calling. After guiding the *Demophalon John* for a few years, she should easily appoint as either the engineer or captain for some Main Fleet Vessel. She'd heard that he did quite a lot for her behind the scenes, managing to push aside some of the less flattering notes that began bubbling up regarding her behavior: unruly, ill mannered, bad tempered … disliked by her crew.

"Not to worry, Gwen," he often told her. "Leave all that to me."

After she had time to cool off and reflect, she once again found herself admiring this man whom most of the Admiralty wished to see fail—this upstart Paymaster from Tyrol who Free Booted his way onto the chair of a Main Fleet Vessel. Look what he'd accomplished. He had been able to get aboard an abandoned ship using a sub-orbital craft, and he had managed to get two total strangers to help him along the way, at great risk to themselves. She wondered if she could have done the same thing, if she could have gotten anyone to assist her in such a fashion. She rather doubted it.

She looked at the cards across the table. "I'm sorry for today—I'd hoped to get off on a better footing. Friends?" she said hopefully.

As she sat there waiting for the cards to answer, her Com chattered.

"Com," she said in her husky voice.

"Com here, Captain. Message from Fleet, Admiral Derlith."

"Aye, Com, I'll take it here."

She took a moment, straightened her hair, and accepted the message. On her Com screen, the stern, iron-haired image of Admiral Derlith appeared.

"Evening, sir," she said. "Well met."

The Admiral didn't mince words. "Gwendolyn, there has been a change in plans regarding the *Seeker.*"

The Admiral was always very informal with her. He was her uncle, after all.

She was elated. "I see. We were at three hours, twenty-two minutes until our link-up with her, sir."

"The *Seeker* is no longer in orbit around Kana."

"What?"

"Yes, Paymaster Stenstrom and his band of pirates are cutting a notorious swath across the face of the Fleet. Seems the good Paymaster took it upon himself to appropriate the tach-scout ship *Westminster* from Dry Dock 275, and is using her as a drive engine. Two hours ago, he broke orbit and is on a slow-speed course to Bazz by way of Onaris."

Gwendolyn absorbed the news. "I see," she said again.

"In light of this development, your mission has changed. You are to intercept the *Seeker,* board her, and deliver Paymaster Stenstrom, Adjutant Josephus, Lord of A-Ram, and Marine Private Taara de la Anderson back to Fleet. There, they shall face any number of charges and fines. You are authorized to disable the *Seeker* in any manner you see fit to safely accomplish your mission, though I bade you to be mindful of Fleet assets and protect them as best you can. I trust to your good judgment. Am I clear?"

Gwendolyn's elation fell. "Admiral," she said, "I request that another perform this task—I do not feel up to it."

"There is no other that I trust for such a mission. We cannot tag out a Main Fleet warbird for this task, as it shall then be out of the Admiralty and a matter of public record. The Paymaster, should such a thing come out, might garner sympathy in the court of public opinion throughout the ranks and manage to get out of this situation enhanced. He might even find help—as no doubt, his father or Captain Davage would come to his aid should his plight become known. We have to keep a tight lid on this, Gwendolyn. I want this matter kept on the hush, and I want that animal from Tyrol before me in irons. We want to rip that mask from his foolish Belmont face and tear that coat right off him. And, for that we need you."

"Who, pray, is 'we,' Admiral?"

"Never mind. Just get him here on the quick."

She closed her eyes. "Admiral, what is to be done with Paymaster Stenstrom?"

"Let us be creative here for a moment. Stockade is an obvious punishment. Work detail, possible imprisonment, and censure from the Fleet and the Sisters are likely. And surely, a date with the sonic lash would be in order."

She sat there for a moment.

"Can I count on you, Gwen?"

"Uncle, were you aware that Adjutant Josephus is an accomplished pilot?"

"Josephus? Of course not! The man can barely see and is afraid of his own shadow. He often scares himself with all the research he does on that Calvert Fiend maniac."

"Apparently, he can see well enough to fly a sub-orbital onto a wrecked ship in orbit. Apparently he has more skill and more guts than you gave him notice for."

"What does that have to do with your orders, Gwendolyn? When you bring Josephus back here, maybe I'll have a talk with him and flush out these skills that I did not know he had. Perhaps I can introduce him to the right folk. In any event, I need you to put this Paymaster's captaincy to a quick end. Again I'll ask, can I count on you, Gwen?"

She nodded. "Yes, yes Uncle, of course."

"That's a good lady. We'll speak again soon. Please be safe and ensure the unharmed return of Josephus and Private Taara. If you have to get rough with the Paymaster, feel free—just remember, I want that coat. Derlith out."

The screen went black.

Gwendolyn sat there for a moment. She sighed and collected the cards sitting on the table. She arranged them back into an orderly deck. "Com," she said in her usual gruff voice.

"Com here, Captain."

"Com, there's been a change in plans. The *Seeker* has broken orbit around Kana and is headed for Bazz. We are to intercept her at once, board her, and return all persons within to Fleet with all speed. Send to navigation to lay in an adjusted course."

"Aye, ma'am."

"Also, inform the boatswain that I want the Christmas guns checked and made ready to be run out."

The Com paused. "The … guns, ma'am?"

"Did I stutter?"

"No, ma'am."

"Are you incapable of following my orders?"

"No, ma'am!"

"Then carry them out. I'll not repeat them, and I'll expect the boatswain's report in short order."

"Aye, ma'am."

The Com went off. She sat there at the table. Outside she could hear the occasional chattering of crewmen as they passed by. She looked at the empty chair on the other side of the table.

There was nobody there, and there probably never would be. That cafeteria at Fleet was, more and more, an idyllic place she could now never go.

PART 2

ALL THAT

RESISTS HIM

1

—A Remarkable Birth—

"So, where're you guys from?" Taara asked. She was sitting at the Missive's chair eating an insta-meal, her feet propped up on the panel. "I'm from the west continent of Bazz, a little village called Dyson-Clampton. Villages on Bazz always have two names—don't ask me why— they just do. Ever heard of it?"

Stenstrom sat down in his chair. "No. I'm afraid I don't know all that much about Bazz. It sounds like a charming place."

"Charming? Nothing charming about it. It's hot in the summer and way cold in the winter; still, it's home."

"I've heard the bugs on Bazz are massive and not to be trifled with," A-Ram said from the helm.

"They sure are big. And mean too. Everything's mean on Bazz. Look at me—I'm mean." She unbuttoned her Marine vest and got comfortable.

Stenstrom laughed. "What's your family do?"

"Well, since you asked, I'll tell you. My mom's a fruit vendor—Galacas mostly when they're in season. My dad and my uncles distil Zemuda. You like Zemuda?"

"I heard it gives you a hangover."

"It can if you're not used to it, and it stops you up pretty good—you never get used to that. Wish we had some right now."

"I like Zemuda," A-Ram said, "in a blue cochina. Very tasty drink."

Taara turned her nose up at the thought. "So, A-Ram, what about you? Where do you come from?" she asked.

He turned the wheel a bit. "From St. Edmund's, a little fishing city south of the forest. A-Ram's a Calvert House. Neither one of you have probably ever been to Calvert."

"I've been to Calvert, and St. Edmund's myself many times," Stenstrom replied.

"You have?"

"Yes. I suppose your being from Calvert is why your thoughts dwell on the Fiend of Calvert so much."

Taara put her fork down and turned to them. "Ok, since I'm not a local, who is the Fiend of Calvert? Can you clue me?"

A-Ram spoke up. "The Fiend of Calvert is a maniac who terrorized the whole of the Calvert region twenty-five years ago."

"Let me guess. He killed ladies, courtesans, that sort of thing?" she asked.

"No, he killed sailors, merchants, drunks—pretty much any dirty man roaming about on the streets was fair game. Since he killed shadowy, downtrodden sorts, nobody really did much about it for a long time, and to this day nobody knows for certain how many people he did away with. After several years of this activity, the riff-raff had had it, and they marched on Calvert Square, demanding justice. The Fiend was like a ghost; nobody could get him, not even the Gifted inspectors from the north they brought in."

"So, what happened?"

"A vigilant from the east called the Mad Lord of Walther came and defeated the Fiend, and he hasn't been heard from since," A-Ram said.

"He killed the Fiend," Stenstrom said.

"No, he didn't kill him," A-Ram said. "The Fiend escaped, fleeing across the rooftops of Calvert. You know, my room in our house was on the top floor. The night the Mad Lord defeated the Fiend, I was just a kid. I distinctly remember lying in my bed hearing footsteps on the roof—*bump, bump, bump, bump*—running across to the adjacent house. That was the Fiend fleeing with the Mad Lord in pursuit. Gives me chills when I think how close I was to him. He ran across my rooftop."

"You sure it's a 'he', A-Ram?" Stenstrom asked. "I heard the Fiend was a woman."

"Oh, that old theory again? It's been debunked by Lord Roderick of Dee."

Stenstrom was about to say something when Taara butted in. "What does your family do, A-Ram?" she asked, trying to change the subject, bored with it.

"Fishing and canning mostly. I never liked the sea much. Flying's another story. My brother had an old 22-Merc sub-orbital. I got it going when I was young, and that's what I learned to fly on. I love to fly."

"How many brothers and sisters do you have? I've got one—one brother, and we fight all the time," Taara said, seemingly enjoying the get-to-know-you session.

"Eight," A-Ram said. "Five brothers and three sisters. I'm the youngest—my mother had a hard time with me and could have no more afterwards. My oldest brother Ephelrood is the pride of our family. He married a Caroline."

Stenstrom thought a moment. "A Caroline—you mean a lady from the House of Caroline? They're Xaphans aren't they?"

A-Ram beamed. "They are. There's an old story about the Carolines that my brother heard of and put to the test. The story goes that, if you venture out to the ruins of Caroline manor bearing gifts and wait there in the moonlight, then you may be rewarded—a Caroline Lady might just pop out of nowhere."

"So, your brother went out and waited amongst the ruins of an abandoned manor with gifts, and a woman just appeared?"

"That's right. Her name is Lady Ezthold. It's a very romantic tale." A-Ram appeared rather envious.

"Hmmm," Stenstrom said. "A-Ram, does the word 'Carofab' mean anything to you?"

"No. Why?"

Stenstrom wanted to say something, but he held his tongue.

"My brother," A-Ram continued. Not only did he have the good fortune to marry a Caroline, but he also had the distinction of participating in the Sister's Program once."

"The Sister's Program?" Stenstrom asked. "Only once? You've never participated, A-Ram?"

A-Ram blushed a little. "Our family—the Sisters normally don't pay us any mind. Calverts—they just don't seem to like us much." He appeared curious. "Bel, have you participated ... with the Sisters, I mean? Belmont is a Zenon House, is that right? Zenons are usually favored amongst the Sisters."

"Yes, A-Ram, it is. And, to answer the first part of your question, I have."

A-Ram stood there behind the wheel—clearly wanting to know more. Taara smiled. "Bel, I think A-Ram's pretty keen on this Sister thing. I think he wants to know how many times you've corked a Sister and is afraid to come out and ask. That right, A-Ram?"

He didn't reply.

"Well," Stenstrom replied. "I've never thought about it in quite that fashion, Taara, but I've participated twenty-seven times."

"Twenty-seven!" A-Ram exclaimed, spitting. "Twenty-seven times? You, by yourself, have nearly quadrupled the output of the entire A-Ram line with the Sisters since it was patented years ago. Why so many?"

"I don't know. I ... really don't. They just come. They come often."

Taara laughed. "Ha! I'll bet they do!"

Stenstrom knew why—he knew perfectly well; he simply didn't want to say. Being spurned by the Sisters was a bad slap and public humiliation that A-Ram appeared to feel quite strongly about. Programmability, as it was called, meant a lot in the League. He looked devastated.

Taara tried to change the subject. "So, Bel, what about you? Where are you from?"

"Tyrol."

"Where's that—I don't know Kana much."

"Esther region, by the sea."

"What's your dad do?"

"He's a Fleet captain. He's commanded the warbird *Caroline* since before I was born. And no, before you ask, his ship, the *Caroline*, has nothing to do with the House of Caroline previously mentioned."

"Why are you a Paymaster then, Bel?" A-Ram asked. "Why—what with your father and all, and apparently the Sisters approve of you," he said with a touch of bitterness. "Admiral Derlith at first could not for the life of him figure out why you didn't simply join the Fleet. He was certain you had some sort of criminal past and was determined to uncover it."

"Really?"

"Yes. He says you're a sorcerer—is that true?"

"I've been trained as a Tyrol sorcerer, yes."

Taara was fascinated. "What does that mean?"

"Not much— it means I have various skills which come in handy every so often."

Taara stared at him. "Do something?"

"Oh, please ..."

"Come on, Bel, do something," she persisted.

"Like what?"

"I don't know, anything."

Stenstrom thought a moment. "All right. Taara, pretend I'm a bad guy. Get the drop on me with your SK."

"You want me to draw on you?"

"Sure."

"Wait a moment." Taara pulled her SK , unloaded the mag, and checked the chamber. She seemed satisfied. "Ok, Bel, you ready?"

"Ready."

In a blur Taara pulled her SK. "Ok, you're covered, I ..." Taara looked around. "Bel? Bel ... where'd you go?"

His chair was suddenly empty. She shot up and touched his chair. "You invisible or something?"

"Nope," came his voice from the other side of the bridge.

She whirled around. "Where are you, Bel?"

"Right behind you."

She turned and there he was, back in his chair.

"Wow!" she said poking him in the shoulder to see if he was real. "Did you see that, A-Ram?"

"I did. Very impressive."

Taara poked him again. "How'd you do that?"

"Sorry, I can't tell—that's a sorcerer's first rule."

"You know what you could do on Bazz with skills like that?"

Stenstrom laughed. She returned to her chair and remagged her SK. "So, Bel, you sneaky guy you, why did you become a Paymaster?"

"It's a difficult story."

"Seems to me we've got nothing but time," she said, taking her Marine coat off and loosening her boots. "You guys mind if I take my boots off—they're killing me."

Stenstrom sat there—contemplating his life.

With two thuds, Taara's boots bounced to the floor. "So, what about your mom then? What about her?"

My mother...

"My mother's dead, passed away. She was a socialite; she had no particular profession. She raised me and my twenty-nine sisters, as our father was often at sea."

"Twenty-nine sisters?" A-Ram asked. "No brothers? That's odd."

Yes, yes it is.

The questions kept coming and Stenstrom, sitting in his chair, fell into nostalgia as he listened to A-Ram and Taara.

Bad birth … *A-Ram had a bad birth.*

Mother/Father …

Sisters. *The Sisters spurned him.*

The House of Caroline … A-Ram's brother married a Caroline from nowhere. Carofab. A fraud?

Zemuda …

Sorcerer … *Tyrol sorcery is forbidden.*

Paymaster … *Your father's a great captain. Why are you a Paymaster? Why??*

How had he come to this place?

"Push! For your baby's life, you must push!!"

Lady Jubilee of Belmont-South Tyrol, sweating and near-delusional, was in dire trouble.

She previously had twenty-nine children. She'd never had a problem carrying or delivering any of them. She could typically wear her expensive gowns all the way up to the end, then, lying on a Tyrol altar, her child would literally fly out of her.

The one she was presently in the middle of delivering was her thirtieth. It had been a rather difficult pregnancy, the two-year period laced with bouts of angina, bleeding, pain, and periods of madness and raving—an odd case to be sure. And the delivery itself was proving to be a challenge, the Tyrol altar beneath her staining with blood, salty fluids and sweat. Five Sisters of the highest order presided over the delivery and appeared concerned. They struggled to save the life of the baby. The Sisters normally showed little emotion, but, in this case, they were clearly frantic.

Lady Jubilee and her partially delivered child were both dying.

With no Marines present, the Sisters had no way to speak with Lord and Lady Belmont. However, their thoughts seemed most plain.

"Push, damn you, Tyrol woman! Push, or we shall tear you apart to get at the child. The child shall live—you are of no concern!!"

"Push!!"

Two years prior, when Lady Jubilee, normally such a vibrant and powerful woman, began showing signs of sickness in her thirtieth pregnancy, her Lord Stenstrom became quite concerned, as any husband would for his wife. He took time away from his duties as captain of the Main Fleet Vessel *Caroline* to personally tend to her. Seeing her in the early stages of deterioration, he took his lady to see the Hospitalers in Tyrol for help, and they were perplexed.

At first they simply thought Jubilee's age was playing a factor—she was over two hundred years old, after all. However, after testing, the Hospitalers determined Lady Jubilee was in model shape. She was fit, typically plump in a modest way as was her body-type, and extremely healthy—a standard Elder woman.

They tested her for signs of sickness or poisoning—nothing could be found. Still, her symptoms were clear: she writhed in bouts of invasive pain, she fell into madness and began to walk a road of slow deterioration that could lead to her eventual death—all the signs were there.

Stumped, the Hospitalers noted everything unusual and pertinent about the lady that they could use to aid in their analysis. Her hair was a bright silver in color—Pewterlock, the shade was called in the east, a trademark of her House Tyrol heritage. Lady Jubilee had a number of vices. She liked to indulge in smoking as was the fashion in the Esther region, and not simply the demure, tiny cigarettes mounted on a stick as ladies often enjoyed; rather, she smoked a large, home-made coal that was almost large enough to be considered a cigar. She smoked them quite often; however, she had given the habit up for her pregnancy—she was loudly eager to take it back up again as soon as she delivered. She also enjoyed the occasional stiff drink, not fruity cocktails, but "men's drinks"—but again had given the practice up for her pregnancy. She was medium-sized for an Esther woman and carried a bit of extra weight, but nothing so excessive that might explain her symptoms.

The Hospitalers also shared with her their pre-natal assessment of the child: a boy, a fairly big one. Though lacking an heir, Lord Stenstrom was reserved at the news of an heir. He had twenty-nine daughters, and twelve of them had false-indicated a boy, so he wasn't holding his breath.

Fearing for her, the Hospitalers, seeing no other course, thought the safest thing would be to terminate the pregnancy—Lady Jubilee's welfare was possibly at stake. Though Lord and Lady Belmont already had twenty-nine children, they didn't want, if at all possible, to give up on the child and decided to go to the Sisterhood of Light for help. Such a visit was their last choice, for Lady Jubilee's House of Tyrol was not close to the Sisters for a number of reasons—still, this was for their unborn child.

They visited the Sister's research facility at Valenhelm and, though graciously welcomed, they got the usual Sisterhood treatment—a smiling disinterest. The Sisters, being the Sisters, had little time for such a mundane thing as a troubled pregnancy. They took the test results the Hospitalers had given them and promised to go over the findings and reply in short order.

In other words, the Sisters weren't going to help them.

So, they returned to their holdings in Tyrol, and Lady Jubilee continued to suffer, her symptoms becoming severe to the point of her being bed-ridden, her husband and her children sitting at her side in their grand bedroom trying to keep her spirits up.

Time passed, and Lady Jubilee fell into protracted madness, eyes blank, fingers trembling. Fearing for his wife, Lord Stenstrom Commed the Hospitalers: please, save his Lady, he said to them frantically over the Com.

End the pregnancy. Save her life.

The Hospitalers arrived the next day from their sanctum in Tyrol, ready to perform the unhappy procedure.

A contingent of Sisters also arrived.

Although they, on the surface, behaved in their usual demure fashion, the Sisters nevertheless appeared a bit anxious—a bit windblown. They intercepted the Hospitalers and, after a lengthy meeting with them and Lord Stenstrom, insisted that the pregnancy continue.

The Hospitalers objected—Lady Jubilee was clearly in dire straits. She had twenty-nine children, and sadly, the thirtieth should be terminated.

The Sisters insisted they be allowed to take action. They went into her room and closed the door. When they emerged some time later, they announced the lady and her unborn child were both fine.

Lord Stenstrom went to Jubilee's side. There she was, resting in bed on a mound of pillows, a little sweaty, but otherwise doing much better than she had been.

"My Lord, my Lord …" she said softly.

Whatever the Sisters did behind the closed door of the bedroom, it was effective; her sanity was restored, her pain managed.

The Hospitalers demanded to examine Lady Jubilee. The Sisters dismissed them outright.

After that, the Sisters became quite interested in Lady Jubilee's pregnancy. They remained in close attendance, visiting often, monitoring Lady Jubilee's progress, and eventually took up temporary residence in a chapel on the green, so that they could stay close by should their help be needed. Their protracted presence was galling, not only for Lady Jubilee, but for the people and Lords of Tyrol, for the Sisters were considered a prying and dangerous nuisance in the region. The Tyrols as a people and the Sisters had never been close.

$$\ast \quad \ast \quad \ast \quad \ast \quad \ast$$

The thing Lady Jubilee had dreaded was finally at hand …

Lord Stenstrom sat by Lady Jubilee's bedside. The grand bedroom room was decorated in old Tyrol signets and inlaid mosaic. Through the many windows, afternoon sun filtered in along with the steady surf from the nearby sea.

Two Sisters sat nearby, each flanked with their usual Marines. The Sisters were asking a series of probing questions, and there appeared to be no way of getting out of it.

Lady Jubilee did not want to answer questions from the Sisters. She had many secrets.

Lord Stenstrom, feeling the tension in the room, tried to break the ice and send the conversation down a suitable path. "Great Sisters, may I offer a thought regarding my Lady's condition?"

"You may, Lord Belmont."

"As you know, there is a long-standing Wirguild placed upon my Lady's head. Perhaps her condition is a result of that death-mark."

"We are aware of the Wirguild placed upon the Lady Jubilee's head. We have determined that no provable malfeasance or similar activities have been acted upon her in such regard."

Lord Stenstrom nodded.

The Sisters turned to Lady Jubilee. "You are in your final weeks of pregnancy, Lady Jubilee," a Marine said for one of the Sisters. "Your distress and continued symptoms are caused by an unusually high demand made upon your body by your unborn child. We have not seen the like in some time. We have, through herbal, botanical and chemical remedies, arrested the problem and you shall carry your child to term without fear or further worry, provided you allow us to continue your treatment."

"We are grateful, Great Sisters," Lord Stenstrom replied.

"We have questions, for both of you, and desire an honest discourse. You need not fear or be modest in this. We simply need all information possible to ensure our diagnosis is sound and our prescribed treatment appropriate."

Sounded reasonable enough.

Lady Jubilee resisted. She did not want to answer questions from the Sisters. She had secrets, many secrets.

They instantly detected this. "We care not of your Tyrol ancestry. We are aware that we are not trusted or well-liked in this area. We know the ancient Tyrol lords did not love the Elders. You need not fear—our interest in this matter lies solely with your unborn child. Any secrets or breaches of Elder law committed by you or your House are of no concern at this time."

Stenstrom and Lady Jubilee looked at each other and clasped hands, the both of them dreading what was to come.

The Sisters began. "The condition of your child does not look to us to be natural. Did either of you take, or otherwise indulge in, anything unusual prior to the conception of this child?" the Sisters asked them. "Please be honest."

As per usual, the Sisters were grappled into their minds, taking their answers both by ear, and directly from their thoughts. Lying would be pointless, and might possibly provoke more questions.

Jubilee swallowed. "I … took an herbal fertility mixture, to promote my body's ability to bear children, as I am getting rather old. I have often done so."

The Sisters noted her admission. "Your body is fully healthy and your age is of no concern. Such an herbal remedy shall, as we understand, promote the production of triple X chromosomes, and most certainly ensure that you shall bear a girl-child. You must have been taking this remedy for some time, as we see you have twenty-nine daughters, and no sons—a statistical impossibility, as Lord Belmont is perfectly virile and his Y counts are normal."

"Clearly," she replied.

"Where did you get this herbal fertility remedy?" a Sister asked.

Jubilee was uncomfortable. "It is a family remedy. I made it myself."

"We see," the Marine said for a Sister. "And you are skilled in the herbal arts?"

"I am."

The Sisters didn't react. "In a normal situation, we would be interested in learning more of this herbal remedy, to test and determine if it is safe and legal for practical use; however, what is done is done. Again, as previously stated, we shall confine ourselves to observation and treatment in this matter."

Jubilee was relieved.

The Sisters turned to Stenstrom. "And you, sir?"

Stenstrom cleared his throat and spoke. "I purchased a serum which was purported to promote the creation of a child with admirable genes."

The Sisters noted his comments. "And you wished for a boy-child, yes?"

"Yes, I have made no secret of that. Our House needs an heir."

Jubilee turned to her husband. She looked like she wanted to say something but held her tongue.

"You wish to add something, Lady Jubilee?" one of the Marines asked.

She faded back into the pillows and said nothing.

The Sisters continued. "And where did you acquire this serum, Lord Belmont?"

"Bazz—it was sold to me by a reputable apothecary and vigorously argued as safe."

The Sisters noted his admission in their usual fashion, displaying little emotion one way or the other. "We have heard of such things and know the potion you speak of. This potion ... it shall certainly guarantee the birth of a boy child. Are we correct?"

"Yes."

Again, Jubilee looked like she wanted to have a private word with her husband, but she couldn't with the Sisters present.

"And that was all you took, Lord Belmont?"

"Yes."

"We have detected certain other compounds present in Lady Jubilee's body—we believe that the potion you took on Bazz was tainted somehow."

"Tainted? The Hospitalers detected no poisons or taints."

"Indeed, we have knowledge the Hospitalers do not, but no matter. We have arrested its effects as best we can."

The interview went on. They insisted nothing was wrong, either with herself or her unborn child and that the herbals and serums they took, even with the odd taint, should not prove harmful. They prescribed a revised retinue of herbal treatments, which appeared to calm her symptoms.

She was in her final weeks of pregnancy.

"Push! Push, woman, push! By the Elders, to protect this child, we shall dash you aside without hesitation!"

Jubilee screamed, the altar beneath her dripping with dark blood. Lord Stenstrom took her hand and whispered in her ear. "Push, my lady, push.

Our child is almost born."

"Something's wrong—something's wrong! She's tearing me apart!"

"Our baby is almost born. Just a little more."

"I can't!"

The Sisters had enough. Their actions clearly indicated that they had little care or sympathy for Lady Jubilee. It was the child they wanted.

They TKed into her, wrenching her flesh aside without regard or mercy.

Jubilee arched her back and uttered a cry of anguish that was soul-shattering.

Through torn flesh and shattered bone, their child was free of her womb. Held aloft by the Sisters, it took its first breath and cried.

✳ ✳ ✳ ✳ ✳

When Jubilee awoke some time later, she discovered the Sisters had departed. The Hospitalers were back. They had labored through the night to save her life, for, as she was later told, the Sisters had nearly torn her apart and left her for dead.

They had worked hard, and she was out of danger. She was a strong woman.

"Child? Where's our child? Where is she?"

The Hospitalers and Lord Stenstrom leaned over her. "The child is fine. Our son is fine, Jubilee," Lord Stenstrom said.

Her eyes, previously heavy-lidded and bleary, snapped open with fury. "Son? A son!" she said, trying to sit up, her voice ragged. "There will be no sons—I have told you that! I have told you that!"

The Hospitalers were shocked. "Lady Jubilee, please try to calm yourself."

"Keep out of this!" She pointed at Lord Stenstrom. "When you are no longer at peril, then you shall have a son—not before!"

"There will be no more children for you, Lady Jubilee. To save you, we had to remove your womb," a Hospitaler said. Lady Jubilee was shocked at the news. Womb gone—no more children? How could this be? Her bearing completely changed. Though she had now thirty children, the fact she could have no more filled her with such loss. "No sons for us ... No sons for my Lord ..." she moaned. The Hospitalers must surely think her mad.

Lord Stenstrom went to the nearby crib and picked up a bundle of blankets. "Here, Jubilee, see our son."

She scowled, regaining her fury. "I'll murder this infant before I've a chance to become devoted to him, you watch! You watch! I'll not be heartbroken! I'll not attend his funeral as I shall yours!"

The Hospitalers stood there, not quite knowing what to make of this display.

But, Lord Stenstrom, holding the perfect baby boy in his arms knelt down and showed him to Jubilee. She looked at the bundle and gasped with joy, her fury instantly forgotten.

"Look, look at our son."

"Our son …"

Their perfect baby boy. All it took was one look.

JUBILEE, LADY OF BELMONT-SOUTH TYROL

2

—THE HOUSE OF BELMONT-SOUTH TYROL—

Lady Jubilee of Tyrol hailed from the eastern Esther city of the same name. Although officially of Esther stock and occupying Esther lands to the northeast, the Tyrols had always considered themselves a separate tribe—the eighth tribe as they liked to say descended from the lost Tartans of old. During the time of the Elders, they mostly shunned the star-faring activities the Vith, Esthers, Remnaths and Zenons took up with relish, contenting themselves to stay in the eastern reaches of Esther, avoiding the stars and concerning themselves with things considered forbidden. They were a silver-haired, smoky people, divested in things arcane and non-Elder. There were supposedly mystical schools located somewhere in the craggy city that taught Black Magic, various sorceries, forbidden chemistries, dark herbals and other questionable subjects to their students, so much so that the Sisters often visited the region hoping to discover more about these alleged schools and what was taught there. The Lords of the City, however, were charming and quick-tongued, always able to side-track the Sisters and allay their sundry fears and suspicions. Tyrol was such a pretty place by the sea, the people silver-haired and lively, and, therefore, what bad things could possibly be going on under all that splendor?

The third daughter of seven, Lady Jubilee of House Tyrol was reputed to be a top graduate of one of those hidden schools of sorcery. It was said she knew how to brew poisons, cast spells, summon demons, construct death totems, and other such blasphemies that, should the Sisters become aware, were crimes punishable by death. She was medium-sized, fair-skinned and a tad plump in an attractive way. She bucked tradition and wore her silver Pewterlock hair short with a large, rather pronounced "swoop" of bangs parted on the side—her short hair becoming her personal trademark, making her instantly recognizable wherever she went. She had numerous "trademarks"—her short hair being one and her rather inflated bowling average being another. Carrying a 260-280 average, she was said to have bowled two consecutive 300 games. Not to be outdone, her confrontational nature was another notable trademark she bore. In her youth she was a feisty, rather catty woman, often feuding with this lady or that over minor slights and perceived insults, and was not above threatening to cast the occasional spell or curse to intimidate a rival or make her point clear. Lady Sephla of Cone once went to the Sisters complaining of an attack of warts—and that Lady Jubilee of Tyrol had done it via arcane methods. A great deal of angry letters and venomous encounters were exchanged after that incident, Lady Sephla demanding justice and hoping to see Lady Jubilee bending in the stocks for a day or two. Jubilee seldom allowed an occasion to pass without making her thoughts on Lady Sephla plainly known whether at home or in public, and she even bedded down her betrothed and wrote all about his various carnal strengths and shortcomings in the local postings.

Lady Jubilee wasn't above a bit of harlotry to humiliate a rival.

Still, unpleasantness aside, Jubilee could be winsome and rather fetching and had the face of an angel with the demeanor to match—case in point— the day she met her husband to be.

She was enjoying a fabulous Nether Day ball in the city of Falz with several of her sisters. She'd had several dances with various gentlemen and excused herself to take a short rest. Smoking her usual cigarette behind the cover of a convenient potted plant, she overheard Lady Sephla of Cone's younger sister Vendra excitedly speaking to her circle of friends regarding a handsome young gentleman of whom she was very keen on. She had invited the fellow, Lord Stenstrom of Belmont, to the ball via correspondence and was positively taken with him. She announced to her friends that she was instantly in love. And they clapped and congratulated her.

Jubilee listened to all this and crushed out her cigarette. A churlish wave passed over her. Where was this man the foolish Vendra of Cone was babbling over—this Lord Stenstrom of Belmont? She was going to steal him, feed him, drink him, possibly bed him, and make a point of being loud about it. Let Vendra's sister wail to the Sisters about that!

With bad intentions, she ventured out into the ball to perform her dirty work.

She spied about, trying to seek him out of the crowd.

Where was he, she didn't know. She had to ask. A gentleman pointed him out. He was standing over there …

Over there.

Oh my…

Just look at him …

Lady Jubilee stopped in her tracks.

There was Lord Stenstrom of Belmont, the eighth son of a prominent Zenon House, standing by the tables, dressed in a Fleet uniform and framed in blue, getting punch for Lady Vendra. It was said she instantly fell in love with the handsome fellow at that moment, open mouthed and heart-struck. What began as a tawdry ploy to humiliate a rival's sister, became the first moment of the rest of her life.

As per usual with Lady Jubilee, none of her exploits could pass without hints of sorcery or under-handed doings floating about. She got him away from Lady Vendra, turning on all of the considerable charm she possessed, casually engaging him, pulling him into privacy. A momentary word became a protracted aside, an innocent inquiry, and then a dance across the floor. It was said by her rivals that she put something in Lord Stenstrom's drink that night, or cast him a potent spell. In any event, after their first dance together, Lord Stenstrom lost his heart to Lady Jubilee of Tyrol, their glittering night of dancing turning into a lifetime of love and devotion, as he soon made her his lady.

$$\ast \quad \ast \quad \ast \quad \ast \quad \ast$$

The enemies Lady Jubilee made that night were many and persistent. No longer was she engaged in social cattiness with a foolish rival, for this was now a matter of the heart and Lady Vendra of Cone became not just a social enemy, but a mortal one as well.

But, as time would tell, Lady Vendra would not vent her rage on Lady Jubilee herself, but on those she loved.

$$\ast \quad \ast \quad \ast \quad \ast \quad \ast$$

It was a usual custom for the lady to relocate to the House of the lord she'd married. However, Lady Jubilee couldn't bear to leave her beloved Tyrol, and her father Carjil, a lord swimming in Tyrol money, put up a fair fortune to renovate an old Merian monastery complex south of the city, complete with gardens, chapels and ballrooms, and offered it to the new couple as a gift. The estate was sprawling with a view of the sea and the secluded, breathtaking monastery, freshly rebuilt and ready to accommodate, was truly lovely. Lord Stenstrom, upon touring the rolling, wooded grounds, agreed it was a fabulous home and promptly relocated from his traditional lands near Brynthia on the flowing banks of the Great Blue Pierce River in Zenon. There they began their life together, the brand new Belmont-South Tyrol branch.

VENDRA, LADY OF CONE

3

—The Wirguild—

The courier rode up the sea-side lane. He arrived in a grand afternoon procession of float cars from the League offices in Armenelos. He and his vast entourage were admitted to the manor grounds and, while they waited outside, the courier was allowed to await the Lady in the parlor.

"Great Lady," the courier said in his polished burr as Lady Jubilee entered the parlor holding her new baby daughter Beryla in her arms. "Well met. I am Lord Marist of Grenville. I have come to your wondrous home by the sea bearing an official dispatch from the League Ex-Commons. The nature of the dispatch compels me to deliver it in person."

It had been a little over two years since Lady Jubilee met her Lord Belmont. After a whirlwind romance, where she was promptly impregnated, they made lavish plans to be married. Several months later, a daughter was born to them.

Lady Jubilee, still carrying her baby, approached him, and he bowed. "Good sir, you are most welcome here. Our home is honored with your presence. I shall be pleased to hear your dispatch."

Lord Grenville bowed again. "I am compelled to deliver it to both yourself and Lord Belmont. Both must hear the dispatch."

"Lord Belmont is at sea in his Fleet ship. He is not here."

"I am aware of Lord Belmont's important duties in space. I have a portable Com, directly fed into the League's communication network. With your permission, we may make use of it to contact Lord Belmont directly."

Lady Jubilee approved, and Lord Grenville pulled the tiny Com from his coat and set it up. Soon, the flickering image of Lord Stenstrom loomed in holographics.

Lord Grenville then pulled a scroll from his coat and began his oratory in a singing, joyous voice. "I, Lord Marist of Grenville, am here in the presence of Lord and Lady Belmont-South Tyrol bearing an official dispatch from the League Ex-Commons on behalf of the Sisterhood of Light. I am compelled to inform you, Lady Jubilee of Belmont-South Tyrol, with Lord Stenstrom of Belmont-South Tyrol in attendance, that a legal Wirguild has been issued and approved against the Lady Jubilee."

On the Com, Lord Stenstrom appeared shocked. "A Wirguild?"

"Yes, my lord. A Wirguild is a public declaration of revenge against an individual Household or against a single person. The Sisterhood of Light holds the final say to whether a Wirguild is accepted and made legal or not accepted and therefore rejected. The League Ex-Commons is then tasked with formally informing the parties involved."

"I am aware of that. Who is issuing the Wirguild." Stenstrom asked.

Jubilee cleared her throat and shuffled uncomfortably. Baby Beryla gurgled.

"The Wirguild has been issued by the Lady Vendra, fourth daughter of the House of Cone, against the Lady Jubilee of Belmont-South Tyrol."

Lord Stenstrom was beside himself. "Why in Creation does Lady Vendra of Cone wish Wirguild against my wife?"

"The Lady Vendra wishes it known that the Lady Jubilee of Belmont-South Tyrol, with malice and intent, did willfully steal a man for whom Lady Vendra of Cone did announce her love."

"Love? Is she referring to me? That cannot be—I barely know Lady Vendra and have only met her in person once. And, by the by, that was over two bloody years ago!"

"A Wirguild, sir, is not something that is happened upon quickly or without much debate. There are appointments to be made, visits to the various strongholds, and cases for and against to be argued before the Sisterhood. Yea, two years is a rather speedy process for a Wirguild to be duly delivered. And, it is here at last." Marist began singing again. "Be it also known that the Lady Vendra did firstly submit a Wirguild against the entire House of Belmont-South Tyrol, but such request was denied by the Sisterhood. This Wirguild is between the Lady Vendra and the Lady Jubilee alone. If Lady Vendra should take revenge against any other of the Household, she shall be in contempt of the law and appropriate action shall be taken against her. I do bade you, Lady Jubilee, to be at your guard and defend yourself appropriately at all times."

After a little more discourse, Lord Grenville gave the Wirguild scroll to Lady Jubilee and took his leave, his mission completed.

Two days later, Lord Stenstrom returned home—he taking a leave of absence from his post.

He was irate. "Why, Jubilee, does Lady Vendra wish to do you harm? I would think, of any of us, she has cause to be angry with me. We had been introduced via correspondence by my late mother Caroline. The Cones are a fine family from Jacarta in Remnath, which isn't too far from our traditional home in Brynthia. We got on well via correspondence—she seemed a delightful young lady. She invited me to a Nether Day ball in Falz. We had only just met, when you caught my eye, and I discarded her for you. Therefore, if that is what she is angry over, then I should sit down and talk with her."

Jubilee sat there, fidgeting with a cigarette. She fumbled with it, eventually tearing the paper, the tobacco spilling out. "My love, she has good cause to be angry with me."

She took a deep breath and started. "I have been a social rival of her older sister, Lady Sephla, for many years. It's just nonsense, a snide comment here, a social slap there—I don't know who started it or when, but we have been at each other's throats in such a fashion for years. At the Nether Day ball, I was sitting with my cigarette, and, over my shoulder, I could hear Lady Vendra talking to her friends. She was very excited. She was talking about you, how it was love at first sight for her. And then I, remembering my rivalry with Lady Sephla, decided to steal you, just to humiliate her."

"Why would you do such a childish, catty thing?" he asked.

"I don't know—that's just what we do—it's almost expected. Sephla did the same thing to my sister Charity on Saluting Day with her fellow several years back—they even got caught in the cloakroom with their knickers down. It didn't occur to me not to try and humiliate her sister."

Stenstrom cupped his face with his hands and listened. "Go on," he said.

Jubilee crushed the remains of the cigarette up in her fist. "Oh, darling, though I started it with all the wrong intentions, the moment I saw you standing there, I fell in love with you too. Everything I said to you at that time, and ever since, has been genuine."

They said a few more words, and Lord Stenstrom forgave Lady Jubilee and took her into his arms.

She then went on to assure him that she could take care of herself; still, Lord Stenstrom took an extended leave of absence from the Fleet and stayed home—ready to defend his wife at all costs.

The days and weeks passed. Nothing unusual happened. As the Cones were from far away Remnath, there was little to no chance of Lady Jubilee happening upon her in the street. There was one story of the two of them being invited to the same party in the city of Lyra. They saw each other, had a few words, and excused themselves. According to the story, they were found on a secluded terrace, Lady Vendra brandishing a pair of long, sharpened hair-pins and Jubilee holding several daggers between her fingers. They appeared to be ready to begin a mortal contest. Interrupted, the two quickly put their weapons away and exited in opposite directions. After that, Lord Stenstrom wrote Lady Vendra a letter stating that what happened at the Nether Day ball was his fault and to forgive Lady Jubilee, but he received no reply.

Shortly after, Lady Jubilee received word that Lady Vendra had tried to kill herself. Having survived her suicide attempt, she had been declared mad and taken away to live out her life in a convent somewhere in the backwater of the League. With Vendra gone off, nothing more happened, the stir the Wirguild caused seemed to have blown over, and life began to return to normal at Belmont Manor.

Except for one small thing.

Lady Jubilee was a consummate worrier—she always had been, and that feature of her personality only got worse after being wed and subjected to the Wirguild. She didn't fret much for herself, as she was more than capable of properly defending against an attack should defending be needed. But, for those unfortunate enough to bear the brunt of her love, she could be unreasonably smothering.

With Lady Vendra's Wirguild lingering in the nether reaches of her mind, Jubilee began looking at everything twice, examining hard to see if any hidden threat existed—regardless of the fact that Vendra was sequestered in a distant convent and insane. Anything, no matter how small or innocent, could be laced with hidden traps and subtle danger. Lady Vendra could have helpers carrying on for her despite her condition.

And she laid a vice down, on both her husband and her growing pool of daughters.

She considered her husband. Lord Belmont was an officer in the Stellar Fleet, a Com Officer of great regard, and was nearly ready to face Appointment to a brand new *Webber*-class starship being assembled in Provst. When her husband got the Appointment at last, Jubilee was excited and rather proud of her handsome husband, as she should be. She bragged to her circle of friends about what her husband has accomplished and how his future was bright. But then, her friends began telling her how dangerous it was being in the Stellar Fleet, how the Xaphans were an implacable enemy, and how many husbands and wives set out in their graceful ships, never to return. She sat there listening, fanning herself, feeling a tightening in her chest as they went on and on.

Hijackings
Abductions
Battles
Spontaneous hull breach
Decompression
Micro-meteors
Micro-Frags
Metal Fatigue
Mid-Space Collision
Stellar Mach
Stellar Mach Dampening
Atomization due to Stellar Mach
Xaphans
Moorlands
Radiation
X-Rays
G-Rays
N-Rays
Spoilt food
Stellar Mach sickness
Stellar Mach Madness
Gift-Valve
Blood bending
Spacing

Boarding
Mutiny
Revolt
Insurrection
Infection
Scurvy
Buggery
Slavery

When they finished the dire list, Lady Jubilee was near ready to pass out with fright. She had no idea Fleet-work was so dangerous. It was said that her arch-enemy, the Lady Vendra of Cone, had—prior to her madness—greased Jubilee's friends to fill her ear full of sordid tales of Fleet work and space travel, playing on her fears, hoping she would do something drastic.

And she did.

Jubilee listened to all the tales and was terrified. She begged her husband to reconsider, to quit the Fleet and do something else—anything. She pleaded with him.

He laughed and assured her he would be fine. What's more, he wanted to honor his beloved wife by naming his new ship after her, for it had not yet been christened.

She flatly refused, so he named it the *Caroline*, after his departed mother and began his long career as a captain in the Fleet.

The years rolled by. Lady Jubilee heard through the gossip circles that Lady Vendra was back, released from the convent and in her right mind afresh.

The Wirguild was on—it had to be. The world seemed a dangerous place to her all of a sudden. Here were Xaphans and battles in space, and there was this maniac she heard of to the south in Calvert—some person slaying the detritus of the wharfs. All these things played on her mind and made her fear.

Soon after, there was "The Incident" which really pushed Lady Jubilee over the edge regarding her husband's occupation. She was delighted when he returned home to Belmont Manor early, his old ship *Amazing* needing a bit of scheduled refitting, which worked out well because the *Caroline* was soon to be ready to launch.

But then she began hearing stories of what really happened to cause *Amazing* to come home early: his ship came upon a derelict in space, sending out a coded distress signal. They responded, investigating in kind.

The derelict was filled with shaddout explosives that ignited, destroying the derelict and slightly damaging *Amazing* in the process, wounding several crew.

Explosives?

In her mind, this incident could mean only one thing—the Wirguild. An attempt had been made on her husband's life; she was certain of it. She went to the Sisters, and they rebuffed her—there was no proof Lady Vendra of Cone had anything to do with the matter. She then confronted Lord

Stenstrom and he laughed it off. It was a Xaphan ship they'd come across—they often have a great deal of explosive ordinance aboard. Nothing to worry about.

Nothing to worry about?

4

—A Need for a Son—

And Lady Jubilee fell into a protracted state of mourning, always expecting her husband to fall, to die in space. She took to wearing black on days when he had to leave with his ship.

However—Captain Stenstrom was a good captain, a skilled captain. He endured and never fell despite many adventures in space.

In a puerile attempt to blackmail Lord Stenstrom out of the stars, Lady Jubilee decided to use their children against him. "You wish an heir, my love? When you place your feet upon the ground for good, then you can expect a son, an heir to all we have. Until such time, you will have girls."

It was said that the lady, falling back on her alleged sorcerer's knowledge, had learned various arcane methods of preselecting the sex of her children, as in the manner the Black Hats can do, and that she was determined to have girls, to keep them from following their father to the stars—more things for her to worry about. The fact that there were great numbers of ladies in the Fleet right next to her husband didn't occur to her. Jubilee expected ladies to behave just like she did: to have no profession; to sit in social circles; to bowl; and, whenever possible, to create gossip. Many in and around Tyrol speculated on the method Jubilee used to prevent the creation of a son: potions, poisons, complicated spells, enchanted items—the list went on and on.

In any event, whatever she was doing worked, eventually racking up twenty-nine daughters as Lord Stenstrom re-appointed to his ship time and time again. Lord Stenstrom, though, was delighted with his daughters, and he loved all of them as they grew into lovely ladies and went their own way. But, as the decades passed and he began to get older, the pressures of succession began to present themselves. They had all sorts of callers at the manor, including demure cousins and discreet distant relatives, friends of friends, even the Lords of the city of Tyrol; each wanted to discuss what was to be done with the holdings of Belmont-South Tyrol should no heir be born.

Everybody, it seemed, was lining up to carve the estate into small lucrative pieces, and nobody wanted to be forgotten or left out. There were already twenty-nine daughters and no sons, and surely none of the latter could be expected by this point. With no heir, all they had would be lost. All their property and wealth would be redistributed to any game enough to seize it, and their twenty-nine daughters could expect nothing; such was the time-honored but rather unfair custom of succession in the League.

Lord Stenstrom began railing Lady Jubilee for a son—the House of Belmont South-Tyrol, needed an heir; otherwise, their branch would fall. If only for their daughters' sakes, they needed a son to protect their assets.

But Lady Jubilee would not budge.

No sons, no lost coffins to cry over. The day he left the Fleet, that's when House Belmont South-Tyrol, would have its heir, not before.

Tyrols, and Lady Jubilee in particular, were rather stubborn and unrelenting.

But apparently, Lord Stenstrom had learned a thing or two himself in his travels. It was said he received a mysterious letter on gray paper one day in his Fleet bag, one with no return stamp. It was said the letter detailed how Lady Jubilee had been taking some sort of potion to prevent the creation of a male child through the years, and that she had no intention of discontinuing its use until he retired from the Fleet. If he ever wanted a son, he would have to fight fire with fire.

Go to Bazz, the letter said, *seek the Elixir of the Gods and you shall have your son.*

And Lord Stenstrom did just that. On Bazz, he discovered an apothecary selling a mystical substance that would, in essence, super-charge his Belmont seed, adding wings to his male YY sperm and lead weights to the female XX. Additionally, these "God Sperm" would be packed with nothing but Stenstrom's best: his courage, his brains, his tenacity, and so on. Paying a healthy price, Stenstrom took the vial and left the apothecary. He returned to his ship and downed the potion, feeling quite invigorated.

He would later hear that the apothecary burned to the ground shortly after he made his purchase.

So, thusly armed, the next time he took his loving, silver-haired lady to bed, something remarkable happened—a battle was waged within her womb, Lady Jubilee's herbal-enhanced male-killing eggs against Lord Stenstrom's "God Sperm."

Apparently, the God Sperm carried the field as, two years later after a very difficult pregnancy, Stenstrom the Younger was born.

✳   ✳   ✳   ✳   ✳

Stenstrom the Younger was a delightful boy; everybody thought so, including his army of older sisters, most old enough themselves to be his mother, and the younger ones as well. Dark-haired in the Belmont fashion, bright and smiling, he lit up Lady Jubilee, she sitting and watching him play with his two next youngest sisters, Virginia and Lyra, for hours on end in the nursery and about the grounds.

Circumstance, though, appeared to be conspiring against Lady Jubilee and her new son. The Wirguild of old was still in effect, and with the birth of her son, Lady Jubilee saw sinister conspiracies and hidden threats floating about more than ever. She was convinced Lady Vendra in far away Remnath was at it again in earnest, and, even though the Wirguild was legally only for Lady Jubilee, as with *Amazing* decades before, it appeared she was going to come at her son, as that's what would hurt Lady Jubilee and the House of Belmont-South Tyrol the most.

Apparently Lady Vendra was quite patient—she'd waited over eighty years.

One evening, Lady Jubilee found a poisonous wasp in Stenstrom's nursery, placed there in a glass vial through the window. She had a terrible nightmare of a spring-loaded, iron-jawed trap lurking beneath the sands of her son's play area. She awoke from bed and ran to the play area, finding nothing, but was certain she'd seen the outline of it in the sand—that it was there and had been removed.

Then, one afternoon, it happened. Her son was abducted. Lady Jubilee had taken her daughters Virginia and Lyra, along with the toddler Stenstrom, to the city to see a children's play in the park. Virginia wanted some candy from an inviting stand. Lady Jubilee turned away for a brief moment to get it for her, and, when she turned back again, Stenstrom was gone, the remains of a Waft cloud quickly dissipating in front of his stroller.

A crowd gathered as Jubilee screamed for help. A hastily organized search of the nearby city streets found nothing.

Lady Jubilee took her daughters and went straight home to get her coach. She was going west to Remnath, to face Lady Vendra of Cone and kill her—perhaps she hadn't given her enough credit for holding a deadly grudge. Perhaps she should have done this years ago. And if her son had been harmed in the least, if one hair was out-of-place, she would kill every last one of them.

When she got to the manor, she was surprised to find a contingent of Sisters waiting for her.

Her son was happily playing at their feet.

The Sisters told her that they had, in fact, listened to her pleas regarding Lady Vendra's improper conduct and, by attempting to abduct her son, Lady Vendra had violated the terms of her Wirguild; therefore, it was immediately revoked, and Lady Vendra had been taken into custody and was to be punished in an undisclosed location.

The Sisters, through their Marines, told her they were glad they could help, and that her son was a joyous, beautiful boy and a testament to the virility of House Belmont-South Tyrol.

Jubilee was elated for the praise and took her son into her arms. She never had much good to say about the Sisters, and they'd nearly been her death during her pregnancy, but they had come to her son's aid. "Whatever we have is yours, Great Sisters, for my son's life."

"Thank you, Great Lady," they replied. "We shall remember that . . ."

5

—THE RUINS OF CAROLINE—

Belmont Manor was divided into several wings. Stenstrom and several of his sisters lived in the east wing, and his parents, along with any of his remaining older sisters, lived in the northern. As he steadily grew and became more aware of his surroundings, one thing was made perfectly clear—the manor home and the grounds surrounding it comprised his entire universe, and that universe was sternly ruled by an implacable goddess.

His mother.

Sitting at the grand table for meals, Stenstrom usually sat toward the back end where he could see outside through the Merian arches to the hillside beyond. His two favorite sisters, Lyra and Virginia, usually sat with him. The rest of his sisters appeared like adults to him, like their mother—regal, elegantly dressed in their Belmont-South Tyrol gowns, their various heads of styled hair a mixture of Pewterlock, half-Pewterlock (black and silver), and black. One of his sisters Ione had blonde hair, the burnished color of a golden candlestick, and nobody was quite sure how that happened. Ione was a blonde oddity at mother's black and silver table.

As Stenstrom grew old enough to understand the goings on around him, he soon discovered that, though he had a great many sisters and only one mother, she was equally disruptive in all their lives. Mother, by herself, surrounded every one of them in a smothering embrace, and the situation, though apparently harmonious on the surface, was anything but.

The game was played many times over the years, with any of a number of his sisters sitting at one side of the board, and his mother, the grand-master, sitting alone at the other.

He recalled his sister Celesta sitting there properly with knife and fork in hand, her hair a gloriously shiny shade of Pewterlock. "Mother, I hate you," she said quietly.

"And I hate you too, Celesta. And no, you shall not marry that fool from Tuk. Whoever heard of such a thing?"

Celesta sat there stiff as a board, with only her trembling utensils held in white-knuckle fingers betraying the rage she was feeling within.

His sister Nylar, sometime later: "Mother I wish to go to the schools in Vithland ..."

"And why do you want to go to the schools in Vithland?"

"I wish to learn mathematics. I believe I would excel at such a course of study."

"I will not have a mathematician for a daughter."

"But I have already filled out the required forms and passed the necessary entry exams. Please, Mother."

"No, Nylar, and that is all, least you wish to face the knife."

Knife and fork trembled in her hands as well.

And on and on it went, each sister being foiled in one manner or another by their omnipresent mother. Of course, there were the short-lived rebellions, the minor schisms—the empty chairs at the table from time to time, Stenstrom's sister Calami being the most persistent at trying to escape, at running away. Her chair was frequently empty at the table, but always—always, there was the flash of smoke, the clap of thunder, and there was Calami, dazed, bewildered under a travelling hat, often holding small suitcases and other baggage.

Always, there was the whirling about and shrieking in frustrated rage, usually right in front of everybody at the table. "Right on time," Mother said. "Come, remove your hat and eat your dinner, young lady—we shall discuss this in more depth later."

Stenstrom came to learn there was no escaping mother—run wherever you wanted, hide wherever you liked, mother would find you and have you home in a literal flash of smoke. He had no idea how mother accomplished the things that she did—but she did, the proof was at the dinner table—an empty chair at the beginning of the meal, an angry, trembling sister occupying it by the end.

Mother was everywhere in the manor—almost as if she were the manor—a living, silver-haired embodiment of the house. She could move silently, and she could vanish from sight and pop up out of nowhere at any given time. The shadows in the manor and on the grounds were full of mother—she could come out of any one of them whenever she wished.

Stenstrom and Lyra often played in the old Merian ruins dotting the grounds, looking through the old telescopes and old astronomical instruments left there.

"What are these things for?" Stenstrom would ask, putting his eye to the viewfinder.

And mother's voice would answer. "They are for seeing the star that only the Merians can see. A star that doesn't exist."

And there she was, like a ghost.

Yet, however stern and unbending Mother was, she was also loving and nurturing, having equal time for all her thirty children. There was enough time in the day to tend to her children—mother would stop time and make the day longer if need be, such was her power, he thought.

He recalled seeing his sister Calami—yes, that same Calami who often tried to run away, Calami the rebel, Calami who said she hated Mother—weeping into her chest, sobbing over a man who had jilted her. "There, there," Mother said holding her heart-broken daughter. "There, there."

* * * * *

"Tighter! By Creation, make it tighter!" Stenstrom heard coming from his sister's room as he walked down the corridor. He was on the prowl for Lyra—that little tart. She had gotten him into a painful wrestling hold and made him say "uncle!" earlier in the day and he was going to get her back.

The door to his sister Constance's room was ajar, and a yellow beam of light came spilling out. He peeked in.

Inside was Constance's large bedroom with an open terrace and a view of the sea. Constance was sitting at her parlor, apparently getting ready for a night out. His other sisters Jonnia and Ione—the weird blonde-headed sister—were there attending to her. Jonnia was working on Constance's hair, and Ione was pulling on the strings of a tight corset, squeezing Constance into a painful, sunk-in hourglass shape.

A holo-terminal image spun on the boudoir—the image of an oddly dressed, green-haired woman was illuminated there.

Ah!—there were Virginia and Lyra sitting cross-legged on the floor watching.

He crept up and got Lyra from behind, pulling her backwards. She managed to turn around and they were arm in arm, rolling about on the floor. Though Lyra was several years older, Stenstrom had matured to the point where she couldn't muscle him around anymore. He pinned her down, though she struggled fiercely.

Constance turned to them. "Will you two cut it out!" she hissed. "If you want to fight, go outside into the hallway and fight. This is important."

Stenstrom had a powerful respect and a bit of awe for his sister Constance. She was seven sisters down the line and, to him appeared as a fully grown woman. She was tall and broad-shouldered and carried herself in a distinctive manner. He let Lyra go and they seated themselves next to Virginia, who was eating from a bowl of fruit. She offered a piece or two to Stenstrom and he took them.

"What are you doing?" he asked as Ione continued pulling on Constance's corset.

"I'm leaving," she said. "I'm going Carofab."

"What? Why?"

She sighed, both from Stenstrom's question and from the tightening of the corset. "Because . . . I need . . . to go. I need to be my . . . own person. I've had enough."

Stenstrom gazed at Constance. She looked odd. Jonnia had made her face up in thick white makeup, especially around the eyes, which were heavily highlighted in black. Her cheeks also were deeply rouged. Her Pewterlock hair was pulled into a strange style and painted a distinct shade of fern green. She appeared to be making herself up in the image of the green-haired girl floating in the holo-terminal.

Ione, her foot placed at the small of Constance's back, tied off the corset. Turning a slight shade of red, Constance stepped into a black silk garter inlaid with sequins. She pulled it up to mid-thigh and arranged it.

"What's that thing?" Stenstrom asked.

"It's my attempt to duplicate a VERY MARY."

"A VERY MARY?"

"You're full of questions tonight, aren't you, little brother?" she said.

Ione then fetched Constance's gown. As she put it on, Stenstrom could see the frilly, somewhat garish gown wasn't what his sisters usually wore. Again, just like the holo-terminal image.

"Before you ask, this is a Caroline gown, Bel," she said, touching up the black makeup around her eyes. "I've spent months putting it together."

"What's a Caroline?"

"An old House that went Xaphan long ago. Their ruins still stand to the west in the Halalands. As the story goes, every so often, a Caroline maiden will simply pop up out of the blue amid their ruins. That's the VERY MARY—that's how it works. If a Caroline maiden gets into trouble, the VERY MARY zaps them back to their ancestral grounds. Gentlemen seeking a bride often go there bearing gifts, hoping to encounter one. I'm going out there tonight and I'm going to win a love—I am going to go Carofab. I'm going to pass myself off as a Caroline maiden. I heard Lord Trevor of Howell shall be out there tonight, and I am going to meet him amid the ruins, disguised as a Caroline."

"What if a real Caroline lady shows up? I heard that actually does happen sometimes," Ione said, tying up Constance's gown.

"Then Lord Trevor will get a show—I'll scratch her eyes out right in front of him if I have to."

Constance stood, looking odd and rather austere in her Caroline gown, weird hair and heavy makeup. "All right, I think I'm ready." She shook her hand and produced, out of thin air, a small, round mirror. She looked herself over. "Yes, yes, I am ready. Oh, this is so exciting!"

Stenstrom was confused. "So, you said you want to be your own person?"

"Yes."

"So, you're going to do that by pretending to be somebody else?"

Constance stopped and thought a moment. "I am going to be my own person ... by ... pretending to be someone who *doesn't* have our mother. How about that?"

That made sense to him. "Oh," he said.

Constance went to Ione and hugged her. She moved on to Jonnia and hugged her too.

"Mother will not allow this," Stenstrom said. "She'll have you back here in no time."

Constance turned to Stenstrom. "Will she?" She pointed to the door. "Look there."

Stenstrom turned to the door. When he looked back, Constance was gone—vanished.

"Constance?" he asked.

"I can do what Mother can do, Bel," came her voice from behind him. *"And, I know her tricks—I know how to avoid the Maidens."*

He looked behind and there was nothing there. He felt a hand touch his shoulder and there she was, all strange-looking again.

She smiled, knelt down as best she could and gave Stenstrom, Lyra and Virginia a common hug. "Oh, you three little sprouts, how I love you. Be good to each other, and don't let Mother put an end to all of your dreams. Promise me that."

"When will we see you again, Constance?" Virginia asked.

"I don't know. If all goes well, possibly never."

With that, Constance vanished again. Her voice called back on a cloud. *"Farewell ..."*

Constance's sad parting was a bit overly-dramatic, as Stenstrom soon learned. He would see his sister Constance again, many times, she sitting at the table on holidays and at other times with her new husband, Lord Trevor of Howell. Though he heard that Mother had been enraged at Constance's antics—passing herself of as a wayward Xaphan maiden—she apparently found favor with Constance's bold inventiveness, and Lord Trevor was welcomed to the family warmly.

In later years, Stenstrom would wonder if Lord Trevor ever realized that his Lady Constance, the woman who appeared before him in the ruins of Caroline manor was not, in fact, a Caroline. He had to, as he didn't seem to be a complete idiot. He wondered if it really mattered. He'd gone out there to find love, and his mission had been accomplished.

6

—THE BLOOD PROMISE—

Lady Jubilee was a smothering blanket, protecting Stenstrom from every harm and perceived threat she could. It could have been that Lady Jubilee, in her fearful mind, was seeing things that weren't there. She continued to see threats coming for her son left and right, from the incarcerated Lady Vendra. If Lady Vendra's hope was to create uncertainty and panic in Lady Jubilee's mind, then she had succeeded. That had to be the most fiendish revenge of all.

Under Jubilee's watchful gaze, Stenstrom grew into a strong boy, bright-eyed and eager to meet the world around him. Though he was several years younger than Virginia and Lyra, he was fully able to keep up with them, his body and face only marginally addled with the childhood Puffies. Lyra, a certified tomboy and self-proclaimed 'Son of Belmont-South Tyrol' at first resented Stenstrom, loudly denouncing him as an intruder. However, as he began to show his prowess, Lyra warmed to her brother and accepted him as "one of the guys."

Stenstrom grew up in a virtual bubble. Smothered by his fearful mother, all he knew was the confines of Belmont Manor and its lands. He rarely got to see the city hugging the coast to the north, and almost never was placed around children his own age. He knew his mother and father, his older sisters, Virginia and Lyra, and the house staff, and that was all.

They were the only people inhabiting his lavish but rather small world.

One thing soon became very clear: Stenstrom had inherited his father's love of adventure. He and his sister Lyra loved watching the vids and posts of bold men and women doing grand things. They thrilled to stories of adventure and quest. They followed the exploits of the colorful vigilant from Rustam—the Mad Lord of Walther, a man of apparent skill and power who took things into his own hands without waiting for the Sisters to tell him to act.

And, they turned to gaze at the stars and all the possibilities that were there. Using the Merian telescopes placed about the manor grounds, he and Lyra often gazed at the stars. They thrilled whenever they caught a glimpse of a Fleet vessel in their viewfinder, watching it soar, off to wherever.

Looking up into the sky—there was freedom, a place where their father sailed. They made a wager between them as to which would become a Fleet captain first, Lyra or Stenstrom.

And there was the steady stream of gifts that flowed in. Pint-sized Fleet coats, hats, leggings, boots, buckles—the works; certainly gifts from his father in space, hoping that his son would want to follow him someday. There were models too—of the *Caroline*, a proud *Straylight*-class warbird, the second to bear the name. There were small toothpick models, large dura-plas ones, even holo-projections with controllers. Lyra and Stenstrom tore into them, putting the clothing on and marching about like little captains, their holo-*Carolines* soaring through the halls. Lord Stenstrom's son and his tomboy daughter both had their hearts set on joining the Fleet.

Oddly, one summer when he was nine, Lyra stopped talking about joining the Fleet and sailing the stars. She also stopped looking through the telescopes and began wearing gowns—something she'd always resisted. What had gotten into her, Stenstrom wondered.

He didn't have long to find out.

SNAP!!

He had that dream again, of sand and something terrible jumping out of it. The dream of his sisters staring at him open-mouthed. The dream of his terrified, screaming mother.

Stenstrom the Younger was roughly pulled from his sleep by several people dressed in black robes.

"What's this?" he said, trying to wake up. In the dark he could see the Fleet coat and hat that he had been wearing before going to bed thrown over a chair.

Even though he was only nine years old, he was strong—strong enough to wrestle Lyra full out. He struggled.

A cloying mist was sprayed into his face. Immediately his strength drained away from him and he fell limp.

Though their faces were covered, he recognized a few of them as he was carried from his bed—Jen, the maid, Laurie, the cook, and Lyra, his sister.

Lyra?

"... sis ..." he managed to say.

"Don't struggle, Bel," Lyra whispered. "Just relax; it's going to be all right, I promise."

Saying nothing further, they dragged him through the interior of the manor, and out into the gardens and pebbled walks.

A fire burned ahead.

They entered a courtyard centered with a large fountain. A brass tripod was set-up in front of the fountain basin, and a fire burned in the tripod's pot. Tending the reddish fire, fueled by various oils and fats, was a robed woman.

He was thrown down to the pebbles. As he watched, the woman picked up a knife and plunged the curved blade into the fire.

When the blade began glowing a rosy red, she pulled it out and approached.

The woman was slight and plump, and her hair was a lilting shade of silver. It was his mother.

It was Lady Jubilee.

He was lifted up off the pebbles and carried before her.

She held the sizzling knife up and let him see it.

"We are not here to harm you, my beloved son," she said in a monotone, her voice amplified in the moonlight. "Rather, we wish to protect you. To save you from death. You will make a promise right now—a Tyrol Blood Promise. You will promise that you shall never become an officer or a crewman in the Stellar Fleet. As you make this promise, I shall cut you with this knife. If, you are true to your word, and promise truthfully, you shall feel no pain, and you shall suffer no injury. Should you break this promise, now or in the future, this wound shall burst open, and that shall be your end. I wish you suffer no harm, either by this knife, or by the perils of the Stellar Fleet. I wish to save you, my son."

She showed it to him again—curved and sizzling. "Are you ready?"

Held in place, drugged, he could do nothing but meekly nod.

Several hands undid his nightclothes and bared his chest.

His mother then reached out and applied the knife to her son's chest. "Will you promise, Stenstrom, my only son, that you will not ever become a member of the Stellar Fleet, as either officer or crewman, as your father has been?"

He looked down as far as he could. He felt no pain, but it looked to all of the world that his mother had every bit of that sizzling knife plunged into his chest, right in the vicinity of his heart.

"Do you promise?" she said again.

In his chest, he could feel the beginnings of heat and pain.

"Yes, Mother, I promise. I promise. Please …"

She moved the knife down the length of his chest, finally drawing it out near his belly button.

He felt dizzy and fell to the pebbles, where his robed sister came to his side and helped pick him up.

Jubilee took the knife and put it back into the fire. A line of robed figures emerged from the dark. They were carrying armfuls of bundled clothing: his Fleet coats, hats, shirts, pants. Everything. They threw them into the fountain's basin, making a little mountain. They also tossed in his models of the *Caroline*.

His mother pointed at the pile, and it caught flames, the orange tongues of fire and smoke leaping up into the night, burning cloth and melting the models.

She watched the pile burn for a bit, then turned to him. "Now, I can rest," she said and kissed him on the cheek. "Lyra, take him back to his bed and stay with him through the night. I shall conclude the ritual here and join you in the morning. Watch over him and call for me should anything happen."

Stenstrom was dragged back to his bed where Lyra tucked him in and sat by his side. Through his window, his could see the bonfire of all his stuff out in the gardens.

It was a rough night for him. Stenstrom developed a sickness—an unheard of thing for an Elder—and he sweated into a fever dream.

"How ... how could M-Mother do this to me?" he stammered, sweating on his sheets.

Lyra sat at his side and wiped his brow. "Because she loves you. It's her way of trying to keep you safe. You're not the only one who's had a knife plunged into your heart. She does that to all of us. And, this won't be the last time you'll be put to The Promise. As she finds things out, if you go off and do something she doesn't like, she'll drag you back out there again and add onto it—she'll update The Promise. I've been out there four times already."

"My d-dreams. I w-wanted to soar, like f-father."

"And so did I ..." Her hand went to her chest.

Lyra kissed him on the forehead, and they watched the fire—both of their dreams turned to smoke. "There's always ways around things, Bel. It might not be what you were expecting or hoping for, but something's always just around the corner. You'll see."

Stenstrom fell into a jumpy sleep, his sister sitting with him all night.

SNAP!! came his dream again—this time a drug-induced nightmare.

SNAP!!

7

—THE WOMAN IN GRAY—

H e had a small bundle of items laid out on his bed; a change of clothes, some of his favorite mementos, and a few bites of food. He took the items and placed them in a small backpack.

Stenstrom was taking a page out of his older sister's book; he was running away from home.

His head full of strange, rebellious thoughts, he was determined to see something of the world, to set out on his own. This manor and its grounds were all he knew—was the whole world; yet, with the memory of the knife entering his chest, "home" began to feel confined and smothering.

Home is where you can dream, and then have those dreams quickly taken away in a bit of oil and the soft glow of a fire.

He was nearly finished packing.

"What are you doing?" came a voice.

He jumped out of his skin with fright. He whirled around. Standing in the open doorway was his sister Virginia. She was leaning in, holding a bowl of snacks with both hands. Her messy head of Half Pewterlock hair made interesting marbled streak patterns on her head.

"You scared the life out of me!" he gasped.

"Sorry—what are you doing?"

He returned to his work as she came to his side, still holding her bowl of food.

"I'm leaving."

"Why?"

He felt a momentary sting—the knife in his chest. "Because I don't want to be here anymore."

He finished packing and walked out of his room, Virginia following. "Where are you going?"

"The city."

"And then what?"

They spilled out in into the night, the dewy grass crinkling under their feet. "Why are you plaguing me with questions? I'm going to the city, and then I'm going to vanish into it, just like the Mad Lord of Walther."

"The who? Aren't you at least going to say goodbye to Mother?"

"Creation no—are you mad? How far would I get if she knew what I'm planning?"

They reached the pebbled walk near the familiar Merian ruins, and Stenstrom turned south, his pack slung over his shoulder.

"What about Lyra? Don't you want to say goodbye to her? She's going to be upset."

He hesitated. "Yes, but … you tell her for me, sis. Tell her I love her, and not to worry."

Virginia looked sad. "I love you, Bel."

He gave her a hug, and she almost dropped her bowl. "Love you too, sis." He started walking south.

"Bel, you said you're going to the city, right?"

"Yes," he said on the hoof.

"Well, you're going the wrong way. The city is that way," she said pointing to the north.

Annoyed, he stopped, turned, and started walking north, moving past her as he did. "I know that," he said.

He moved down the walk, passing all the old haunts of his childhood, the places where he, Lyra and Virginia played and crested a low hill. Beyond, the coastline stretched out in the dark blues and pearly grays of night, heading northwest in a rocky curve. About a mile away, straddling the coast and the swampy interior was a huddled, semi-lit collection of stony buildings—the southern proper of Tyrol. As he walked, the city unfolded in front of him in little stages—scattered buildings, a few outlying streets, all mostly dark under the moonlight. Looking back, he could see the manor sitting in the dale, lit up in cheery yellow window light. He could see his room from where he was standing—his bed was there, his toys, his sisters. All he knew was back there in a rectangle of yellow light.

He had a sudden urge to go back. Overhead, a blinking vessel of some sort rumbled by, winged, lit-up, whistling. It banked inland and disappeared, gone as quickly as it came. He was reminded of the Fleet, of the stars, and of the knife in his chest.

He turned back toward the dark mosaic of Tyrol ahead and continued.

He eventually reached the outskirts of the city where the pebbled walk gave way to a wider cobbled street. The whole cityscape around him was relentlessly dark and deserted, the houses and other assorted buildings mostly lightless and without noise. The street he walked was deserted. He wondered, in his child's mind, why it was so dark—why he appeared to be the only living soul around. Shouldn't it be more lively? Shouldn't there be people? He looked up—the night sky appeared odd, littered with stars in unfamiliar constellations.

He thought he heard something, a slight breaking of twig or stirring of rock. He turned to see what had made the noise.

Crouching near a small house on the other side of the street was a shape, like that of a small person pushed up against the wall of the house. The shape sat there, looking at him intently.

"Hello?" he said, surprised at the sound of his own voice, at the loudness of it.

Testing his own courage, he walked across the street toward the figure. "What are you doing there?" he asked.

The figure didn't move, nor did it speak.

As he neared, a storm of some sort, a sudden gust of wind mixed with grit and swirling debris, welled up from the house. Stenstrom coughed and covered his eyes. He gasped for air and quickly stumbled away from the house as fast as he could. After several steps, the cloud of wind and grit abated, and he could breathe. He looked back once and could clearly see a boiling ball of churned-up debris moving down the street away from him.

Astonished, he continued northward, shaken from his encounter with … whatever it was. He approached a small park that was dark and partially wooded. He wanted to find someplace to sit down—to consider his poorly thought out escape attempt. He hadn't expected the world to be so dark and lonely—so full of strange winds and unusual stars. He didn't know what to make of the world. He wandered into the park to gather his wits.

He found a large statue of a fox, carved in a cat-like sitting position, its head pointed upward to gaze at the sky.

Sitting next to the statue, he saw the slight figure of a slender woman.

"Hello?" he said, remembering his encounter with the thing near the house. Could this person be real?

The woman slowly lifted her head. "Good morning," she said quietly, her voice inflected with an odd accent. "What is a little boy like you doing out all alone at this hour? Please come here."

The woman was sitting on a small bench to the left of the fox statue. It was difficult to see in the dim moonlight, but she appeared to be wearing a gray suit of some sort, with a knee-length skirt. Her slender legs were crossed, and she wore a pair of button-up boots. Her face was thin, with a pair of thoughtful eyes and a pointy chin. A large, flat-brimmed hat sat next to her on the bench. She appeared frail, and slightly bent.

She looked at him. "Why are you out here all alone?"

"I'm running away from home," he said. Having had little contact with strangers, and having been taught to never lie, it didn't occur to him not to answer the woman truthfully.

It also didn't occur to him to not be completely trusting.

"So, your mother does not know where you are?"

"I don't think so. That's the whole point."

The woman reached into the lining of her suit. She appeared momentarily saddened. She pulled her hand back out.

She was holding a knife. Stenstrom stared at it in horror.

"I'm so sorry," she said. "You are such a handsome young fellow—I see so much of your father in your face."

He backed away. "What are you going to do with that knife?" he stammered.

"I'm going to kill you with it," she said standing up. "I've been waiting for you for a long time, to come walking down that road. Please, do not make this harder than it has to be. I truly do not wish to make you suffer any more than is necessary."

  He turned to run. The park was alive with shapes—men all around emerging from behind the trees. They were dirty and mangy. They looked to him like the vids of sailors and pirates he and Lyra liked to watch.

  "There is no place for you to go," the woman said walking toward him.

She raised the knife over her head. "Again, I am so sorry ..."

He backed up against a tree. The woman approached, the knife gleaming.

Thinking fast, Stenstrom changed his tactics. He ran to her and put his arms around her thin waist. "Please don't hurt me."

The woman hesitated. "I ... I remember holding you when you were just a little baby, those chubby cheeks, those wonderful bright eyes. I couldn't do it then. I should have, but I didn't. And now here we are ..."

"You ... you needn't do this. What have I done to deserve this?"

Her free hand came down and lifted his chin. "You haven't done anything. This is a closed circle that we are trapped in, and there is no way out of it. I'm sorry."

She reared back, knife gleaming.

Something appeared next to him in a cloud of black veils. Something breezy kissed him on the cheek.

"No!"

Stenstrom rose in a gasp. He was in his bed, his room smothered in a layer of night mixed with starlight.

He was in his pajamas. His toys were neatly arranged in the corner. There was no lonely road, no Fox Park, no Woman in Gray.

He lay back and pulled the sheets up to his chin.

What a terrible nightmare.

8

—THE MAD LORD OF WALTHER—

When Stenstrom was ten years old, he and his entire family went into the Barbary North Esther city of Rustam for a family gathering. His mother's side of the family had a grand get-together every five years to celebrate the ongoing history of the Tyrol line. His immediate family was fairly large, consisting of his parents, himself, and his twenty-nine sisters, coupled with his aunts, uncles, brothers-in-law, and cousins, creating a veritable army of people. The Tyrols had rented the entire Labyrinth of Rustam for the event, a place of vast gardens and twisting, hedged corridors.

From barely having contact with anyone outside of Belmont Manor to suddenly being thrust into a literal army of people, the get-together was bewildering for Stenstrom. Most of his sisters he barely knew—they were much older, had married and moved on long before he came around, and he only saw them on holidays and special events, like this one. He was closest to his youngest sisters, Lyra and Virginia. Lyra had a lovely head of dark black Belmont hair like he did, while Virginia had Half Pewterlock hair, a mixed head of black and Tyrol Pewterlock which reminded Stenstrom of a marble cake.

They sat outdoors in the maze of gardens and hedges, enjoying the mild Rustam weather. Music played, and people laughed as the afternoon wore on. There were many tables set up in the sprawling gardens of the labyrinth to accommodate the near thousand assembled Tyrols. An army of staff moved about attending the people. Stenstrom, wearing his finest little boy clothes, sat at a huge feasting table in the center of the labyrinth with nearly fifty of his sisters, brothers-in-law, and cousins. His parents weren't at that particular table, and he hadn't seen them in some time—he assumed they were off, mingling with other family members. Stenstrom sat somewhere in the middle of the table, flanked by Lyra and Virginia. Lyra's plate was only partially filled as she looked about trying to see if she could recall the names of all these people she barely knew. "There's Celesta over there," she said. "And I think that's her husband. What's his name?"

"I don't know," Stenstrom replied.

Virginia was fully tucked into her heavily-loaded plate of food and wasn't listening. She leaned over her plate, a huge bib was stuffed into her gown.

These Tyrol get-togethers were normally rather dull—just a lot of people eating and talking. However, it wasn't long before the proceedings were rudely interrupted.

A group of armed men appeared from nowhere, Wafting in and covering the hedged exits. They pointed all manner of swords and pistols at the people seated at the table. The staff, that happened to be around, hit the deck and put their hands over their heads.

The band stopped playing. Someone screamed for help.

The sky grew odd, turned a frightening blackish-blue color, and soundless lightning flashed.

"*Shhh, quiet,*" came a commanding voice in a hard Dirge. "*Don't move... Don't move.*" The screams muffled and then stopped all together. The Dirge kept them quiet and still; all those seated at the table appearing as unwilling statuary.

With that, the leader of the villains Wafted in with aplomb. He was a broad, portly man wearing a red coat and a garish hat. His thick, black beard looked like it was composed of animal fur rather than mere facial hair. He looked about and smiled.

"Afternoon, darlings," he said in a flamboyant accent. "I hate to be a bore, but we are to be robbing you of your valuables. I promised my mistress I would be paying the lot of you a visit—she was most keen on it in fact."

"It's Lord Sedgwick of Kold," Lyra mouthed under her breath, unable to fully move or speak under the influence of the Dirge. "The Pirate of Remnath."

Virginia was frozen opened-mouthed, with a forkful of saucy meat halted in mid-flight on its way to her mouth. "What's he want with us?" she mumbled.

Somebody else arrived, a tall woman wearing gray ladies garments and slim, button-up boots. She *walked* in from far away, it seemed, across the dark sky, arriving like a goddess. Stenstrom didn't understand what he was seeing. Things didn't quite make sense—time and distance were distorted. The woman's face was mostly obscured by her large, flat-brimmed hat. Stenstrom could see hints of a pointy chin, but that was about it.

He'd seen her before, in a dream, he thought.

She looked around and spoke in a ghostly voice. "He's here, at this table. Fetch him for me. I want him alive!" Lord Sedgwick listened to her instructions intently.

She then walked away, again covering miles across the odd sky, and was gone. When she left, the sky cleared and things appeared to melt back into normalcy—except for Lord Sedgwick's armed pirates roaming about.

Sedgwick pushed his hat away and wiped his beefy brow. "Well, there you have it. Therefore, we're to be robbing the lot of you, and kidnapping someone in particular. We shan't inconvenience you any longer than necessary, but make no mistake, 'Puddings'; do not attempt any heroic use of weapon or Gifts, I warn you. I would hate to have to kill anyone here."

Lord Sedgwick's men fanned out and, holding open bags, began taking items of value, removing rings, necklaces, brooches, watches and anything else they could find that looked valuable. They also leaned over and inspected the faces of all the young men seated at the table.

"Who're we a-lookin' for, Sedge?" one of them called out.

"A boy, should be around ten or twelve, I think. Look for the Puffy ones."

The men began searching anew, carefully inspecting all the young boys.

<Mother! Mother, help us!> his sister Lyra tried to send via telepathy, calling for help.

<Now, now,> came a reply. <Let's keep this amongst ourselves, shall we. I'd hate to have to harm any here that I do not need to.> It was Lord Sedgwick—he had intercepted her thoughts.

Lyra fumed.

The passing tide of ruffians approached, robbing some, pawing others. They were just a few place settings down.

"Check that kid there!" one of them said, pointing as he worked to get a large ring off one of his sister's fingers.

The dirty brute turned to Stenstrom.

There was a blast from the near end of the labyrinth. A man appeared in a cloud of wind. He was wearing a blue and green coat, black pantaloons, black bucket boots with spurs, and a Vith-style triangle hat.

Lyra and Stenstrom, unable to move their heads, turned their eyes to him.

The man was wearing a jeweled mask over a well-trimmed mustache. "Dear Sedgwick," he said in a proud voice. "This is a low, even for you, interrupting these good people's dinner."

It's the Mad Lord of Walther, Stenstrom thought. He and Lyra had thrilled to his exploits in the vids and posts for years. He was a notable vigilant from the west, and here he was, in the flesh.

Sedgwick grimaced. "Everywhere I go, I find you close behind, Walther, sniffing my wind! Kill him!" he yelled to his underlings. They dropped what they were doing, produced a rusty assortment of weapons, and attacked with a shout.

The Mad Lord smiled and threw himself into action. *"Hide, you people!"* he said in commanding Dirge. *"Protect yourselves!"*

"No, stay where you are," Kold Dirged back.

Stenstrom felt sick as the two Dirges clashed and competed in his head.

"I said hide—and that's final!" the Mad Lord's Dirge ripped into their heads as he clashed steel with the first of many henchmen to reach him.

They were free. Stenstrom was seized by his collar and pulled under the table by his sister Lyra. Virginia landed at his side with a *"whuff!"* still wearing her bib. The whole family had thusly taken refuge. Stenstrom couldn't see much under the table. He saw many pairs of booted and shoed feet moving about in confusion, some running in various directions, others Wafting in and out in a cloud. He could hear weapons discharging, shouts and curses, and steel clashing. He could see the Mad Lord's spurred boots mixed in with the other pairs. He could taste the dust that was being kicked up

A pair of boots suddenly were yanked out of sight, followed by a rough crash onto the tabletop above them. A limp hand bounced into view, lightly clutching a Hit-6 fraglock pistol. Lyra quickly grabbed it and placed it in her sash.

People Wafted in and out in sprays of wind. Men collapsed—some apparently pummeled, others shot or stabbed by the Mad Lord.

The sound of fists crunching into faces and biting steel echoed.

Shoed feet approached at a run. "Gah! Take hostages—kill a few!" a henchman yelled. He looked under the table; there was his wide-eyed, scruffy face. "Wait—he's here! Here's the kid we're lookin' for!" he said as he reached out for Stenstrom.

Lyra raised her hand, and in a blur of movement, shook it. In an instant, she had three silver daggers nested between her slim fingers. With a sweeping motion, she let them fly, burying one in the lout's chest, another in his neck, and the last in his cheek.

He fell dead. Lyra shook her hand again and had three more daggers ready to go.

Another henchman arrived and knelt down. "What'd you say, Tort?" he cried. He saw Stenstrom. "Ahhh!" he gurgled as Lyra again let fly with her daggers, and, mortally stabbed, he fell next to the first man. She put two protective arms around Stenstrom and Virginia, ready to fend off any further attacks.

"You people could help me, you know!" came a Dirge from the Mad Lord.

Now that they were Dirged free by the Mad Lord, lots of daggers were flying around the yard, sent flying by Stenstrom's older sisters, as well as gun fire and sword-play from his brothers-in-law and cousins.

"Damn you lot! Damn you!" Kold cried as a cloud of daggers flew in his direction. He Wafted away, leaving his men to their fate.

Eventually, after a good deal of jostling about and noise, things got quiet in a hurry. Pockets of fallen men lay everywhere. Men babbled in pain; some called for their mothers.

"Hold fast, you!" somebody said.

"Oh, do drop your weapons and sit down will you!" the Mad Lord Dirged.

All around, people dropped their weapons and plopped down to the ground as ordered, nobody able to match the Mad Lord's Dirge.

A single pair of boots approached the table, spurs jingling with each step.

The man knelt down, the leather of his boots creaking.

There he was, the Mad Lord of Walther, hardly even out of breath after all that. He inspected the dead henchmen. Finally: "Everyone all right under here?"

Stenstrom looked at him: the hat, the mask, the glittering eyes, the handsome face underneath.

Stenstrom thought: *He's not a man—he's a machine—a robot, look!* For a moment, the Mad Lord's face appeared gilded and jeweled, like a high-quality mannequin made of delicate silver and bits of inlaid gold. But, after a second glance, the Mad Lord appeared as nothing more than flesh and blood.

"What are these contretemps?" Lyra gasped. "Where are the Sisters? This is an outrage!"

"It comes with the territory, my lady." He kicked at the dead henchmen. "Did you do that?"

"I did."

"Well done. You Tyrols are always full of surprises. You and your lot fought well. I'll ask again, are the three of you all right?"

"Yes, yes, we're fine," Lyra said, holding onto Stenstrom. "They were after my brother!"

"Were they?" The Mad Lord looked at Stenstrom and did a double-take. Something about the young lad appeared to have gotten his attention. He shook his head and smiled. "Well, what do you know? You're a fine fellow. What's your name?"

"Stenstrom," he replied quietly.

"Well, Lord Stenstrom, keep a clear head and grow up fast, will you? I'm getting too old for this."

"What in the name of Creation is that supposed to mean?" Lyra said, protective of her brother.

The Mad Lord stood. "It means exactly what I said. Good day."

And he vanished with a mighty blast as a crowd of shouting people and their mother and father arrived through the hedge.

9

—The Black Maidens—

I mmediately after the incident at Rustam Labyrinth with Lord Sedgwick of
Kold, Mother's demeanor became even more frantic than normal.

He overheard his mother and father talking in the parlor the next
evening.

"*The Wirguild is on in earnest, and she is coming at our children! Our children!*"

"*No, no, I heard she is mortally sick ... on her death bed.*"

"*Then, she has helpers, assassins. We have to take steps!*"

The next morning, Stenstrom, Lyra and Virginia were taken down to a
small Merian ruin near an outcropping of rock.

Mother was solemn. "The attack on us at Rustam has proved to me that
the enemies of our House are many, and will not hesitate to come at you, our
children. Therefore, it is time to begin your training. Lyra has some pre-
indoctrination to it, so she is a little ahead."

"What training?" Virginia asked.

"Training in matters not spoken of outside of these grounds. Tyrol
sorcery."

She laughed. "My friends in the city told me Tyrol sorcery is a myth."

Mother raised her hands and shook them. Six silver daggers appeared
between her fingers. She approached Virginia and held them to her throat.
"And, are these not real, my daughter?"

She shook her hands again, and the daggers vanished. "As I have done
for your sisters before, I will teach you as well. When you have mastered
these skills, never again will you be defenseless; never will you be disarmed.
You shall walk unseen. No lock shall hold you, and no truth shall bind you."

She produced out of thin air several brightly colored balls. One was
magenta purple, one was speckled silver, and the last was solid black.

"What are those?" Stenstrom asked.

"Holystones," Mother said. "I am determining if we are being watched."

She placed the Holystones on the flat surface of one of the Merian
telescopes. She watched them for a moment—they just sat there, glinting in
the afternoon sun.

Stenstrom stared at the Holystones—they almost looked good enough to
eat, like large gumballs. Far away, someone trimmed the lawns west of the
manor.

"Good," she said at last, apparently satisfied. She produced an odd-looking key and thrust it into a hidden slot in the rock face. A narrow door opened, sliding inward. "Through here," she said leading them down into the darkness beyond. "Be careful with your footing."

"Where, where are we going?" Virginia asked hesitant of the dark.

"The culverts. They run for miles. They once were just below the surface, taking the drainage water from the Estherlands to the sea. Now, they lay covered up in layers of modern stone and metal framing and are forgotten, the water long since dried up. It is here in these trackless forgotten spaces that I shall teach you all you need know."

They made their way down a narrow stone staircase, the air quickly becoming cool and damp. Light blossomed—Mother was holding something in her hand that created a soft yellow light. "Continue down. Quickly. No dawdling!"

Stenstrom could see a vast artificial cavern stretching off into the gloom as they exited the staircase. The floor was a flat 'U'-shaped basin about two hundred feet wide. The roof, about twenty feet above them, was a confusion of metal lattice and buttress work. It was amazingly quiet in the depths.

Feet crunching on grit and crushed stone, they walked into the dark for a ways until they came upon a small area that had been cleared out. Stone slabs were arranged in a circle. A line of several large chests sat in the darkness nearby.

"You will find several robes in the first chest on the left. I want you to put them on."

Lyra opened the chest and pulled out three white robes. She passed them out and they scattered into the darkness and changed. When they returned, Mother was sitting on a slab, smoking her usual cigarette, her face lit-up in the orange glow of her coal. Her hand was shaking. They seated themselves around her, and she began.

"You must know by now that your mother has made enemies over the years, some more dangerous than others. I believe these enemies are seeking to harm me through you."

"You're talking about Lord Sedgwick of Kold—the man who attacked us in the labyrinth?" Lyra asked.

"Yes, and perhaps others as well."

"We aren't helpless, Mother," Lyra said. She shook her hand, and three daggers appeared.

"Yes, and those skills you possess I am now going to teach your sister and brother."

"Mother," Virginia said. "I am elder. Why have you previously instructed Lyra and not me in these arts?"

Lady Jubilee pulled on her cigarette, stoking the coal up to bright orange. "Because, Virginia, you can barely walk erect without falling over. I do not wish to be blunt, but your lack of coordination has given me pause. And you, Bel, you're so young. It's time to grow up and face the world, and you must have these skills."

"Again, Mother," Virginia said, uncharacteristically defiant, "They say there is no such thing as Tyrol sorcery."

Mother smiled and took a pull from her cigarette. Stenstrom looked at the glow of the coal, orange-red in the dark.

Suddenly, mother vanished.

"Mother?" he said, his voice lost in the quiet vastness of the culvert.

"They know nothing in the city," they heard Mother's voice say, from the shadows. They looked around.

And there was Mother again, sitting right where she was previously. "As I was saying, you three have much to train."

She set up a brass tripod with a pot hanging under it and started a fire. She tossed in a handful of something granular, and the fire leapt up, turning purple. "You shall learn the ways of nature and of the elements, how they relate, how they react with one another—and I'm not simply talking about chemistry. I'm talking about herbalism, cabalism—all the things of the hidden natural world that the Sisters seem to find so repugnant. I am going to teach you skills that shall protect you. You will learn to walk unseen, past both living and non-living eyes. No lock shall hold you; no locked door shall hinder you as well. So, it is time to begin. First, I am going to introduce you to some friends that you all shall soon become very familiar with. I am going to summon spirits that will guard and keep you safe."

"What spirits?" Lyra asked.

Mother smoked her cigarette. "Spirits your elder sisters are quite familiar with, some more than others. Have you ever wondered why we have no expensive security system installed here in our home? Have you ever considered why we have no private army at hire prowling the grounds as other Houses do? That is because we have something better, more seeing, more tireless. We have the Black Maidens. They are manifestations of spirits of the air. They hover over our grounds, seeing everything. Additionally, they are wonderful chaperones. Once summoned, they will follow you wherever you go, and should you need instant assistance, or should I feel you are in danger, they will spirit you away, back home to me. You three have not vexed me much, however, I've been using them on your rebellious sisters for years."

Mother continued. "I shall require a bit of your blood. All of you, I need blood for the summoning. Now, pay attention, the Black Maidens are given lease to locate your position via smell and sight. They can detect you at great distances via smell, and then home-in precisely by using sight. If your face is covered, they shall not be able to see you. Remember that—your face must be uncovered."

Stenstrom stirred. "Mother, is this really necessary?"

She put her cigarette down and held out a small bowl. "Yes it is. Now, Bel, I shall demonstrate. Give me a bit of your blood."

He took the bowl. Mother produced a dagger and cut him in the arm. He bled into the bowl for a few moments, and she handed him a cloth to tend to his cut. Virginia, watching this, appeared horrified about having to cut herself. Lyra was nonplussed.

Mother added various herbs, salts and metals to the bowl of Stenstrom's blood. She poured the contents into a pot and began stirring. "This process is very delicate—the potential to go wrong is high. What you want is a Black Maiden—and they are fairly harmless."

As Mother stirred, a cloud of steamy smoke issued from the pot. It coalesced into the form of a tall, gaunt, and pale maiden with a sunken face. She wore gossamer veils of black that floated about her on phantom winds. She drifted about, tilting one way, then another. "Please sit next to my son," Mother said.

The Black Maiden looked at Stenstrom and, in a lilting fashion, sat next to him.

"See, perfectly harmless and submissive." Mother crushed out her cigarette. Her tone became dark. "Now, prepare yourselves."

The three sat there looking at the ghostly form sitting next to Stenstrom.

Mother continued. "There are other things protecting our House beyond mere Black Maidens. Something cruel and utterly evil. When a Black Maiden encounters someone hostile on our grounds, they summon what I am about to show you. I am going to let you see, so that you will know the difference. Dredged up from the shadow-lands, from the lightless places, are the Soul Devourers, hungry, restless, always seeking their next soul to eat."

Jubilee added something to the pot and the smoke coming out of it became dense and choking. They coughed, sickened with it.

Something rose up in the distance, backlit in a brackish light. It appeared to be a naked female rising up with a ballerina's grace, her lean body perfectly formed.

She raised her head. There was no face there, just a huge mouth full of chattering teeth and a seeking tongue.

Virginia, and even Lyra, screamed.

"There is my son," Jubilee said quietly.

The Soul Devourer raised her arms and clenched her hands into grasping claws.

"You may have him."

The creature shouted with feral passion and sprinted toward Stenstrom, eager to tear into him. "YOOOOUUUUURRR SOUUUUULLLLLLLLL!!" she wailed.

Stenstrom sat there, horrified. Lyra dashed in front of him, daggers in hand, ready to stand and fight the unholy thing.

Mother sat there, allowing it to approach. Then she said: "Save my son," and the Black Maiden leaned over and kissed Stenstrom on the cheek.

He was instantly teleported home. He spun about. He was all alone in his room.

10

—His Greatest Enemy—

They sat in the stony darkness of the culvert. Stenstrom was wearing the now familiar white robes. His sisters Virginia and Lyra wore the same. Their training had been going on at a steady rate for nine years, around the calendar without protracted pause. He was now nineteen years old.

Their mother, sitting before them, wore black robes. As usual, Mother slowly smoked a large cigarette with a burning ember that sizzled with every pull.

This old culvert, once flowing with drainage waters from the interior swamps of Esther, became like a second home. They sat in a semicircle in the quiet dark with all manner of arcane flotsam from their years of study scattered around them. There were tripods full of boiling oils and gels heated with purple, red and blue flames. Mortar and pestles, aromatic with the crushed remains of herbs and rare salts, sat pushed aside along with various scrolls and books opened to mystical pages. The books were thick, made of hide and stout vellum, each page meticulously hand copied from mother's originals. Over the past nine years, they'd worked hard, writing down the knowledge Mother shared with them, and each student now had a small library of arcane learning written by their own hand. Lady Lyra's books were very studious and similar to Mother's. Stenstrom's were craftier with generous hand-drawn art, and Lady Virginia's were overflowing with expanded insets and detailed, step-by-step instructions. Near Lady Jubilee was a holo-pedestal—the cheery image of Lord Stenstrom the Older slowly spun, something she always kept near her when he was away on his Fleet vessel that she hated.

Lady Jubilee was, as before, putting her life in jeopardy—she was teaching her children the shadowy and seldom spoken of subject of Tyrol Sorcery, an offense not easily forgiven by the Sisterhood of Light should it become known. Lady Jubilee, as she often said, didn't care about the Sisters and potential punishments that could be in the offing; her children needed these skills and they would have them—the repercussions to herself would be dealt with at another time.

"Now, do it again," she said, her voice echoing around the vastness of the culvert. All heads turned to Virginia as she raised her hands. Virginia had inherited a body shape very similar to Mother's, and therefore was a tad plump in her robes. She shook her hands and, in a blur, two bright blue balls appeared between her fingers.

Jubilee was elated and critical at the same time. "Decent technique, Virginia, but slow hand speed," she said, pointing with her cigarette, the ember making a reddish trail as she moved it about. "I could see how you did that, even in the dark here. You must practice with your dexterity—I have told you so before. Let me see one of your Holystones, please," she said.

Virginia handed one of them to her. She looked at it in the dim light. "There are a number of imperfections in the plaster casing—and it's too thick in spots—it will be difficult to break." She cast the Holystone away, where it bounced off of a stone slab and didn't crack open.

"I expect better next time. It should be hard enough for safe handling, yet thin enough to crack open with the slightest of tosses."

Even in the dark, Stenstrom could see Virginia flushing up a bit.

"Now, Virginia, come here and turn around."

Virginia was shy and apprehensive. "Mother, I'm not ready."

"Come here, Virginia! By Creation, you're as apprehensive and uncoordinated as your sister Deneba was years before."

She slowly stood and approached her mother.

"Turn around."

Virginia winced and turned around. There was a small "click," the sound made loud in the quiet culvert, as Virginia's wrists were bound with a stout set of manacles.

"Now, get out of them, Virginia!"

As Virginia struggled, Mother turned her attention to Lyra. "Lyra has long completed her training. Watch her skill and technique."

Lyra pushed back the sleeves of her white robes and displayed her hands. In a blur, she had six Tyrol MARZABLE daggers nested between her fingers. Mother was clearly impressed.

"Well done, Lyra!" She reached out and took one of the daggers. "See, impeccable balance. This is what you two have to do." She held it by the tip and sent it tumbling into a solid rock face where it buried to the hilt with a thud. "We often forget the LosCapricos weapon of my family—the MARZABLE, your father's NTH pistol being a bit flashier. But, do not forget your Tyrol heritage and the MARZABLE dagger that comes with it. Make it well and keep it hidden, and you will never run out of them—you will never be disarmed."

Virginia cried out and fell over, her wrists still hopelessly shackled, her robed butt slightly sticking up in the air as she struggled. "I can't, Mother, I can't get out!"

"You have much to train, young lady. Slow hands, thick fingers—you require improvement in every category of the art. Lyra, please save your sister."

Lyra scooted over and reached out. Virginia disappeared.

"Leave me alone!" they heard her voice say.

Mother looked around and pulled on her cigarette. "I will stand corrected, Virginia. You have mastered the art of walking in the shadows—yes, you do that quite well."

There was a clatter off in the darkness. "Oww!" they heard her cry. "These damn things!"

Mother laughed. "Virginia, come back here, and Lyra will take them off."

Virginia re-emerged a moment later, still hopelessly shackled. Lyra approached her, and in an effortless movement had the manacles off.

Jubilee took a pull from her cigarette. "We shall discuss this development in further detail later, young lady," she said to Virginia. "Now, Lyra, shackle your brother."

Lyra smiled and approached. Stenstrom calmly turned and let her put them on.

"Do not be kind to your brother, Lyra. Make them tight."

Lyra squeezed and the manacles clicked tightly into place. She then resumed her seat.

"You forgot something, Lyra," Stenstrom said.

"What did I forget, Bel?"

"These." Stenstrom held out the manacles and handed them to her. She gasped at the speed and ease with which he'd escaped them.

Jubilee sat there in silence, her cigarette glowing brightly. "Now, Bel, I wish to see your MARZABLE."

He shrugged and felt on-the-spot. "I'm not finished with it, Mother."

She held her hand out and motioned with her fingers. He hesitated, then pulled the small silver dagger from the folds of his robes. It had a classic stiletto handle with a tapering blade, sharpened on both sides. He had stained the handle black and embossed tiny stars at regular intervals.

Lady Jubilee carefully inspected the dagger, testing its weight, trying its balance. "Bel, I don't see anything wrong with this MARZABLE—it looks completed to me. I'm very pleased."

Jubilee smiled and gazed at him with a mother's pride. She handed it back to him, where he returned it to the folds of his robes.

"Now, turn it into many."

He raised his hands. He shook them, and six identical daggers appeared between his fingers.

She approved with a nod, as did Lyra. Virginia stewed a bit. "And your Holystones? Let's see those."

Stenstrom shook his hands and the daggers vanished, replaced by four shiny balls of pastel green.

Mother took one and looked at the surface—it was like an enameled ping pong ball. She hauled back and threw it. It smashed against a stone slab and burst into a confusion of spider webs.

"Excellent, Bel—well made!"

Jubilee looked over her shoulder. "Now, Bel, for your final test of the day, I wish you to get up and start walking."

"Walking? Where, Mother?" he asked.

Jubilee pointed into the darkness of the culvert beyond. "That way."

Confused, Stenstrom stood, straightened his robes, and started walking. The stone floor of the culvert was strewn with old pebbles and other bits of wash once carried along by the swamp run-off, and he crunched with every step.

The culvert was vast, stretching off into the dark for as far as his straining eyes could see.

He had no idea how far he had walked when he barely heard his sister Lyra cry out: "Come back, Bel!"

He turned and made his slow way back, seeing nothing at first, then the low purple glow of the tripods came into view along with the three huddled shapes of his mother and two sisters.

When he returned, his mother looked up at him. "Do you know what your trouble is, Bel?"

"No, Mother," he replied.

"You're too compliant. I ask you to walk off into the dark, and you do so without a question." Jubilee turned to his sister, Lyra. "Lyra! Get up and start walking!"

"Why would I want to do that, Mother?"

Jubilee smiled. "You see, Bel—your sister didn't simply take a bizarre order, and nor should you. Are you afraid of me, my son?"

"Mother, you have put me to the knife three times by my latest counting and …"

"There is occasion for the knife, Bel, and there is time when you need to be a man. I have put you to the knife because I love you. I love my children beyond all reason. I have taught you my secrets, and I have made you strong, fully able to see to yourself. Now, with your skills fully matured, I do not have to worry about you quite so much. I would wager your skills against anybody's—Gifted or not, Blue or not. You're a good son, Bel, but I want you to stop being such a good son all of the time. I want you to resist my demands—confound me, challenge me. Look at your sisters before you— they challenged me, and yet they still sit at our family table. Though I am your mother, consider me your enemy. Consider me your greatest, most vile enemy. Henceforth, I shall attempt to confound you and set you to my will. I want you to resist—to confound me in turn. Thus, using your wits, I shall make you strong. Nothing more than your best effort do I expect of you. To give you the will to become your own man—that is the final bit of sorcery I have to teach you, for you have mastered all else."

Jubilee leaned back. "So, Bel, I want you to get up and start walking."

He sat there a moment, then got up and again started walking down the culvert.

After a minute or so, he heard his mother's voice. "Come back, Bel!"

This time, he kept on walking into the deep dark of the culvert.

"Bel!" he heard from far away, but he didn't listen, he kept on going.

After a time of wandering through the dark, he decided he'd gone far enough and turned to go back, but quickly found he was quite lost—he had no idea which way he'd come from. "Mother?" he cried. "Mother!"

No answer.

He spun around, not really sure what to do. He couldn't see a thing, and he had no Holystones on him that would make light.

He heard a sound. It was a soft hiss, like the grating of small bits of dry rock rubbing together. It seemed to be coming from far away, but was rapidly approaching.

He felt he was in terrible danger. He backed away. He felt something dry and abrasive wrap around his ankle, like a coiling snake made of sand or grit. He tried to free himself, but whatever it was had him tight.

He heard something. He heard: "...*bellllllll*..." in a sort of grating hiss.

His first inclination was to panic; however, he managed to recall his untested training. He shook his hand and created three MARZABLE daggers. He quickly let two fly. He could hear the creature moving around his throws in a gritty, snakelike undulation. The MARZABLES bounced off the stone floor of the culvert with a clatter. He heard the creature tittering slightly, as if it were toying with him.

He lined up his third dagger and let it fly. It hit something.

Stenstrom was seized about the waist and held fast for a moment—it felt like a soft beach full of sand—and then it gave him a firm shove, sending him sprawling. He lost his footing and roughly fell to the ground.

Something metallic clattered in front of him—his MARZABLE, returned to him, by the creature?

"...*bye...bye*..." it hissed. He heard something sliding away in a gritty fuss, and then it was gone.

Three globes of light approached. "Bel!" came his mother's shaking voice, his sisters close by.

✳ ✳ ✳ ✳ ✳

"Boy, Mother was mad," Lyra said snickering.

Stenstrom, Lyra, and Virginia sat in their favorite Merian ruin down the hillside. Virginia fumbled with her gown.

"She said to resist, so I resisted."

"I don't think she expected you to resist quite so quickly," Virginia said. She shook her hands and nothing happened. "Why am I so bad at this? I don't understand!"

"Keep your hands closer to your chest," Stenstrom said, trying to help with her form.

Virginia got frustrated and vanished into the shadows.

"Virginia, come back here, please," Stenstrom said.

"No! I'm terrible!" came her voice from nowhere.

"Get back here!" Lyra said, annoyed.

Virginia reappeared like nothing, still holding her hands in the same position.

"Thank you," Stenstrom said. "So, what are we to infer from this? Is Mother going to allow us a bit of roam from now on?'"

"Perhaps, but I doubt it," Lyra said adjusting Virginia's foot placement.

"She might say she wants us to spread our wings, but I don't know if I believe her. I think she's going to sic the Black Maidens on us anytime she wants us home. She's done it before."

"She used them on me last month," Virginia said, readying her hands for another try. "I was visiting at the House of Copperwell when, out of nowhere, a Black Maiden appeared, kissed me on the cheek, and teleported me straight home. It was galling, and a little embarrassing."

"I don't know about you, but I am tired of being sequestered," Lyra said. "I want to stretch out, see the cities, and find a love on my own. Those Black Maidens shall make it impossible—she'll have us back here on a whim."

Stenstrom reached into Virginia's gown. "Don't put your MARZABLE there; it's too difficult to extract. Here is better." He adjusted it.

"Thanks, Bel."

He stepped back and leaned against the old, weathered telescope. "I know almost nothing of the cities, or of the people in them. You two are my best friends. I have no others."

Lyra approached him. "And in that Mother has done you a disservice. How are you to properly interact with your fellows if you've rarely been allowed to do so? There's a big world out there beyond these manor grounds."

"And I've seen almost nothing of it."

Virginia lifted her hands to try again. "Watch your hands," Lyra said. "Now breathe and produce them."

Lyra looked at Stenstrom. "I'm afraid, when you do get out, you're going to be horribly unprepared, have no idea how to act, and probably will get homesick."

"I think you'll do just fine, Bel," Virginia said. She shook her hands. Again nothing happened.

"Not on the upstroke, Sis. On the down stroke. Try again," he said.

"You two and Mother make this look so easy," she said, flustered.

Lyra began toying with the telescope and swung it around to look at the smaller moon Solon which was high to the south. "I've been looking through these old Merian telescopes since I was a child. I've never seen anything other than the ordinary."

"What?" Virginia asked as she flexed her fingers and prepared herself.

"That funny star the Merians say is out there. I've never seen it. How do you hide a star? It cannot exist. The Merians have been deluding themselves, just like we have been."

"How so?" Virginia asked.

"That we'd ever get to live a life that we truly wanted, free of knives and Black Maidens," Lyra said.

Virginia shook her hands and produced one knife between her fingers. "Ah!" she cried in triumph. "For one thing, Lyra, you're looking for the Merian's star in the wrong place."

"What do you mean?"

"You've got the telescope pointing to the south. The star is over there," she said pointing with the dagger to the north-west."

Stenstrom and Lyra looked at each other. "Come again?"

"That big, funny star over there. The yellow one with the red cloud swirling around it, plain as can be. Right over there! Don't you see it?"

Stenstrom and Lyra looked to the north-west and saw nothing but the afternoon sky.

"You see a large yellow star over there?" Stenstrom asked, shading his eyes, seeing nothing.

"Yes," Virginia replied.

"How is it you see a large yellow star to the north-west?" Lyra asked.

"How is it you do not?" she replied. She shook her hands, and her dagger vanished.

11

—THE NTH—

S tenstrom the Older was home for the holidays. It was always a happy
time when father was home—Mother had a rare light in her eye as she
hung on his arm like a school girl. The family together at last.

✳ ✳ ✳ ✳ ✳

Father pulled the old wooden chest off the shelf in his private study. He
held it happily for a moment, and then set it down on the desktop.

Stenstrom the Younger sat in the chair opposite him. His sister Lyra sat
in another chair nearby. She was in a lovely Belmont gown—that's all she
wore anymore.

"Do you know what's in this chest, Bel?" Father asked.

He looked at the chest. "No, Father, I don't."

"A bit of your heritage," he said.

Stenstrom the Older opened the lid. Inside the felt-lined chest were two
rather ancient-looking flint-lock pistols. Bel and Lyra leaned forward to get a
better look.

The two pistols were mostly made of smooth wood, stained an old
reddish-brown and curved in a gentle fashion, like a lazy "j." The stocks were
pitted with age, dotted with imperfections. The bases of the grips were
capped with ornate brass bulbs, inlaid with fine filigree of gold, silver and
lapis. The barrel was, apparently, a simple iron tube that was banded at
regular lengths with gold, holding it fast on the stock. It had a large and
elaborate hammer mechanism. The hammer was shaped like a large steel "S."
The base of the "S" was attached to the pistol via a large, button-like black
screw. The top of the "S" held a cherry-red stone of some kind locked in
place with a screw vise.

"I think it's time I gave you these, Bel. I've been meaning to for some
time, but didn't have the occasion. The NTH pistols have been a Belmont
family tradition since the time of the Elders. This set once belonged to
Haveral, your grandfather, a great man of Zenon. Now, they belong to you."

Stenstrom sat there and looked at them. Lyra reached into the chest and
pulled one out. She held it out to him. "Go ahead, Bel, take it."

He took the pistol and was surprised how heavy it was. He thought about
his sister sitting there in her gown. "Father—Lyra is elder; she should have

these."

She smiled and shook her head. "I can't use these, Bel." She pulled the other one out of the chest and cocked the hammer with a fussy, springy-sounding click. She aimed at the far wall and pulled the trigger. The large hammer swung around in a dramatic fashion and clanked into the breach.

Nothing happened.

"The NTH pistol only works for men, Bel," Stenstrom the Older said. "There are a number of LosCapricos weapons that are gender-specific one way or the other—the NTH is one of them. Our family being an old Zenon line, the ladies were traditionally expected to be rather demure and above such things as brandishing a firearm—thus the classical image of a Zenon-girl."

Lyra smiled. "It's fine, Bel—take them. None of the elder sisters wanted them. I once had hopes of offering these to my son one day, but these are yours by right."

Bel took the second NTH, the two of them heavy and solid.

"What can you tell me about the NTHs, Bel? What do you know about them?"

He thought a moment. "They are able to destroy nearly anything they hit. They do a great deal of damage, if my reading is correct."

Lord Stenstrom laughed. "That's called a 'Rumalore'—a ruse. Every LosCapricos weapon has to be registered with the Sisterhood of Light, and the Sisters have an exact description of what the weapon does. A Rumalore is a false description that has been registered and is made generally known to the League, though the Sisters know it to be false. The Rumalore for the NTHs is the amount of damage they do—the NTHs actually do no damage to objects such as walls and furniture and so forth because the NTH shot actually passes right through them. I will stress that you take extreme care with these weapons, Bel, though I know you shall use them in a responsible manner. These pistols might look rather quaint and nostalgic, but know you this—they can slay anything set against them. They are sometimes known as "Ghost-Slayers," and they live up to their name. They function to the Nth degree. They may slay any, alive or dead, real, unreal, intangible, or incorporeal, and no matter how huge and powerful. They also work against robotic and mechanical foes. Do not expect any large hole or damage to be created, and there is no wounding either—hit a target and they simply fall over and die. The range of this weapon is roughly three hundred yards."

Stenstrom the Older pointed at the red stone held in the hammer's vice. "There is some maintenance that goes along with these. The red stone there—that is a cinnabar. You must have a sharpened bit of cinnabar to enter the chamber; otherwise, the NTH will not fire. Cinnabar, as you might know from your studies, is rather toxic and creates mercury if crushed, so, handle it as infrequently as possible. Occasionally, the cinnabar will crack with use and will be rendered useless. It shall then have to be replaced. I have a whole case full of replacement loads, so you shan't have to worry about that for some time to come. As long as you have a whole piece of cinnabar, the NTH shall fire."

Stenstrom the Older smiled. "I've always found it odd that the NTH requires a red stone to fire, yet creates a glowing green blast—rather interesting I might say."

Stenstrom sat with the pistols. He was troubled.

"Why the long face, Bel?" Lyra asked.

"I still feel you have been slighted."

She laughed. "You've always been such a thoughtful young fellow."

Stenstrom slid the two NTHs into his sash. He was struck with inspiration. "I know. Father, will you promise that, when the time comes, you will give your set to Lyra, so that she may in turn offer them to her future son as she wanted to."

Stenstrom the Older leaned back in his chair. "Would that arrangement please you, Lyra?"

She blushed. "Yes, Father. My brother is always thinking of me."

She pinched his cheek and gave him a hug.

"Then it's settled, Lyra. You shall have my set of NTHs to present to my grandson when the time is right. As for now, Bel, let these NTHs keep you safe from any that might wish to harm you."

12

—The Death of the Mad Lord—

Stenstrom was looking all over for his sisters. Lyra was nowhere to be found, and neither was Virginia. Virginia usually wasn't too hard to find—she could usually be found in or near the kitchens, either eating or making something to eat. She was actually a pretty decent cook.

But, today, she wasn't there. He roamed the manor, all their usual haunts empty.

On a lark, he went to the other side of the manor, in parts where he and his sisters rarely went.

He thought he heard something.

"How could they? How could they?" he heard his sister's voice.

He went into the library. Virginia and Lyra were sitting by an open holo-terminal. Lyra was in tears, Virginia was comforting her.

"What's wrong?" Stenstrom asked walking into the library. "I've been looking all over for you two."

Lyra didn't respond; she continued weeping. Virginia looked back. "Sorry, Bel," she said.

Stenstrom came to their side and put his hand on Lyra's shoulder. "You're sobbing like they cancelled Nether Day," he said cheerfully.

Floating in front of them was a posting. "Are you crying about the news?" he said knocking her in the shoulder again.

The Posting read:

VIGILANT FROM THE EAST SLAIN BY THE SISTERHOOD OF LIGHT

RUSTAM (Synthnet)—Terrance, Lord of Walther, also known as the "Mad Lord of Walther" was killed by the Sisterhood of Light Sunday evening. Declared a public menace after engaging in a horrific and damaging battle in Rustam with Sedgwick, Lord of Kold, the self-styled "Pirate of Remnath", the Sisters presided over the evacuation of Rustam and were instrumental in ensuring the safety of the citizenry. In said battle, Lord Walther allegedly killed Lord Kold and was wanted for immediate questioning by the local authorities. He refused to turn himself in, and the Remnath magistrate declared *Prata-Envita*, a writ granting unquestioned authority to the Sisterhood to handle the matter. The

Sisterhood censured Lord Walther and seized his holdings, pending results of an investigation. After repeatedly being asked to surrender, Lord Walther refused, making his slow way south toward a heavily populated area. The Sisters then slew him outside of Rustam, as confirmed by local authorities. The Sisters had nothing further to add on the slaying.

Although considered a vigilant and was openly censured by the Sisterhood on many occasions, Lord Walther was well-liked in the Green Sabre area of Esther for his repeated and well-documented acts of heroism and bravery. Lord Walther is best known across Kana for his uncovering of the "City of the Dead" in Remnath and his defeating of the Fiend of Calvert twenty years ago.

A vigil has been organized at the site of Lord Walther's former holdings in Rustam by the local citizenry, to both celebrate his life and decry the Sisterhood, whom they claim "murdered" Lord Walther.

Stenstrom read the posting and couldn't believe it. The Mad Lord, an object of his fascination since he was a child, dead …

He recalled his handsome face in Rustam, at the Tyrol dinner, and his actions. He was a good man.

He was a good man.

Stenstrom joined his sister in sadness.

13

—LILLIAN OF GAMBOA—

"Father, we have discussed this," Stenstrom the younger said as the two walked the south gardens. The Belmont-South Tyrol manor, once a Merian monastery, sat on a hillside in the distance. With its random placement of white, black and red bricks, its exterior often reminded Stenstrom of a vast gingerbread house covered with candies. Surrounding the manor were mystic walks lined with pergolas and primitive-looking observatories full of star-watching equipment. They were scattered about the hillside and gardens, some in ruin, others used as landscaping features. The Merians once used the equipment to gaze out at their mythical Star of Merian—a star that only they could see. Stenstrom and his sister sometimes tried to use the equipment to locate this mythical star, but could never see anything. Virginia said she could see it to the northwest, but he never saw anything but empty sky.

It was a holiday across the League: St Porter's Day, a holiday for family, friends and new loves. Many of his married older sisters were in attendance at the manor to celebrate. Stenstrom was incensed; Mother had trucked in yet another young lady for him to meet, an annoying habit she'd acquired.

Lord Stenstrom the Older laughed as they walked the lovely paths. "I know we have; however, it means a great deal to your mother. And, besides, it's St. Porter's day—good things are supposed to happen on St. Porter's Day."

"Happy coincidence—clever of her to arrange it that way. Mother has been trying to control every aspect of my life since before I can remember. Additionally, per her insistence and direction, I am to defy her wishes and make my own choices. Therefore, as before, I will not see this woman."

"Your mother might seem a bit overbearing, and in some aspects she certainly can be; even so, she does it because she loves you. And, as an added bonus, I think you might like this one—got spirit, I think."

Stenstrom the Younger shrugged. "So, who is it today, just out of curiosity?" he asked.

"A lovely young lady from Esther, Lillian of Gamboa. I know what you're thinking—many of the Gamboa ilk have made a name for themselves for being rather homely and uninteresting, but this one seems a tad different. I saw her get out of the coach myself as she arrived—she's pretty and seems a vibrant young lady. Let's take your mother out of the equation for a moment, shall we? She's come all this way—the least you can do is spend a moment with her and determine for yourself if you wish to get to know her better or not. It's not her fault you and your mother have this on-going contest to one-up the other."

Stenstrom shook his head. "True, but out of sheer principle, I'm not going in there. Mother has to learn that I am not interested in her continued efforts to locate me a bride."

"She's done that for all the children. She's paired off at least ten of your sisters and ..."

There was a crack of thunder. As they walked the garden path, the weather began to quickly turn. The clouds grew angry and a strong wind kicked up from the sea.

"I wasn't aware of any storms in the forecast for today."

The two Stenstroms held their hats. This was no usual spring up of bad weather. The clouds banged into each other like two opposing armies and were red-rimmed. The center of the conflagration seemed to be right over their heads.

Sorcery was involved; Stenstrom knew it. Suddenly a thick, reaching fog sprang up.

"Father?" Stenstrom said groping about. "Father!" No reply came.

He whirled around in the fog. This was his mother's doing, and he could expect anything to come running out of the mist, ready to put him to yet another dangerous trial. It was amazing to him how many times his mother mortgaged his soul to simply prove a point, sending a rotting host of minor demons after him, knowing full well he could get rid of them easily with his NTHs—weapons that could slay anything set before him.

The problem today was that he didn't have his NTHs—they had been missing from their felt-lined box that morning.

Mother ...

He thought he could hear the babbling of a creek, and smell the stagnant odor of dirty water and drenched mud—odd, there was no creek in the area.

A few feet distant in the thick fog, he saw it—the tepid banks of a creek that had appeared from nowhere. Something swam in it—something with red, beady eyes that watched him intently from the calm water's surface.

A huge, demonic creature in the form of a giant catfish came leaping out of the creek with a drenched roar. It leaned on its fins, clambering toward Stenstrom in a malevolent fashion. The demon fish was a skillet-full of clashing colors. Its scales were a mottled mixture of awful greens and dead ochres, stretched out over a backdrop of blazing, sun-burned red. Its fins were mostly the same shade of blazing red webbing over a scalloped rib-work of black, over-sized fish bones, ending in rather lethal-looking spines. Its reaching whiskers moved about, like a slimy moustache. Its catfish mouth was enormous and glowed slightly from the reddish tint within.

"Morning, Lord Belmont!" it said. *"I have been summoned to ensure you don't forget to go see your lady friend today! Fail to keep your appointment, and I get to eat you! Isn't that lovely?"*

* * * * *

Lady Jubilee had, for many years, attempted to pair her son, Stenstrom the Younger, to various ladies of standing whom she deemed worthy. One of her favorite social functions was pairing her children off to the various offspring of Great Houses she favored. As Stenstrom was her only son, she threw herself into his pairing with unusual gusto. As per everything Lady

Jubilee did, she was very exacting, and rather unflattering in her appraisals of potential candidates, having sullied and greatly angered various Houses with her blunt assessments and quick dismissals. She was looking for an impeccable pedigree, a comely bearing and a high degree of knowledge in the finer things and social graces. Most importantly, Lady Jubilee was looking for a grounded, mundane woman: no Gifts of the Mind, no telepathy and no knowledge of sorcery; she thought it important to counter-balance her son's sorcerous training. As such she ruled out the heroic Vith with their Gifts and a good many of the Zenons. She wanted a nice safe Halagirl, or a trusty Esther woman. She was no longer on speaking terms with several Great Houses whom she'd so insulted. She nearly touched off a disturbing social incident when she publically proclaimed that no Houses of Barrow stock were to be considered for her son: the Dares, Cottens and Tuks reacting strenuously with a fruitless letter-writing campaign to counter her position.

Sorry—no Barrows, Vith, Zenons, Calverts or Remnaths. Nothing out of the ordinary for her son.

It was quite a shame that she was mortal enemies with the Cones of Remnath (having suspected them of repeatedly trying to murder and abduct her son throughout his early youth), for they had several daughters of fine quality—truly regrettable.

When a potential candidate did emerge who happened to pass all of Lady Jubilee's standards, she would be invited to visit the Belmont-South Tyrol estate and be introduced to Lord Stenstrom the Younger. Normally, the lady would be given a fine breakfast, and then asked to wait in a large ballroom on the north manor grounds called the Chalk House for its white limestone walls. Then, Stenstrom the Younger would be summoned and entreated to go into the Chalk House and see if a rapport was struck.

Stenstrom, however, was on a vendetta in this matter. He was bound and determined to show his mother up—as she fervently requested. She herself asked him to not be such a compliant young man—to thwart her will and set himself against her—though she never failed to get angry when he made a showing of such independence. Many times, he would not go into the Chalk House at all simply to annoy and embarrass his mother; many times he avoided it and allowed the poor lady within to sit all day unattended—she a victim of their ongoing struggle. Other times, he would take one look at the woman sitting there in her gown and walk right back out.

As Stenstrom knew, Lillian of Gamboa, a fine Esther woman, had been asked to House Belmont several times. She was reputed to be a bright young lady, the tenth of fifteen Gamboa children. Usually attired in festive pastels, she was a tallish girl, blonde-headed and blue eyed. She was a noted painter and sculptress with a lovely eye for color and form. Some of her more ambitious works had sold for a fair amount of money, and she had a small but burgeoning gallery in Gamboa where her works were admired by all.

Lady Jubilee had taken a great liking to Lady Lillian. She personally visited her at her home in Gamboa, had stood in her gallery and marveled at the fabulous works of art she had created, and was generally taken with the lovely young lady. This woman was perfect, so grounded and pretty, so mundane. Lady Jubilee wanted a mundane woman for her son, to keep him properly balanced. When dealing with the arcane, it was a simple matter to become lost in it. Having a decidedly non-arcane companion, specifically a spouse, would provide him with the grounding he needed.

And Lillian of Gamboa seemed perfect. Stately and prim, talented and artistic, but rather dry and humorless, she would do well for her son. Lady Jubilee happily showed her pictures and holo-vids of her son Stenstrom and was pleased that Lillian found him handsome.

So, with a hopeful spirit and an open mind, Lillian boarded her House transport and made the trip across the marshes of Esther to Tyrol to meet Stenstrom the Younger. She certainly didn't quite know what to expect, but she was apparently game to give it a try.

The afternoon came and went. Stenstrom never showed up. Lillian sat in the huge, empty Chalk House all afternoon alone.

Lady Jubilee's rage was memorable. *"How could you let that woman sit there unattended?"*

"I did not wish to see her."

"I do not care about your wishes in this matter! You've your House and your name to consider!"

After a vigorous set of apologies from Lady Jubilee, Lady Lillian agreed to give it another go. She said there had been a scheduling error, and that it had been her fault. She begged Lady Lillian to forgive her and please grace them with her presence a second time. Lady Jubilee, with her short head of Pewterlock Tyrol hair swooped in the front, was, above all things, quite ingratiating when she wanted to be, and Lady Lillian forgave the first incident. Not being one to hold a grudge or allow an honest mistake to go unforgiven, Lady Lillian agreed, and again made the trip to Tyrol to meet Lord Stenstrom.

Again, he was a no show. Sitting there alone in the Chalk House a second time, the table full of elegant treats, she sat there in her teal gown and felt humiliated.

Again, she returned to Gamboa—this time in quite a huff.

Again there was a dreadful row that evening in Belmont Manor.

"I am considering making you a guest of our dungeon, boy, or worse!"

"Mother—you yourself have insisted that I confound your various machinations with wit and stratagem. Be relentless, you stated. What think you of it?"

"So I did. Very well, such a position shall force me to take drastic measures! Be at your guard and do not forget that you've only yourself to blame for the consequences!"

Again Lady Jubilee contacted Lillian of Gamboa full of apologies and, this time, said that Lord Stenstrom had been called away at the last moment on urgent business in Tyrol.

Via correspondence, Lillian informed Lady Jubilee that she wished nothing further to do with the House of Belmont and that was that. She then went on a rather scathing letter-writing campaign letting any who would listen how she was treated at the House of Belmont-South Tyrol.

But, apparently, time heals all, and eventually Lady Lillian sent Lady Jubilee a correspondence stating she would forgive the first two incidents and, for a third time, agreed to meet Lord Stenstrom. She wrote it was becoming a matter of pride for her—she would make this foolish Belmont Lord see her, by Creation. She was determined. Full of thanks and promises, Lady Jubilee made the required preparations.

Sitting there in the Chalk House a third time, Lady Lillian waited.

This time Lord Stenstrom showed.

Stenstrom ran for his soul—the demon in hot pursuit. For being, quite literally, a fish out of water, the demon covered the ground rather well, pulling itself along on its fins and grabbing passing trees and other large objects for leverage with its whiskers, leaving a definite trail of slime as it went. The beast was clearly steering him toward the Chalk House and the lovely lady waiting within.

Not having his NTHs, and seeing no other choice, Stenstrom made a break for it. He flew into the Chalk House and slammed the door shut, rattling it in its frame. Outside he could hear the maelstrom of wind and angry smoke. He thought he could vaguely hear the demon tittering about, waiting for him. If he came out of that ballroom alone, the demon would have its prize.

"Come out here, Lord Belmont! I have been promised your flesh!"

This time his mother's sorcery had gone too far.

He turned and looked into the interior. The Chalk House was a large, gilded ballroom used for select occasions: Nether Day, Valentine's Day, and other special events. It had been made especially for Lord Stenstrom and Lady Jubilee, being built on the site of an old Merian altar. It was rather modest in size as far as grand League ballrooms went, but it could still hold several hundred people rather comfortably. The floor was made of rare woods from Hoban, and the walls were covered in fine pink and yellow silk paper—his mother had designed the print herself. When she wasn't busy summoning demons and plunging knives into his chest, his mother had a delicate touch for decorating. The four massive chandeliers hanging over the ballroom floor were priceless.

Lady Jubilee had good taste.

Sitting erect on a padded couch at the far end of the hall was a slender young woman wearing a festive pink gown. She had golden blonde hair that was done up in a partial bun, with long, slightly curled tendrils hanging down past the nape of her neck. Her face was nicely painted, her bare back was provocatively curved and her blue eyes sparkled. She looked at him quietly.

Stenstrom was wearing a dark green Belmont coat with a pair of gold knee britches and a pair of shined Tyrol-style boots.

So, what to pick—the lady or the demon? He could go back outside and fight the demon, and he would probably figure out a way to win, or, he could stay and speak with the young lady, offer his apologies, and escort her back to the manor house, where the demon would be dispelled. But then, he would be caving into his mother's wishes, and that prospect galled him.

After a few seconds of introspection, he chose the lady—seemed the more sensible of the two—this whole situation was, in fact, not her fault. He removed his hat and approached. Her eyes were locked on him; he could feel them all the way across the room.

"My Lady," he said in a cheerful voice, still somewhat out of breath. "I am sorry that my mother has wasted your time today, and on other occasions previously. She is determined to locate me a bride, and I have repeatedly informed her that I shall discover one on my own. I am sorry you have been inconvenienced today. Please, allow me to escort you back to the manor."

Lady Lillian said nothing, and slowly stood.

"Good sir," she said after a lengthy pause. "This is my third visit to House Belmont. This is the third time I have journeyed across the marshes of Esther to come and make your acquaintance. I have been told, by the Great Lady Jubilee, that there was a scheduling misadventure upon my first visit, and an urgent matter that required your immediate attention on my second."

She paused. "I am to infer that the Great Lady misspoke herself? There was no scheduling issue, was there? You were not called away on urgent business the second time, were you? I would appreciate an honest answer."

Stenstrom looked down at the fine, wood floor. Perhaps he should have selected the demon after all. "You are correct, my lady."

"You simply did not wish to come in and see me, is that it?"

Stenstrom blushed. "Yes, my lady. I am sorry. Again, it has nothing to do with you. It's an issue I have with my mother. I would like to offer my apologies."

Lady Lillian seemed to tense up. "I am not interested in an apology, sir." She reached down behind the couch and drew a long, slim rapier. "Have you a weapon?"

Stenstrom was shocked. "I do not. You wish to have a duel, my lady?"

"I do. I have been repeatedly insulted. I came here in good faith, to meet a promising young gentleman, whom I found rather handsome. Now, sir, I will have satisfaction."

She began walking forward, her blue eyes flashing.

"I do not have a weapon."

"Then I shall simply deal you a minor wound and take my leave. I shall not be back, as you have proved yourself a lout and a bore."

Stenstrom was stung. "I am neither a lout or a bore. I am offended."

Lillian raised her rapier and thrust, rather skillfully.

Stenstrom side-stepped her thrust and attempted to grab her by the shoulders.

She moved away with considerable skill, creating space to use her weapon—Stenstrom was impressed. "I have been thoroughly trained by my brothers and my father," she called out, her voice echoing across the ballroom. "I am your match and more. I suggest you simply take my satisfaction the way that a man does, then I shall depart. Fall on the floor and bleed, sir, and I shall be appeased."

Stenstrom looked to the door.

"Come out here, Belmont!" he thought he heard the demon yell. *"Heheheheh…"*

He raised his left hand. With a vigorous bit of sleight-of-hand, four brightly colored stones appeared between his fingers.

"Do you know what these are?" he asked. "These are Holystones, and they may be cast for a variety of effects. Please lower your weapon."

Lillian was undeterred. "I do not believe in Tyrol magic," she said side-stepping to her right.

"Nor do I," Stenstrom said. "However, here they are. I can blind you with them or make you sneeze, or ruin your gown. Please lower your weapon. I have wronged you, and wish to apologize."

"Where's my apology, Belmont, for my empty belly?" the demon roared.

Lillian feinted to her right then applied a thrust, getting him slightly in the coat. "I entreat you to use them, sir," she said. "Use your stones. Do something with them!"

Stenstrom took a teal one and threw it to the floor where it burst in a noisy flash.

Lillian covered her eyes. "How dare you!" she cried, still covering her eyes.

There was a huge crash of stone and glass.

The demon had broken into the ballroom.

"Hahaha! I'm not going to have come all this way to return to my poisoned stream with an empty stomach!"

"You stated your pre-conditions. I have not violated them."

"I care not! I want you in my rotten belly! And, I think I'll eat her too!"

The demon, bounding on its fins and slashing with its catfish whiskers, pulled itself with a fuss into the ballroom.

Lillian stood there with her sword and was horrified. "What in the name of Creation?"

Stenstrom threw a gray Holystone at the demon where it burst into a grainy cloud around the demon's catfish face. It got the stuff in its gills sneezed. It then cleared its gills with a blast of mucous dripping down the wallpaper. *"So, a little pepper with my dinner. That's fine!"*

Lillian backed away from the creature into the ballroom. She was incensed. "So, you scoundrel, it took a summoned demon to get you in here with me today, did it?"

The demon lunged. Stenstrom backed into a corner and threw a sky blue Holy Stone and hit it in the head. The demon immediately was covered in polka-dots.

Roaring with anger, it shot out with its whiskers and got Lillian around the waist. She dropped her rapier with a wood and metal clatter/thud. It opened its huge mouth to swallow her.

Stenstrom shook his hand and threw six MARZABLE daggers at the fiend, getting it in its bony fish head.

It turned to Stenstrom with incredible speed, opened wide, and swallowed him whole.

As he slid down the smelly, rotten gullet, a flash of cold steel suddenly ripped in. Lillian, with her little rapier, sliced the demon in two separating its head from its body where it vanished back to wherever it came from with a cry of misery.

Stenstrom, covered in blood and slime, came climbing out of the remains.

Lillian, holding her gory rapier, raised it. "I am going to make you wish you'd selected the demon today, Lord of Pigs!" she said.

She charged forward and was met with a freezing cascade of iced punch that had been set out on the table. Stenstrom, still dripping with demon slime and stinking of innards, was holding the now empty punch bowl.

Lillian stood there open-mouthed. Her face and gown covered in red punch, bits of pink shaved ice trailing down the stainless blade of her rapier, mixing with the demon's blood in a dripping pool at her feet. She was aghast. "V-villain …" she piped.

They stood there looking at each other, Stenstrom holding the punch bowl and Lillian, wide-eyed, her blue eyes standing out like two aqua-marine wheels on a snowy pink landscape, punch dripping off her.

"Quite a pity," he said still holding the bowl, "I was hoping to have a refreshing glass of punch just now after such vigorous activity."

Lillian smiled a little and gave a short laugh. "And I usually enjoy my fish lightly breaded and seasoned with a hint of lemon."

Soon, they both laughed in earnest.

Stenstrom, slimy, took Lillian, dripping, by the hand and they went back to the manor on the hill to get her out of her wet, stained gown and he out of his ruined clothes. There, she changed into a robe, and her gown was taken away to be cleaned by the staff. They chatted for the rest of the afternoon on the terrace overlooking the sea and enjoyed a well-made lunch.

The air cleared and an experience shared, they warmed to each other. Despite himself and his desire to humble his mother, Stenstrom found this spirited woman from Gamboa to be well worth the adventure and the "I told you so" he was sure to hear. She had proven that she was fiery, skilled, had a back-bone, and had a sense of humor as well—all things Stenstrom found very admirable.

"I'm sorry I chose to avoid you on your first two trips—look what company I missed out on," Stenstrom said eating his lunch.

Lilly sat there in her fluffy robe and smiled. "I'm glad I came again, and I'm glad I didn't stab you in the heart with my sword."

Stenstrom thought about her rapier. "That was quite a blow you struck to the demon."

"It's the MARTIN, the LosCapricos weapon of my family."

"I'm not familiar with that one."

"It works just like a rapier, except when you get really mad; then it always cuts the head off the victim."

"Gods—"

"It's all right. I wasn't going to chop your head off, though I sort of wanted to at first."

"I told you so!"

It was an amazing summer. Lillian of Gamboa was a grand hit around the Belmont Manor.

"And you liked her, my son, truly?" Lady Jubilee said, walking arm in arm through the garden paths with her son. For once they weren't fighting about something—they talked about Lilly. Lady Jubilee was all smiles—something that didn't happen often.

"I did, Mother. She was beautiful, and she had spirit to match."

"Wonderful. You see, I have good taste. I would not have invited some awful bore or society fool to our home to dally with my son. I was certain you would find favor with her."

Stenstrom looked down at his mother: silver-hair, sparkly eyes, a bright smile. "I wonder though, was it really necessary to summon a demon?"

"A demon? Why, I'm sure I don't know what you're talking about."

"The big, scary catfish you summoned to tear my soul apart. He half destroyed the Chalk House."

They stopped, and Jubilee put her hands on Stenstrom's face. "I care not about the antics that went on in the Chalk House between the two of you— that can be fixed. My son, the last thing in the world I would want is for a demon to feast upon your soul. I have been guilty of subjecting you to bizarre things and putting you to steps I'm certain other young men have not had to face. The love of a Tyrolese mother can be severe."

They reached the end of the path. Ahead, a coach came into view, floating down the lane.

"I have had the good fortune to have thirty wonderful children: twenty-nine daughters, and one fine son. I can't imagine life without any of you. Perhaps I am over-protective. Perhaps I impose my will on you too much. There are times when I am in the wrong, and need to be told as much—your father is good for that. Of course, he's out chasing the stars again."

The coach stopped at the gate, and Lillian of Gamboa got out, lit-up in a fine teal gown and holding a small matching parasol to keep her out of the hot sun.

"But, sometimes, I am right."

Lilly saw him and waved. He waved back.

"I told you so."

Lilly's skill as a painter was obvious. She stood by the large canvas holding the brush. She looked at her subject with a careful eye. She mixed her paints and smoothed them onto the canvas with easy, learned strokes.

She was painting a portrait of Stenstrom. She had been planning to give it to him as a future birthday present. She refused to let him see it. It was going to be a surprise.

Stenstrom was lying there in the garden, naked, watching her paint. "I hope you're not planning on giving me a nude portrait, Lilly. I might have a hard time finding a place to hang it."

Lilly was also naked. "It's not a nude, silly."

They'd been lovers for some time now. Their rocky start well past them, their relationship quickly had escalated into a passionate one.

Stenstrom lay back and looked at her naked body, partially obscured by the large canvas. "So, Lilly, would you really have stuck me with your sword upon our first meeting?"

"Oh, yes. I was hurt, and angry. I wanted you to acknowledge me, so, yes—I think I would have stabbed you—not to kill, if that means anything to you."

She put her brush down and joined him on the couch. "I'm glad I didn't. I'm glad we were able to find each at last. It was worth the wait."

They gazed at each other in the fading afternoon light. "I'm settled, Lilly. I would like to announce ourselves. I am happy with you, and want no other."

She closed her eyes. "Me, the first Countess of Belmont-South Tyrol?"

"Would you accept such a distinction?"

She lay back and thought a moment. "Right now, at this moment, yes— yes I would. Gladly. But..."

"But?"

"Just look at us, Bel. We're both still so young. There is so much we haven't seen or done. There is a whole League out there, and beyond. If we committed to each other now, what if something else came around the corner? I'm not saying something will, I just want us both to know for certain."

She saw the disappointment in Stenstrom's face. "Oh, darling—please. I don't mean it as a rebuke or rejection. I just want the both of us to be assured that, when we commit to each other, that there will be no *maybe's* and *what if's*. I mean, how much do you really know about me?"

"I know all I need to."

"You should be careful with that, Bel. We all have our secrets, and I certainly have my share." She took him into her arms. "Here's what I propose. Let us take five years. During that time, we may both choose to explore the world and the League at large as we will. If in that time we find something different or new, we may be free to explore it. I pray such a thing doesn't happen, but I cannot predict the future. I simply want it to be that when I give my heart to you, or you give yours to me, there will never be any question that we were meant for each other."

"I don't want anybody else, Lilly."

She kissed him. "I pray that, at the end of five years, you still feel the same way. I don't want to lose you either." She took a deep breath. "So, is this what it feels like to be in love? It's wondrous. I don't want it to stop."

"Then let us present ourselves."

She lay back. "No, Bel—five years. Please, that is what I must ask of you."

Stenstrom got up and approached the painting. "No, no, no," Lilly said. "You promised not to look." She laid back, her naked breasts pointing up at the sky. "I have a gift for you, Bel, I've been wanting to give it to you for some time now.

She placed a small golden locket on a delicate chain in the dimple between her beasts and waited for him to take it. He picked it up. "May I open it?" he asked.

"Of course."

Inside was a tiny picture of Lilly's golden face, hand-painted and meticulous. "Did you paint this, Lilly?"

"I did, Bel. I've been working on it for some time. I wanted it to be perfect before I gave it to you. Do you like it?"

"I love it. I'll carry it with me always." Lilly beamed.

He turned, cradling the locket in his hand and went to fetch his clothes. A few minutes later, partially dressed, he returned.

Lilly lay prone on the couch.

"Lilly, will you stay for dinner this evening, I …"

Lilly was gone. In her place was an intricate sculpture of her nude body in sand, perfect in every detail. Everything about it was perfect, the shape of her face, the curve of her legs, her soft, delicate feet.

Lilly often did this—disappearing at a moment's notice and leaving behind a wonderful sculpture of her likeness in sand. It amazed him how fast she could put these sculptures together—such care and detail—surely such a thing should take hours, but he'd been gone only a few minutes.

The canvas of his portrait was gone too.

Written in sand near her head in a fine cursive hand was: "Bye, bye …" That was another thing Lilly did on her departures. "*Bye … bye …*"

Oh Lilly, he thought. He always felt so sad when she abruptly left like this. He got out the locket and stared at her beautiful face. "Bye, Lilly. Don't be long."

Five years—a lot of things can happen in five years.

Though he could probably expect to see much less of Lilly around, she would, nevertheless, come to dominate his thoughts and his doings. Just as Stenstrom began to emerge from his mother's wing and openly challenge her, he replaced one domineering woman with another—Lilly.

Everything that happened from then on out she had a hand in determining. Just like she could sculpt a statue of sand, she could sculpt him too.

Five years …

14

—A Question of Occupation—

There was an unspoken disconnect rumbling around Belmont Manor. It had been there for years, and was largely—and wisely—undiscussed.

The disconnect: what sort of occupation would Stenstrom the Younger be allowed to pursue as he matured into a young man. Such a topic was new around the House with Stenstrom being the only son of Belmont. Lady Jubilee assumed that all of her daughters would simply become ladies, countesses and socialites, like she was. Only a few of her daughters, Lady Celesta and Nylar, for example, and more recently, Lady Lyra, had openly antagonized Lady Jubilee on the matter and promptly found themselves outside in the moonlit garden under the knife.

As for Lord Stenstrom the Younger, clearly, his father wanted him to join the Fleet and clearly Lady Jubilee did not.

Lord Stenstrom at one time was rather keen on the idea. He sent his young son all sorts of Fleet memorabilia to fill his thoughts, and spun grand tales of his adventures when he was in attendance at home—both Stenstrom and Lyra soaking them up eagerly. Lady Jubilee frowned on the subject, her hatred of the Fleet most clear.

To further push the matter, Captain Stenstrom took his son on a trip to Onaris aboard his vessel, the *Caroline,* when he was nine—his first trip into space. It was just a quick run to gather supplies, a task great warbirds normally didn't partake in; however, Captain Stenstrom was eager for a chance to take his son on a brief introductory spin around the stars.

He hoped more would follow.

Stenstrom the Younger was intoxicated with the whole thing: the launch from Esther Bay, listening to his father command the ship, barking out orders, and watching the bridge crew follow them without pause or question. Sitting in his office, the ship under full sail, he looked out the window at the dark gallery of space moving by.

"Do you see that great glowing thread stretching off into the distance, my son," he asked.

"I do, father," Stenstrom the Younger said, his face pushed up against the glass. "What is it?"

"It's a cloud of gas called Druries Belt—just a harmless oddity one finds while at sea. There are many such things, each more wondrous than the previous, all just waiting to be discovered."

"When will we arrive at Onaris?" Stenstrom the Younger asked.

"Oh, in just a few hours."

"What's out there?'

"Here—nothing, just a bit of empty space between Kana and Onaris. Pay it no mind. There's nothing out there except Druries Belt and some ice."

When they returned to Tyrol, Lady Jubilee was incensed, and though she was missing her usual cigarette, she smoked nonetheless.

That was the first time he ever heard his parents engage in a bitter, shouting argument, their voices exchanging back and forth through the halls of the old monastery, he covering his ears so as not to hear the hurtful words being hurled back and forth.

As time passed, Stenstrom the Older's zeal diminished a bit. He never saw his son wearing any of the clothes he sent home to him, never saw him playing with the toys and models he'd bought. Perhaps he really didn't have an interest in it after all.

So, what was he to do? He was getting older and the question could be ignored no longer.

The question of Stenstrom's future occupation, the thing Lord Stenstrom and Lady Jubilee always had avoided discussing at any length, finally came to a boil one day when Stenstrom the Younger was seventeen. Lord Stenstrom again took his son for a ride to Onaris, this time bringing Lady Lyra along as well. As he had when he was younger, Stenstrom was full of excitement—so was Lyra. This time, Lord Stenstrom put it to them directly.

"So, would either of you like to join the Fleet, sail the stars with your old man? There is a place waiting for either or both of you. Many clamor for such an opportunity, I beg not to waste it."

Both of them looked at each other and respectfully said, "No."

"But why—you both seem to love it. I don't understand."

Stenstrom the Younger spoke up: "Mother will not allow it, and has seen to it."

Ah—Stenstrom the Older now understood.

They returned to Belmont Manor the next day. It was time of the Yearly Reasoning, when a League Auditor from the city of Armenelos came to check the House of Belmont's assets and determine if enough tax had been paid—it was a dreary and sometimes infuriating exercise to have to go through.

The auditor, a Lord Belamy of Koff—a small, meek man from the League office, sat there going through all of House Belmont's assets as Lady Jubilee and Lord Stenstrom had a raging fight all around him.

"I have told you that our son will not join the Fleet and have nothing to do with it! I have made that most clear, have I not?" she shouted. "They call you Stenstrom the Brave. Instead, they should call you 'Stenstrom the Deaf', or 'Stenstrom the Forgetful'!"

He returned the favor. "How about these appellations, madam:

'Stenstrom the Pained'. 'Stenstrom the Encumbered', and 'Stenstrom the Determined'! Jubilee, you cannot protect our son so; he has all of the tools needed to be a fine officer in the Fleet, and should be permitted to make his own choices as he sees fit. He loved his trip to Onaris—he has a passion for faring the stars—just as I do. I know he does!"

"We are under Wirguild!"

"The Wirguild is suspended, and has been for years! There's glory to be had for him in the Fleet!"

"And death and destruction and pain for his mother!"

"You are talking nonsense!"

Lord Koff continued checking his papers, trying to blend in with the tabletop. In all his travels, he'd clearly never seen a Lord and Lady behave so.

"He has a world of choices before him—just not the Fleet! Not the Stars! I forbid it! Additionally, I have set him to the Blood Promise—he has promised not to join the Fleet."

Ah—so there it was—there it was. She and her damned rituals. Her superstitions. Stenstrom slammed his hand down on the table, causing Lord Koff's terminal to jump.

"That is a piece of Tyrol nonsense! How could you do such a thing to our son?" he roared.

"I have protected our children from all that may harm them—I have stood guard over their souls, and the Blood Promise is part of that protection! It is my guarantee!"

"Tyrol nonsense!"

"Tyrol nonsense, is it? I should turn you into a fly and swat you flat right now for your temerity!" Jubilee shouted back.

"I wish you would—I truly do! You have been threatening to transform me into this creature or that for years. Go ahead! Do it! End my suffering!"

Amid this thunderstorm, Lord Koff meekly spoke up. "My Lord, might I command your attention for a moment?"

Lady Jubilee turned her fury to Lord Koff, her eyes smoldering. "You!" she spat. "What, in the name of Creation, do you want?"

Lord Koff trembled under her gaze. "My Lady, I have some figures that I would like to go over with you. I feel, and the data support it, that there has been an underpayment to the League ..."

"An underpayment?"

"Yes, Great Lady ..."

"AN UNDERPAYMENT?"

Lord Stenstrom approached and looked at Lord Koff's figures. He threw his hands up. "Yes, yes, I agree. I will authorize a payment to you, Lord Koff, this very moment."

His gaze went to Lady Jubilee. "I will go and get the funds. I find the company in this room fairly distasteful at present."

Lady Jubilee watched him exit and lit a fresh cigarette.

Lord Koff tapped his keys. "I certainly hope Lord Belmont understands there shall be additional fees and penalties for the tardy nature of the payment."

Lady Jubilee appeared not to care about taxes and money at the moment. "The hallmark of any sound relationship, Lord Koff, is the ability to fight with vigor with the one you love and make up later, would you not agree?"

"I... well, I..."

She began to choke up a little and pulled from her cigarette to hide it. "We often fight about this and that, and never fail to properly make up. This time will be no different. I love that man—cherish him. That's why I act as I do. He and our children, that's why I care so much."

She pulled herself from her reflections. She turned back to Lord Koff. She looked at the little man sitting there with his terminal and papers, and she sneered with disdain. "You sir, you are an accountant, correct?"

"Yes, Great Lady. I am a fully accredited accountant for the League and a proud member of the IBBAANA brotherhood."

"Truth be told? How nice. And this 'Banana' organization you mentioned, that is some sort of accountant gathering, yes?"

"IBBAANA, Great Lady, and yes, it is a proud brotherhood of accountants and other similar occupations."

"I see. And, have you ever been shot at?"

"What? Shot at? No, Great Lady."

"Have you ever faced death in space?"

"In space? No, Great Lady."

"Has an accountant ever died of botulism?"

"What? Well, I ..."

She leaned down and gritted her teeth. "And, do you not believe that I could turn you into a fly, should I so choose to do so?"

Lord Koff sweated. "I ... do not know, Great Lady."

Jubilee intimidated Lord Koff for a few minutes more; then Lord Stenstrom returned with a chest of coins.

"An accountant!" she declared as Lord Stenstrom sorted through the coins. "Our son shall become an accountant and join the—the. . ." Jubilee snapped her fingers in Lord Koff's face. "What is the name of that insipid brotherhood you grovel in fealty to, sir?"

"What? The IBBAANA, is that what you are referring to? I do not gro--"

"Yes, yes, the 'BANANA'—our son shall belong to such an organization and elevate it to new heights." Jubilee pointed at Lord Koff. "Just like this insignificant man sitting right here! And to ensure such a thing, I shall put him to the Promise."

Lord Koff was open-mouthed in outrage. "Insignificant?" he sputtered.

Stenstrom threw down the chest. "You will force our son into mediocrity? You will force upon him the life of a faceless Hack?"

"Mediocrity?" Koff shouted with indignation. "Faceless Hack?"

"If it ensures a long, uneventful life for our son, then yes I will!"

Lord Koff, a partially forgotten man in the midst of this row, opened his coat and pulled out a holo pedestal. He set it on the table and turned it on. Soon the flickering images of a number of young people began floating about the room. "I will have you know, Great Lady Jubilee, that I am the proud father of fifteen wonderful children. I am not insignificant."

Jubilee stopped shouting at her husband and looked at the smiling images orbiting around his head.

"I see," she said studying them. "And did you have any children that lived, Lord Koff?"

"Lady Jubilee!" Lord Stenstrom said, aghast, dropping his coins. "Where are your manners?"

"Manners be damned! Behold these tawdry waifs, with naught to look at but this man's bald head as he stumbles home after yet another uneventful day. At least they may expect no harm to come to their father. That is what I crave for our son—a simple, uneventful life, free of danger. And that, by Creation, is what he shall have!"

15

—Favored of the Sisters—

Shortly after the big row with Lord Stenstrom, Lady Jubilee was distressed to learn that a contingent of Sisters was coming west from Valenhelm to pay her a visit.

The Sisters always made her nervous. What did they want? What did they know?

Their intentions soon became clear. With Lady Jubilee and Stenstrom the Younger sitting in the parlor, the group of ten Sisters laid it out for them with uncharacteristic haste and frankness. The Sisters didn't seem to care about Lady Jubilee at all—it was her son they were interested in.

"We have watched your growth, Lord Stenstrom, with great interest. You have matured into an admirable young man," the prim Marine said.

"Thank you, Great Sister."

"We shall be blunt, as we are certain your time is short, as is ours. We wish you to participate in our Program, sir. You have been found to be of fine lineage, and you would honor us with your participation."

Stenstrom was nervous. He knew of the Sister's "Program," where they invited select males throughout the League to inseminate fertile Sisters. He'd heard it was a complicated procedure, requiring many visits and a lengthy negotiation, and to be selected was an honor.

He didn't feel honored. He felt rushed and on-the-spot. He looked to his mother. "Mother, I …"

"This request does not concern your mother, the Great Lady Jubilee. She has no say in your response, either yes or no. Please refer your answer to us."

Stenstrom didn't know what to say or do.

Jubilee spoke up. "Sisters, this is most irregular. Normally, a House may expect a reception and proper sitting before …"

"This is hardly, regular, Lady Jubilee. Do not forget that it was we who saved your son's life on repeated occasions. We expect a small recompense for our assistance."

Lady Jubilee forgotten, they gazed at Stenstrom. "We require an answer, sir. The matter is completely voluntary, and you shall not offend us in any case. Therefore, what say you?"

Stenstrom wanted his mother to answer. "I … perhaps I am a bit too young. I might better serve you in a year or so, when I am more mature."

"You are optimally mature at present, Lord Belmont, hence our presence in your wonderful home. Again, what is your answer?"

Their eyes bored into him.

He swallowed. "Regretfully, I ..."

"We certainly hope you will accept our offer. We would leave here ... most disappointed otherwise. We would not wish to have to investigate your mother's doings at length. It would pain us to discover that she was engaging in anything ... forbidden."

Lady Jubilee stood. "Do not threaten my son! I care not what you do to me! My son is ..."

"Sit ... down ..." the Marine said in a quiet but commanding tone, the Sisters' eyes flaring. Jubilee sat, unable to match the iron wall of their will.

Stenstrom, fearing for his mother, spoke. "Yes, Great Sisters, I accept!"

Jubilee was panicked. "Bel, don't ..."

"I accept! I accept! Please, I shall participate!"

The Sisters were silent a moment. Then: "We are most pleased."

Stenstrom felt awkward. "I am not informed regarding what shall happen next. I do not know what is expected of me. Who am I to ... assist in this matter?"

The Sisters smiled. "Why, all of us, Lord Belmont. 'Tis a great honor we pay you. And you need not fear—we shall handle this and take a good treatment of you."

They turned to Lady Jubilee. "Get out," the Marines said.

Lady Jubilee was silent and rather helpless in her own home. There was nothing she could do. She stood and left the parlor.

The Sisters then took command of Lord Stenstrom, rendering him helpless within his own body.

He had a vague memory of being led into a guest bedroom. He remembered something about being pushed against the wall, strong arms around him and the softness of heated skin pressed against his.

He thought he recalled the sting of primal release, over and over.

And when it was over, they left as quickly as they came.

But, it wouldn't be long before they returned. Again and again, a roomful of Sisters demanding servicing, always the same.

✳   ✳   ✳   ✳   ✳

"They come, all the time, Lilly. What am I supposed to do?"

Lilly sat there with him in the moonlight, her arms around him. "Isn't participating in the Sister's Program a great honor?"

"Yes, so I'm told, but this many times? And they threaten my mother if I show the slightest inclination to resist."

Lilly thought a bit. "Obviously you have something they desperately want. There have been instances in the past where the Sisters have taken particular shines to certain League men—why is not plainly clear. The Sisters are inscrutable. It seems to me that, if you weren't here anymore, they might leave you and your mother alone."

"What do you mean?"

"I mean even the Sisters are supposed to conform with social protocols. Having you service them so often actually violates some of those protocols—they are supposed to 'spread it around,' if you follow my meaning. And, they are supposed to schedule their Program over several visits—not just show up and demand servicing. I'm afraid with you hidden behind the walls of Belmont Manor and out of the League's eye, they may do as they please."

"So, what am I to do?"

"I think it's time you left home, Bel. Get out, and see the world. If you were out in a public place and not secluded at home, the Sisters would have a much harder time getting to you. Out in the public you are protected—the Sisters could not simply ride in and take you whenever they want."

"What sort of public place?"

"School. University. There are many to choose from."

"I don't want to go to school, Lilly. According to Mother, the only course of study I'm permitted to follow is accounting, and that sounds like a slow death to me."

"Really? Does your mother dominate you so?"

Stenstrom looked at his chest and remembered the searing knife that was plunged into it.

You will study nothing in the schools but accounting ...

"Yes ..."

"Your course of study is really quite pointless, Bel—what difference will it make? Go to school and study accounting—do as little as possible to pass your courses if the subject matter bores you. There, you shall be out in public and shielded from the Sisters. Additionally, I think you need to blossom as a person. You are secluded here in this manor—you see nobody, you talk to no one other than your parents and your sisters and me. You need to get out and interact. School's great for that."

"Why don't you come to school with me?"

"Shall we go over this again, Bel? We have our five years—they have just begun. Fear not—I will come and see you often, and I shall write constantly. Our hearts will not be far."

16

—The Astral Traveler—

With a fair amount of trepidation, Stenstrom enrolled in the University of Bern far to the west in Vithland. The University of Bern was a rich, well-known school across the League. Not a school known for sciences, as the University of Arden was, or a liberal arts school like the University of Dee, Bern was best known as a trade and business school. Many of the most successful traders and merchants across the League were alumni of the U of B.

As typical, his House spared little expense for his maintenance and board. They bought him a lovely terraced apartment on a green near the university grounds complete with several guestrooms so that they could visit often. They furnished the apartment with fine things and filled his closets with the best clothing.

Though Stenstrom often dreamed of leaving home often when he was younger, to be free of his mother's leash, he immediately found himself badly homesick in his lovely apartment. He recalled many of his sisters, loudly rebellious at home, bemoaning their freedom, clamoring to take flight, found themselves right back at home of their own volition once they came of age. He recalled his sister Lenta actually came to live at home even after she had been wed, she and her husband moving into her old bedroom—Belmont Manor was a nest that was soul-shattering to walk away from. There were also Calami, Phaedra, Kormanda and Io who were often in attendance at home for months at a time for no particular reason.

Lilly was right. The grounds of his South-Tyrol home and his family were all he'd ever known. He realized he truly didn't have a friend in the world, and didn't have the first clue as to go about making one. He'd been taught to look at people twice, to mistrust and suspect treachery. The trusting little boy who was almost killed in the Fox Park in Tyrol was gone. Strangers, he had learned, were the enemy, in the employ of the enemy and doing the work of the enemy—whoever that was.

From his terrace, he could see the school and the city buildings of Bern not far away. He saw the students coming and going and the floating traffic moving in an orderly fashion down the street. He saw groups of students milling about, laughing, talking, and interacting with each other in a simple yet utterly alien fashion for him. None of his mother's sorcery had prepared him for this, to be a simple student, to be a citizen of the League. He saw young ladies in gowns of all kinds from all over the League. He saw young gentlemen wearing clothing in the style of Vith, Remnath, Zenon, and Hala.

And he felt completely alone in his somber Tyrol clothes, having little if any idea how to go out and fit in.

The last time he'd been truly out of his own was the Fox Park debacle—which he still didn't know if that had been real or simply an elaborate dream. He nearly hit the Com and called home for Mother to come and get him.

After a bit of inner turmoil, he decided to go out and walk about the campus, get a feel for the place. He had to remember that he was no longer a little boy with his possessions in a sack; he was no longer helpless.

He walked down the stairs of his building and made his way onto the green, passing groups of people along the way. He felt out of place in his Tyrol clothes, not seeing anybody else in the familiar Tyrol jacket, leggings and boots. The people seemed friendly enough as he wandered down the green, the ladies curtsying and the gentlemen tipping their hats. He thought to introduce himself several times, to strike up a conversation, but found himself with nothing to say and on the defensive.

He continued on, eventually wandering deep into the mass of tightly packed campus buildings.

He noticed his surroundings change a little; everything seemed dark and quiet. He looked up at the early evening sky—it wasn't a Kanan sky, it was something else, a negative image of what it should be, peppered with unusual stars. He heard a strange wind and odd sounds. After another few moments, the sky reverted to its normal cheery blue.

He remembered a strange sky like that, from his Fox Park dream and from the incident at Rustam Labyrinth. After nine years of arcane study, he knew what it might be—the Astral Plane, a sort of pocket dimension that was always there but seldom noticed. It tended to warp the perceptions of any in close proximity to it, and therefore mundane things might appear unusual, such as the sky. The Astral Plane was difficult to access, daunting to navigate, and dangerous to traverse. According to his mother, the Sisters made Astral travel illegal centuries ago, though the Xaphans sometimes still used it at their peril.

The Astral Plane could be opened by strong emotion. No doubt the boiling uncertainty he was feeling might be responsible for it. Part of him, still reminiscing in the Fox Park dream, wanted to run home and hide. The new man in him, however, refused. With the Astral Plane, he could expect to see what he feared most.

Something approached him from behind. He quickly turned.

A lady wearing a summer gown beneath a knit sweater stood there—surprised by his abrupt turn. "Oh," she said, hand over her heart. "You startled me."

Stenstrom looked her over. She seemed innocent enough. "Your pardon," he said.

She stood there for an awkward moment. "Are you new? This is my first year, and I was just exploring the grounds. Are you new here too?"

Stenstrom didn't answer. She awaited a reply, and, when one didn't come, she rocked back and forth uncomfortably. "Ummm, my name is Corvene of Dan. I was trying to locate the student union, and I thought to have a bite of dinner there. This campus is quite large. Would you care to join me? Perhaps we could locate it together."

"No."

She blushed and adjusted the sleeves of her sweater. "Well. Sorry then. Please, have a good evening." She walked past him and continued around the side of the building.

He felt a little crass for treating the girl in such a manner, and had a thought to follow her around the building and apologize. Still, the Astral Plane was present in the immediate area near enough to warp his perceptions, and her arrival seemed awfully well-timed.

He had a sudden feeling that he was in danger. Quickly, he faded into the shadows and hid by the side of the building.

Someone came around the corner of the building just then. It was her—she'd returned. She walked right past where Stenstrom was hiding and looked around. "Sir?" she said. "Sir, are you still here?"

He noted she bore an odd smell with her this time—not perfume, but something basic and primal. She smelled like a dog in heat, and he found himself drawn to it; aroused by it. She panned around, clearly wondering where he had gone. She walked to the building's edge and looked some more, her neck bending from one side to the other.

What was that smell? It was now more of a stench, filling his nostrils. He could barely contain himself.

Her bearing changed. She straightened, seemed angry, poised and rather sinister. She dug through her bag and produced a smoky vial from within along with a small copper sphere. She set the sphere on the ground, unstoppered the vial and poured out its contents, covering the sphere. She stood over it waiting for something to happen.

The sphere twitched all on its own and began rolling in his direction, picking up steady speed until it rolled off the walk into the shrubs nearby.

The woman looked in his direction, not seeing him, but seemingly knowing he was there. She slowly reached back into her bag and, when she pulled her hand back out, she wore a form-fitting metal assembly around her knuckles. It appeared to be some sort of weapon.

Stenstrom shook his hand, producing his MARZABLE.

He and the woman were engaged in a tense standoff, neither flinching, both ready to strike.

At that moment, warning sirens went off all around campus. The skies darkened and through the clouds came the terrifying rope-like tongue of a cyclone. It had appeared from nowhere and threatened to touch ground right in the middle of the campus. Students from all over scattered for cover.

The woman looked up, saw the cyclone and scowled. She got something out of her sweater, and a gaping hole in the universe opened in front of her.

The Astral Plane, he was sure of it. Things got dark, and the sky changed once again into a nightmare of itself.

She had just opened a door to the Astral Plane. She took one last look in his direction, turned, and walked up the steps of a long bridge, her movements exaggerated, and she walked away into unfathomable chaos, her strides stretching off into the distance.

The Astral door closed. He just caught a glimpse of the lady moving down the bridge as the threshold sealed behind her. She was no longer wearing a gown and a sweater. She was wearing a gray suit and a broad-brimmed hat.

And the frightening cyclone overhead that had everyone on the campus scrambling dissipated and vanished just as quickly as it had come.

Since the incident with the Astral traveler, he'd been doing research into the topic of the Astral Plane. He finally found interesting reading.

PLANAR BRIDGE

(qv: teleportation device) Any of a number of devices/artifacts used for rapid travel through the Astral Plane. The existence of the Astral Plane and its exact nature is currently in dispute and no effort has been made to further the technology within League space. The Planar Bridge was first developed by the Xaphan branch of the House of Conwell in 00002ax when it was discovered the Type II world they settled on was a Planar World often lapsing in and out of the Astral Plane. The Planar Bridge is an arcane pendant capable of opening a threshold to the Astral Plane and could be programmed to transport the user to a predetermined location. The assumed nature of Astral travel minimizes the considerations of speed and distance. Bearing is critical and any slight deviation can cause an Astral traveler using the bridge to become hopelessly lost. One of the effects of opening a threshold to the Astral Plane by way of Planar Bridge is the tendency to pull nearby objects into the Astral plane where they are lost forever. The effects upon perception for those near the open threshold is said to vary. The Sisterhood of Light successfully blocked many key points of interest from Astral incursion in 00021ax, thus rendering the use of the Planar Bridge for military purposes moot.

Interesting. So, given this information, he assumed that the woman whom he met on the green weeks earlier was using a Planar Bridge to travel via the Astral Plane. It made sense. Given the odd appearance of the sky and the gray clothing she was revealed to be wearing, he assumed that she was the same woman who attacked him in the Fox Park, and again at the Labyrinth of Rustam as a boy.

Whoever she was, she was persistent—if she existed at all, and that could be in doubt. He had a notion that this Astral Traveler, this Woman in Gray could simply be a projection of his fears given life by the Astral Plane. His elder sister Nylar once let it slip that he had been abducted as an infant, that the person who had abducted him had been a woman wearing gray who was captured by the Sisters. Such a traumatic event might have imprinted itself in his young mind, and the Astral Plane brought her back out at select moments. He had been under great stress as a boy and encountered the Astral Plane in Fox Park—and saw the Woman in Gray there. When the pirate Sedgewick of Kold came upon him in Rustam, his fear might have triggered the opening of a doorway to the Astral Plane, and he saw the Woman in Gray a second time. And now, here at school, alone, unsure, here again is the Astral Plane and the Astral Traveler, the Woman in Gray—a possible phantom of his own mind.

He set to work, using his array of arcane books and knowledge. He knew from his reading that Planar Bridges were fairly easy to block. He created a number of cyan Holystones made of jasmine, carbolyte and wormwood. Such Holystones would prevent the incursion of thresholds from the Astral Plane and provide him protection. He then set them all over his apartment and all about the university, hiding them in gutters, alcoves, rooftops and anywhere else he could find where they would be safe. He cleaned out a local silver shop of candlesticks, ashtrays curios, and other such items and used them to create a whole retinue of arcane devices and aids designed to detect the presence of the Astral Plane. Thus armed and never without his NTHs and MARZABLE, he could feel reasonably secure that whoever this woman was, if she existed at all, she could no longer simply step out of thin air on a Planar Bridge.

He stayed wary, examining any who came near twice and three times, always waiting for his arcane Astral Plane detectors to come to life.

They never did.

As the semester began and he settled into school, no further incidents were noted and, though never forgotten, the matter fell farther and farther back into his thoughts. He did not encounter the Astral Plane or the Astral Traveler again.

17

—The Bones Club—

One thing that Stenstrom could count on when he was really feeling blue was either an appearance in person or a letter from Lilly. It seemed she could read his thoughts and his state of mind from far away in Gamboa and always came to his spiritual rescue.

Today was no different.

Sitting merrily in his stack of daily posts was a letter in a square envelope, scented with a touch of lavender. Great Lords and Ladies always corresponded in hand-written letters—they were so much more personal and heart-felt than a holo-post or insta-type.

Stenstrom savored the letter for a moment before opening it.

It said:

I've being thinking of you lately. I always think of you, but more so as of recently. I hear from your mother that you are all alone down there at school. She tells me you've not made any friends.

When I suggested our five year hiatus, I never intended for you to become a hermit. I wish you to take this time that we agreed upon and use it to your advantage—live, see what's out there. And, should your travels bring you into the arms of another, then that is something that I shall have to accept. I wished for this time, and you are blameless in whatever comes of it.

I have taken the liberty of making some inquiries for you. I certainly hope you will not be angry with me, and I hope you shall keep to an open mind and do a good effort to make friends. If only for me then, please try to enjoy yourself.

Thinking of you, as always…

Lilly

Stenstrom read the letter several times and replied. He wrote her that he would do as she asked and not go out of his way to be a hermit. If only for her, he would try to enjoy himself and make a friend or two.

What could it hurt?

★　★　★　★　★

After lunch the next day, Stenstrom retired to the library to study for a pending exam. Characteristically, he was behind on his studies, but didn't feel overly put off—a bout of furious cramming and he should be up-to-date without undo fuss.

And, characteristically, he sat at the large table alone. Lilly's concern for him passed through his thoughts, but he didn't have time at present to be sociable. It was second nature to avoid strangers and sit by himself—he still really didn't have the first clue how to go about making a friend.

But, all that had to wait because his studies were in peril. He had a selection of books piled in front of him and several holo-term cones floating about for additional research. He was so behind.

Before long, two people approached his table and stood there.

A smallish gentleman in a sumptuous gold and green coat and a skinny lady in a brown gown hovered over his table, staring at him. The woman, her brown hair pulled away from her face and laced into a long, single braid, cooled herself with a black silk fan. She wore fingerless lacy black gloves.

They stood there for what seemed like a long stretch of time.

Eventually, Stenstrom pushed his books aside and looked up, feeling his personal space invaded in a big way. "What's this all about?" he asked.

The pair took Stenstrom's question as an invitation, and they sat down, pulling their chairs out with a draggy, woody fuss that leapt across the open air of the library. The gentleman drew a small silver case from his coat pocket and opened it. Neatly housed within the case was a line of slim cigarettes, leafed in a natural brown color. The gentleman took one out, tapped it on his sleeve, and held it aloft, as if expecting Stenstrom to offer a light.

"I do not have a lighter, if that's what you're hoping for," he said.

The woman lifted her slender hand and, with her thumb and forefinger, pinched down on the end of the cigarette. After a moment a thin trail of smoke curled through her fingers. She slowly let go, and his cigarette was fully lit.

Some sort of sorcery or hidden technology in her palm or on the pads of her fingers—Stenstrom was unimpressed. He returned to his reading.

The fellow in the gold jacket took a puff and let the smoke come out his nostrils, the delicate gray feathers of smoke rising up toward the distant ceiling, getting lost in the wood paneling.

Stenstrom didn't indulge in smoking, but he found the soft, woodsy smell of the smoke pleasant enough.

"I don't believe smoking's allowed in the library," Stenstrom quietly remarked, looking up from his books.

The gentleman smiled slightly and continued smoking, enjoying his cigarette with deliberate slowness, pull after pull.

Finally, as his coal began to fizzle, he spoke. "Are you Stenstrom, Lord of Belmont-South Tyrol?" he asked in a smooth tone.

"I could say no," he replied, "but I'm fairly sure you already know who I am."

"True enough. I am Bannaster, Lord of Tartan, and this lovely lady with me is Alitrix, Lady of Zama."

The woman smiled and ripped her fan. "I am of the Hoban Zamas, sir, not the wild Onaris Zamas. That is a common misconception." Apparently, she found that an important distinction to make plain right off the bat. She gestured with her fan as she spoke.

"Great!" Stenstrom said. "Glad to know you. Now, I have a pile of studying to catch up on, so if you don't mind, could you two please push off?"

Lord Bannaster was unfazed. "We have an opening in an exclusive club that we belong to. You have been highly recommended, and we wish to invite you to join us this evening. I guarantee there will be rich foods, entertainments, and feats of mind and body to freeze your blood. Only the best people shall be there."

"Really?" Stenstrom replied, uninterested.

Lady Alitrix spoke in a greasy accent. "Are you willing to place your soul at risk? Are you willing to face the Sisters' wrath? If you have courage, if you call yourself a man, meet us at this address tonight." She placed a small card onto the tabletop and slid it toward him. "Only those of good blood may join—that shall be your first test."

"Test?" Stenstrom blurted out. "As in the test I'm going to fail if you both don't clear my space."

The two of them stood and walked away, the wooden floor of the library creaking under foot as they went.

Stenstrom thanked Creation for their departure and continued with his reading. After a bit, his curiosity got the better of him—that damn card sitting there on the table. It might as well have been a crowd of people, a flashing light, or a blaring noise, for the card troubled his thoughts and made studying impossible. He picked the card up and had a look at it.

It was blank, just an ivory white card with a faint smell of myrrh.

$$\ast \quad \ast \quad \ast \quad \ast \quad \ast$$

Stenstrom was annoyed and rather unhappy about his visitors in the library. Though he sat there all afternoon, he got relatively little studying done.

He returned to his apartment, tossed his things aside and sat there—as Lilly's letter had noted, he was alone and had no friends to call on. His last visitor was his sister Lyra. It was always good seeing her, and, in fact, the bed in the guestroom where she had slept was still unmade.

He felt quite lonely all of a sudden, the fine walls of the apartment closing in around him. He longed for home, for Mother, and for Lilly. He got Lilly's letter out and read it again.

I have taken the liberty of making some inquiries for you. I certainly hope you will not be angry with me...

He wondered—were the two bores from the library, Lord Bannaster and Lady Alitrix, responding to an inquiry Lilly had made on his behalf? They had to have been—so, in such an instance, he couldn't be overly sore at them for disrupting his study session. They had, after a fashion, been invited into his presence.

Maybe they were friends with Lilly. Maybe they would tell her that he was a cold fish.

Or, maybe they were in association with the Woman in Gray: the Astral Traveler.

He went through his books and picked up the scented card Lady Alitrix had given him. Again, it was nothing more than a plain white card—no embossing, holo-triggers, 4-D tattoos or stamping. He had created several simple tools capable of detecting the presence of the Astral Plane. The most effective was a hollow, silver pyramid filled with certain salts and minerals that he had gathered. If the two of them had recently been to the Astral Plane, he should be able to determine that—the components within the pyramid would react and rattle about inside. He ran the smooth bottom of the pyramid over the face of the card.

Nothing happened. The card had not recently been to the Astral Plane.

Determined to be safe, he lost interest in it. He tossed it aside; he had no time for such intrigues.

He put his pyramid away. He sat down.

The clock near the door ticked. Through the window, he could hear traffic floating down the street.

He thought about it some more. Lilly asked him to try and make friends. Lilly had taken the time to reach out for him and start the process; Bannaster and Alitrix—an odd sort, but still.

He picked the card back up. "All right, Lilly, for you, I'll give it a go," he said into the air.

He looked at it—plain and white—what was he supposed to deduce from it? He considered Lord Bannaster and Lady Alitrix, two obviously gentile types who enjoyed a spot of mystery and gothic flaunt in their stuffy, blue society circle. They encoded this card with information of some sort, and he was supposed to be suitably mystified and would have to labor to discover its secret, matching his wits against theirs. It was a tawdry game he truly didn't feel like playing, but, for Lilly . . .

He took the card into the bathroom and held it up to the bright lights, hoping something would be revealed. Nothing was.

He looked at it in the mirror, again nothing. He held it under the faucet and ran the water over it—nothing.

He thought about Lady Alitrix's parting words:

"Only those of good blood may join—that shall be your first test."

Blood . . .

Oh dear—the thought crossed his mind that he might actually have to smear blood on this card, and some cryptic lettering might react and show up. Bannaster and Alitrix seemed slightly off-putting, and they appeared to have a thirst to boldly break little rules that had no punishable consequences, as with Bannaster's smoking in the library.

Stenstrom sighed, cleaned off his shaving razor, and cut his finger. He squeezed the small cut and allowed several drops to fall on the card.

Something appeared on the face of the card. He rubbed the blood around.

"22 Stang at 24 bells" it read.

✳ ✳ ✳ ✳ ✳

Stenstrom stood there on the deserted street holding the bloody card. 22 Stang—here was the place. The building was a neo-Remnath design, being constructed of grayish sandstone in a boxy footprint, boldly windowed and framed, with a domed roof of metal and glass popping out of the center. In front of the building was a gated yard landscaped in low hedges and beds of colorful flowers.

Number 22 was placed at the wooded end of a quiet side street named "Stang," just off the main drag in downtown Bern, about twenty minutes walk from the university. Surrounding the street on all sides were the capped domes and tall, squarish buildings of Bern, lit up in the evening air. An orderly string of quiet residences lined the street, and, though there was a large bustle of activity at the mouth of the street (traffic coming and going, blinking lights from the shops, people walking), its tree-lined lengthy interior was rather sleepy.

He was dressed in his best: a fine gray Tyrol coat and shirt, black knee britches, and his beloved, Tyrol boots shined to perfection. Tyrol boots sometimes caused a stir in Bern for they, at first glance, looked rather like Hala ranchers' boots. They had a very elongated toe area and always had a mix of leather and metal, the finest using generous amounts of silver, gold and copper at the ankle and the tip. They looked like boots from a suit of armor.

The rustic stocks of his duel NTH pistols stuck out of his sash, and the MARZABLE was hidden, untraceable somewhere in the folds of his clothing. As usual, he was hatless, his wavy, black Belmont hair combed and cut short.

Also hidden in his coat was a special white Holystone—one that would warn him should any Astral travelers become present.

He grappled with his thoughts a moment and truly wished to be elsewhere. Again, Lilly won out—he imagined the door to 22 Stang swinging open and lovely Lilly coming out, bounding down the steps in her festive gown and parasol to great him. He went through the gate, climbed the marble stairs, and tried the main door.

It was locked. He banged on it with his fist.

After a minute or so, the door unlatched and slowly swung inward. A thin man in servant's attire stood within. He gazed at Stenstrom impassively. "Do you have your invitation?"

Invitation? Stenstrom didn't have an invitation—only this bloody card. He held it out. The servant took it and opened the door wide. "If you please," he said, motioning for Stenstrom to enter.

He walked in. The interior of the building was well appointed, scented in the savory aroma of expensive foods and knee-deep in idle chatter. Fine lengths of polished granite and marble lined the floors and the walls. Rich fabrics draped the walls, and vast hangings decorated quiet sitting rooms.

Young people, all dressed in their best, roamed about, holding drinks and smoking scented cigarettes. They turned and looked at Stenstrom as he passed, neither approving of his presence or disapproving.

"May I check your weapons, sir?" the servant asked. "They shall be well cared for and returned to you as the evening concludes. It is a House rule. I shall even request our attendants polish and clean them for you."

Stenstrom pulled the NTHs out of his sash, pocketed the cinnabar strikers to prevent an accidental misfire, and handed them over.

"Thank you, sir. Do you have anything else?"

"No," he lied, knowing full well he had his MARZABLE hidden in his coat.

The servant placed the NTHs on a small table and produced a scanner. "May I? Again, it is a matter of House procedure."

Stenstrom raised his arms and the servant waved the scanner about his chest and legs. He knew the scanner could never locate the mystical MARZABLE.

The servant seemed satisfied and put the scanner away. "This way, please," he said. Stenstrom followed him through a maze of sitting rooms and luxurious halls. A steady stream of foods and drinks came and went from the kitchens as they walked deeper into the building.

Stenstrom knew what this was: an exclusive club—a den of the rich. His mother and father had belonged to such clubs at various times. It was just a place to pay extravagant dues and sit with other rich people, talking about nothing and feeling superior.

The servant led Stenstrom away from the main area to a large, oaken door carved with some type of sunburst design. He opened it with a creak, and motioned for Stenstrom to enter.

At the end of a short, dark corridor was a circular room about sixty feet in circumference, domed, about three stories high. The curving walls were painted a sooty black and were lined all around with books and various arcane decorations. The walls were so black and lusterless, in fact, that it looked as if a fire had raged in the room at some point. Above, two evenly-spaced wooden catwalks ringed the room and, beyond that, the glass dome at the top admitted the starlight outside. Shadowy hints of telescopes and other astronomical equipment were placed all around the dome. He'd seen the dome from outside—this must be the very center of the building. At floor level, axes and halberds, morning stars, and pikes of various sizes hung on the walls, giving the place a torture-chamber sort of feel. There was a hint of spiced incense floating about, and its woody smell quickly became unpleasant in his nostrils. The floor was a smooth green marble with a golden design hammered into the center.

It was an odd design. He looked at it further as he stepped in.

It was a Xaphan symbol.

Four people sat spaced out along the perimeter of the wall. They sat in the shadows in large, throne-like gothic chairs—two gentlemen and two ladies.

He noticed all four were wearing black from tip to top: black coats, black gowns, black shirts, black shoes. And, not only that, they had painted their faces and hands black so that the only thing that stood out on them was their well-cared for teeth and their eyes—blues, browns and greens on beds of white.

One of them spoke. "Good evening, Lord Belmont. This is our sanctum sanctorum—the heart of our club. Here you soul is at risk."

"Is it?" Stenstrom replied.

"As you have probably guessed, this is an exclusive club. The best of everything can be had here ... should you pass muster."

"Here, we do things abhorrent to the Sisterhood," someone else said. "Here, we openly mock them, and deliberately violate their tenets. We are not afraid. Here we do what we will. Here, we are free."

"I see."

"We know your mother's House of Tyrol is on the Sisters' list, for sorcery. We find favor with that. That makes you of interest to us. We would, if you pass our tests, like you to join our club. It is an exclusive offer, and not presented to many."

Stenstrom looked around. "No thanks. I'll have a pass."

One of the women smiled, her white teeth lighting up as if back-lit. "Are you afraid of the Sisters? Are you afraid for your soul?" Her accent was heavy and slightly unpleasant.

He thought of the Sisters, coming to him, their fingers digging into his flesh, their legs around him ...

"I have nothing for or against the Sisters," he said. "And there is nothing here that endangers my soul. This is a place of spoiled indulgence and fathers' wealth ill-spent to entertain wayward children."

The woman laughed. "Allow us to put your courage to the test." She produced a black box which she placed on the floor. With a flick of her wrist, the box slid across the floor on its own accord and stopped a few feet in front of him.

The box gave a shudder. He sensed danger and backed up a step or two.

The box lid opened, and a black leg popped out, padded and spider-like, followed by a second, then a third. Each leg was quite a bit larger than the box that had been confining it.

Soon, ten black legs waved in the air, followed by a hairy bloated body and glittering, jewel-like eyes.

"Have you ever been to Onaris, Lord Stenstrom?" the woman asked, watching the creature emerge from the box. "If you have, then you might have encountered one of these before—it's a demonweb, and I assure you it is quite poisonous and rather bad-tempered."

Stenstrom looked at it with horror: huge, with a leg span nearing four feet and a belly sac full of poison.

"I thought you said you were from Hoban," he said to the woman, who was clearly Lady Alitrix from the library. She cocked her head and gave a slight titter. She raised her hand again and, either through TK, some arcane method, or cleverly hidden technology, began pushing the huge demonweb toward him without touching it.

It didn't like being pushed and reared up aggressively, exposing its coiled-up fangs. It hissed slightly.

Stenstrom replied in kind. He waved his hands and produced two lime green Holystones, and two red ones. He threw a green one at the terrifying creature and webbed it up solid, its legs flexing feebly as it tried to free itself.

Stenstrom then threw a red Holystone, and the webbing caught fire, the room soon full of the smell of roasted demonweb.

The four people in black then clapped in approval. "Well done, Lord Stenstrom. Well done. We had been told that you can create Holystones in the fashion of Tyrol sorcery, and that such things are forbidden by the Sisterhood."

Stenstrom headed for the door. "Yes, and with that I bid you a fond farewell. I wish nothing to do with this club or you lot in particular."

Lady Alitrix waved her hand and the door locked with a heavy click. "But, you've only just arrived …"

He tried the door and it was locked tight.

One of the gentlemen in black stood, wound back and threw something which spiraled through the air. A rectangular card impacted the door frame near Stenstrom's face and stuck fast in the wood. The card was adorned with several colorful numbers and letters:

$$I \quad M \, M$$

$$II \quad M$$

$$III \quad M$$

$$IV \quad *$$

$$V \quad P$$

"The night has only just begun, Lord Belmont. We insist you share it with us," Lady Alitrix said.

After a moment, using tools unseen and speed unheard of, he had the lock picked, and the heavy door swung open. He marched out.

A trapdoor opened beneath him, and he fell down a slide, plunging into pitch black, emerging in a rather shapeless cave-like room that looked like a dungeon. The irregular walls were made of boulder-like, black rock mortared with ash cement. Five archways, each barred by a stout portcullis, led off in different directions.

In the center of the room was a lone figure standing in white.

"Be our guest, Lord Belmont," came Lady Alitrix's accented voice from above. "However, you shan't wish to stay for long."

He could hear and smell gas entering the chamber from hidden nozzles at various locations. He ran to one of the archways and looked through the portcullis. He could see a passage leading off in some twisting direction before it shortly disappeared into darkness. Stenstrom could feel a breeze passing through the bars. He rattled the portcullis—it was solid and locked to the ground.

"Pick a way out, but be warned: only one way leads to a happy ending."

Covering his mouth with his sleeve, he ran to the figure in white in the center of the room. It appeared to be a Sister. She was in white robes, headdressed in the usual fashion. She stood silently pointing at one of the archways.

"Sister, Sister?" he said through his sleeve.

She didn't respond. Upon closer inspection, she was a well-made, fully dressed life-sized dummy.

The gas was quickly getting into his head. He ran to the archway the dummy was pointing at. It was an archway guarded by a solidly placed locked portcullis. Again, a twisting passageway beyond led off into the cool darkness and disappeared.

He looked around, trying to figure some way out of this.

Beyond the portcullis, about four feet away, he noticed a panel had been cut into the stony wall. A large round button sat in the center of the panel. The button must open the portcullis.

He reached out for it, but it was beyond his grasp. He shook his hand and produced a MARZABLE. He lined up the shot and threw, hitting the button easily.

The portcullis quickly rose up into a slot in the ceiling.

Coughing, he made his way into the twisting passageway beyond. He could feel a stiff breeze pulling on him from around the bend.

Stenstrom saw something carved on the floor as he took his first step. It was "IV", the ancient numerology for the number 4.

He suddenly felt an extreme sense of danger. Lady Alitrix and her lot seemed to have a great apathy for the Sisters. Here was a dummy of a Sister pointing at an archway labeled IV; therefore, he reasoned, this door was probably not the way to go to get Lady Alitrix's "happy ending." Something really bad must be waiting for him at the end of this passage.

Holding his breath, he took a quick glance around. He saw, carved into the floor before the other archways: I, II, III, and V.

He recalled the card the gentleman had thrown into the door frame. The card must contain a clue as to which archway he was supposed to take. He recalled seeing I, II, III, IV, V, along with some other lettering. The IV had a star next to it, if he was remembering correctly. The V had a *"P,"* and the rest had *"m's."*

The gas was clogging his brain.

He didn't have any time to bat this around. IV must be a starting point of some sort, hence the star. V was also different somehow with its *"P."* It made sense to him to add V to IV, five "plus" four, giving him nine. Obviously there was no archway labeled nine, so he assumed the rest of the numbers with the *"m's"* might mean to subtract; III, "minus" II, minus I from nine was three.

He moved to the archway labeled III. That must be the correct way to go. Wait …

Didn't one of the numbers have two *"m's"* next to it? That might indicate that that number needed to be subtracted from twice.

Which one was it?

It was I or II—he was sure of it.

It was I—it had to be I. Then, if his gas-clouded reasoning was correct, the archway he wanted was II.

He didn't give himself any time to mull it over. He went to the II archway, produced another MARZABLE, hit the button, and the portcullis rose up into the ceiling.

He ran into the narrow, twisting corridor and went around the bend.

He was instantly sucked off his feet by a powerful updraft and pulled through a dark hole in the ceiling. He seemed to be going up for a time in a twisting fashion, and then started going down.

He emerged through a small door and landed in a sea of pillows. He looked around. He was in a richly furnished room lying on a vast couch. The room was lit in pleasing yellow light and soft music played. On the other side of the room, a great number of people stood holding drinks and smoking slim cigarettes. The four people in black he'd seen in the sanctum sanctorum stood at the front. They were wiping the black paint from their faces.

After a moment, somebody said "Bravo!" and everybody clapped.

Stenstrom pushed the pillows aside. "What is this?" he demanded, his brain hurting a little from the gas.

Lady Alitrix, her face free of black paint, and her accent gone, spoke. "You pass, Lord Belmont. You passed our test, and well done! You are truly full of surprises!"

"You tried to murder me tonight—a demonweb, a gas-filled dungeon!"

"The demonweb is a very convincing and very expensive robot we use. We call him Arthur and he's been 'killed' lots of times in the past. The gas in the dungeon is a harmless sedative—it might have caused you a bit of a headache later on should you have not escaped."

"And the alternate routes out of the dungeon, what of those?"

"Oh, one of them leads to a lesser, Outer Sanctum room somewhere here in the building—you would have been 'in', but you would have been in an inferior circle. The rest head out into the alley—one of them, the worst one, lands you in a dumpster full of food refuse. Should you have taken any of the alley ones, you would not have been offered a membership in our club." She smiled brightly. "You, however, picked the good door—you made it to the Inner Sanctum. I had a feeling you would be successful and was pulling for you."

Lord Bannaster stepped forward. "We do enjoy a bit of theatricality from time to time. We enjoy challenging each other—but all in good fun, if you've the intellect to appreciate it. We must say, we were talking before you arrived—we have no idea how you did some of the things you accomplished tonight, most impressive. We've heard about Tyrol sorcery of course, but to see it firsthand, to witness it in action—remarkable! People usually slay Arthur with a weapon pulled from the wall, or with Vith Gifts—we've seen those on occasion. But you—you actually appeared to conjure Holystones from thin air! And the locked door—you were supposed to fall through a trap door *inside* the sanctum sanctorum, but you got through it so fast we had to use the extra one outside the door. Again a spectacular display."

"And the locked portcullis? How was I to open those without sorcery?"

Lady Alitrix sat down next to him. Her real voice was rather pleasing, and, smiling, she was a beautiful young woman. "If you had inspected the mannequin of the Sister in the dungeon, you would have found that she is held upright with a long stick which you could have pulled up out of the floor and run through the portcullis to press the button. Again, you did something we've never seen before."

"We call her Alice," Lord Bannaster said.

"And I suppose the 'Stick up the Sister's butt' is a metaphorical reference to your continued disdain for the Sisterhood?"

Lady Alitrix smiled. "I guess so, yes—excellent point! So, Lord Belmont, we would like to invite you to join the Inner Sanctum of the Bones Club. It's a large club—this simply being the Bern Chapter. There are chapters all over the League. Here, we gather often to delight each other, help each other when it's needed, and, on occasion, to challenge one another with intrigues—all in good fun. Helps keep the mind sharp. When you're a member of the Bones Club, you may rest assured that, wherever you go, you have friends waiting for you."

She looked at him. "So, what do you say? We'd love to have you."

Stenstrom's first inclination was to walk out and leave these people behind. However, in reviewing the events of the evening, he had to admit he had fun—these people had him completely fooled. He could picture himself bringing Lilly here.

"Sure, why not? And call me Bel. All my friends do."

Stenstrom had made great strides as the year progressed. No longer an aloof, friendless man about the school, he was now a well-liked and active member of the Bones Club. He even participated in the selection ritual, painting and dressing himself in black and sitting in the sanctum sanctorum, as various prospectives came and went, sometimes using his Tyrol sorcery to liven things up. He was amazed how few people actually made it through the process, almost all either ending up in the alley or curling up and becoming incapacitated in the dungeon.

He had a new best friend as well—Lady Alitrix. She was like a dual person—in the Bones Club, she was rather cool and sultry, exuding confidence and wit. She asked him to show her his skills and was amazed how he could make things appear and disappear with only a shake of his hand. Even up close, watching intently, she had no idea how he did it. She wanted to know, but he was mum.

Never tell ... his mother's voice rang in his head. *Never give up your secrets.*

Away from the club, however, out in the school, she was timid, shy, and uncertain. She cried out for attention and positive reinforcement, becoming almost sick with worry when she didn't get it.

They became lovers at her suggestion one evening as they gazed through the telescopes at the top of the sanctum's dome; just a bit of harmless fun between friends, no entanglements, no expectations. Just two people enjoying each other; that's what she said.

Lady Alitrix' thinly veiled insecurities came shining through as they made love.

"Do you like that? Do you like that?" she often said, seeking affirmation throughout the encounter.

After the first awkward session, Stenstrom was certain Lady Alitrix wouldn't want to repeat it—she seemed to not have enjoyed a moment. But, she kept coming back for more—always insistent and demanding, quickly fading to lost and fragile as the deed wore on. She liked most of all to go into the "dungeon" and have sex on the stony floor with the dummy "Alice" watching.

One thing that was always a given, at least in Stenstrom's mind, was that when Lilly came calling, Alitrix would have to retreat. They were, after all, just friends. And, for a time Alitrix was agreeable, disappearing without a second word whenever Lilly chose to grace him with an appearance. After a year or so, Alitrix began to change her tune a little. She once suggested she be allowed to accompany him and Lilly during her visits—she'd be quiet, simply a friend hanging about, and Stenstrom agreed. However, the two ladies quickly began sniping at each other.

"Is this 'person' someone you are experimenting with, Bel?" Lilly asked, rather bluntly.

"What we share together is none of your business," Alitrix said.

"Quite true; nevertheless, I'd hope, Bel, you might select someone a little more to your level."

Alitrix blushed and was clearly hurt. "What do you mean?"

"I mean, look at you. Rather scrawny and not overly pretty—and clearly not a great intellect or wit either, like a little puppy dog nipping at his heals. Making love to a handsome man like Bel must be ... humbling for you at best."

Alitrix sat there and shivered. Stenstrom had never heard Lilly speak so cruelly.

18

—The Paymaster Solution—

Stenstrom had cast aside all of his old inhibitions. He'd gone his whole life
with virtually no friends—his parents, and his two youngest sisters were
all the people he knew. Thus far, in the Bones Club he found himself being
liked, accepted, and he functioned as a vibrant member. He often invited his
sisters Virginia and Lyra to his club meetings, and was delighted when they
were able to come, for seeing the two of them mingling and enjoying
themselves made him feel good. As Lilly had hoped, he was finally enjoying
himself, out every evening with his new friends, Alitrix being his closest.

And, his encounter with the Astral Traveler was a mere distant
memory—his various warnings and protections went unused.

All of the old baggage he carried with him was, for the most part, gone.

Except for one thing.

Many members of the club often arrived at 22 Stang wearing brand new
Fleet uniforms—they having been newly admitted. Stenstrom looked at
them, wearing the fine blue coats and hats he knew so well, and all of his old
dreams returned. His desire to soar the stars and see what was there had
never really left him—just been beaten into place by a knife in his chest.

Listening to his friends chatter about what ship they had joined and
where they were going made him maudlin—sometimes even angry.

What was he to do?

* * * * *

A knock came at the door of his apartment. Stenstrom had quit 22 Stang
early that evening, feeling rather sorry for himself as he listened to Lord Wills
of Narrow talk of shipping out on the Fleet scouting ship *Centerville* at term's
end. He'd felt rather jealous.

He assumed it was Alitrix, come to see what was wrong with him.

Stenstrom opened the door, and there was Lilly, elegant in her pink
Gamboa gown and parasol. "Hello, Bel," she said, all smiles.

Stenstrom hadn't expected her, but, as usual, Lilly came and went as her
whims dictated.

And she was always welcome.

They embraced warmly in the hallway, and then kissed. "Is this a bad
time?" she asked. "Is your little puppy dog here?"

"That's not a nice thing to say, Lilly."

"No, I suppose it isn't. I'm sorry."

They sat down and caught up. He told her that he now had many friends, mostly from the Bones Club, that Lilly had suggested he join. He told her about the dark, posh confines of that exclusive club, where he did many silly things that the others in the group thought were shocking—'look', they gasped, 'look what he just did', and the Sisters would be outraged.

Lilly clapped and listened, glad her Bel was making friends and enjoying himself. "The Bones Club, though a bit off-putting at first, is a fine club to be in. All of the best people belong to it—you'll find wherever you go, you'll have friends from the club waiting for you. I knew you would spread your wings there."

Still, he couldn't hide anything from Lilly. "You outwardly appear to be in fine spirits, but you can't hide anything from me. I can tell something is troubling you—tell me, please. I'm here just for you."

Stenstrom laughed and shook his head. "Nothing goes past your notice, does it? Just silliness really. I saw some of my friends at the club had joined the Fleet. They were wearing their newly fitted uniforms and discussing the ships they were soon to join. I felt left out. I felt jealous. I don't know, Lilly. Sometimes I have thoughts of clearing out of school all together, leaving Kana and heading to who knows where." He laughed. "I'm sorry—just dreams I used to have."

They stepped into the apartment, Lilly hugging him tightly. He could hear her heart beat, and he thought it an odd chain—Alitrix drawing strength from him, and he drawing strength from Lilly, one person feeding on the next.

Lilly was the perfect tonic for his soul; with a fresh dose of Lilly he could go on, do his schooling, entertain his new friends, and become the dreary, land-locked man his mother had envisioned for him.

That evening, Lilly put an odd seed into his head.

They finished the fine meal that Stenstrom had brought in from the kitchens of the Bones Club—room service yet another perk of membership—and asked if Lilly wanted to step out, to see Bern, possibly enjoy a theater or go to 22 Stang and sit.

Instead, they fell into each other's arms and retired to his bedroom.

"So, just who is this Lady Alitrix?" Lilly asked as they lay together in the dark, entwined.

"A friend," Stenstrom said in return.

Lilly considered the thought. "I did tell you that you are free to seek your heart; still, I cannot help but feel a little jealous," she said. "That girl certainly didn't seem up to your level. I almost thought to challenge her."

"Challenge her? You mean to a duel?" He was alarmed.

"Yes, but don't worry. I'm not going to hurt her."

"She is a fine person and I cherish her friendship. So, if you feel that strongly are you prepared to end this five year experiment, Lilly?"

She thought about it. "Frankly, I am a bit put off, but our experiment shall continue. How could you ever take me seriously should I do such a thing over a bland little person like Lady Alitrix of Zama."

Stenstrom was shocked. "Zama—did I mention she was of the House of Zama? I don't recall doing so."

"You didn't. I make it a point to know your doings. I might warn you that girls from Onaris might diminish your House, should you choose to pursue her further."

"She claims she is of the Hoban Zamas, not the Onaris Zamas."

"She's lying."

Stenstrom tried to disengage, but Lilly held him fast. "I'll pose a question that you once asked me, Lilly. Are you enjoying this time apart? Are you seeing anyone?" he asked.

"I'm not really looking."

"Are you wasting your five years? These are the years you asked for, remember?"

"Yes, I remember, but I'm not going out of my way to find somebody else, either. I never meant for these five years to serve as a replacement for you, Bel—I simply wanted to see if, in the natural course of events, something else came along. So far, nothing has."

She tried to change the subject. "How are your studies coming along?"

"Fine. I'm not really interested in studying accounting. I'm sure you know that."

"I listened to you this evening, lamenting your friends, lamenting the Fleet. If you wish to soar the stars in a Fleet ship so badly, Bel, then why don't you?"

"You know full well why. That door has been shut to me."

Lilly jumped out of bed and went to the desk. Her slender naked body glistened in the pearly moonlight coming in through the window. "Where are you going?" he asked.

She turned on the holo-terminal and rejoined him in bed as a carousel of lights began jumping out of it and swirling around the room. "You know, Bel, if you have any faults, I'd say one of them is too heavy a reliance on conventional thinking."

"Conventional thinking?"

"In some ways, you're the fastest thinker I've ever seen—when properly tasked and motivated. In other instances regarding your mother, like this one, you are guilty of very uninspired thought. There are ways around everything, if you want something badly enough."

She paused a moment, her face full of longing. "Look at me; there is something that I want very badly and am currently taking steps to see that I get it."

"Oh, and what is that?"

She reached out with her foot and manipulated the holographic glyph controls. "Let's focus on you for the moment, Bel, and not worry about me, shall we? Let's see …" She worked the floating glyph with her foot, moving it about. Soon a banner popped up.

"What do you have there?" Stenstrom leaned over to look at it as it danced around the room.

It read:

Inter-Stellar Brotherhood of Barrs, Attorneys, Actuaries, Notaries and Accountants.

"What's this?"

"The IBBAANA."

"I think my mother's mentioned something about this organization. I truly had no interest."

"You should listen to your mother in this case. The IBBAANA is your ticket to the stars," she said happily. "And, more than that, it's your ticket to glory."

Stenstrom sat up from the bed and looked at the banner. It was a dry, uninteresting posting. He saw nothing of glory or honor in the drab, business -like construction of the holo.

Barrs . . .

Actuaries …

Notaries …

Attorneys… Good Creation.

"All right, Lilly, out with it. What's on your mind?"

"If you peruse the rather dry subject matter of this posting, you'll see that all sorts of occupations are covered by this society … including this one … Let's see …" She highlighted a notice with her foot, and it jumped to the forefront. Stenstrom squinted to read it.

"Fleet Paymaster?"

"Yes, indeed," she said with a hint of triumph. "Sounds impressive, doesn't it: Fleet Paymaster. I've been doing some research. Every Fleet vessel manning fifty or more souls is required, by rule, to carry a Paymaster. A Paymaster is basically a third party who arbitrates the dispersement of funds to the officers and crew. The Paymaster also ensures that all parties entitled to pays from the vessel in question are properly and timely compensated."

"It sounds like a do-nothing to me."

"Well, that's what it is, Bel. But, it's a shipboard do-nothing. You'd be on a ship, but you wouldn't be in the Fleet officially; you'd be a shipboard civilian. See, you've got to learn to be sneaky."

Stenstrom thought about it and the notion began to take flight in his head. "My father's never mentioned anything about Fleet Paymasters before."

"It's not a prestigious thing, and your father, being ship's captain, probably never really dealt with the shipboard Paymaster much—it's more of a clerical thing, probably something the boatswain had to deal with most often."

"Lilly, you really sound like you know what you're talking about."

"I always make it my business to know what I'm talking about."

Stenstrom began reading the notice. His promise to his mother stated he would never join the Fleet as either an officer or a crewman, and she'd updated the Promise over the years. She'd added: the Stellar Marines, the Merchant Marines, Space Traders and Astro-Tenders—anything she had heard of requiring frequent space travel she knifed out of him. And, there was one thing she had knifed *into* him: *accountant.*

But, all of his promises failed to include a shipboard civilian accountant— Mother hadn't thought of that. Perhaps Lilly was onto something. He continued to read, saw the requirements, and his heart sunk.

"No, no, Lilly—look here. You didn't read carefully enough. To be a Fleet Paymaster, you have to be an attorney."

"Ah, Bel, it appears *you* didn't read carefully enough. True, most Fleet Paymasters are attorneys, but, if you read here, (she pointed at a line of text with her foot) an accountant of ten years or more tenure with experience in public financial arbitration may also qualify as a Fleet Paymaster. I mean, to do this job, all you need is a pulse, an impartial mind, and a bit of bookkeeping skills."

Stenstrom snorted. "Lilly, I'm not even graduated yet—I have zero tenure, and I've never arbitrated a public financial deal."

Lilly kissed him on the cheek. "Again, Bel—think creatively. Your lack of experience and tenure is nothing that a few Belmont sesterces placed snuggly in the right pockets won't fix. Come on, Bel—are you so innocent you won't up and bribe a fellow or two? A good, well-thought out bribe can be a noble thing."

Stenstrom sat up and thought about it. Bribe someone? In all his wranglings with his mother in their game of brinkmanship, he had never even considered trying something underhanded or unethical. In his mind, the only way to play the game was above board.

"I … can't bribe somebody, Lilly—that's unethical."

Lilly pulled him back down and lay on top of him. "What a virtuous young man you are, Bel. Consider this though—great men are often self-made. There are no great, self-made men lacking an unsavory component somewhere in their make-up. If you can make your way through life and say that the worst thing you did as a young man was bribe a fellow or two simply so you might have the opportunity to start your career and live your dream, then that's saying something. There are worse things you could do, Bel."

Stenstrom, feeling Lilly's weight on top of him, thought it over. "You'd not think ill of me?"

"No, Bel. Would you think ill of me, should I tell you some of things I've done?"

"What things?"

"Just things, Bel—so, will you do it?" She held onto him tightly.

Stenstrom fought with the thought for a bit more. "A bribe? What reputable gentleman would succumb to something as pedestrian and poorly thought out as a bribe?"

"Then I would avoid dealing with a reputable gentleman and confine your activities to the disreputable ones. And where are they? I would say in a place where anything goes if you have the coin to make things happen: Calvert."

Stenstrom lay there under the heat of Lilly's body and watched the posting swirl around the room.

A Fleet Paymaster ...

19

—Flight from Bern—

The following spring, Stenstrom graduated. At the Bones Club, he was hailed with raised glasses and fond, overflowing toasts. Several graduating members standing with him were, as usual, decked out in new Fleet uniforms.

This time, Stenstrom felt none of the sadness and envy he previously had when seeing the new recruits.

This time he had a plan.

He returned to his apartment to pack. When he got there, a message awaited him on his Com. He began getting his baggage ready and played the message, his back turned to it as he worked, glancing occasionally.

It was his mother and sisters Lyra and Virginia. Virginia was holding a large cake frosted in white icing. "Bel!" Mother said warmly. "We are so proud of you—a newly graduated alumnus of the University of Bern."

"Congratulations, Bel!" Lyra said, chiming in.

"I made you a cake, Bel," Virginia said.

Mother continued. "We are sending a coach for you tomorrow, to pick you up in grand style. You may expect the coach promptly at twelve bells. We have been laboring to restore your old room here at home and cannot wait for you to return. I'm also very excited to say that a Lord Fulmar of Bass shall be stopping by in a few days. Lord Bass is the proprietor of several successful firms here in Tyrol and he is eager to make your acquaintance. If you speak and present yourself well, Lord Bass might offer you a job."

He hastily filled his baggage. "Sorry, Mother, I've got other ideas for employment."

The Com continued. Virginia was sampling a little of the cake she had made, unable to resist. Mother spoke again. "It will be so nice to have you home again, where you belong. Don't forget, tomorrow at twelve bells. Do not be late—I would hate to have to come looking for you." The Com closed.

Stenstrom looked at the Com in horror.

… have you home again, where you belong.

Tomorrow, she's coming for him tomorrow. No doubt, the moment she gets him home, she'll ply him for information and update the Promise as needed.

It was imperative that he not be anywhere near Bern tomorrow.

He had to fly. He threw his clothes into the baggage without pausing to fold or arrange them.

There was a knock at his door, and he nearly cried out in fright.

Who was it? It had to be his mother—or a Black Maiden.

Forgetting his baggage, he went to the window and started to climb out. He got his leg out into open air when the door swung open.

"Bel?" It was Lady Alitrix. She was peeking her head in through the door. "Hi, Bel—what are you doing out there?"

Stenstrom sighed in relief and pulled himself back into the apartment. "Hey, sorry, I thought you might be somebody else."

"May I come in?"

Stenstrom returned to his baggage. "Sure, sure, come in."

She opened the door and entered. She was holding a large straw basket. "I was hoping to share a small private celebration with you—to commemorate your graduation." She held out the basket. "I brought some nice food and cheeses from the Club, and some aged wine. I was ..."

She saw his open baggage and clothes tossed in. "Are you... are you leaving so soon?"

"My mother is coming for me tomorrow, at twelve bells."

Alitrix approached him. She knew of his smothering mother—he spoke of her often. "Your mother? Are you worried?"

"I'm terrified as a matter of fact. If she manages to get me home, she'll wring out of me what I'm planning to do, then she'll put me to the knife and that shall be the end of it."

"Oh. What can I do to help?"

"If you really want to help me, help me pack. I have to flee the region as soon as possible. I'm not going home. I'm going where I've always wanted to go."

He grabbed another handful of clothes from the closet. "I really should have been more prepared. I should have..."

Alitrix put her hand on his wrist and pulled herself into him. "Stop, for a moment. Take a break with me, please."

He resisted. He tried to pull away and continue packing.

"Please ..." she said.

They fell into each other's arms, Alitrix dropping her basket.

✳   ✳   ✳   ✳   ✳

Later that night, Stenstrom and Alitrix lay on his bed. He could see the squared-off landscape of open baggage beyond the foot of the bed and the partially empty closet. Alitrix smelled of perfume and fine soaps.

He thought she was asleep, but she wasn't. "Do you know where you're headed?" she asked.

"Southeast, to Calvert."

"Why Calvert?"

"There are some gentlemen I plan to call on in Calvert. I'm planning on plying my new trade in earnest."

"Oh?"

She was quiet for a minute or two, then: "You know, my father owns several banks in Inari. I've mentioned you to him—I'm certain he would be glad to offer you a position, and, who knows, with good work, you might quickly rise through the ranks."

Stenstrom looked at her in the dark: her thin, doll-like face, her hopeful eyes. "I appreciate that, I really do, but I've got other plans. I need to go to Calvert."

"Am I to never see you again?"

"Never's a long time. I'm certain our paths shall . . ."

"Bel—I love you."

Stenstrom didn't know what to say.

"I know when we began this that it was simply two friends sharing the pleasure of each other's company, and that I promised I wouldn't expect anything beyond mere sex. I allowed the silly little girl in me too much sway, and I fell in love."

"Alitrix, you know I value you as one of my best friends. You helped me come out of my shell—taught me how to behave and interact as a friend. And the experiences we've shared over the past year and a half I'll always treasure. What can I say that will not break your heart? I love Lilly. You know that."

Tears fell down her face. "Yes, your Lilly, always Lilly. I didn't want to say anything earlier—and I know you'll think I'm just trying to make up a story to keep you from her, but I cannot remain silent any longer. Please, hear me out."

"All right."

"There is something odd about Lilly—I don't know what, but I just know. Haven't you thought it peculiar that she seems so in-tune with your thoughts and emotions? Always she's there to save the day just when you need her most. I would see you looking at the Club-members in their Fleet uniforms, and I knew you were feeling sad. Often, I wanted to come to your side, to try and comfort you, to make you smile. And always, there was Lilly, from out of nowhere walking up the steps, and I would sit there and wish that, for once, I could be the one to offer you comfort. I'm just a woman. Lilly is not a woman—she is something else. It's almost as if she's steering you to some predetermined destination. I don't know; I'm talking non-sense, but that's how I feel. I don't know what she is, but she's not a woman."

Stenstrom patiently listened and let her get it all out.

"I am a woman, and you have earned my love. That's all I have to give. That's all that I am. I'm nothing but a woman while Lilly is something else. How was I to ever compete with that?"

They lay there in silence, Alitrix sniffing slightly. "I'm, sorry," she said, "it's just the bitter little girl in me talking. I didn't mean to trouble you with this. Will you do me a favor?"

"Anything," Stenstrom said.

"Will you hold me tonight? I know you have to pack and are eager to leave before your mother's procession arrives, but I can help you in the morning. I shall meet the procession and stall for you, to give you added time to be clear. If I'm questioned, I'll tell them you're off to Barrow to seek adventure there."

He pulled her into him.

"Also, I would like you to write to me when you can—just so I know you're safe. And, one final thing. I will give you a year. Your Lilly gave you five years. I shall offer you one. One year, and if in that time you discover that I was correct about Lilly, then you may come to me and take my hand."

And they held each other all night long.

They had a busy morning. They rose with the sun and finished packing. Stenstrom had a lot of baggage, and Alitrix promised to have the Club take care of his stuff until he called for it.

Alitrix showed remarkable toughness that morning. She must have been hurting inside, but didn't show it; she'd come a long way since he first met her. She was a big help.

Carrying a small overnight bag, he went out into the street with Alitrix and nearly ran into the procession of float cars Mother had promised to send—several hours early it seemed.

Pulling Alitrix aside, he gave her one last kiss and then made his way down the street toward the station. He caught a glimpse of Alitrix approaching the procession, his mother getting out and questioning her.

He had to act fast. He got to the station and booked a ticket for the first coach out—it didn't matter where. It was heading to Falz. Fine. He bought a ticket and got in.

After getting to Falz, he then booked freight passage to the smelly city of Bezzel in the heart of Calvert. Calvert was certainly the last place his mother would expect him to go, and it was also the best place for him to begin his career as a Paymaster.

GRAND DAME MIRANDA, LADY OF ROSEL

20

—CALVERT—

Calvert—the veritable tossed-salad of Kana. There, among the know-nothings and ne'er-to-dos dotting the wharves and seedy streets, he set about his business.

Here was Calvert, a sliver of land against the sea east of the Great Armenelos Forest, a collection of crowded cities and bad architecture, where showering and basic hygiene was, apparently, optional in some quarters. Still, walking the tight streets crowded with riff-raff and smelling the salt in the air, Stenstrom felt a sense of jubilation, of release. Not like the well-tended and stuffy city of Bern, this was real, full of Barbary-style buildings that have been lived in by real people.

He found he liked the place as it unfolded around him.

Moving about in the streets in the salty sunshine marred only by seabirds and the tall masts of sailing vessels, he noted a thriving cottage industry was at work everywhere—the Fiend of Calvert, that murderous madman who had terrorized the place for years was now like a second-son. Stenstrom saw inns and taverns called "The Fiend's Hideout" and the "Madman's Pleasure." He saw vendors selling Fiend merchandise and, most prevalently, he saw people dressed in a variety of garbs offering Murder Tours, where the curious bystanders and amateur sleuths could visit the murder sites for themselves and try to figure out who the Fiend was.

As he made his way down the street near the docks, he became aware of a tall woman following him—a woman dressed in gray and wearing a broad gray hat.

It was her, the Astral Traveler!!

She closed the distance. From behind, she reached out for him.

Quickly he turned and seized her by the wrist, hauling her down and drawing a MARZABLE.

He put it to her throat.

"Oh!" the woman said as she fell, her hat falling away revealing a head of blonde hair.

"Who are you!" Stenstrom roared.

"I ... I just wanted to see if you would be interested in joining us for a tour, sir ... Please ..."

Scattered at her feet was a stack of pamphlets. They read:

THE Fiend of Calvert MURDER TOUR

Spanning two cities
(Bezzel, St. Edmund's)

✢See all of the most notable locations where the Fiend plied his trade from the mobile comfort of your seat.

✢Witness his escape route across the rooftops of St. Edmund's.

✢Pick from a list of notorious suspects and try to guess who did it!

Calvert's Best Guided Tour given by

Grand Dame Lady Miranda of Rosel,

A noted authority on the Fiend and author
of several acclaimed books on the subject.
Lunch served.
Midnight Lantern tours available during Summer months.

The Fiend of Calvert Murder Tour

Spanning two cities (Bezzel, St. Edmund's).

—See all of the most notable locations where the Fiend plied his trade from the mobile comfort of your seat.

—Witness his escape route across the rooftops of St. Edmund's.

—Pick from a list of notorious suspects and try to guess who did it.

Calvert's Best Guided Tour given by

Grand Dame Lady Miranda of Rosel,

noted authority on the Fiend and author of several acclaimed books on the subject.

Lunch served.

Midnight Lantern tours available during Summer months.

She looked up at him, wide-eyed. He checked his white Holystone—it was silent. She was just a woman dressed in gray.

"Good Creation, ma'am, I am so sorry!" he said picking her up. "Are you all right?"

She checked herself over. "I think so."

Stenstrom picked up her stack of pamphlets and her hat and gave them to her. "Please forgive me. Is there anything I can do to make this up to you?"

She put her hat on. "No, no, it was an accident. I shouldn't have sneaked up on you like I did. This is Calvert after all. I should know better."

Stenstrom felt miserable. "Please, I would like to purchase a tour."

He paid the lady his money, and she showed him to a large, fairly classy open-air hover float parked by the docks. Several people were already seated inside, awaiting the tour to begin. As Stenstrom took his seat, she handed him a rather thick packet of pamphlets detailing the layout of Calvert, the scenes of some of the Fiend's more gruesome crimes, and his escape route in the city of St. Edmund's. As Stenstrom looked it over, more people joined him in the hover float, lead by other ladies, also dressed in gray.

The lady he assaulted seated herself on an opposing bench and readied herself for the tour.

"What is your name, please, ma'am?" Stenstrom asked.

"I am Grand Dame Lady Miranda of Rosel."

Stenstrom looked at his pamphlet. "Ah, our hostess for the afternoon?"

"Yes."

"Again, I apologize for my behavior earlier. I have a rather sour history with ladies dressed in gray."

"Do you? May I ask what you've encountered? Obviously, as I make this subject my trade and chief point of interest, I am most keen to gather all information I can."

"Is a woman in gray a facet of the Fiend of Calvert lore?"

Lady Miranda became excited as she spoke, clearly a devotee of the subject. "Oh yes, sir, yes. As we shall discover on the tour, the Mad Lord of Walther, who engaged and pursued the Fiend across the rooftops of St.

Edmund's, is the only person who ever saw the Fiend in person and lived to tell the story. He claims, and my colleagues dispute this, that he saw the Fiend of Calvert as a lady dressed in gray. That's why I and my assistants dress in gray, for I believe the Mad Lord's account. I believe there is evidence to support the notion that the Fiend of Calvert was indeed a woman."

She got out a roto-pad and took down Stenstrom's account, of the incident at the Fox Park when he was a boy, at Rustam Labyrinth, and again at the university, nodding as she took the dictation, Stenstrom adding repeatedly that he believed the woman to be nothing more than a bad dream.

When he was done, she smiled at him. "Well, I think you've given me some remarkable information to think about. I shall perform research and ... are you staying in Calvert? You do not look like a local. I should be happy to call on you if I have further questions, and I know I shall. Oh, this is most exciting. I finally have mounting evidence to argue with Rodrick of Dee."

Stenstrom told her he was staying in town for a few days and would drop in on her in a day or two.

She was thrilled, and the tour began.

He settled into Calvert the next day and began his task. He was armed with a ton of Belmont sesterces, which went a long way and opened a great many doors. He'd been stealthily deducting the money from his account and saving it over the past year—moving the loot from one unmarked account to another, his newly won skills at accounting helping him hide the deductions so that Mother would not get wise. Flush with cash and determination, he prowled the crooked streets and windblown allies, looking for scalawags and pinch-pricks, and not having a hard time finding them, much he mused as the Fiend of Calvert had thirty years prior. Soon, he discovered just the men he was looking for. He found the seediest Notary he could, a Lord Gissel of Wheeze, down on his luck and ready to deal. Stenstrom sat him down in the bars, filled his cups, and greased his pockets. Before long he had a whole stack of notarized endorsements, each more impressive-sounding and outlandish than the last. With Notary Gissel happily stamping anything put in front of him, Stenstrom could have proclaimed himself the governor of Planet Fall and gotten a notarized stamp to prove it. With this pile of bought paper, he could claim as much tenure as he wanted.

He bunked out in a fallen-down cricket shack near the wharf called "The Toothless Dame." Despite his lavish upbringing in Belmont Manor, he found something of an affinity with the peeling paint and the dirty flooring of his room, the air tepid with the smell of old stockings and people's dinners. Hiding out in Calvert, he felt like he was on one of the adventures he so longed for as a child, and he didn't want it to end. He decided to unpack and take his time. Nestled in his bag, he found a small card placed there by Alitrix as he unpacked. It read: "One Year" with the date and her holo-account information at the Bones Club. He set the card out on his desk, feeling close to her. He wrote her as he promised, using the seedy VX terminal in his room.

She wrote back stating his mother was not happy at all and looked the devil to pay.

So much the better.

She also wrote saying one year was provisional—that she would wait as long as he needed. She wrote she missed him terribly.

So far, Calvert had been fairly safe, his mother clearly not suspecting he was anywhere near the region. His most persistent caller was Lady Miranda of Rosel. He must have whetted her appetite for information, and he saw her prowling the streets, inquiring at every inn she could find, apparently looking for him. He was sitting in the tavern of the Toothless Dame having an ale when she happened to walk in. A casual fade into the shadows, and she walked right past him, marching up to the counter and persistently speaking to the innkeeper.

The innkeeper pointed at the table where Stenstrom was sitting.

She looked over. "Well, I don't see him," she said. She left her card with the innkeeper and departed, giving his table one last look as she walked past. He laughed and fetched the card.

He would be sure to meet up with her later once his task was finished and answer whatever questions she had. He still felt he owed her for knocking her down the other day.

On a more serious note, as the days passed, the net around him cast from distant Tyrol was finally beginning to tighten.

While walking back from Notary Gissel's office with yet another ream of bogus papers under arm, he was sure he saw the gossamer veils of a Black Maiden in the crowds, sniffing the air, heading in his direction.

Black Maidens, the airy watchdogs and nursemaids of his mother and bane of his wayward sisters—they were on the prowl, and were closing in on him. They closed in on his scent, and no hiding in the shadows could protect him. Sooner or later, they would have him right back at Belmont Manor with his mother ready to pounce.

He felt the hand of desperation. What was he going to do? Some of his sisters had been adept at evading the Black Maidens, at prolonging the chase. Constance was one, and his other sister Xantrope held the record for running from the Maidens, having successfully eluded them for two months. But, others were terrible at evading the Maidens: Calami the wayward was one, Nathalie, Elma and Lenta were others, rarely lasting more than a few hours.

Now it was his turn to run.

He tore down an alley, the reaching veils in slow but steady pursuit. He emerged on a crowded side street—the now familiar vendors and tour guides arranged in a row down toward the docks plying their "Fiend" trade in earnest. He saw Lady Miranda standing amid the crowd in her usual gray dress and hat looking for customers.

Thinking fast, he ran in her direction. "Lord Belmont!" she said seeing him. "Lord Belmont, there you are! I have been looking all over for you. You promised we could sit down and discuss matters in greater detail. I have a whole slew of new questions for you, sir!"

Breathless, he approached her. "Lady Miranda, I promise, you can ask me anything you want, but first I must ask a novel favor of you." He whispered in her ear, and she was shocked.

"What? You're not serious?"

"I'm deadly serious!"

"And, you'll answer my questions?"

"Yes, yes!"

"Well, all right, if you must."

Quickly, he got down on all fours and put his head up the folds of her petticoat as the Black Maiden passed.

Some people laughed. She stood there, clearly embarrassed, but determined to get her information. "Oh, do mind your own business, please," she said to some gawker.

After a minute or two, Stenstrom emerged, Lady Miranda red-faced, louts across the street clapping and hoping for a turn. "Will you kindly tell me what that was all about, please?" she asked.

"It's complicated. Suffice to say, I am pursued by unusual forces. Standing in your presence with my face obscured shielded me from being discovered. Your scent protected me."

"My scent—I see. I didn't notice anything just now."

"No, you wouldn't, unless you know specifically what to look for."

She got her rotopad out and added a few notations to it. "Well then, sir, I have delivered on my part of the bargain. I shall expect you to be at my disposal this evening, for I have many questions, and I expect a dinner to be provided by you at a place of my choosing."

Stenstrom just had his head up her dress; he couldn't refuse.

✳ ✳ ✳ ✳ ✳

That evening, he and Lady Miranda sat at dinner, she with her roto-pad out, peppering him with questions.

". . . And, going back to the Fox Park incident, you say there were many men there with the Woman in Gray?"

"Yes."

"What did they look like? How were they dressed?"

Stenstrom thought back. "I don't know … like sailors, I suppose."

"Like Calvert men? They looked like men from Calvert?"

"I suppose so, yes."

She added a few notations to her pad. She smiled. "Ah, see, this all ties together."

"What does?"

"I have long conjectured that many of the men suspected of being killed by the Fiend were actually abducted—there were no bodies found in many cases. The missing men were simply assumed to be murder victims, their bodies hidden and not found. The Fiend, however, took no pains to hide his work in most cases; therefore, I believe that those men were not murder victims after all, but abductees, somehow spirited away and kept hidden. See, many of my colleagues have failed to take the Mad Lord of Walther at his word—they considered him to be a drunken and unreliable source of information. Though he tended to freely embellish his exploits in his memoirs, there is a kernel of truth to everything he writes. The Mad Lord suspected that the mindless men he encountered in the City of the Dead were somehow under the sway of the Fiend of Calvert, a theory that has been debunked by my colleagues as poppycock.

"I recall reading about the Mad Lord's exploits with my sister when I was a child. Something about zombies and lost men in a hidden place."

"Yes. I think those men you saw in Fox Park were more abductees from Calvert."

"I really don't think the Woman in Gray exists. She is an apparition of my fears. If she did exist, then she would be in league with the Fiend"

Lady Miranda tapped the tablecloth with her fingers, her excitement clear. "No, no, the Woman in Gray you encountered at Fox Park *is* the Fiend of Calvert. The Mad Lord wrote that the Fiend of Calvert was, in fact, a woman in gray—it fits; it all fits. Oh, by Creation, how I wish I could have been there with you."

They talked a bit further and concluded the meal, Stenstrom tired and ready to return to his rented room.

Lady Miranda, though, had other ideas. She went to the clerk and bought a room for the night and bade him join her for a nightcap, and there she invited him to make love to her. Every bit of Stenstrom told him that this was a trap—that he was in mortal peril. However, Lady Miranda did not read as having been to the Astral Plane, and she did not smell of strong woman scent. She obviously had little skills beyond the scholarly.

No, this was simply a woman who desperately wanted to be close to someone who had stood in the presence of the Fiend of Calvert—her life's passion.

He obliged her, spending a steamy night, and then took his leave come morning.

21

—Stenstrom's Baggage—

B ack in his rented room, he was again to his task, and the growing troubles that dogged him.

Mother. He saw five Black Maidens as he made his way back to the Toothless Dame—the lingering smell of Lady Miranda upon his body still offering him a bit of cover.

Mother was going to magic him back to Tyrol, and to fight fire with fire, he needed his books. He had them in a chest back in his room at the university in Bern; he had to leave them behind after his hasty flight from the city. He wrote Alitrix to send for his baggage, and he gave her the number of a locker at the air, sea and land port in St. Edmund's which was just up the coast.

In disguise, moving in the shadows, he staked out the place and waited for his baggage to arrive. He had to be careful. His mother had ways of finding people, both worldly and other worldly. Her vast network of friends was formidable. Any passing person could be on the look-out for him, hence his disguise. Additionally, any number of summoned entities could track him down if it got close enough, and he had no protection, other than his NTHs, which were overkill and sure to alert other entities should he use them. He needed a way to quietly detect the spirits and devise countermeasures.

He needed his baggage, and, specifically, his chest full of his books.

A few days later, the baggage arrived. Trying to be discreet, he carefully spied the surroundings, and waited for a good moment to collect and be off with them.

Drat! Was that Lady Chatstra of Owens standing over there? What in Creation was she doing in Calvert? She was a friend of his mother's from Mercia, and she saw everything.

True to her name, she was chatting with friends near the counter where his chest was held, and she didn't seem to be in a hurry.

He waited in the shadows for her to depart.

Black Maidens! They were emerging from everywhere, and no hiding in the shadows would suffice against them—they were going to sniff him out.

He could not linger—he had to flee the port, his mother having clearly won this round, and he seethed with frustration.

* * * * *

He waited in his small room, not daring to go out. He paced the floor, impatient.

There was a knock. He moved silently to the door and gave it a small rap with his knuckles. Three raps came in reply. He smiled and opened the door.

Lady Miranda quickly walked in, pulling a float litter behind her.

"Lord Belmont, I have fetched your baggage as you requested. I saw no one at the station. I felt no danger."

There was his baggage—four large trunks emblazoned with a garish "B" and a slightly smaller wooden chest containing his books. They appeared innocent enough, but …

"Thank you, my lady. These trunks are trapped."

"Trapped?" Her attention turned to the baggage, and her interest began to peak. "I think you should explain in further detail, Lord Belmont."

"My mother … she is a Tyrol sorceress. And she has trapped my baggage with out-worldly snares. If I open these trunks, I'll be back to Belmont Manor in a flash."

Lady Miranda stared at the trunks, her eyes wide with interest. She then curtsied and lifted the front of her skirt. "Well then, let's see it. I'm not afraid. I offer you protection, as I did before."

Stenstrom knelt down and put his head up Lady Miranda's skirt. "The baggage, except for the chest, should be unlocked. Go ahead and open them—don't be afraid, it's me they want, not you."

"Will they not see you?"

"Not like this."

Stenstrom could hear Lady Miranda opening the trunks, her smooth legs flexing slightly as she worked. Her skin smelled of soaps and powders.

"I don't see anything," she said with a hint of disappointment.

However, there was no question they were there in the room with them at that moment, coming out of the baggage—he could feel it. "You're not looking correctly. Look to the shadows. Forget the obvious and mundane; see the improbable and the half-formed around you and you will notice things few have ever seen."

"I don't understand," she said, rocking back and forth.

"Relax, close your eyes, and then open them—truly open them."

She stiffened up a little. Then: "Oh, what is this? I see them! I see them! They appear rather ghastly. Are they evil?"

"No. No, they are not. They simply appear rather odd. Do you have all the trunks open?"

"Yes, all except for the wooden chest. It's locked."

"How many are there?"

Lady Miranda counted. "Twenty-six. They seem to be sniffing about."

"Let them sniff their fill. They will then present themselves to you. When they do, simply tell them to go away, and they will. It's me they want, not you, and they cannot detect me clothed in your scent."

Lady Miranda then did something he never would have expected. She suddenly crossed her legs, trapping his head between her thighs, her muscles cabling up in a taut manner. His ears muffled, he could vaguely hear her saying "Go away. Do go away, please."

She wrenched up the pressure, and then finally released him. He came rolling out of her skirt, face red gasping for air, the Black Maidens gone. Lady Miranda didn't say a word. Instead, she fell on him, tearing at his clothes, grabbing his hands and moving them to rather private places on her person. Apparently, her sexual desires and her intellectual curiosities were strongly linked together—as discovering new things deeply aroused her.

They had a rather torrid night, Stenstrom taking her several times, discovering for himself that she had a rather sadistic side to her, as he found himself scratched and rather bloody as the night wore on. Her voice changed. She uttered obscenities as they had sex. She performed fellatio upon him and demanded he take her from the rear. She then demanded lengthy cunnilingus.

In the morning, she plied him with questions. She wanted to begin research on a new book uncovering the hidden truths of the world—Black Maidens and sorcery chief among them. She insisted he check out of the inn and come with her, to her home on the hill north of the city. She said she was alone, a widow, and would be glad to have him. "Think of the things we could do for each other ... and to each other ..." she said.

He promised he would consider it and sent her on her way, she first securing his various Com, holo-mon and holo-mail account information, and a flurry of promises that he visit her soon, for research ... and other things.

At last, he was alone with his baggage. The important one, though, his chest of books, was still locked—he'd forgotten all about that one. Lady Miranda couldn't open it.

He grabbed his NTHs and cocked them. He touched the surface of the chest, for he truly didn't want to hurt a Black Maiden. They were kind and benevolent, and though they were a tad gaunt, they were a glad presence. His sister Nylar knew how to tickle them and make them laugh. It wasn't their fault Mother had sent them after him. "I'm sorry, I'm sorry," he said as he pointed and fired. The throbbing mass of green energy passed through the wooden lid of the chest and didn't come out the other side. He took a deep breath and unlocked the chest, revealing the cache of books within.

There was no indication that anything had been in the chest waiting for him—perhaps it had been empty after all. He kept that thought with him as he unloaded his books. He vowed he would never point his NTHs at a Black Maiden, ever. He would run, he'd confound and divert them, but not kill. They didn't deserve that.

Finally, with his arcane library in hand, he set up a small apothecary in his room. He bought brass pots, tripods to hang them on, flame burners, mortars and pestles, an assortment of knives, tongs and other required utensils, and a laboratory's worth of salts, chemicals, flowers, herbs and metals. He also bought bags of plaster for Holystones.

The first thing he did was create a bolabung, which was a small bit of wormwood infused with a few chemicals. Bolabungs were normally used to shield one's mind from unwanted telepathy, but with a little modification, they could protect one from a variety of things—Black Maidens included. He infused the bolabung with a healthy amount of Lady Miranda's scent (he acquired a fair amount of it during their previous night together), strung it on a leather cord, and put it round his neck. The bolabung would require refreshing. Cooking down various oils and bees wax, he made a salve of her scent, strong and odorous, which he could smear on the bolabung every day.

Thus equipped, he began making Holystones.

Holystones were marvels of chemical design, and could be made to perform any number of useful, one-time functions. They took a skilled hand and a learned mind to properly make them—Mother had spent three years teaching their lore to him and his sisters. He prepared the plaster and cast them into hollow spheres, not too thin, not too thick, and readied them for filling.

Some of the more basic ones were quite easy to create:

Yellow: Creates a soft light equal to four or five candle power. Duration: 1 hour.

Ingredients: Tungsten, Salt (sodium chromate)

Red (rose): Creates a hot, energetic fire and shall burn until chemicals are used up.

Ingredients: Hydrogen-infused gel, kerosene, flint;

Green: Creates an expanding, sticky substance similar in appearance to a spider's web.

Ingredients: Titanium, Bromine, Mercury, Silk and Whisperwill (a flowering plant)

Blue: Creates a powerful Vitriolic acid.

Ingredients: Sulfur, Pyrite, Manganese and water.

Those Holystones were nice to have and fairly easy to make. In one afternoon of crushing and stirring and heating over a fire, he had quite a few of them ready to go. Then he set to work to the more advanced ones—ones that could aid him in the detection and defeating of demons and invisible spirits. Those were the ones he needed most:

Purple: Oscillates or "Rumbles" in the presence of invisible creatures.

Ingredients: Cadmium, iron, Henbane (a flowering plant), Yew

Black: Detects mystical objects or persons.

Ingredients: Hornblende, antimony, zinc, Monks Hood (a flowering plant), beryl (crushed), natron, bismuth, Hardaway (a flowering plant), quartz, and obsidian

Pink: Renders those who touch it for too long unconscious.

Ingredients: morganite, carbuncle (garnet), gypsum-weed, beeswax, rose oil, peyote, nightshade berry

White: Prevents the body from going into shock.

Ingredients: granite (crushed), manganese, rhodium, and menthol.

The pink ones, or "Pinkies," were difficult to get used to, as in handling them he could just as easily be incapacitated as the person he was planning to use it on. During his training, he had gotten used to its effects to the point where he could hold one for an extended length of time and not be addled. His sister Virginia, for all her various failings, was a champion Pinky holder, easily able to out-last both him and Lyra back-to-back.

He purchased several silver candlesticks and ground them down a little, ensuring they were perfectly level. He then placed a Purple and Black Holystone on the top of the stick where a candle would normally go. If the stones started rumbling, or if they jumped off the stick and began rolling on the floor, he would have immediate warning. Those, along with his Astral Plane detectors and his bolabung, should keep him reasonably safe.

Now he could relax a little and continue his business.

He now felt he had more than enough false papers and fake tenure to sustain him. The matter of officiating a public financial deal was a bit more challenging, as he needed witnesses.

A visit to one of the drop-down waterfront bars in Bezzel easily corrected that problem. He slid up to the bar one noisy evening, nursed a watered-down bottle of spirits, and kept a sharp ear. Before long, he eavesdropped on two toughs in great need of arbitration.

"Garh, Morbagg, you Xaphan-spawn! I rolls sevens, sevens!" a painted-over merchant-man spat, pointing his crooked finger at a pair of grubby dice. "Ye' owes me the lot and more!"

The man sitting across the table begged to differ. "Ye' rolls sixes, Nosspin. See, three e' four equals six. Now hand over the till, lest I feels inclined to char-broil yer lungs!"

Stenstrom pulled a chair and sat down. Two pairs of blood-shot eyes turned to him. "Gentlemen," he said. "Well met. I am Stenstrom, Lord of Belmont-South Tyrol, and I couldn't help but overhear your small financial dispute. I would like to offer my services and assist you through this unsettling situation as a fair and impartial arbitrator. What do you say?"

"I says ye' best be moving' along, 'squire, les you be findin' these dice knockin' about inside yer body."

"Yeh'," Nosspin said, "an' you'll not have eaten them, either." The two men laughed in a phlegmy fashion.

Stenstrom was unfazed. "Yes, well, I think we can clear this up pretty fast, gentlemen. You see, Sir Morbagg, four plus three indeed equals seven, as currently displayed by these dice here. However, these dice appear to be rigged to unfairly land on seven a disproportionately high percentage of the time, and, therefore, the roll is invalid."

"Yo' sayin I'm rolling loaded dice, Slime-hauler!" Nosspin shouted.

"Yes, I am. My judgment in this matter, therefore, is swift. This roll is invalid, as are any previous rolls using said loaded dice, and you two shall receive all payouts back and let the matter be forgotten. The dice in question shall be impounded or replaced with fair set of dice with all speed. I additionally rule that you two shall be entitled to a small reimbursement equaling four thousand sesterces each for your inconvenience."

Stenstrom plopped two small moneybags down on the table.

He smiled. "There, that was easy. Now, I require that you two follow me down the street to the office of Notary Gissel, where you shall sign a sworn affidavit that I, Stenstrom, Lord of Belmont-South Tyrol, fairly and promptly arbitrated this matter in a public place."

The two grubby men gawked at him a moment. They suddenly drew a set of dirty blades. "Get out o' town, Wench-wanker!"

A massive brawl broke out in the bar. Courtesans screamed, things flew out the windows.

Sometime later, a rumpled Morbagg and bloodied Nosspin arrived at the office of Notary Gissel and signed, at gun-point, the sworn affidavit Stenstrom had asked for.

He was now all set.

22

—The Quest for IBBAANA—

H is next stop was to join the IBBAANA brotherhood. The problem was that there was not an IBBAANA office anywhere in Bezzel, or in the whole of Calvert for that matter. The nearest office was in the Remnath, city of Mercia, about twenty-five hundred miles to the west. Apparently, one had to present oneself in person to join.

Armed with his dubious stack of notarized papers and phony affidavits, Stenstrom made his way to the station.

The purple Holystone hidden in his coat rumbled so hard in its pocket he thought he might go into palpitations. The station was blanketed with invisible entities, and he caught glimpse of gaunt maidens in black occasionally lifting their heads and sniffing the air.

If he went into the station, he would be overwhelmed—even his bolabung would not protect him from them all. Dragging his baggage, he headed north and wandered into Bezzel's small town square. He needed to think; he needed a plan. He thought about running to Lady Miranda, but quickly thought better of it. She was becoming obsessive and rather demanding as of late, and was starting to treat him like a lowly husband. She might not be inclined to let him go should he enlist her for help. He needed something else—something his mother wouldn't have expected and pre-saturated with Maidens.

An opportunity soon presented itself. He saw a modest caravan of ten weather-beaten float wagons covered with faded white tarpaulins. The tarpaulins were decorated with a series of red and green symbols and squiggles, highlighted in gold. Stenstrom easily recognized the designs—he'd seen them all his life adorning the old Merian ruins dotting his manor.

It was a caravan of Pilgrims of Merian. The Merians were sect of religious zealots preaching non-approved Elder lore. They roamed the countryside of Kana delivering good news, that the Elders were not gone and that all one had to do was look up into the sky to see them. They were tolerated at best, jeered and censured by the Sisters at worst.

They were sitting out in front of their caravan dressed in their usual: loose -fitting, white smock-like garments that went down to their knees. Over that, they wore longer green robes sleeved in gold cloth. They wore numerous thin necklaces of wooden red and green beads. The women all had their long hair held up in elaborate combs, while the men's long hair went down unkempt past their shoulders. They were all either shoeless or shod in simple sandals.

They'd set up several modest stands before their wagons and were attempting to sell hand-crafted trinkets and bolts of homespun cloth to the masses assembled in front to gawk at them.

As per usual wherever they went, the Merians were getting laughed at, and, worse, the uncouth of Bezzel were turning out in force to harass and torment them.

"You want to sell something, missy—I'll pay for something of yours all right …" a lout said.

"I'll buy the lot of you, and make you into fine street-walkers … You men too …"

The various people in the crowd who appeared to want to buy some of the Merian's wares were being overwhelmed by the hecklers and the uncouth gropers.

One burly man strode forward and seized one of the Merian females by the cheek. "Lemme' have a look at you, missy!"

She struggled. "Please … sir …" she stammered, trying to pull away.

"Hold still!" he yelled, knocking her little stand aside, scattering her trinkets.

None of the Merian men and nobody in the crowd seemed to want to help her as she struggled.

"Now, let's see yer' goods!" the man yelled as he began ripping her clothes.

He'd seen enough. Stenstrom pushed through the crowd. "Take your hands off her!" he said with authority.

The man gave him a quick look, snorted, and returned to what he was doing. Stenstrom produced a pink Holystone in a blur and casually dropped it down his shirt. Immediately, the lout went limp and fell to the ground.

Everybody turned to Stenstrom.

"He killed Gasser!" someone yelled. "Get him!" A dirty fellow drew a Hertamer energy gun out of his coat.

Stenstrom drew his NTH and stuck the iron muzzle in the man's face. He cocked the hammer. "Care to join him?" he asked.

Another man raised his fists and rushed Stenstrom from behind. In a moment he was webbed up solid with a green Holystone.

With that, the crowd backed up and gave Stenstrom space.

"But he killed Gasser!" the first man protested. "Where's the justice?" Most in the crowd appeared unsympathetic.

"He's not dead, just incapacitated," Stenstrom said. "Take him and clean him up, will you, and make sure he gets a shower with plenty of lye to defeat his stench."

The man began dragging the fallen Gasser and the webbed-up fellow away in stages, moving one for a time, and then the other. "We're going to be looking for you, mate—mark my words! You'll be seein' us again!"

"Grand, I'll be happy to serve you up the same a second time."

Stenstrom turned and helped the Merian woman right her table and gather her scattered trinkets. "Are you all right, ma'am?"

"Yes, yes, I think so."

"Why did none of your group help out just now? That man could have hurt you."

She gazed at him, her eyes serene. "Our Star would not have allowed him to harm me."

"But, had I not been here, you might have been …"

"But, you were here. The Star sent you to me, and I was not harmed."

Stenstrom couldn't really argue with the logic and hope to get anywhere. "May I ask—what are you doing in Calvert? Not a place I'd expect to see a band of Merians."

The rest of the Merians gathered around. "Several of our wagons are in need of repairs," she said. "We stopped here to try and raise money to have them properly serviced."

"In Calvert? Nobody has money in Calvert."

"Our Star will provide. We must simply have faith. If we do that, then we shall be provided for."

He checked his coat—the Holystone within was quiet—so far he'd been unnoticed.

"How much do you need?"

"A thousand Calvert solaris. That's what we were told the price would be."

He had a thought as he looked at the unassuming Merians gathered around him. They appeared to want to thank him, that they were grateful for his help, but truly didn't know how to respond. Apparently, they weren't used to people being kind to them. He reached into his coat and pulled out several notes. "A thousand Calvert solaris … Here, this should be enough."

He handed the girl the money. She stood there holding it. "Our Star has indeed provided. If I may ask, why have you done this for us?"

"Because I wanted to. Because my home is on the grounds of an old Merian monastery and I've always felt a bit of a kinship with your order. Also, my sister can see the star you claim exists."

"Your sister? She can see our star?"

He had to be off. "Yes. She says it's in that direction," he said pointing to the northwest. "And, that it is a large yellow star with a red cloud swirling around it."

The girl smiled. "I see. Well, this is a wonderful day, as our Star intended. I am Nefia, and we are a humble band of traveler Merians from Westwood, seeking to offer good news to the people. May I ask your name, sir, so that I may properly thank you?"

"Stenstrom, Lord of Belmont-South Tyrol. I suppose that I am in the market for a little good news."

"Lord Stenstrom, we are at your service for the unexpected kindness you have shown us."

"I was also hoping I might catch a ride with you. Are you heading west, by chance?"

"We head in no particular direction. The Star has sent you to us with purpose and speed. We will take you west, all the way to the sea if need be."

✳   ✳   ✳   ✳   ✳

With the money Stenstrom gave them, the Merians repaired their meager float wagons and gladly made their way out of Calvert. Safe with the Merians, an unlikely bunch, he was free of his out-worldly pursuers, his Holystones remaining quiet. He had out-foxed them and his mother to boot.

The caravan made its slow way west, up the coast, through St. Edmund's, around the bay, and into the wild lands of southern Zenon. To the south was the rocky, sea coast and to the north were the towering pillars of clouds covering the vast stretch of Lake Monama where the pale people lived.

Two days into the trip, he found the Merians had an old Maxim-style Com screen in one of the wagons. It had been over two weeks since his graduation and flight from Bern. He felt homesick and wanted to at least let his mother know he was all right. With this old Maxim Com unit, he could probably send word to her, and she wouldn't be able to trace him.

She appeared on the screen in bed. Her face was haggard and spent. Her breakfast on a tray was sitting off to the side, barely touched.

"Bel, is that you?" she said trying to squint into the screen.

"Yes, Mother, it's me."

"I've been so worried about you. How could you do this to your mother?"

"I'm sorry. I didn't mean to worry you. As you can see, I'm fine."

She smiled a little. "Bel, why did you not come home after your graduation? Your sisters and I had had a lovely reception planned. Lyra and Virginia were so very disappointed. They had prepared a wonderful celebration for you." Her voice was tired and thin.

"I will apologize to them when I can. I have some business to attend to, Mother. I'm trying to accumulate my accreditations so that I might ply the trade you and father paid for me to learn."

His mother seemed so tired. "I'm glad you are embracing your schooling." She appeared pained for a moment. "You always talked of the Fleet and of the stars. I see you, even now in my dreams, as a boy wearing the little clothes your father sent home. I always see you as a little boy in my dreams. What have I done, Bel? Have I robbed you of what you wanted most?"

Stenstrom thought about his answer. "What's done is done, and I am no worse for it."

She smiled. "I'm glad. If I had it to do over again, I would have let you do whatever you wanted. Are you coming home soon?"

"When time allows; again, I am pursuing a lead."

Jubilee leaned back and sank into her pillows. "I ... really think you should come home for a bit ... to visit and catch up. It won't take long, I promise. Then you may pursue your matters in earnest."

"Why, is there anything the matter? Why do you look so tired?"

"No, Bel, no … nothing's the matter. I was worried, and I simply miss my son, and would like to see you."

"I'll be home when I can. I have some matters to attend, and then I'll be home."

Lady Jubilee gazed at her son through the Com. "All right then. But please, when you've concluded your business, will you promise to come home and see your old mother?"

"I promise Mother, yes."

It struck him as he concluded the Com that his mother was uncharacteristically timid and accommodating. He had expected her to be frothing with rage, full of recriminations and threats. He was used to speaking boldly to his mother; otherwise, she might have had him twisted in knots.

Perhaps she was mellowing, or possibly trying a different tactic.

As he rode the hovering wagon across the Zenon lowlands with the vast, cloud-shrouded plume of Lake Monama to the north, he began noticing something. In the far distance, he saw four thin figures in shroud-like robes following his procession.

The Black Maidens. They were slowly zeroing in on him. He'd almost forgotten about his mother's determination to forcibly bring him home.

Seeing them in the distance reminded him of the dire contest his mother insisted he play: *Resist. Be your own man.*

Very well—be it so. The game was on, Mother. She almost had him fooled.

✳   ✳   ✳   ✳   ✳

Once in Mercia, the Merians dropped Stenstrom off at the local office of IBBAANA—the Inter-Stellar Brotherhood of Barrs, Attorneys, Actuaries, Notaries and Accountants, a modest red-brick structure in the center of town. He got out of the wagon with his chests. He bade the Merians a fond farewell and went inside the office.

He announced he wished to join the Brotherhood. Getting a stern eye, he was taken into a backroom, and his qualifications were reviewed.

As it turned out, it was his membership in the Bones Club that got him into the IBBAANA brotherhood, for the fellow reviewing his papers spotted them as fabricated at once. However, he, like Stenstrom, was a proud member of the Bones Club, so, after a bit of chit-chat and a healthy "entrance fee" was collected, Stenstrom was at last made an official member of the brotherhood, no further questions asked. Chosen Occupation: Paymaster, Status: Active.

So, he had come to Mercia and gotten what he came for—he was now an IBBAANA. As he exited the building, he saw four tall women in black standing at the end of the street waiting for him.

His mother—the Black Maidens. He had a quick thought that this game was becoming rather silly, that he was getting too old for such things. If he had had a more timid nature, he would simply go home and see his mother.

But, she herself had drilled into him: *Though I am your mother, consider me your enemy. I shall attempt to confound you and set you to my will. I want you to resist— to confound me in turn. Thus, using your wits, I shall make you strong. Nothing more than your best effort I expect of you.*

Not wanting to disappoint her, Stenstrom determined to get the better of this situation. Avoiding the front door, he found a convenient window out the back and bore away from the building through the craggy allies leading to the side-streets of Mercia.

With the Black Maidens dogging his heels, he waited in town, never allowing himself to stay stationary for more than a few hours at a time. He also avoided being alone as he bought one courtesan after another to stand with him. The Black Maidens couldn't get to him if he was in constant company. Female company was best. He would need to be careful. These Black Maidens appeared to be showing no sign of giving up.

Two days later he received a message from the Brotherhood. A Fleet vessel, the *Sandwich*, a small frigate making berth in Atalea, was in need of a replacement Paymaster at once, for theirs had died.

What was the reason for the man's death, Stenstrom wanted to know.

The official word was food poisoning.

With the Maidens close at his heels, he accepted. Courtesan in hand, he immediately booked passage to Atalea and met up with his first charge, the Fleet Frigate *Sandwich*. If he could get on that ship, he would be victorious.

23

—THE *SANDWICH*—

He had to admit, he was a little disappointed when he first saw the *Sandwich*. She was little more than a flying wreck. An ugly *Mermidon*-class frigate assigned the lowly role of hauling Fleet freight, refuse, and assorted goods back and forth across the League, the *Sandwich* was squat and saucer-shaped and in desperate need of both a painting and a fumigating. She was at one time white, but was now a patchy, unidentifiable red with the outer few millimeters of her thick, tough hull rusted. The capsule-like bridge sitting atop the saucer looked like a virus implanting its DNA into some unsuspecting bacteria cell.

Still, she was a Fleet ship and was going to the stars. After taking a moment to get used to her meager shape and rusty hull, she became like a magic carpet, ready to speed him away to adventure.

The Boatswain of the *Sandwich*, an untidy man named Pike, was waiting for him on the gangway. He was terse and unpleasant from the get go. "You shall confine yourself to the areas of the ship assigned to you, namely, your office, your quarters and the crew's mess. You are forbidden from entering the bridge, period. You shall not, under any circumstances, enter or dine in the officer's mess, nor shall you eat in the crew's mess during peak dining hours, unless you choose to take your chow to your office or your room. You shall be allowed on the boat deck for two hours a day at times so designated by myself or the captain. You shall be assigned one crewman as an aid when their duties allow. You shall not fraternize with the officers or the crew, and you shall not be permitted to sit in at the nightly film. Just remember, you are on this ship, but you are not a part of it in any way. Do your job, make sure we get paid, hide our expenses if you can, and be quiet about it."

And with that warm welcome, Stenstrom boarded the ship, walking up the bouncy gang plank. He could smell the heavy salt water in the air by the wharf, and he could almost hear the *Sandwich's* foot-thick duraplate hull rusting.

He looked back over his shoulder—the Black Maidens were just arriving on the dock, sniffing the air and swaying slightly.

✳ ✳ ✳ ✳ ✳

Moving through the small, poorly lit corridors of the ship, Stenstrom found himself a bit appalled. The ship was a mess—dirty walls, peeling paint, marred floors, and the crew was motley in the extreme: mismatched uniforms in various stages of serviceable repair, filthy shoes, tarnished buckles, paunched bellies, and unshaven faces. The crew, full of dirty looks and second glances, were also inked up in an assemblage of gaudy 4-D tattoos in the images of naked ladies, obscene gestures, grotesque body parts, and varied, profane verbiage spelled out (and occasionally misspelled) on arms, shoulders, faces and necks. As he descended farther into the ship, he was painfully reminded of the two times he'd been on his father's ship, the *Caroline*, and the difference between the two was night and day. His father's warbird was a brightly-lit paradise of gleaming metal, spotless appointments, ram-rod crew, shaved faces, and rigid discipline.

In comparison to his father's ship, the *Sandwich* was a veritable cave populated by a squad of unwashed, stinking cavemen. He found his tiny cabin, which appeared to have been a bathroom at some point in the past, and he went inside and wondered if he really wanted to be here. He could de-ship, avoid the Black Maidens, and return to IBBAANA and announce his desire to wait for another more serviceable vessel.

The thought passed through his mind several times.

There was a knock at his door. A young lady stood there. "Hi!" she said in a cheery voice. "I'm Crewman Kaly! I've been assigned to help you!"

Stenstrom was pulled from his gloomy thoughts. He regarded her for a moment—again, as with most things on this ship, here was a lady standing in the doorway, presumably a member of the crew, without an ounce of military bearing or protocol that he had assumed was a staple of the Fleet, no matter the ship. She could have been a lady walking down the street, a co-ed at school, a waitress from Onaris, or an urchin from Calvert, anything but an active crewman in the Fleet aboard a commissioned ship.

Still, unlike the dirty looks he got from the other members of the crew that he passed, this Crewman Kaly smiled in an inviting and genuine way.

What the heck; he stood and held out his hand. She shook it. "Wow, strong grip," she said. "I like that."

Kaly sat down on his small bed and began talking—she appeared to be a real yapper. "I man the forward sensing station on the bridge, day bell. Between ten and twelve bells after my shift, I'll be down to help you out."

Kaly studied him intently. "You're a lot taller than our last Paymaster, and a lot more handsome."

"Thanks," he said, not expecting the compliment.

"So, you're a Great Lord from Kana?"

"I am," Stenstrom replied.

"What House? Not that I'll know what you're talking about or anything, I'm just curious."

"Belmont. Officially, Belmont-South Tyrol, an off-shoot branch."

Kaly's eyes lit up—she had fascinating green eyes. "I have no idea what that means. We don't see many Great Lords on this ship. Our last Paymaster was just some guy—I didn't know much about him. I think he was an attorney—I don't like attorneys much. Oh ... you're not an attorney, are you?"

"No."

Kaly was relieved. "That's great! So, what do I call you? I'm not well-versed on Kanan customs and such. Do I call you *Lord* or *Sir*, or *Great Lord*? I really don't have a clue."

"Call me Bel. All my friends do."

"Okay, Bel, I'll do that. You're sort of alone on this ship—no other Great Lords around, I mean other than Dunks. Do lords from Planet Fall count, in the social scheme, I mean? Planet Fall is where Dunks is from. We're pretty much all Browns here. I'm from Fig on Onaris."

"Who's Dunks?"

"Oh! He's our commander. Sorry."

"How long have you been in the Fleet?"

"Five years. I ... didn't score too well in my exams and got stuck with ship duty on a frigate. When they don't know what to do with you, they put you on one of these ships. S'ok, it pays the bills, I guess, and we're pretty informal around here, if you haven't already guessed—that's a perk I imagine. I'm told every ship is in the image of its commander—Dunks is an informal guy, and so are we. I've got a big family to help support back home on Onaris, and a deadbeat ex-husband whom I have to pay for by court order—I guess that's why I don't like attorneys. Yeah, I think I'm going to like you; you're a heck of a lot better looking than the last guy. Did I already mention that?"

Stenstrom was mystified. "I believe you did. Um, will my superior pulchritude be a plus in your assisting me in the ship's financial matters?"

"Oh, yeah."

"I hear tell the previous Paymaster died of food poisoning. Is that correct?"

"Well, yeah, I guess so."

Stenstrom tried to make sense of that as Kaly chirped away. She seemed a happy-enough person, smiling; she had those stunning eyes and a piled-up head of messy brown hair held in some bit of order with a pink hair band. Her skin was a pearly shade, and she had nice bone structure.

She saw his chests full of books.

"What are those?" she asked, looking at the old brown covers.

"Just old books."

The pipes overhead made a loud hissing sound, and Stenstrom could hear many doors clanging shut. His lights flickered for a moment.

"Oh," Kaly said, "looks like we're about to take off. You want to come to the boat deck and see?"

"The boatswain said I was forbidden to go to the boat deck except at designated hours."

"Don't worry about him; he's a knob. Come on. Taking off is always my favorite part."

She led him down the cramped corridor, up a gangway, and up two decks. There was the *Sandwich's* modest boat deck, just a long corridor lined on one side with windows. They went to the glass and looked down on the wharf. There was a jarring clank coming up from the bowels of the ship.

"Any moment now, the engineer is just building up pressure," Kaly said as people on the wharf began to back away from the ship.

Stenstrom looked around and felt weak. He remembered his father and the stars and the trips to Onaris, he and Lyra running through the manor halls playing with their models of the *Caroline*.

He remembered the knife in his chest, the clothes burning in the fountain. So, here he was at last, standing on a Fleet ship, ready to blast off.

The journey he'd taken to arrive on this rusty old vessel ...

He leaned against the glass.

"Hey," Kaly said looking up at him. "You okay?"

He smiled. "I'm fine. I'm just fine. I've waited a long time for this."

"Yeah?" she said. "Well, welcome aboard, Bel, Lord of Belmont. I really think I'm going to like you. I'm glad you're here with us."

And the ship lifted away from the wharf and slowly soared into the heavens.

$$\star \quad \star \quad \star \quad \star \quad \star$$

Stenstrom stood there on the boat deck for hours. Kaly had left sometime back, and he stood alone, the occasional crewman passing by idly. He watched the sky turn to black and Kana fade away. He stared at nothing but little speckles of distant stars, barely able to take it all in.

Footsteps came clanking in approach.

A slender man in a Fleet coat was walking down the corridor holding a triangle hat under his arm. He saw Stenstrom and stopped.

"Are you our new Paymaster?" he asked.

Stenstrom turned. "I am."

The man smiled and held out his hand. "Well then, glad to know you. I'm the captain of the ship, though my official rank is lieutenant. Lt. Dunkster's my name. I'm from the House of Carew on Planet Fall. Just call me Dunks."

Stenstrom took his hand and shook it. "Stenstrom, Lord of Belmont-South Tyrol. Please call me Bel."

Lt. Dunkster thought a moment and tapped the felt of his hat with his fingertips. "Isn't there a Lord Belmont in the Fleet? Yeah, Captain Stenstrom, of the *Caroline*, right?"

"He's my father."

"A warbird captain's your father, and here you are, a Paymaster? What's the story on that?"

"No story—I just never joined."

Lt. Dunkster looked a little dubious. "Hmmm, well, I'm certain we'll be fast friends in no time. It's a good ship here, good crew. Might not look like much, but we manage a decent service. Frigates—you know in ancient times a 'frigate' was a term that meant warship, a small warship, but a fighting vessel none the same. In our modern Fleet, however, a frigate is nothing more than a small ship relegated to small duties. But, somebody has to do this job, and I might say, we do it pretty well, and I pride myself on always managing to get my mates a little extra come payday—our Fleet earnings are a travesty. You'll see. Have you met Kaly? I assigned her to you."

"I have. Very nice lady."

"You … like her? I mean, I can get someone else for you if you want."

Stenstrom was puzzled. There was something fishy going on. "I like her just fine."

"Good, good. If you change your mind, let me know. Well, I've got to find the boatswain. Good meeting you."

"And you."

They shook hands again, and Lt. Dunkster continued on to the aft of the ship.

✶ ✶ ✶ ✶ ✶

As the first few days rolled by, Stenstrom began to get the hang of the ship. He could move around fairly well through the tight metal interior, and he'd met most of the crew. Most seemed friendly enough in a silent sort of way, while others looked at his nice clothes and seemed a bit jealous—he was obviously a man of wealth, a man beyond them socially and financially.

His duties as Paymaster were quite simple. Come payday, the money rolled in from the Fleet and dispersed to the crew—he just had to validate it and witness the computerized transactions. He was amazed how little they got paid. It didn't seem fair.

Every day, Kaly came down to his office after her watch ended and logged him into the ship's lists—he not having clearance to access them on his own. They then would go through all the ship's transactions, and he would validate them as OC: "Observed and Correct" and send them on.

His newly won knowledge of forged documents and his experience in hiding money from his Mother instantly told him the transactions he was looking at were faked: "cooked," "doctored"—call it whatever you will. Clearly Lt. Dunkster, the mate, and the boatswain were trying to hide money by moving it figuratively from one pocket or purse to another—it wasn't much, just a few coins here and there, but it added up and was fairly clear to see, if one knew what to look for. Once he validated them, the documents were sent on to Fleet, where they piled up in a dusty database somewhere and were probably never looked at again.

Kaly saw him puzzling over the documents. "Something wrong, Bel?" she asked.

He thought about it a moment. "No, no." He validated the documents and sent them on.

Perhaps it was simply an error.

As the days went on, the errors continued, always the neat little tricks, the missing coin or two here, and the extra money piled up there. It became obvious that there was more money floating around and exiting the ship than was coming in. Lt. Dunkster, the mate, and the boatswain were up to something shady. Some of the crew had to be in on it too—the dirty, mistrusting looks he got walking the corridors hadn't abated; in fact, they'd gotten worse. He wondered sometimes when he headed to the chow line or the showers if he was going to get jumped.

Let them try—they'd have a sore surprise coming. He could handle himself against this sorry lot any day.

Kaly seemed to be his only friend. She tried at first to be aloof and standoffish, but her friendly nature won out every time. She chattered about her home on Onaris and her friends, and she peppered him with questions about his home and his house—"Twenty-nine sisters, wow!" Her tendency to give tongue to her random thoughts made her appear to be a scatter-brain, a real ditz; in truth, such was not the case—she had a good head in there, somewhere, but simply didn't act like it. She appeared to be incapable of being anything other than herself, anything other than genuine. Her visits were the happiest parts of his day. He'd become genuinely fond of her.

After two weeks, he decided to level with her. "Kaly, tomorrow, I'm going to go speak to Dunks."

"About what?" she asked, a little alarmed.

"About whatever it is he's doing here on the side."

She turned a little pale and didn't try to deny it. Clearly she knew. "I don't think you want to do that, Bel," she said.

"I'm sorry, I must. I'm bonded to be honest, to report what I see. I want to know what he's doing—if he's running illegal goods and pushing things that harm folks, I'm not going to put up with it."

She sat there and looked sad. Stenstrom headed for the door. "Where are you going?" she asked.

"To the mess to get some dinner. I'll bring you something back."

He went down to the crew's mess and grabbed a tray, feeling eyes on him as he did so. He selected some chow and two cans of gasol and headed back to his cabin.

He was in for quite a surprise when a got there.

Kaly was in his bed, the covers pulled up to her bare arms and shoulders—her clothes scattered on the floor. Her voice changed from her normal perky one, to a more seductive, low-pitched drawl. "Why don't you put down the tray, close the door, and come to bed."

"Kaly," he said holding his tray, "what is this?"

She smiled. "Just doing my job, and, like I said, you're a lot better looking than the last Paymaster—I actually want to have sex with you. I've been thinking about it a lot over the last few days. I was wondering when it would come to this."

She pulled the covers aside, and there she was, naked and steaming. A strong smell came out—she'd applied The Weed. It began to cloud his head.

"Kaly—we needn't do this. Please put your clothes on."

She looked a tad hurt. "Don't you like me?"

"I like you just fine."

"Then come to bed."

"I'm not going to come to bed, Kaly. I spoke to the captain the other day before we blasted off. I got the distinct feeling that sexing me is part of your duties—am I correct?"

She sat up, staring at him hard with her lovely green eyes. "It is, though again, it is one duty I was looking forward to."

"Why are you to serve me in such a capacity? I'm certain such a thing isn't a standard Fleet practice."

Her smile faded. "You're on a frigate, Bel—we both are. We do what we have to do. And, I think I'm a little insulted. Sex is something we share on Onaris. To reject me is a huge slap. Do you think I'm beneath you, Lord Belmont? Is that what you think? Am I not good enough for a Great Lord like you?"

"Don't call me that, Kaly, and no, I don't think such a thing. I consider you my friend."

"Friends have sex on Onaris all the time—no big deal. You really must think I'm ugly."

He sat down on the bed. She sat up and put her arms on his back. "I think nothing of the sort. I just don't feel that having sex would be properly honoring you at this time."

"Bel," she said, a hint of desperation in her voice, "do you know what could happen to me if we don't do this—if you go to the captain?"

"No. What? What could happen? I don't understand."

She looked like she wanted to say something.

"Go on, Kaly, you can tell me. You have my word as a Great Lord, I won't tell or think ill of you, and the word of a Great Lord is something you can depend on."

He stood and got her the can of gasol that he'd brought for her from the mess. She took the can and tossed it back. "I'm supposed to have sex with you," she said, swallowing. "We should have been having sex days ago—all the other fellows I've been assigned to took me right away. I was starting to think I'd lost my touch."

"Why?"

"To keep you keep you occupied. To keep you from asking questions."

"Why?"

She finished her can and stifled a burp. "You've seen by now how little we make. To supplement our purses, we do a little extra on the side—it's no big deal; all frigates do it."

"What extra on the side?" he asked.

"I don't want to say. It's no big deal—but you're not supposed to know about it."

"Why not?"

"Because you're not part of the crew, because you are bound and notarized to be truthful when questioned. And, in your case, because you're a Great Lord. I don't want to say anymore. It's not a big deal, but if I can't keep you in here, if you start snooping around, I'm going to get in serious trouble. I could just disappear, you know?"

Stenstrom took her empty can and put it on the desk. "I certainly don't want to get you in trouble, Kaly, but I can't just let Dunks carry on. What if he's pushing something that's hurting people?"

"I would never party myself to something like that, Bel—honest! Please, it's nothing—nobody's getting hurt. If he was hurting people, if he was pushing Maggs or Remax or something, I'd turn him in myself. Look, I know I talk a lot. I know I say out loud pretty much anything that rolls into my head, but usually everything I say is the truth, and what we're doing here is harmless, small potatoes. We're just trying to get by is all."

She stared at him. "And I was also hoping to share an open relationship with you. I'm not a whore—if that's what you're thinking."

"Of course not, though, the sex ploy seems to be lacking a tad in sophistication."

"Yeah?" she said, "it's always worked before—we stick with what works on this ship."

"So, you can assure me that none are being harmed by whatever Dunks is doing?"

"Yes, yes …"

Stenstrom gave her hair a toss. "Fine then—I trust your word. Don't worry about it. I won't go snooping about."

"Especially on Wednesday nights."

"Fine then. On Wednesday nights I'll just linger here, eat my dinner, and look at the Air Net."

"Am I still invited to share your evenings on Wednesday nights?"

"Certainly—I was hoping you'd ask. We can talk, or hit the Net."

"Or, we can have sex. I really want to." She put her hands on his face.

"Perhaps another time. He stood up, got his tray, and began eating.

He froze. In the mirror opposite the bed, he thought he saw a shadowy figure standing there. It reached out for him with clawed hands.

He jumped back.

"Bel?" what is it?" Kaly asked. "What's wrong?"

He turned to the mirror again and the figure was gone. Even in the middle of open space, his mother's servants pursued. It was time to get out his gear.

"Nothing," he replied. "I need to unpack a few things. Would you like to help me?"

"Oh, Bel, come on … Well, okay. You promise we'll do it later, after I've helped you."

"Um, sure, sure."

Kaly sprang out of bed, and wrapped herself up in a sheet. Stenstrom pulled out his chest of books. She knelt down and looked at it.

"What's this one? It's got a funny lock."

Stenstrom considered his words. "You've shared a secret with me, Kaly. Now I've got one to share with you."

"Yeah? A secret? Okay, what is it?"

"You promise not to tell?"

"I promise."

"I'm an … enthusiast in certain seldom-studied arts, Kaly. That chest is full of all my arcane learning and instrumentality."

Her eyes got wide. "You mean you're a magician, or something like that?"

"Yes, after a sort."

"Cooool!" she said. "Can I see?"

"The chest is locked tight right?"

She tried the lid. "Yep."

He reached out and put his hand against the lock and then pulled his hand back. "Try it now."

She did, and the lid opened easily. "How'd you do that? Is it a trick lock, or one of those neat palm-sprander locks on Bazz?"

"No, it's a real lock. No lock can deter me for long."

"Can you teach me that?"

"Maybe later. Can you bring me the wooden box within, please?"

Kaly, still wrapped up in the sheet, tentatively rummaged around in the chest. "You mean this one?" she said pulling out a brown wooden box.

"That's it. Bring it over here and open it, please."

Kaly brought it to the desk and carefully pulled the lid off. Inside was a silver device. It looked like a tall candlestick with a recessed pan at the top. She pulled it out of the box and stood it up on the desk. "What is it?"

Stenstrom reached up, waved his hand, and placed a black Holystone in the pan at the top.

Kaly gasped. "What's that? How did you do that?" she asked.

"It's a Holystone. It shall alert me if demons should come near. If you're going to be helping me, Kaly, you might as well know that creatures not of this world are after me, and might well tear my soul apart should they catch wind of where I am."

"Ok," she said staring at the black Holystone.

"Does that prospect disturb you?"

She thought for a moment. "They're coming for your soul, right?"

"That's right, yes."

"Just yours, not mine?"

"Just mine."

"Nope. I'm fine. I'm good."

24

—A Stain on His Soul—

E very three days, toward 18 bells, there'd be a knock on his door, and Kaly came in.

They had become very good friends. Sometimes they'd watch the Air-net, other times she'd bring a game or two. Sometimes they'd just sit and talk—Kaly going on and on for hours about her life, her dreams—whatever came into her head. He didn't mind; he liked listening to her stories. Eventually, Stenstrom's inhibitions fell to the point where they started having sex, Kaly being remarkably casual with it. She was also completely uninhibited, willing to do or try anything.

He lay there one night, Kaly wrapped around him. He began to wonder what was going on that he wasn't supposed to see. He took a pink Holystone and put it in Kaly's hand. She was already asleep, but the pinky would ensure she stayed out.

He rose from bed, dressed, and prepared to creep out. He looked back—there was Kaly, quiet and peaceful. He came back and gave her a quick kiss on the forehead and then sneaked out. Using his training, he was remarkably stealthy. He could silently slip from shadow to shadow, blending in with the dark. Several people passed by as he roamed about, not one realizing he was there.

He wasn't sure what he was looking for. Given what Kaly had said, he assumed there was some improper or possibly illegal enterprise in progress on the *Sandwich*. For decency's sake he could only hope it wasn't something too outrageous, though she had promised him it wasn't harmful. Moving silently, he eventually made his way to the hold. He had to be careful, as he could hear quite a few people talking within.

When he thought the moment was right, he drifted in.

Inside the hold, he saw Dunks, the boatswain Pike, and several other people tending a huge vat in the center of the hold. There was a heavy smell of chemicals and various herbs floating on the air. And, he saw a large apothecary full of all sorts of ingredients in shelved glass bottles and jars against the far wall. Normally, there was nothing but a blank wall in that area.

It looked like they were brewing some sort of potion. He silently made his way into the hold and crept up on the pot Dunks was stirring. Within was a clear bubbling liquid that reeked of chemicals.

"Keep stirrin'," the boatswain said. "It has to be just right."

Dunks agreed. "No worries, pops. This is going to be a fine batch of sun tan lotion. Now—everybody out 'cuz here's where I use my secret technique to polish it up. Come on—out!"

People set their things down and exited the hold.

The boatswain Pike lingered. "I think I'll hang about. You promised to give me your procedure, and I've waited long enough. I want it."

"You'll get it when I'm good and ready to give it to you, not a moment sooner," Dunks snapped. "Now, get out!"

The boatswain turned in a huff and nearly plowed into Stenstrom. Alone in the hold, Dunks donned a breather mask and began adding components into the vat. The fumes that poured out were enough to incapacitate Stenstrom. Clinging to the shadows, he staggered out into the corridor, the fumes soon mixing with all the other bad smells on the ship, and they were lost. That was a near thing, for the mixture was foul and nearly had him on the floor. He worked his way out of the hold unnoticed and back to his quarters. He undressed and climbed back into bed. Kaly, with the pinky in her hand, hadn't even moved.

✱　✱　✱　✱　✱

Two days later, Stenstrom still puzzled over what he'd seen in the hold. What exactly were they up to? He wasn't naïve enough to believe they were making "sun tan lotion," as Dunks called it. Perhaps it was a certain tincture, spirit or snake-oil remedy—though it smelled terrible, whatever it was.

Feeling himself a little flushed, he went to the basin to splash water on his face.

He looked into the mirror.

Behind his reflection was a demonic landscape. Strange objects festered under old cobwebs.

As he stared at the mirror, he saw four indistinct figures sitting in the distance.

He heard a voice *"Lone Rider... The Star that does not Fall. It man... You belong to us..."*

Hands reached for him.

And he felt a ripping in his chest, a sundering of soul from flesh.

His soul was being attacked. For the love of Creation—what had Mother set against him this time?

Wheezing, holding his chest, his staggered out of his cabin and blundered into the corridor where he fell to the metal floor.

A moment later, Kaly came by. "Bel!" she squeaked seeing him lying there.

She knelt down and tried to pull him up. "Bel! Bel, what's wrong?"

He struggled to catch his breath. "Kaly … I'm in trouble …"

She looked down at him. She seemed whole-heartedly disappointed. "You know, Bel—I've really come to look up to you. We were going at it hard having sex the other day and I thought—*you know, I respect the heck out of this guy*. And then I had a monster orgasm. I really thought you might be a different sort."

"Kaly ... please ..."

"I mean, I'm not one to talk. I had my fill yesterday, Creation knows. But you—I don't know, I had you up there. I thought you were above this sort of thing, you know?"

"Kaly ... I'm dying ..."

She put her hands on her hips. "You filthy drunk right now, Bel?"

"Help me ..."

"You Balled-out? Kooked up?"

He wheezed for breath. "It's nothing like that ..."

She leaned down and sniffed him. "I don't smell any booze. I do smell a little BO—no, wait, that's me. And your pupils aren't dilated so you're not 'Kooked' up either."

"It's my soul ... it's sorcery .... I'm under—attack!"

She finally seemed convinced. "Sorcery, really? Oh, that's so cool! I'm so happy you're not strung out or drunk! What can I do?"

Stenstrom struggled to stay conscious. "Need ... salts ... chemicals... and a bit of tin or antimony ..."

"Where—where am I going to get that stuff?"

"Cargo hold—I saw a hidden a—apothecary. Should have w-what I need."

"How do you know about that?" she asked.

"I saw it ..."

Kaly thought about it for a moment, then slung his arm around her shoulder and helped him down to the hold, stumbling often.

They passed several people on their way. They saw Stenstrom, apparently in bad shape, and they laughed and shook their heads. "Would you look at that—Paymaster Stenstrom, all Kooked up. Guess we're rubbing off on *his lordship...*"

They got to the hold a few minutes later. Kaly sat him down against the wall. "Now, you think this is just an apothecary, right?" she asked. "Nothing more?"

Stenstrom felt his soul rip. He held his chest. "I don't ... don't care what it is, Kaly ... help me."

She stood and went to the far wall. She pressed a hidden lever and a portion of the wall spun about revealing a vast cabinetry of shelves and drawers brimming with lined-up jars, beakers and bottles. "Ok," she said. "What do I need?"

"N-Natron ..."

"What? What's that?"

"S-soda ash ..."

Kaly looked around the shelves and browsed through the bottles, clinking them together. "Soda ash, soda ash ... ah, here's some!" She pulled out a clear glass vial full of bluish salt. "What else?"

"Bismuth ..."

"Bismuth, bismuth ..." She looked around. "Ok—bismuth, this silvery metal here?" She showed him a clear glass vial with two bits of metal sliding about inside.

"Now, fox ... fox glove ..."

"What's that?"

"A purple ... flower, hooded, bell-shaped."

She looked around. "I don't think we're going to have that ... wait—what do you know? Fox glove—wow, Dunks has this thing stocked!" She pulled an earthen jar out of the shelving and removed a stalk of dried purple, hood-like flowers."

"Now ... I need either tin ... or ... anti—mony."

She looked around. "Ha—we have both!"

"A-Antimony ... It's better."

"What else?"

"Get a pot and start a small fire."

Kaly rummaged about and found a rough iron pot. She turned on a gas burner and put the pot on it.

"No ... no, Kaly, I need fire, not ... a gas flame."

She spun around. "Where am I going to make a fire, Bel?" She went to a stainless steel basin in the corner. "Here' I'll make one in here." She grabbed bits of paper and board and tossed them into the basin. She tried lighting bits of papers on the nearby gas burner and tossing them in, but she couldn't sustain a flame in the basin. "You got a lighter?"

"Kaly ... take this and be careful." He produced a red Holystone. She ran toward him and took it. "Throw it into the basin and step away."

Kaly threw the Holystone into the basin, and a hot yellow fire erupted, licking up the side of the metal wall. It subsided after a few moments and she put the iron pot into the basin, careful not to burn herself.

"Now, carefully put ... the natron into the fire. Be-be careful, it's going to jump up again."

Kaly unstoppered the natron and tossed it into the flames. The fire turned cobalt blue and leapt up. "Wow! Okay! What's next?" she asked.

"Put ... the rest of the ingredients in the pot and crush them—don't stir, crush... them with something."

She threw all the ingredients in and, finding a large wrench, began crushing the ingredients. She sweated with the heat of the fire. "Ok. Everything's starting to melt together. Smells kind of good."

"Help me over there ... Kaly."

She put the wrench down and helped him up. She then led him to the basin.

"Now, find a cloth, a h-handkerchief or similar ... sized rag."

She propped him up against the basin and went to find a cloth. Stenstrom readied himself, then reached into the pot and seized the contents in his fist.

Kaly returned with a length of course linen. "What are you doing?" she asked, looking at his hand. "You'll burn yourself!"

"That's the ... price for ... saving my ... soul ..." he said as the metals burned his palm.

He opened his hand. There were three small ingots of antimony, mixed with bismuth and foxglove, rapidly cooling though still hot in his blistered hand.

"Lay ... the cloth out ..."

Kaly cleared a spot and laid the linen out. Stenstrom then arranged it into a band with two triangular flaps coming down. He then rolled the three irregular ingots into the cloth and put the whole thing around his head. The flaps came down over his eyes. Sighing with relief, he tied the back.

"You okay?" Kaly asked.

"I am now. Thanks, Kaly, I really owe you." He put his arm around her and gave her a kiss on the cheek.

She gave him a large hug in return. "It's okay—I'm glad I could help. That was pretty neat, actually. What did we just do, by the way?"

"We made a set of hermelins. They are a sort of magical rock that protects your soul."

The cloth was pulled down over his eyes.

"Why don't you push the cloth back so you can see?"

"It has to go over my eyes—that way the spirits won't be able to find me as easily. Eyes are the route to the soul. Obscure them a little, and they'll have a harder time."

Kaly found a knife and they cut small holes into the cloth. "Oh," she said. "What sort of spirit is after you?"

"The worst kind. My mother summoned it."

25

—Calling on the Eryne—

"Hey, Bel! Over here!" Dunks yelled as Stenstrom entered the mess. Dunks was a chatty fellow from Planet Fall. He was an able, if disinterested, officer, having long since resigned himself to the dregs of Fleet command. Stenstrom had heard he had a history of bad behavior and erratic manners, always the darting eye and the hand in the pocket. His Fleet uniform was rumpled and worn in places, his handsome face unshaved, and his blonde hair often uncombed.

And, without question, he was conducting some sort of illicit side-enterprise, all the stuff in the hold, the thinly veiled transactions, and the coin payouts to the crew that Bel noticed. In several of their past conversations, Stenstrom could tell that Dunks was trying to get information out of him, to determine if he knew anything. Stenstrom couldn't care less what he was doing—Kaly had promised him that the "Side Venture," whatever it was, wasn't harmful, and he trusted Kaly, so he took her at her word and left it alone.

By this point Stenstrom had seen a great deal of the League. He'd seen plenty of Onaris and Xandarr, they being frequent stops on the *Sandwich's* route. He'd also been to Hoban, Brindval, Poteete, and Goima.

The problem that dogged his heels was his mother and her Black Maidens. Every port the *Sandwich* arrived at, there they were, lurking in the background waiting for the first chance to get him. They seemed dark and sinister—as if Mother had something more terrifying than just Black Maidens set against him.

And, he had to wear his mask with its protective hermelins all the time now. If he took it off, even for a moment, he instantly felt the clawed hand tearing at his soul. The crew certainly thought it amusing seeing him walk around in his mask. "What—you think you're a pirate now—ahahahahar!" they'd say.

"We surrender, Captain Mask-face!" they chortled.

He refined the mask over time, replacing the original linen with fine black silk from Hoban. He also had redone and refined the mystical hermelins, adding a tiny bit of cadmium to the ingredients—the cad allowing him to sleep better.

He was now able to fold and situate the silk better, rolling the hermelins in with precision—now the mask was little more than a black headband with two modest diamond-shaped corners of cloth pulled down over his eyes and cutout so he could see.

Eventually, the crew stopped making fun of him—Kaly didn't even notice it anymore.

Lt. Dunkster sat there with him in the mess. Every so often he gave Stenstrom's mask a second look, but if Stenstrom's masked face puzzled him, he kept it to himself.

"Bel, I need you to do me a favor."

"Sure thing, Dunks, you name it."

"We're soon to anchor on Z-Encarr, Planet Fall."

"Z-Encarr? What is that, please?"

"It's a floating continent, one of three on Planet Fall. Being a gas giant, there's really no ground to walk around on except deep in the core where nothing can live, so we've built three massive platforms that float in the upper atmosphere—Z-Encarr's one of them. Marvels of modern engineering. I'm from Planet Fall. You know that, right?"

"Yes."

He placed a small money bag on the table. "I need you to off the ship once we anchor-up and take this moneybag to a lady I know. Can you do that for me?"

"A lady?"

"Her name's Christiana …"

"Just Christiana? No *Lady Christiana of*…and what not?"

Dunkster smiled. "No, Bel. She's an ex-dirty courtesan, and she's also my wife."

"I thought your wife was on Poteete?"

"She is on Poteete, and she's on Bazz too, and on Hoban, and here on Planet Fall as well. I have fourteen wives when last I counted, I think."

Dunks jangled the moneybag. "This one's important—this one knows certain things, and I need to keep her quiet. I need you to pretend you're me and take her this moneybag. It's for her and the kids."

"Kids? I didn't know you have kids."

"I do—I've no idea how many, but it's a lot. Christiana has four, I think. She needs this money to help her survive, and I'm very late with this current payment."

"Why don't you put it into her account?"

"Christiana doesn't have an account—she's too stupid to know how a bank works. Come on Bel—can you be a pal? All you have to do is go to her address, hand her the money, and leave."

Stenstrom looked at the bag. "I'm not nearly as good-looking as you, Dunks. I'm certain she recalls what her husband looks like."

"I got you covered on that one, Bel. She's nearly blind—got a dose of bad Weed some years back and lost a good deal of her sight. Of all my wives, she's probably the most broken down and threadbare—kind of embarrassing, you know. I'm used to something a little bit more polished up at my side." Dunks pulled his coat off and laid it on the table. "Just wear my coat and she'll never know the difference. She can sort of see shapes, I think."

Stenstrom stared at the coat. A Fleet Lt.'s coat. "Why? For feel or," as Stenstrom noted, "for the smell?"

"Both. Christiana knows the smell of her hubby sure enough."

Stenstrom thought it over. "Sure, Dunks, sure. Just give me her address."

Dunks wrote it down on a slip of paper. "... Appreciate this—you're saving me a lot of trouble. Oh, just between the two of us, you can bed her down if you want—I don't care. Maybe she'll have a heart attack right in the middle of it and save me a lot of further trouble and expense. I was hoping she would have keeled over a long time ago."

Stenstrom found Dunk's attitude toward his wife a little annoying—how bad could she be? He took Dunk's coat and went back to his room. Staring into the mirror, he put it on. It was a little dirty and somewhat threadbare in places, but he stared none the less.

A Fleet coat ... Some of his lost little boy dreams returned to him, wearing the clothes his father had sent.

He was missing something, but he couldn't quite put his finger on it.

Ah, a hat! He needed a triangle hat, just like they wore in the Fleet. He went down the hall and knocked on the boatswain's cabin.

Nobody answered. The door was locked, but with a fast shake of his hand and nimble movement of his fingers, the door swung open. "Mr. Pike?" Stenstrom asked, peeking in.

The cabin was empty. He stepped in and borrowed one of the boatswain's hats, as they appeared to have a similar head-size.

He popped it on. Not used to triangle hats, it felt strange. Ah, well—he'd get used to it.

He locked the boatswain's cabin up, headed back to his room, and loaded up with MARZABLE, Holystones, and his trusty NTHs. He then left his room and exited the ship. Address in hand, Stenstrom walked off the plank of the *Sandwich*. He was wearing Dunk's coat and the boatswain's hat, and though it was dirty and rather seedy, the ensemble felt wonderful—even the hat. How he always longed to wear such a thing.

Kaly was walking out of the ship as well. "Hey, Bell!" she called. "I'm heading out to the bars with some of my friends. Want to come? Hey! Where'd you get that hat?"

"I borrowed it from the boatswain."

"Borrowed it, huh—looks like we're starting to rub off on you a little. Such a shame to mess up your handsome face with that hat."

She noted his coat. "Oh ... Dunks has you on a mission, right? He wants you to go see one of his wives, doesn't he?"

"Something like that. Just a quick errand."

She looked a little concerned. "Well, you're a big fella'; you'll be just fine."

Stenstrom was apprehensive. "I detect a hint of concern in your voice."

She hesitated and pulled him aside off the gangplank. "Ok, look. Dunks has a thing for ex-Erynes. Do you know what those are? I mean, we're talking some pretty trashy stuff here, and I'm not sure a classy Great Lord like you divests himself much in that—I hope not anyway."

"Erynes? Those are courtesans if I'm not mistaken."

"They're more than just that. They're either the best or the worst, depending on how you look at it. The Erynes can do things to you unholy, Bel. You name it, secrets, thoughts, blind obedience ... they can screw it right out of you, or into you as the case may be. You laugh, but they are nothing to trifle with. They use some sort of super-charged strain of The Weed and they know how to make the most of it. It gives them glowing red eyes. The Weed they use takes a toll on their bodies, wears them out, makes them old, and Dunks has a thing for those old, broken down Erynes. He marries them at a whim, and collects them like discarded bottle caps. Sometimes he uses them to find out things or to get into people's heads. Virtually every port we stop in, he's got an old Eryne wife stashed somewhere, and Planet Fall is no exception. And, just like an old attack dog that's all beaten up and tired, they still have teeth. They can still bite. Be careful, okay?"

"I will, Kaly, thanks."

She gave her lips a tap with her finger and Stenstrom shot her a kiss. She smiled at him and walked down the wharf. "If you change your mind, we'll be at one of the wharf-side bars!" she called out. She pointed at her neck. "I've got my Holo-mon, so just Holo me up if you need to find me, 'kay?"

He waved her goodbye. "I don't carry a Holo-mon, Kaly, but thanks."

✶   ✶   ✶   ✶   ✶

Planet Fall was a turbid gas giant with several floating continents drifting through its upper atmosphere—it had no habitable surface. The vast metal continents floating on air were marvels of engineering and completely self-contained and featuring a sort of reverse-gravity, to counteract the crushing gravity of the planet below. Looking up, Stenstrom could see a banded lace-work of white, red and orange clouds swirling past at high, wind-driven speeds. Used to the soft blue sky of Kana, the perpetual clouds of the place with its orange tint made him feel a little uneasy. He walked at a brisk pace into the interior of the massive, skyscraper-clogged city, his boots clacking on the metal street. Despite Kaly's rather ominous warning, he had a spring in his step. As he worked his way into the man-made canyons of Z-Encarr, many people stopped and tipped their hats.

"Evening, Lt."

"Nice day, Lt."

"Care for some company, Lt...."

"Got a dime, Lt.?"

Only a few people stopped and noticed he was wearing a mask; it was hard to see under the boatswain's hat.

He felt true joy wearing Dunk's seedy coat and the boatswain's hat. The clothes made him feel ... whole.

He had to be careful, though. He looked around, peering twice into the shadows and the distant reaches. He was certain he'd seen the hint of darting black robes and hooded faces looking at him in the far distance. His Holystone was rumbling steadily.

The Black Maidens. They were here. They had to be. He wore his mask and his bolabung, refreshed with Kaly's scent, and together they gave him protection as the Maidens couldn't see and smell him—but they could still sense him, feel his presence. And they appeared to not be giving up.

Moving on, Stenstrom found the address—it was a smallish, row house tenement on a seedy side street.

So, an Eryne lives here, he thought. *Like an old pet that still has teeth.* He wondered what sort of hellion raged within.

He walked up the steps and knocked on the door. After a moment, a red-headed woman with squinting brown eyes emerged. She was wearing a brown dress with an apron tied over the top.

He remembered Kaly's warning: *The Weed they use takes a toll on their bodies, wears them out, makes them old.* He was expecting a proverbial "old crone" to come out—bent and withered, like in his picture books he and Lyra thrilled over when he was a child—the ones Virginia was too scared to look at. Old crones were monsters from fairytales—nobody got old in the League, except for the sick and the badly bred.

Upon seeing her, he was a tad disappointed. Christiana certainly didn't look old and worn out. She was tall, nearly six feet, and stood with practiced posture. Her skin was a pleasing pearly shade. Her brassy red hair was thick and full, held back with unseen pins and clips. Her face was pretty, heart-shaped, with well-formed cheekbones and a large pair of striking brown eyes, lost in the confusion of blindness. Her waist was very thin—he imagined she'd probably spent years suffocating in a laced-up corset.

"Dunks, is that you?" she said tentatively, her voice accented in a brogue Planet Fall burr, opening the screen door.

Stenstrom didn't quite know what to do—Dunks hadn't briefed him on how to interface with his wife. He hadn't thought of that. The way Dunks described it, he figured he'd knock on the door, a gnarled hand would come out, accept the money, and go back in, shutting the door behind it with little or no interface.

But, there she was, standing in the door.

He tried to disguise his voice and sound like Dunks. "Uh, yeah, Christiana, it's me."

She smiled and reached out. "Let me look at you." Probing with her hands, she found his face and began feeling his chin with her fingers. Her hands found his hat.

Her hands—they were the hands of a hag: bony, withered, and the skin, dull and parchment-like. So that's what The Weed did to her.

"Have you lost weight, Dunks?" she asked.

"Umm, yeah, yeah. Stellar food, it's terrible."

Her bent fingers found the fabric of his mask. "What's this?" she asked.

"Oh, I got hurt—just a bandage. It's nothing."

Christiana pulled him forward and gave him a kiss on the cheek. "I've made lunch for us. Please come in and share it with me."

His Holystone gave a rumble. Stenstrom looked down the street and clearly saw four figures in black standing in the distance, teetering about, sniffing the air. Here, with Christiana nearby and his mask, he should be safe. "Sure, sure," he said, stepping in.

The interior of the apartment was small and modest. Childrens' toys lay scattered about. Piled up on the couch were sorted stacks of children's clothing. In a small closet, a primitive manual wash-basin full of soapy water and an old air-oven were crammed in. A scratchy program played on her battered Aire-net receptor in the sunken living room.

Christiana, holding his hand, led him to her tiny dinner table. Feeling her way about, she sat him down to a strange meal of meats and sauces he couldn't identify. He watched her carefully serve the food—her hands so terribly withered and gnarled from the degenerative effects of prolonged contact with The Weed. She held her ladle with the hands of a dead woman.

Standing there in her tiny, galley-style kitchen wearing an apron, he felt sorry for her as she put the finishing touches on the meal.

Dunks said she was stupid, but she didn't appear to be stupid; on the contrary, she seemed to be getting on and dealing with her blindness rather well.

Dunks said she was broken down—an embarrassment, yet, except for her hands, she was beautiful.

Dunks hoped she'd die, to spare him further expense.

"I've been practicing, Dunks—my cooking. I think I've gotten much better at it."

She served the food, and it was good. He had no trouble finishing it. Christiana sat next to him, eating with polished manners and grace, all of her very beautiful, except for her horrid hands. She held her knife and fork court-style, taking tiny bites, chatting happily with Stenstrom whom she thought was her husband. He could imagine her sitting in some lavish castle or manor—a prim and proper lady of the house.

And here she was, living in near squalor, married to a man that had collected her as a prize and probably didn't know their children's names.

She pointed out a small trophy sitting on the mantle.

"What's that?" Stenstrom asked.

"It's a merit award. Our son was at the top of his class again." She beamed with pride.

"That's wonderful. Um …which one?"

"Nathan."

"Nathan, he's the one who looks like his beautiful mother, yes?"

She blushed. Christiana was clearly attention-starved. As she ate she was wincing a tiny bit.

"Are you having trouble with your teeth, Christiana?" Stenstrom asked.

She shook her head. "It's nothing."

"Let me have a look." He leaned in, and she swallowed and wiped her mouth with her napkin. She opened her mouth. Several of her teeth were obviously rotten. "You need to see a Hospitaler for your teeth."

"I'm fine."

Stenstrom stood up. "Get dressed," he said.

She looked up at him. "What? Why?"

"I saw a Hospitaler sanctum a short walk away. We're going to walk there now, and you're going to have your teeth looked at, this very afternoon. And then, do you know what we're going to do?"

"What, Dunks?"

"We're going to walk the town, arm in arm, and when we've worked up a healthy appetite, we're going to eat at the finest restaurant we can find. I want to serve you, today, and show you off to the people, as a lady deserves. Go on, I'll take care of the dishes here. Where are the children?"

"I sent them away for the day. That sounds so expensive, Dunks," she said. "My teeth, a fine meal? We don't have the money for that."

"I ... had a big score not long ago, and I've coin a-plenty. Come on—who better to spend it on than my beautiful wife?"

She smiled at the compliment. She got up and made her way into the bedroom. He began cleaning up their lunch, and he could hear her clinking around in the bedroom as he worked. A short time later she emerged. She changed into a slender black dress with a pearl heart charm about her neck. In her dress, her corset-created, hour-glass figure was clear. She had put her hair up and was wearing a curved straw hat with a ribbon hanging from the back. Thankfully, she'd put on a pair of black gloves.

She was still such a beautiful woman.

Stenstrom took her arm and led her outside. After a short walk they arrived at the Hospitaler sanctum, and they admitted Christiana. Their assessment—six teeth needed replacement, and they wanted to see the color of his money before they began. Stenstrom got his money bag out and paid them: one hundred and four sesterces, equaling four hundred Planet Fall billets.

As they worked on her, his Holystone rumbled again, warning him of danger. He went outside. Sure enough, four black-robed Maidens wandered down the lane, their noses in the air.

He knew as long as Christiana was with him, her love, though misplaced, would protect him and mask his scent. It was a simple counter-charm he knew worked.

The Maidens appeared different from how he remembered them—more covered up, more sinister. He could simply shoot them with his NTHs and be rid of them for now, but he didn't want to shoot a Black Maiden; they were harmless and benign—and persistent and inconvenient as well. That, however, did not give him lease to kill them. He had made a promise to himself in Calvert not to harm the Black Maidens ever again.

A short time later, Christiana emerged from the sanctum. She had a brand new smile and didn't mind showing it off. What a face when she smiled—a classic beauty.

Stenstrom took her arm and led her outside. He watched the Maidens disappear into the distance, his scent masked. He strolled the streets with her, people tipping their hats as they passed. He walked her to a market and bought her a modern fabric cleaning unit, to replace the ridiculous wash basin she'd been using, and arranged to have it delivered to her apartment. He bought some toys for the children—again having them delivered.

He spent more money on her in one afternoon than Dunks probably had in their entire marriage. He wanted to do nice things for her because it felt good. He felt responsible for her somehow—that this afternoon she was his to care for, and he'd not spare a dime.

They passed a bank. "Christiana, do you have a bank account?"

"You know I don't, Dunks. I've never learned to use one."

Stenstrom pulled her toward the bank. "Well, come on. We're going to go inside, and I'm going to create an account for you, and I'm going to deposit money into it every month for you and the children. I'll show you how to access your account from home when we get back."

They finished at the bank and continued their stroll. He could see the rusty bulk of the *Sandwich* sitting at the wharf. He took her to an expensive-looking restaurant and let her have whatever she wanted. Through the meal, he told her about all the places they had recently been, she closing her eyes and listening.

As the gas-giant sky faded to a night-time brown, he walked her back to her apartment. There, using the Holo-net, he showed her how to access her new bank account. Using voice commands, she picked it up rather quickly. She wasn't stupid at all.

"That was a wonderful meal, what a delightful evening. And my teeth, to eat without pain. The children are gone, Dunks," she said trying to pull him into their bedroom, but he talked his way out of it. He then led her back to her small sitting room, put her feet up, and tucked her in with a blanket. He put the moneybag Dunks had given him in a drawer and told her where it was.

"Will you come back soon, Dunks?" she asked, looking at him with mostly blind eyes. "Please say you'll come back."

"You bet. I'll be back tomorrow. I promise."

He kissed her goodnight and took his leave, watching for the Black Maidens. He didn't see any, his Holystone quiet.

"Good night, Christiana," he said.

"I love you …" she returned.

As he began walking down the street, his Holystone suddenly went wild.

Four Black Maidens appeared all around him. They surrounded him, groping with their bony arms. They pawed at him, trying to see him.

He had no place to go. He felt his soul churn. They fell upon him. They reached out, grasping with their fingers, acting in an aggressive, belligerent manner that was unusual for Black Maidens.

They found his mask and tore it from his face along with his hat and his bolabung. They threw them aside.

Stenstrom put his hands up. "All right, all right—you got me. I guess it's time to go and see Mother."

"Mother ... "

One of them tore away the veil covering her face. She had no face—only a large smiling mouth and chattering teeth. *"You are ours! We shall feast upon your soul ... "*

Holy Creation!! What had his mother done? These weren't Black Maidens—these were Soul Devourers! Mother had put a stain on his soul!! He was doomed!

"YOUR SOUL!!"

He drew his NTHs and fired, getting one in the chest. She bent over and disappeared.

The rest pulled him down. He fired his other NTH and got another one. She disappeared too.

They closed in, giving him no space, no room to aim his guns. They pawed and tore at him. He dropped one of his NTHs and fell to the street.

A moment later the remaining two Soul Devourers seemed to recoil in pain and quickly retreated, covering their faces.

Stenstrom cocked his NTH. He fired, hitting one in the back where she vanished in a gristly spray. He picked up the NTH he'd dropped and then got the last with a longer range shot, the green blasts lighting up the street as he fired.

Something touched him from behind. He whirled around.

It was Christiana. She had emerged from the apartment. She was holding his mask in her hand. She reached out, searching. "What's going on? I thought I heard something. Did you drop your handkerchief? I can smell your cologne on it."

Her presence had driven them away, giving him a chance to be rid of them with his guns.

"It's nothing," Stenstrom said, panting. He took his mask and put it back on. His thoughts spun in a panic.

Soul Devourers. What had his mother done? He was doomed. They'd be back. They'd get him sooner or later.

"It's nothing. Let me take you back inside and tuck you in again," he said, his voice shaking.

Stenstrom helped her inside while figuring out his next move. At least, now that he knew they were Soul Devourers, he would feel empowered to shoot and kill them—he hadn't wanted to treat a gentle Black Maiden in that fashion if he could help it.

Suddenly, there was Christiana.

She put her gloved hands on his face and kissed him with fire. "I was to question you today, to discover what you know," she whispered, kissing him. "My husband thinks you know something. He thinks you're a spy sent from the Fleet, and I was to uncover it. He wants to know who you're working for.

And here you are, such a fine young man who knocked on my door today. You've done much for me: you entertained me, listened to my stories, and told a few in return. You asked the name of my son—something my husband has never done. You walked at my side and held my arm, as a Lord does for his Lady, and I was proud to stand there with you. I've not been admired as I walked down the street in some time. You took away my pain, and mostly, you've helped restore a shred of my dignity that I'd long lost. During our afternoon today, I indulged myself. I pretended that you actually are my husband and that the two of us share a love seldom seen. Wouldn't that be nice—to have a husband who actually loves me and our children? I am not a puppet, and I care not what my husband wants—you have earned my adoration. I invite you into my bedroom, not because of my husband, but because I want you. You've shared much with me today, and I want to share with you all I have to give."

He pulled away. "Please, Christiana."

"I'm blind, but I'm not dead, and I'm still a woman. You're not my husband—you're a good man, and I want to be with you."

She pulled him back into the apartment. He was feeling shaky from his encounter with the Soul Devourers. He didn't have the strength to resist.

And soon, he was in Christiana's bedroom, she all around him. She was still using a lesser strain of The Weed, and it belted him into places he'd never been before, stabbing him with frenzied jolts.

Making love to Lilly was a joy, a smooth scent of perfume.

Making love to Alitrix was fragile and private, she unsure and remarkably in need of assurance and tenderness.

Making love to Lady Miranda was weird and a little painful.

Making love to Kaly was fun and carefree.

But this? This was savagery. This was very nearly a fight to the death. This was top to bottom, skin and sweat, body against body. He could barely breathe, and he couldn't think. Christiana used The Weed relentlessly, prolonging the act, taking him to unbearable stages, flawlessly playing the notes of a complex tune on his body, whipping up small pieces of him into a lather of ecstasy and moving on when he could take it no more.

This was what it was like to experience an Eryne in action.

He thought he could hear her speaking to him. Not with her mouth; somewhere she was making a lot of noise with her mouth, but he was only partially aware of it—he was making a lot of noise too.

His heart pounded. He saw stars. He saw through time. He heard her voice.

"I was a queen once, a dame respected and feared—all my needs doted on and cared for. I've enslaved many—I've even killed and wrung out secrets. I had only to ask, anything I desired was mine. Then, I grew old, my body beginning to fail me, and I was a queen no more—cast out, used up, with no skills other than my lexicon of the night. You've nothing to fear, and I'm not going to harm you. Let me worship you."

Kaly's green eyes and pink hair band flashed into his thoughts. *"Dunks has a thing for old Erynes—he collects them like discarded bottlecaps. I have no idea how many he's married to—but it's a lot. Watch out for the Erynes—even old, and used up, they can do things to you unholy. Man or woman, they can make you talk—no secret you have is beyond their reach. They can even kill you if they want—and that's old and rotten, using a crap Weed... just imagine a fit one on a mission, with that Red-eye stuff they use!"*

They can kill you if they want ...

Christiana was a master—she certainly could kill him if she wanted, or extract secrets. He was hers to do with as she would. Christiana, who walked with him in his arm, basking in the attention and eating her dinner with perfect grace, was now a fierce warrior using her body and The Weed as a terror weapon and execution tool.

She asked him no lengthy questions. The only secret she extracted from him: "What ...w-what is your n-name ...?"

"Sten—Stenstrom ..."

In psychedelic jolts, he saw techno-color splashes of Lilly. In psychotropic mush, he saw Alitrix, devastated, crying for attention and Kaly, smiling, ready to try anything.

And soon, when he thought he could endure no more, it was over, Christiana lying next to him, her lazy, gloved fingers dabbing away jewels of sweat from his chest, the both of them soon passing out.

✳ ✳ ✳ ✳ ✳

"And you banged her?" Kaly's green eyes were huge as she leaned over her lunch in the mess. They were back on the ship, both Planet Fall and Christiana far away.

"Must you be so crude? But, yes, I didn't have the strength to resist."

"You returned to her the next day, didn't you?"

"I did—but not for the sex. I returned for the company. I found her a lovely woman."

"But you still had sex the second time, right?"

"Of course."

"See. Told you. They're tough. So, how was it?"

"Remarkable. It was remarkable."

"You okay, you look a little tired."

"I'm exhausted."

Kaly took a bite from her sandwich. "Well, you better buck up, 'cause I'm feeling it for tonight and I don't want to hear any excuses."

26

—The HRN—

"Where in the name of Creation have you been?" Captain Stenstrom yelled through the Com. "Your mother is ready to die of worry." He was sitting in his large office on the *Caroline* and he looked positively livid. "This is very irresponsible of you, Bel!"

"I'm sorry, Father, I'm simply doing what Mother has told me to do—to be my own man. If she wouldn't continually harass me with Black Maidens and Soul Devourers, maybe I'd be in touch more often."

Captain Stenstrom squinted and tried to look past his face at his surroundings through the screen. "Are you in a brig somewhere—and is that a mask you're wearing?"

"This is my office, it's not much, but it's mine, and I am wearing a mask to keep mother's demons from tearing my soul apart."

"Your mother has done no such thing. Your mother loves you." Captain Stenstrom's interest seemed to peak, his anger diminished. "So, where are you? Are you on a ship? You can tell me."

"I am on a frigate."

"A ... *frigate?*" he said with some distaste.

"Yes. It's a fine frigate, and I am its Paymaster."

"A Paymaster? You're the Paymaster of a frigate?"

"That is correct. Mother never thought of knifing a shipboard civilian out of me. I always wanted to join the Fleet, to soar the stars. I suppose this is as close as I am able to get."

"You never showed any interest in joining the Fleet."

"I always wanted to join the Fleet, Father—Lyra too. I wore the clothes you sent home to me, and I played with the toys you bought for us. Mother wouldn't have it. So, here I am, a Fleet Paymaster on a frigate. It's not much, and it's not how I expected it to be, but I am living my dream."

Captain Stenstrom, despite himself, beamed, smiling from ear to ear. "Well, what do you know? You are something, my son—you've got some wit. What ship are you on? Maybe I can swing by if I'm close. I'm very proud. Very proud indeed."

"I'm on the *Sandwich*. Again, it's not much, but it's home. The places I've been to, the things I've seen—remarkable."

The captain noted the name down. "Is there anything you need? Just say the word, and I'll get you whatever you require."

"I'm fine, Father, I think."

"Well, I must admit, this is a great surprise. The *Sandwich*, and my son is its Paymaster. Still, as to my previous point, when you're close, I do bade you come home and visit your mother. She ..."

"She what?"

"Nothing. She would love to see you, is all. And your sisters too. You will be happy to learn that Virginia is betrothed."

"That's wonderful. To whom?"

"Lord Cobbleshem of Pole. She's very excited, and, as usual, your mother is home fussing over the details."

"How about Lyra?"

"She's actually planning on going to school. She managed to talk your mother into letting her go—can you believe that?"

Stenstrom was nearly open-mouthed with shock. "That's ... amazing. What school, what is she studying?"

"University of Arden—she's studying stellar cartography. Your mother is mellowing, and I cannot believe she would conjure up demons to harass you. Come home, Bel. Tell her what you've become, and she will be as proud of you as I am."

$$\star \quad \star \quad \star \quad \star \quad \star$$

The *Sandwich* made berth in Mercia several days later to load up on supplies. Stenstrom and Kaly disembarked. He'd promised to take her out on the town.

As they walked down the gangplank, his felt his Holystone go off. He stopped and scanned the area. "What?" Kaly asked.

"Something's about ..." He cleared his coat and put his hand on his NTH."

Kaly looked around. "Demons?"

"Possibly."

He looked around and didn't see the usual black robed figures sniffing about. Instead, he saw a familiar shape standing on the dock.

He smiled. "Hey, Kaly, I'm going to have to take a rain-check. I promise I'll take you out tomorrow, okay?"

"What, what is it?" she asked. "Who are you ditching me for?"

"I see a friend down there. I promise I'll get you tomorrow."

"All right—tomorrow then. I wish you carried a Holo-mon so I can get a hold of you. Watch out for demons, okay?" Kaly gave him a wink and trotted down the gangplank and disappeared into the streets.

Stenstrom slowly walked down to the dock. A familiar person stood there waiting for him. "Hello, Lilly," he said.

"Hello, Bel," she replied, spinning her usual parasol. "I heard you would be in town here in Mercia, and I wanted to see you."

He took her hand and kissed it. "It's been quite a while, Lilly. Where have you been?"

"Here and there. Come on, Bel—take my hand and let's enjoy the afternoon."

Together, they strolled into the city.

"I tell you, Lilly, it was wondrous, wearing Dunk's coat. I know, I know, it's just a coat, but it felt so good wearing it. I felt safe; I felt whole. I felt like I was a part of something."

They were sitting at a café on the water's edge. His Holystone was rumbling constantly, but he saw no demons and felt no particular danger. He could feel his NTHs at his side with fresh cinnabar strikers just in case he needed them—that was a comfort at least.

Lilly finished her lunch. "You young lords and your love of uniforms and pageantry." She gazed at him hard. "You look good in a mask. You have a face for it."

He closed his eyes. "The things I have to do to overcome my mother's efforts. I can't take it off, or else I feel my soul ripping apart. Even ashore I feel it—I'm not safe anywhere I go. Kaly suggested branding the hermelins within into my forehead, but I really didn't want to do that."

"And who is *Kaly*?"

"She's a friend."

"I see." Lilly appeared to flush for a moment. "So, you enjoyed wearing a Fleet coat," she said, reverting to the previous subject.

"I did."

"And you enjoyed it because it made you feel like you were a part of something? You reveled in the comfort of wearing a uniform?"

"I suppose."

"Well, perhaps you might wear something similar—something that looks like a Fleet ensemble, but actually isn't. There's nothing to stop you from doing that, is there?"

Stenstrom finished his lunch. "No, but ..."

"No buts," Lilly said dabbing her lips with her napkin. "Come with me. Let's go shopping."

"Shopping for what?"

"For your uniform, Bel."

Together, they plunged into the lovely city and prowled the many shops lining the streets. Lilly looked him over with a discriminating eye, not unlike his mother's. "I think you shall need a white shirt, a pair of black pants—knee britches if you must, and a new sash. Do you have any particular color in mind?"

"Green is the designated color of a Fleet Paymaster."

"All right, we'll get you a lovely green sash."

The pants and shirts were easy enough. His pants were simply black cotton pantaloons that they bought at a nice tailor shop along with several white shirts. Lilly insisted on a frilly shirt, though Stenstrom resisted at first. She also tried to get him to buy a different pair of boots, but he refused, having a love of his old Tyrol boots.

They moved on to a fine haberdashery. They looked at the assortment of men's hats, concentrating on Vith triangle hats, as they most resembled those worn in the Fleet. Lilly picked him out a large black one, inlaid with silver swirls.

Now, for his coat. That was the hard part. They looked all over, trying to find a coat that was similar to the long, tailed coat worn in the Fleet, but wasn't overly garish or mocking. That was a tall order. All of the tailors they went to had nothing like what he wanted. Too overblown. Too simple. Too dainty. Too modest. Too costume-like. Most of the coats they found that were cut in the Fleet style were for going to the opera, or a night at a ball.

Lilly finally had the answer. She pulled him down a side-street, the fine shops fading to run-down, rusted facilities and steamy, workman-like warehouses. Stenstrom looked around dubiously—what could they possibly find here?

At the end of the street was a large warehouse selling used and damaged goods at a discount to those encumbered with a more meager budget.

"Let's look in there," Lilly said, pulling on him.

Stenstrom didn't want to go in. "What could they possibly have in there, Lilly? It's a thrift store offering nothing but used sundries."

"Oh, come now, what could it hurt? We've had no success at the more prestigious establishments. Sometimes one can find lost or hidden treasures in second-hand stores."

Stenstrom stopped. "I really don't want to, Lilly."

"Please," she cooed, "for me …"

He sighed and took her hand. Together they went in. The warehouse was vast, offering boxed and unboxed articles of clothing, shoes, stockings, undergarments, old pieces of furniture, and the like. None of it was displayed with any regard for presentation or aesthetics; everything was laid out no-frills and functional, nothing more.

They rolled around in the vast aisles, sorting through this and that. The other shoppers in the warehouse were dressed rather poorly, and gave the richly attired Stenstrom and Lilly reproachful looks: what did *they* need in an establishment like this?

Stenstrom half-heartedly looked at the used wares on display. "Shockingly, I'm not seeing anything I like."

"I don't think you're trying."

"May we go?"

Lilly pointed to a corner of the warehouse they hadn't checked yet. "Let's look over there, first. Then we can leave."

They walked to the far side of the warehouse. The items on display there were a bit more expensive than the goods laid out elsewhere and got little attention from the usual shoppers. The boxes laid out on the tables all were stamped: HOBAN. Stenstrom looked into the boxes—Hoban turned out some fine items, and he was mildly impressed by what he saw.

"Bel," Lilly said from behind. "What about this?" He turned around.

Lilly was holding up a long, dark green coat—it was so long it dragged on the floor in front of her. Stenstrom took it from her and held it up. It was a fairly heavy coat made of terlamane, a fine fabric made from the hair of a livestock animal native to Hoban—the finished product mixing the feel of silk with the toughness of wool. The entire surface of the coat was embroidered with twisting ivy, highlighted in silver thread, mixing in lightning bolts and some sort of fruit-like objects. The stiff black collar and cuffs were heavily embroidered in silver and gold. It had silver buttons and silver clips. Centered on both sides of the collar, riveted in place, were the letters "HRN" in gothic, flawless silver.

He stood there holding the coat—it was the loveliest thing he'd ever seen.

"What do you think, Bel—I think it's a wonderful coat."

He continued to gaze at it.

"Try it on, see how it feels."

Stenstrom put the coat on, and it fit almost perfectly. The sleeves were just the right length and the tails were just an inch or two from dragging on the floor. It was almost like it was made just for him.

The terlamane fabric breathed well, so the coat wasn't too hot or too cold on him, and it had numerous pockets sewn into the interior—perfect places to put his Holystones, MARZABLE, his Astral Plane detectors, and other bits of arcane equipment. He imagined a coat like this could serve as a mobile office, housing everything he needed.

"Oh, yes, Bel—this looks wonderful on you—look how handsome. How does it feel?"

"Feels nice."

Lilly backed up a few steps. "Yes, it's elegant and Fleet-worthy, yet not too-overdone as to appear like a costume. From a step or two away, you almost look like an Admiral."

He was sold. He checked around and didn't see any other coats like this HRN one, and bought it as is.

As they left the warehouse, wearing his HRN coat, he felt like a new man. He felt like he was bursting with power.

It was getting late and the *Sandwich* was soon to blast off. Stenstrom and Lilly made their way back to the docks. As they did, Lilly's demeanor seemed to change a little. She looked lost, desperate even. Worse, she looked positively sad. He asked her what was wrong.

"Nothing, I suppose it's getting late and my job is done … for the day. I'm glad we found clothes to your liking."

They arrived at the docks, and Stenstrom gave her a kiss on the hand, as there were many people about.

Lilly's usual cool demeanor completely fell away. She wept bitterly, her mouth pulled back in anguish.

"Lilly, Lilly, what's wrong?"

She looked at him with her tear-streaked face. "I love you, Bel," she said putting her arms around him. "I love you so much. Don't ever let anyone tell you I don't love you. Don't let anyone tell you what I feel isn't genuine."

"I love you too, Lilly. I've been around, I've experienced life, and I've not met your equal. I want you, Lilly. I want to make you my countess, the first of the Belmont-South Tyrol line. I want it now more than ever. I've learned a lot in these two years, I've learned there is no other but you."

She managed a smile. She put her hands on his face. "Then, I've plans to make. I've steps to put into place. I don't know when you'll see me again, Bel, but I promise you will. As I have tried to impress upon you—there's always a way around a challenge if you want something badly enough."

"Lilly, your tone has a certain air of finality. It is frightening me."

She dried her tears and smiled. "Don't be scared, Bel. There's nothing to be scared of."

They kissed one last time and, slowly, Stenstrom mounted the gangplank and walked into the ship.

He turned as the door closed, expecting Lilly to be gone—Wafted away like she normally did, but, she was still standing there on the dock, her hands to her face, her parasol lying on the planks.

Blasting off from Mercia was terribly emotional. Lilly was still standing there, crying as the ship lifted away. Hands on the boat deck glass, he watched Lilly's weeping form quickly fade into a speck and then gone.

He felt such a tide of loss.

Returning to his quarters, he fretted for awhile. Lilly was strange and rather odd toward the end of the day. He thought for a moment that she was going to break it off and cut ties with him for good. He was sure of it, but something had prevented her at the last moment.

He'd parted ways with Lilly many times, but this seemed different. It seemed like the end. He got her locket out and opened it, seeing her smiling, hand-painted face.

There was a knock at his door. "Come in."

The door creaked open and there was Kaly, carrying a few bags from her day in the city. "Hey, Bel, did you have fun today? I almost didn't make it back aboard. I had to run."

He didn't say anything. He stood, grabbed her, and kissed her hard. He spun her around, her bags went flying, and he threw her on the bed, her legs going up in the air as he closed the door.

"Ohhh," she said in a sultry voice as she popped off her shoes and began unbuttoning her pants, *"okay, okay…that's how you want it. Come and take it …"*

He was sick of feeling out of control. His whole life—his mother, Lilly, Lady Miranda, even Alitrix, at every turn there was a woman in his way, tripping him up, confusing him, making him hurt. *Plunging knives into his chest.*

Tonight, just for one night, he was going to take out all his frustrations on a woman, and Kaly, ever eager to try new things, appeared to be more than willing to play along. With the locket open, Lilly watching, he tore into Kaly.

* * * * *

They sat at breakfast the next morning. Stenstrom was wearing his new stuff. "I'm really sorry about last night."

"Why?" Kaly said, smiling. "I thought it was fun—not a side I see of you often, though, we might have to sit out tonight—*I'm a little sore, you know?"*

He gave a short laugh and continued eating his breakfast.

"I like your new clothes," she said looking at him.

"I went shopping with Lilly. She was waiting for me on the docks as we departed the ship."

"I didn't see anybody on the docks with you yesterday."

"How do you mean?"

"I didn't see anybody. I looked around. I thought I saw you walking off with a mannequin or something, and I was thinking 'Hey, if he's going off to have fun with a sex mannequin or something, I want to join in', but I couldn't holo-mon you."

Stenstrom laughed. "That wasn't a mannequin; that was Lilly."

"If you say so." Kaly looked at his clothes. "You look like an Admiral, or something close to it. I've only seen a couple of Admirals—they make me sort of nervous."

"Yes, I found this coat in a second-hand store of all places. Can you believe that—a beautiful coat like this. I wonder what HRN stands for."

"Hoban Royal Navy, that's easy."

Stenstrom was surprised. "HRN? The Hoban Royal Navy? You know it?"

"Yeah—I might be stuck on this old tub, but I'm still a crewman in the Fleet. Everybody joining the Fleet has to pass a Fleet history course right off the bat, and there was a whole chapter on the Hoban Royal Navy. The Fleet *hated* the Hoban Royal Navy."

Stenstrom was curious. "Tell me."

"I think they were a bunch of guys from Hoban, obviously—sort of like you, rich, highly placed. They tried to replace the Fleet around Hoban a few years back—said they could do a better job of protecting Hoban from the Xaphans than the Fleet could. According to the course, they were actually there to protect the Governor of Hoban, as he was an incognito pirate running contraband to the Xaphans and raiding passing ships. I guess they didn't last long. I think they lost the only battle they ever got into with the Xaphans and had to have the Fleet come and rescue them. A lot of them got killed, and some were thrown in jail for gross incompetence. But they wore coats just like that. I'm really not surprised you found that coat in a second-hand store as they're all washed up and outlawed now. Seeing it up-close, it is a really neat-looking coat."

The morning bell tolled.

"Well, there's my cue," Kaly said, standing. "Time to go to the bridge and stare into the little visor for awhile."

She put her tray into the trash and then leaned down and whispered into his ear.

"Hey—I know your lady must have troubled you yesterday somehow. I know you were hurting. I'm glad I could be there to help ... to take your mind off things, you know? You're my friend, Bel—never forget that. If your lady broke your heart, or chose to discard you, she must be crazy. You are a wonderful man, in every way."

"Thanks, Kaly."

She gave him a quick peck on the cheek and headed off to the bridge.

He returned to his office and checked his mailings. There wasn't much—his duties were miniscule at best. He looked up the Hoban Royal Navy on his terminal. As he read, Kaly appeared to have summed up their history quite well: The Governor of Hoban, a Lord Crowe, had gotten into a tiff with the Fleet over a bit of contraband goods that had been seized. Apparently, the

Governor had a little streak of pirate in him, and was enraged that the Fleet had busted up his ring. He then forbade the Fleet from approaching Hoban, instead forming a small navy of old Planet Fall *corvettes* and called it the Hoban Royal Navy. He was quite proud of it at first, and even thought that such a thing would become a trend, each local planet having its own small navy to protect against the Xaphans. Perhaps the Fleet was no longer needed.

The Navy proved to be a disaster. Sloppy standards, dubious morals and motivations, ships in worn out shape and barely space-worthy. The Fleet had to come and save them from breakdowns time and time again. The only battle they ever fought with the Xaphans at Two-Pitch Nebula was a complete rout. The great Xaphan hero, Princess Marilith of Xandarr, was, for once, victorious in battle driving the HRN *corvettes* before her until the Fleet came and covered their retreat.

Soon, red-faced, the Navy was disbanded, and the Governor sought to hide all traces of their existence. He scrapped the ships, threw several officers into prison, and sent the uniforms off to be burned. All trace of the HRN was made to vanish almost overnight.

Not quite everything—this lovely coat, made with care and fine materials, still stood. Stenstrom would wear it with pride.

27

—An Incident at Terrabus—

Stenstrom's mask was feeling rather hot on his face today, and his skin beneath it was getting chaffed and red. He wished he could take it off, but he didn't dare remove it for the clawed hand searching for his soul found him almost instantly without it.

There was a knock on his door. He was sitting behind his desk trying to catch up on some paperwork, but his mask was bothering him too much to get anything done. "Come in," he said, hand on his face trying to adjust the mask into a comfortable position.

The door opened. There stood crewman Forest, one of the Sensing Station crewmen from the bridge. "Bel, you got a moment?"

He looked up from his work. "Sure, Forest. What's up?"

Forest blushed a little. "Can you please come to the bridge with me?"

"Why?"

"It's better if you just come."

The Bridge? "I'm not allowed on or anywhere near the bridge—remember? The boatswain gave me the lecture."

"It'sokay, really. Just for a second. You're not going to get in trouble or anything. The boatswain—he's a dork, you know that."

Stenstrom had no idea why he was being summoned to the bridge—maybe he was in trouble for something. Maybe Dunks wanted to let him in on their secret operation. "All right," he said, feeling a bit of mild excitement despite himself.

He stood up and put his HRN coat on, Forest waiting quietly as he did so. Stenstrom popped his hat on and then followed him through the seedy corridors, his Tyrol boots clunking on the thick, riveted metal flooring, to the *Sandwich's* tiny and rather primitive bridge at the top of the ship. Within, several crewmen sat at their stations. There was no holo-cone or viewing screen on the bridge—just an array of large, head's up infused windows all around, like a cathedral of glass lit up in occasional, computer-generated color. The far wall of the bridge was a solid pane of strong pyro glass, with small panes wrapping around either side trailing just past where the helm and the navigator sat. It was like being in a fishbowl.

The helmsman sat at his chair and looked nervous. So too did the navigator.

Through the windows, Stenstrom could see the ship was nestled in some sort of space-borne junkyard—the murky outside lit up in some sort of blue filter through the windows. There were a number of old corroded relics floating about outside, nudging into each other in the solar tide. There were layers of wrecked ships above as well. It looked like an asteroid field of twisted and collided shipping.

"Where in Creation are we?" he asked, noting the melancholy hulks floating about outside.

"We're in the Kills, Terrabus Field—Xaphan ships. The site of an old battle a couple hundred years back," Kaly said, waving at him from her station.

Stenstrom thought a moment. "Terrabus field—isn't that near Xaphan space?"

"Yeah, Bel, it is."

"What are we doing near Xaphan space? That's not on our route, is it? What's going on here? Where's Dunks?"

"There, there's Dunks," Forest said, pointing.

Lying on the floor, on the far side of the command chair, was Lt. Dunkster, flat on his back, arms splayed out, the tips of his boots pointing toward the glass ceiling of the bridge. Kaly went to his side and took his limp hand. She was wearing her usual pink hair band. Stenstrom went to him and knelt down next to Kaly, Forest following. "What's this? What's wrong with him?"

Kaly cleared her throat. "Well, we're not sure, but we think he's in toxic shock. We think he got hold of a bad dirty courtesan on Bazz and is all tox'ed up with her."

"One of his wives?"

"eh …yeah …"

"It just hit him all of a sudden," Forest added. "Up one moment, down the next."

"He needs a Hospitaler," Stenstrom said.

"We don't have a Hospitaler aboard, Bel. You know that. We, umm, were hoping you could do something for him," Kaly said quietly.

"Me? What do you expect me to do?"

"Kaly tells us you're a sorcerer," Forest blurted out. "She was bragging on your powers the other day, says she's seen you do some remarkable things. We were hoping you could 'magic up' some sort of cure until we can get him to a Hospitaler sanctum. Cabril 17 is not too far. We just need to keep him alive until we get him there."

Stenstrom looked out the windows again and adjusted his mask. The *Sandwich* was not moving; it was stationary within the drifting masses of blasted Xaphan shipping.

"Why are we just sitting here?"

"We have a slight issue and need to sit here for a time. Please, Bel—Kaly told us that you could help any who is in medical distress," Forest said.

Stenstrom shook his head. "Kaly is mistaken."

She looked a little desperate. "But, Bel, I saw you remedy yourself that one time—I helped you."

"You're confusing what addled me with this—this is a totally different thing. My soul was at stake. I hadn't tox'ed up on a dirty courtesan."

Dunks began to convulse. "Please, Bel. Is there anything you can do for him? Anything at all—it couldn't hurt in any case. I know you can do something for him. Please …" Kaly said.

Stenstrom reached out and felt his pulse—his heart was racing. He touched his forehead; it was burning up. "Forest, go get cool water and some towels." Forest got up and ran to the door of the bridge. "Kaly, I need merriander and a spring of rosemary from the hold, okay?"

"Merriander and rosemary," she repeated.

"Go now." Kaly ran out of the bridge.

With the crew watching, Stenstrom spread his fingers and shook his hand. A white Holystone appeared.

"What's that?" the helmsman asked. "What do you have there?"

"Holystone. This should slow his heart rate and stabilize his system a little. But, it's no cure—he needs a Hospitaler with all speed."

He checked Dunks' pulse again, and it began to slow. The Holystone appeared to be working. "Okay, once Kaly returns with the stuff I asked for, he should be stabilized for now. Where's the mate or the boatswain? Come on—we need to get moving."

The helmsman swallowed. "Can't, Belmont … Dunks is just going to have to hope you know what you're doing for the time being, as we have a slight problem."

"Yeah? What is it?"

Stenstrom looked out the windows again—junked out hulks floating about everywhere in a filtered blue tint. He thought he saw something move in the distance.

A warning buzzer went off.

"We have a proximity alert! Vessel moving at 8:52 AM, mark 2:45PM," the navigator said to everybody and nobody at the same time.

"That's our problem, Belmont," the navigator said. "That ship out there."

"What? Why?"

The Com chattered. "We have an incoming message," Lt. Varnay at the Com said. "What do we do?"

"Ignore it," the helm said.

"Play it," Stenstrom said.

The Com ignored the message.

"What is going on here?" Stenstrom asked as Kaly and Forest returned. Stenstrom took the sprigs of merriander and rosemary, bent them in two, and stuck them in Dunk's mouth. He then cooled his forehead with a wet towel.

"Will that stuff work, Bel?" Kaly asked, a little out of breath.

"For the time being, but not for long. Go, back to your station, okay?"

She got up and ran to her visor.

The Com went off again. "It's him again," Varney said. "What do we do?"

"Elder's Balls, ignore him!" the helm barked.

Stenstrom spoke up. "Com, accept the message. Accept it."

The Com sighed and hit the button. A wheezy voice came on through the speakers. "Dunks, where are you?"

Everybody on the bridge looked at each other.

"Dunks, answer me!"

Stenstrom cleared his voice and spoke up. "My good sir, Lt. Dunkster is indisposed."

There was a pause. Then: "I see. Drink a little of that poison he tried to pass off on me, did he?"

"Poison?"

"Yes, your mate and your boatswain, who are now in my lucrative employ, have come clean and told all to me. Tell Dunks he's going to be more than 'indisposed' in a moment once I get my crosshairs on ya'! Selling me ten years worth of cheap Zemuda tinted and scented to pass for Kanan grain spirits is a bad mistake and a crime punishable by death. On second thought, I think I'll tell him… personally. Yes, this is about to get very personal …"

Stenstrom looked around—everybody on the bridge was wide-eyed with fear. "I'm … certain there has been a mistake. I'll inform Lt. Dunkster of your dissatisfaction at once and …"

There was a flash through the windows. Stenstrom saw a hulk in the distance go spinning off, a gassy chemical fire lighting up its dented hull.

"That was a cassagrain attack beam," Kaly, manning her sensing station, whispered.

Stenstrom made a cutting motion across his neck, and Lt. Varnay muted the Com. "Look, I know Dunks is running some sort of enterprise here on the side and, if this Xaphan out there has something to do with it …"

The Helmsman spoke up. "Yeah, and just what do you know about it?"

"Only that most of the ship is involved in one form or another. Out of respect for Kaly, I didn't choose to pursue the matter further. But, I'm but not blind and I'm not stupid either."

"Could have fooled me," the helmsman said.

Stenstrom shot up. "How would you like to join Dunks on the floor? Huh? One more ill word out of you and that's where you'll be, got it?"

The helmsman started to reply, but then silenced himself.

The Navigator pitched in. "Look, Bel—you see our pay. You know we don't make a whole lot manning a wretched frigate, and none of us are society men like you are. I've a wife and four children to tend to. We all have families to support. Have you ever known a day when you didn't know where your next meal was going to come from for lack of money? Have you ever had to watch your little girls go shoeless—what sort of a father can't afford to properly shoe his children? We joined the bloody Fleet to make something of ourselves, and look where we are, stuck on this rusting tub going nowhere.

The captain supplements our purses with the occasional sale of contraband to Xaphans. There's a big market for Kanan spirits in Xaphan space—that good Zenon whiskey they distill using water from the Great Blue Pierce—best water in the universe. That's some high-quality stuff, and the Xaphans have a real thirst for it. They buy up any that they can get for premium prices in silver."

Stenstrom stood there and listened. Kaly looked distressed and fidgety. "All frigates do it, Bel—just a little something to supplement our purses. We're just providing goods that the Xaphans really want and can't legally get, that's all," she said.

"Ok, that's fine—I don't have a problem with that," Stenstrom said. "So what's this guy talking about—Zemuda?"

"Zemuda's a cheap, crappy liquor from Bazz. It's colorless and tasteless, and you can get it by the thousand gallon drum for nothing. With a little tending, Zemuda can be made to look and taste like most anything—Dunks is an artist with it. It's bad for your regularity, and it deals you a rocking hangover—not like the smooth, easy ride you get from the Kanan stuff, but normally, these Xaphan stiffs can't tell the difference."

"At least not until that Jo-Boy, Boatswain Pike, and the mate, decided to turn their coats and rat us out," the helmsman said. "Pike's been wanting in on Dunk's racket for a long time."

Stenstrom thought about it. "So, this fellow out there paid for a certain set of goods and Dunks cheated him? Is that right? So that's the reason for the hidden apothecary in the hold—to chemically alter the smell, tint and taste of your counterfeit spirits?"

Kaly wrung her hands. "Well, Bel, this is business—and when you're in business, that's what you do. Real Kanan grain spirits are too hard to get through League regulators, and just a few small casks are ruinously expensive. The fake stuff Dunks sells is pretty close to real and the Xaphans just love it."

"Except for the mind-wringing hangover and issues pooping afterwards," the Helmsman said.

"Hope you're not too disappointed in us, Bel?" Kaly said.

"You don't have to ask for his approval, Kaly—who is he?" the helmsman said. "Just a cock-balled Paymaster, and a rich one at that."

"He's our mate, and he's my friend," she responded.

"Yeah, well he's not my mate. He's a rich, worthless Paymaster."

"Shut up!" Kaly screamed, anger cracking her voice.

The Helmsman threw her an obscene gesture. "See that's how our last Paymaster bought it. He saw the money Dunks was making and tried to horn in on the racket. He even tried to come up with his own fake brew. Got tox'ed up pretty nasty taste-testing it and the old boy never woke up."

Stenstrom turned to Kaly. She nodded, verifying the story.

He stood there, looking at the people sitting in the bridge and the captain lying on the floor. "It's fine, Kaly. Don't worry about me," he said. "As was just pointed out, I've never been without or had to worry about money. Who am I to judge? Still, I believe that even a Xaphan deserves to be dealt with honestly and—"

There was another flash from outside. Another hulk, a bit closer this time, went spiraling.

"Good Creation!" the navigator cried. "We're going to get blasted into small bits over a load of fake booze!"

The helmsman was a little frantic. "Dunks! Wake your Planet Fall-ass up and get us out of this!"

Stenstrom thought a moment. "Can we give the Xaphan trader what he wants?"

"We don't have any Kanan grain spirits."

"Can we fight?"

"With what? We've got a pair of penny-toots in the fore-quarter, but that's it!" the navigator said.

"Penny-toots? Those are stationary guns, yes?"

"They're only good for clearing out unmoving targets like asteroids."

"Then let's call the Fleet for help."

"The Fleet?" the helmsman said, shocked. "Assuming we survive until they get here, we could all then expect a nice stay in Hagthorpe prison for running contraband to the Xaphans, Zemuda or not."

"Alive and incarcerated is preferable to a free corpse floating, is it not?"

Another blast nearby.

Stenstrom sat down in Dunk's seat. "Com, call the Fleet—when they get here we can make up a story and talk our way out of trouble."

Lt. Varnay hesitated, and then began punching buttons to put the call out.

"What are you doing?" the helmsman barked.

"Saving my skin! I want to live,okay! I'm calling the Fleet. Bel will get us out of trouble."

The helmsman threw his hands up. "Well, we're good and stuffed now!"

Stenstrom looked outside, at the maze of old hulks lit up in the blue filter. "Helm, can we run?"

"That's a Ghome 15 out there—got three times our speed."

"We're going to have to vacate this position and find suitable cover."

Stenstrom stood and walked to the windows and looked out. "I see a craggy mass of junked vessels over yonder and a rather large vessel of some sort behind them—might provide us a wealth of places to hide. I think our ship will fit into those spaces just barely. Helm, let's go there now."

The helmsman looked confused. Another blast. "Go where? What—what's our course?"

Stenstrom pointed. "That way, to my left."

"*To my left?* What does that mean? What orientation? What declination? What speed?"

"Can't we improvise here? This is an emergency."

"No!" the helmsman cried. "We don't make things up on the bridge! Go back to bean counting!"

There was a marked lack of coordination and initiative on the bridge just short of full-blown paralysis. Everybody appeared to know their jobs, but without Dunks screaming orders at them, they were quite powerless and unable to act. They were the proverbial body with its head cut off.

Stenstrom strode up to the helm. "That way!" he yelled pointing to his left. "Go that way!"

Baffled, the Helmsman pressed a few buttons, and the *Sandwich* lazily moved from its hiding spot. A mass of twisted metal moved into the windows. "There, there—tuck into that mass just there!"

"Where?"

"There! Go in there!"

The helmsman saw the space in the wreckage Stenstrom was talking about and slid the *Sandwich* in. Behind, a cassagrain shot blasted the hulk where the ship previously was. The helmsman skillfully backed the ship into the recess.

Through the glass Stenstrom could see the Xaphan ship drift into view. It was a white, somewhat potato-shaped vessel with a flat bottom. He could see the welded outer plates of the hull and its blinking running lights. It was decorated with long red streaks in the shape of lightning bolts painted on the sides of the ship. The engines were housed in cylindrical tubes attached low. It was about twice the size of the *Sandwich*. The Xaphan ship puttered about, rummaging through the ruined ships. Bluish searchlights panned. Stenstrom could see its gun ports were open.

Stenstrom stared at the Xaphan ship. "He doesn't seem to be able to detect us."

"There's too much metal in the vicinity; it's fouling his scanners, no doubt," Kaly said.

A pair of pulsing red beams burst out of the nose of the ship and several wrecks careened away.

"He's going to smoke us out sooner or later," the helmsman said.

Stenstrom went to the windows again. "What's behind us?"

Kaly looked into her sensor. "There's a burned out area, looks to be the remains of a large A-H freighter."

"Is there room for us to maneuver?"

"Yes."

"Let's go further in there. What do we have to lose?"

The helmsman was flustered. "Go in there? I need orientation and declination, AM and PM. I'm sitting here blind. Every button press I make is recorded, and I'll get court-martialed if I damage this vessel! Besides, I'll probably tear the bottom out of the ship!"

Kaly turned to Stenstrom. "*Bel...*" she whispered. "*Come here.*"

He walked over to her sensing station. She put her arm around him, showing him various readouts in her sensor."

"Well, what's this over here?" he asked, pointing.

"That's the ..." she said whispering in reply as they hashed things out.

"I have the coordinates!" Stenstrom said. "Can I send them to you, helm?"

"No!" he said.

"Why not?"

"The helm is isolated on frigates, Belmont. Xaphans in the past have been able to get through our encryption and take over frigates in battle, using our console to control the helm. So, the helm isn't connected. The captain has to tell me what coordinates to set."

Stenstrom gazed into the sensor. "Helm, turn to… 7:30…AM by 2:52PM."

The helmsman looked dubious, but then he slowly began turning switches. The ship spun around slowly, and a vast, dark space within the wreckage came into the windows.

"All right," he said. "7:30AM mark 2:52PM, moving at station keeping—hope you know what you're doing, 'cause I'm going to tell the court-martial that you hijacked the bridge and I was under your orders for fear of my life."

Stenstrom bent down over the sensor. "Now, turn to … 7:45AM by 6:12PM."

The helmsman slowly entered the settings. "Ok," he said.

Stenstrom moved away from the sensor. "Good. Now, stop the ship and turn us around.

The helmsman thought about it for a moment, glanced over at the fallen Lt. Dunkster, then slowly stopped the ship and turned it around. In the distance, the opening that they had just come through could be seen, lit up by occasional weapons flashes. The ship was within the cavernous hold of a Xaphan A-H Cargoer. The *Sandwich* was swallowed up by it, like a goldfish in a large metal bowl.

"Let's wait here a moment," Stenstrom said.

The Com chattered. "Bel, the Fleet has answered our call. MFV *New Faith* is nearby and is proceeding to our location with all speed. She's broadcasting fair warning to all Xaphan vessels not to damage Fleet shipping on pain of retaliation."

"When will she arrive?"

"Advised fifteen minutes! We're lucky she was in the area."

Through the opening beyond, several spotlights shined in through the passages of metal.

"I don't think we've got fifteen minutes, Bel!" Kaly said. "And I don't think he cares about fair warning right now."

Stenstrom thought a moment. "What were those guns you said we had?"

"The what? The pennytoots?"

"Can we get them ready?"

"What for?"

"To buy us time."

The crew looked at each other just before the navigator opened a voice tube and called for the guns to be run out. A minute or two later a reply came. "The pennytoots are ready, Bel, for what that's worth."

Stenstrom went back to the windows and looked around. "Seems to me that, if we set two charges behind us, when they detonate, the Xaphan will believe that we are trying to blast our way out and go to the source of the explosion, thereby leaving the way ahead clear for us to make a fast exit through the wreckage field and out into open space. There, with luck, the *New Faith* should arrive and protect us at that time."

"That's a big gamble, Bel."

"Does anybody have a better idea, and did anybody think to do an honest, under-handed deal with this Xaphan in the first place?"

"But, Bel, we didn't know this guy was a—"

"Shh!" Stenstrom said. "All right. Let's plant two in the aft walls behind us, and, when they go off, let's exit the area in a hurry."

The navigator looked exasperated. "Fine. Don't expect a big explosion or anything." He spoke into the voice tube. "Fire the pennytoots to our aft, will you?"

Stenstrom waited a moment. "Did the weapons fire?"

"Yeah ..."

"Fine, helm, move us back toward the opening and be ready to make a break for it."

The ship began moving. Through the windows, the opening approached. As they neared, there were two feeble explosions coming from the rear of the enclosure. "Were those the weapons?"

"Yeah ... see!" the navigator said. "They stink!"

There was no time to wonder over it. The *Sandwich* came rocketing out of the enclosure through the hole of wreckage.

As they emerged, Stenstrom saw the rear-end of the Xaphan ship disappear around the side of the wrecked ships—his ruse worked, and the way was clear.

"Helm, get us out of this maze, best possible speed!"

"Aye!" the helm said, incredulous that the scheme worked.

Though hardly burning it up, the *Sandwich* clawed its way out of the field of wrecked ships, barely avoiding becoming a wreck themselves. Stenstrom bent down over Kaly's sensor. "Helm, steer 5:22AM by 1:15PM and make for clear space! Best possible speed."

"5:22AM by 1:15PM, Aye!" the helm said.

An explosion came from the Terrabus field and out charged the Xaphan ship. He turned after the *Sandwich*, and his starboard engine caught some wreckage and was fouled with it. He cleared it, squared himself, and came in a hurry, closing the ground with speed.

Stenstrom looked at Kaly's sensor. "Kaly, what does this bit of data here mean?"

"It means he's heating his weapons!"

"Helm, evasive to port!"

The helmsman moved his levers and the ship moved to port. A lance of red energy shot out, passing the ship. The beams panned into them and hit the *Sandwich* in the far starboard side, tremoring the ship.

The Com chattered. "It's him, Bel!" Varnay said. "It's the guy trying to kill us!"

After a moment the Xaphan's voice filled the bridge. "Where do you plan on going, Dunks? You must know you can't outrun me."

"We've called the Fleet—they shall be here any moment!" Stenstrom replied.

"That's a daring move considering you're all a bunch of criminals. We detected your tranmission, but thought it was a ruse. You wouldn't dare bring the Fleet in on this. Who am I speaking to, please?"

"I am Stenstrom, Lord of Belmont."

"Really ... Lord Stenstrom of Belmont? Ah, Boatswain Pike tells me you are the son of Captain Stenstrom of the warbird *Caroline*. Ha! The boatswain tells me he thinks you're a spy sent from the Fleet to bear evidence again Dunks. Is that correct?"

"The reason for my presence here is none of your concern. And, be it known, should you damage or destroy this vessel, the Main Fleet captaincy shall know of it and be none too pleased. I shan't think you'll make it back to Xaphan space in one piece what with the armada of warbirds—my father's included—that shall descend upon this theatre, seeking your worthless hide. Ask Boatswain Pike the truth of that."

The Com was silent for a moment. Then: "Lord Belmont, I have been cheated for years. Should this scandal become generally known, not only will my reputation be ruined, but I could lose my life as well. I simply wanted my spirits—I wanted what I paid for in good silver."

Ahead came a clatter of light, as the huge bulk of the *New Faith* slid into the theatre. The *Sandwich* went to its side like a baby duck to its mother.

✳   ✳   ✳   ✳   ✳

The *Sandwich*'s crew, all sixty of them, stood in the hold of the *New Faith*. The first officer, a tall woman with long, brownish hair, had them all lined up and was dressing them down loudly. In comparison with the dapper Marines and immaculate first officer, the crew from the *Sandwich* were an unshaven, slouching, spotty, and rather motley bunch.

Lt. Dunkster, still holding the Holystone in his limp fingers, was taken to the dispensary on a stretcher.

The *New Faith*'s captain, a tall blued-haired Vith man, stood and watched as the first officer prowled through the ranks.

"The fine Xaphan gentleman trying to kill you, I'm happy to say, has quit the area after a bit of parlay. However, as he departed, he said he was here to purchase contraband liquor from you, and that you cheated him. Is that true?" she demanded to know.

Nobody said anything. Kaly wiped her nose and nervously adjusted her pink hair band. The helmsman held back a belch and scratched himself.

The first officer was irate. "The jig is up here, people!" she said. "We want to know who was running this contraband operation and we want to know now; otherwise, we'll have the lot of you in the brig!"

"Will all of us fit in your brig?" the helmsman said in a smarmy fashion.

"We'll excavate some brand new ones just for you, how about that?"

"I'll excavate something, all right," he said.

The captain strode forward. He was breathing fire. "I'm pleased you are enjoying yourself, sir," he said, towering over the helmsman, the point of his triangle hat bopping him in the forehead. "Yes, I'm told a pending stay at Hagthorpe prison is often cause for merriment. In the meanwhile, you are in my charge and I am permitted to deal you up to 100 lashes whilst you await trial and conviction. Don't think I won't go out of my way to make a career out of you, crewman. Therefore, open your mouth again at your peril—am I understood?"

The helmsman swallowed hard, looked at the wall, and said nothing.

The *Sandwich* crew was now thoroughly quaking in their shoes. The captain stepped back, and the first officer resumed.

"My question remains unanswered!" she yelled. "Who's ready to fess up?"

There was silence.

"I better hear somebody owning up real quick, or we're going to start flaying skin off people's backs!"

Stenstrom stepped forward. "It was me, Lieutenant."

She strode up to Stenstrom and looked him over, clearly baffled by his mask and his coat. She was a tall lady, but Stenstrom was a fair amount taller. She looked up at him, the point of her triangle hat nearly knocking into his. "I see. What is your name please, Sir?"

"Stenstrom, Lord of Belmont."

The captain seemed to take a bit of exception. He stepped forward and addressed Stenstrom. "Belmont? As in Captain Stenstrom, Lord of Belmont? Of the *Caroline*?"

"My father, Sir," Stenstrom replied.

The captain rubbed his chin. "Good man—great man. I've had the pleasure of sailing at his side many times. Is he aware that his son is conducting a criminal enterprise at sea?"

"I don't believe so, Sir."

"Very well, and what is your role aboard the *Sandwich*, other than running contraband?"

"I'm the Paymaster, Sir."

The captain was startled. "Really?"

"Yes, Sir. In this criminal matter, I ran, planned, and financed the whole of the operation. It was my doing alone—the crew had nothing to do with it."

"Pure as the driven, huh, this lot?" the first officer said.

"Indeed. In fact I can say the crew vigorously voiced their objections; however, I forced them to accede to my whims."

"Yeah?" the first officer said. "How'd you manage that all by yourself?"

"With fist and NTH, I terrorized this lot and haunted the ship, though they remained unblemished."

The first officer laughed. "Wow—we normally don't see such sterling character coming from frigate crews. This is inspirational."

"It's the truth, Lt. This is all my doing and my fault."

The captain looked him over again. "I see." He turned to the rest of the crew. "Does anyone here have anything else to add? This man is about to go to the brig for the crime of running contraband goods to the enemy. He's about to face any number of charges that could lead to his lengthy internment at Hagthorpe Prison, and I am seriously considering putting him to the lash as well for imposing his malign will upon your stainless souls. So, with that in mind, does anyone have anything to say?"

The crew fidgeted about a little, but said nothing. "Very well," he said turning to a Marine. "Take this man to the brig."

The Marine came forward and clapped Stenstrom in irons. He reached out to pull Stenstrom's mask off.

"No!" Kaly shouted. "He needs his mask! Don't you touch it!"

The Marine looked back at the captain, who nodded and said, "Let him have his mask."

He then led him away.

As Stenstrom was marched out, he passed the bridge crew all lined up in a row. Kaly looked up, her face red and streaked with tears.

"... *thanks, Bel* ..." she choked out as he passed.

Though he was manacled, he raised a shackle-free hand and wiped the tears off her cheek. "It's all right, Kaly. I'll be all right."

The Marine was shocked—clearly he couldn't understand how Stenstrom had gotten out of his irons. He refastened them and marched him through.

The other crewmen responded quietly as he passed. "Bel ... Bel ... Belmont... " they said.

"That's our mate!" somebody said.

"Better treat our mate right!" came another.

Though he was being lead away to the brig and a possible session with the lash, Stenstrom reflected on what had just happened. He had led his ship in battle and had gotten his mates out safe and sound. And he had the guts to stand for them. Now they sang his name, albeit quietly, as he passed.

"*Bel ... Belmont* ..."

The joy he felt as he passed by. So this is what it feels like ...

✶　✶　✶　✶　✶

A day later, Stenstrom was fetched from the brig and led into the captain's office. What a difference from the *Sandwich*: clean carpeting, lush paneling, and shining brass. Waiting for him there was the captain, his first officer, and a smallish beautiful woman with red hair, wearing a blue gown. She had a strange mark around her right eye.

Stenstrom stood there as the Marine removed his irons.

The captain looked up at him. "Paymaster Stenstrom, I believe you've already met my first officer."

"The name's Kilos," she said sitting there, all arms and legs.

"And," the captain continued, "May I introduce my countess, Sygillis of Blanchefort."

"Great Countess," Stenstrom said, bowing to her, and she nodded in a courtly way.

"Finally, I am Captain Davage, Lord of Blanchefort."

"I believe I've heard my father mention your name, sir, as an esteemed colleague," Stenstrom replied.

Davage offered Stenstrom a chair, which he accepted.

"Sir," Stenstrom said, "before we begin, may I ask how is Lt. Dunkster?"

"He's fine. Just fine. My Hospitaler informs me he was tox'ed up rather severely, but he's in weather shape now. He had some plants in his mouth and an odd ball in his hand with unique chemical properties. My Hospitaler said those items helped calm his system and prolonged his chances of survival."

"I see," Stenstrom replied.

The first officer chimed in. "Yeah, a cautionary tale, you see—mixing a potent strain of The Weed with a bellyful of Zemuda—not good for the body at all. It hits you all of a sudden—you're fine one minute and flat on your back the next."

"Which brings me to it, sir," Davage said. "I'm in quite the situation, aren't I? You claim to be the ringleader and unchallenged potentate of a contraband outfit aboard the frigate *Sandwich*, is that right? Am I correct?"

"Yes, Sir."

"Such operations can be rather profitable. I'm certain you had to twist the crew's arms to get them to cooperate, yes?"

"Indeed, Sir."

"Yet, according to our records, you have only been aboard the *Sandwich* for a year, while, at the same time, I have here a rather extensive dossier on the activities of the ship's captain, Lt. Dunkster." He thumbed through a thick file on his desk. "Let's see ... originally from Planet Fall, a lord of the House of Carew. Long suspected of bootlegging, piracy, counterfeiting, and polygamy, with over thirty-four dirty courtesans in varying degrees of disrepair belonging to his harem—which, might I say, is an offense punishable by death on Planet Fall."

"He told me he only had fourteen wives."

"Yes, we'll add the inability to perform simple arithmetic to his list of crimes. He has thirty-four, not counting the ones who have passed away on him."

The countess spoke up in a regal voice. "And that is not all, Sir. His various wives are suspected of being ex-members of the Erynes, a rather potent and feared band of dirty courtesans based on Planet Fall by way of Carina 7. Not a sedate bunch, they. Again, Lt. Dunkster appears to enjoy a dangerous lifestyle."

Stenstrom thought about Christiana on Planet Fall: a little weather-beaten, but unbroken, still beautiful, and a loving woman worthy of honor, with her son's merit trophy sitting on her mantle. Christiana was not a dangerous woman.

"Additionally," the captain added, "the fine Xaphan gentleman who was spoiling to cassagrain you into small bits says that he's been dealing in contraband with Lt. Dunkster for years. As we escorted him back to Xaphan space, he sang like a lark. Painted quite a lurid picture for us."

"Sir, I ..."

"Let's not mince words, shall we? We know all about Fleet frigates, and the little operations they often carry on. Of course, there are all sorts of rules and punishments regarding such a thing; however, let's be practical. We're out here in the Kills, far away from Fleet ballrooms and all the niceties that go along with that. We both know the crew of a frigate barely make enough to subsist—and that is truly a shame, for those are good people on those tiny ships, doing a rancid job that must be done. Other captains may feel differently, but I frankly do not care what side enterprises go on aboard frigates, as long as the merchandise being passed isn't harmful. Pushing dangerous things that have no good use, such as Remax and Magga-tabs is one thing, but selling a reputable product that is in demand is another. Xaphans might be conniving and evil, but they do enjoy a fine grain spirit as well as the next person."

Lt. Kilos objected. "Yeah, but Dav, they were trying to pass off Zemuda as Kanan grain spirits."

"Yes, and I imagine that's what got our fine Lt. Dunkster into trouble. He was probably taste-testing his batch of fake spirits after having had at one of his ex-Erynes wives, apparently while soaked in The Weed. A poor combination to be sure. Well, no harm done, I suppose."

"No harm done? Have you ever tried to survive a hangover from a night of Zemuda? And don't even try to go to the bathroom afterwards—you'll be in there all day," Kilos said.

The countess, who was sitting rather properly, laughed a little.

"Thank you, Ki, we get the picture."

Stenstrom stirred. "Sir, you mentioned that the lash might be in the offing for ..."

"Paymaster, I've never lashed a soul aboard my ship, and I don't intend to start now. Sounds impressive though, doesn't it?"

Stenstrom was relieved.

The captain continued. "I am most interested in you, Sir. Are you still purporting to be the sole mastermind behind this Zemuda-counterfeiting ring aboard the *Sandwich,* when I have reams of evidence to the contrary?"

"Yes, Sir."

Davage held up a small report. "Such loyalty—I value that. I have here a signed confession from your fellow mates. Apparently, they had an attack of conscience over the night and claim that you had nothing to do with the operation. Additionally, they claim it was under your leadership that they survived the affair with the Xaphan scalawag in the first place, after the captain was incapacitated."

"Sir, what's to be done with my mates?"

"Nothing. I've dropped the charges, and they've already set sail—off to who knows where. They were hoping you would be joining them; a . . . Crewman Kaly did not want to leave without you—made quite a fuss, I'm told, but I'm not quite done with you, am I?"

They sat there in silence for a bit. "I had a little talk with Lt. Dunkster as he convalesced in the dispensary. I informed him that, if he is purporting to sell Kanan grain spirits to the Xaphans, then that is exactly what he better be selling. I was most strenuous about it and I think he got the point. I can't fault the Xaphans for wanting Kanan grain spirits—it is a very lovely beverage."

"It's the best, Dav—come Saluting Day, that's all I drink," Lt. Kilos said.

Countess Sygillis smiled. "I must admit, I do enjoy a touch of it mixed together with …"

"No mixing, Syg," Kilos cried. "You'll ruin it with girly mixers and flavorings and little accessories that are meaningless. It's straight or nothing!"

Davage looked at Kilos. "Well, I suppose straight with a bit of ice …"

"No ice, Dav. Lukewarm, or, if you must, warm it up a little under your armpit, and then kill it."

"You are a bizarre person, Ki," Countess Sygillis said.

The first officer turned to Stenstrom. "So what's with the mask?" she asked. "What's the matter? You scarred under there?"

Stenstrom stirred, but didn't say anything.

"Yes, you were quite the picture, weren't you—standing there in the hold all shackled up," the captain said. "An apparently handsome fellow in a Hoban Royal Navy coat and a mask to boot. I haven't seen one of those coats in quite some time. And, I must say, you standing up for your mates was probably the bravest act ever performed while wearing a Hoban Royal Navy coat. That coat, that mask, like a vigilant right out of a penny-vid. I've not quite seen such a thing … ever, and I've certainly been around."

"I wear the coat because someone dear to me picked it out," Stenstrom said. "Because I once had hopes of joining the Fleet, and this is as close to wearing a uniform as I'll ever get."

"Yes, about that. Your father is Captain Stenstrom, an esteemed warbird commander. With such a father, your place in the Fleet is assured, why didn't you simply join? The three of us were bandying that topic about yesterday at dinner, and couldn't come up with a suitable reason. Perhaps you'll care to explain."

"It's complicated, sir. I really do not wish to go into it."

"Well, perhaps someday you'll feel at ease to reveal your reasoning."

Countess Blanchefort spoke. "Your mother is the Lady Jubilee, formerly of Tyrol is that correct?"

"Yes, Great Countess."

"I know of her—a stern matriarch and, purportedly, a difficult personality to get along with."

"I have been told that on occasion, yes."

"I understand she has been under Wirguild for over a hundred years."

"Yes, though the Wirguild had been revoked."

"Yes, for violation of terms. We also understand that you have sorcerous abilities, is that true?" the countess asked.

"Yes, Great Countess, that is true. My mother taught me."

"May we see? We do not wish to gawk; however, we are truly fascinated."

Stenstrom leaned forward and showed them his empty hands.

He shook them. Six silver daggers appeared between his fingers.

The captain, the first officer, and the countess all gasped.

"These daggers are the MARZABLE, the LosCapricos weapon of my mother's house."

The captain was truly amazed. "You had those on you the whole time? We disarmed you prior to sending you to the brig."

"With the MARZABLE, one can never be disarmed."

"And these ... MARZABLE are the LosCapricos weapons of House Tyrol, is that right?"

"Yes, Sir."

The captain thought a moment. "I don't think we have a MARZABLE in our collection, Syg. Paymaster, we have a hall in our castle where we've collected what we thought was the complete family of LosCapricos weapons from all over the League and proudly display them. We do not have a MARZABLE."

"Yeah, you do, Dav," Kilos said. "It's by the ..."

"No, Ki," he replied. "We don't. Paymaster, I would be greatly interested in purchasing one from you. It doesn't have to be a functioning example—it can be a mock-up. I would love to add a bit of your mother's heritage to a place of honor at our home where it may be properly appreciated."

Stenstrom shook his hand, and they disappeared. He shook it again, and one dagger appeared, shiny and silver. "Sir, for your fair-handed treatment of my mates, and for your understanding of the Xaphan trader's position ..."

Stenstrom placed the dagger on the desk and slid it toward him. "I offer it to you as a gift."

Captain Davage took the dagger and looked at it with wonder. He then opened his desk drawer and pulled the NTHs out and placed them on the desktop. "I believe these belong to you. These I have on my wall. Remarkable weapons."

Stenstrom picked them up and returned them to his sash. "Thank you, sir. So, may I ask, what is to be done with me?"

"That is an interesting question. What shall we do with you? Have you ever been aboard a *Triumph-class* vessel?"

"No, sir."

"We have over a thousand souls aboard: officers, crewmen, a smattering of civilians, and a changeable number of Sisters; they come and go as they will. This is a big ship, a complex ship, and, in order for it to function, I have to know that I may count on every soul aboard to do their duty, to be their best. There are no unneeded souls aboard my ship. All have worth; all have value. All are people of quality, from top to bottom. You, Sir, you were willing to give yourself up for your mates after I had promised prison and the lash. As an eye-opener and attention-getter, threat of the lash has no peer, and I saw how scared your mates were. You saw it too, and you took it upon yourself to bear the brunt of our wrath. I'm certain that you, with your family name and Belmont fortune, could have bought your way out of any troubles that might have been pending; however, such a thing is inconvenient, troubling, time-consuming, embarrassing— the list goes on. You jumped in front of your mates without fear or hesitation. Your actions say a lot about you, and, though I don't know you personally as of yet, I know your father, and I see him in you. I find favor with your character. You sit there in a mask and a Hoban Royal Navy coat, and odd sight to be sure. All the same, if those accessories empower you to be yourself, then they are well-served and most welcome."

"What are you trying to say, Sir?"

"I'm saying that Paymaster Milke, my Paymaster of old, is soon to retire. When he does, I would like you to replace him."

"Me?"

"We believe you would make a fine addition to our family aboard the *New Faith*—there is certainly no shortage of characters here," Countess Sygillis said.

"We mix it up a lot," Kilos said. "Get into it with the Xaphans all the time. Somehow, I think you'd like that."

They talked for a bit more, Stenstrom soon warming to these people.

28

—A Regretful Competition—

A few days later, the *New Faith* dropped Stenstrom off in Bern, where he took up residence in the IBBAANA apartments. There he caught up with Lady Alitrix, and she marveled at his attire and his stories. He was glad to hear she'd moved on, found a good man with whom she could be happy.

He also sent word to Kaly, who was frantic. She was certain he'd been lashed raw and thrown in prison. He told her what had happened, and she was overjoyed—though she was also very upset that he wasn't to be returning to the ship. He met up with her when the *Sandwich* arrived in Mercia again, and he was hailed as a hero by the crew. He and Kaly also shared each other's bed a few more times—"one for the road," as she said. He was going to miss Kaly—she was a good friend.

He also wrote to Lilly to share his good fortune. Lilly was silent. He received no reply.

As he waited in Bern, Stenstrom's Com chirped.

It was his sister Lyra. "Hello, Bel," she said.

"Lyra! This is a great surprise." It had been a long time since he'd last seen her. She wore a university pin on the shoulder of her gown.

She seemed sad. "Bel ... you need to come home."

"Oh, Lyra, you're starting to sound like Mother. What is it this time?"

"Bel, Mother's dead."

He sat there and tried to comprehend. "What? How? It can't be ..."

"Mother was old, Bel. It was just her time. I think she knew it was coming. She asked us all to come home. I think she wanted to see us all one last time."

He thought about that for a moment. He hadn't come home. He did what she asked. He resisted.

"We are all lingering here, to hold vigil with Father and celebrate her memory. You need to come home, Bel. We need you here—I need you."

"Yes, Lyra, yes. I'm coming at once."

$$\ast \quad \ast \quad \ast \quad \ast \quad \ast$$

The four hour trip to Tyrol on the large liner was guilt-ridden and phantasm-filled. His mind was ablaze.

I knew something was wrong, I knew it. Why didn't I come home?

His mother's voice rang in his ear: *I told you to play the game, Bel. To the very end, I played the game. There're no give-backs.*

The Black Maidens, the Soul Devourers ... creatures in the mirror and the stain on his soul—Mother was playing the game.

Why didn't she tell me?

As he waited for the liner to come in from Bern port, he wondered at the lack of Black Maidens—they were crawling after him previously, but now there were none; he even took off his bolabung. Nothing. Now that he wanted one to zap him home straight away, there were none.

He thought about finding a quiet spot and summoning a Black Maiden or two. The bad thing was he was terrible at it. The summoning was quite hard despite the fact Mother made it look rather easy—even Lyra wasn't very skilled at it. Virginia was quite adept. Even if he could summon one, it wouldn't do any good. They weren't a taxi service—"take me here, take me there"—they would send him back to the place where they'd been summoned, period.

So he waited for the liner and felt the pounding throb of guilt seep into his mind.

He wondered about all the usual things. Did Mother know how much he loved her? Did Mother know how grateful he was for all she'd taught him? The recriminations could go on and on.

Surrounded by ghosts and pointed fingers, he drifted off to sleep as the liner lifted off and headed east.

SNAP!!

The old dream again. The sand pit, the afternoon sun, and the stars shining in broad daylight.

This time, the dream was different. This time, all twenty nine of his sisters and his father were there, watching him sailing through the air.

He landed in the sand. Something lurched out of it.

Everything went black, just like always.

"Open your eyes, Bel," he heard a voice say.

He opened them, and there was his mother, leaning over him, her swoop of Pewterlock hair shining in the sun.

"What's bothering you?" she asked.

"You died."

"What's so strange about that? I was two hundred and fifty years old. How old do you wish I get?"

"Why didn't you tell me?"

"Because I told you to resist me. Telling you I was dying would have been cheating."

"Mother, I wasn't there when you died."

"No, but you were there all the other times. You were in your crib every morning, snoring away—how I loved to watch you sleep. You were there in the manor, filling the halls with your laughter. You were there at the dining table, sitting right where I could see you. You were a good friend to your sisters, and a good son to your mother. I'm glad you weren't there, Bel. I'm glad your last memory of me wasn't one of weakness, of me on my deathbed. Remember me as I was, as a strong woman and a proud mother. Perhaps you'll tell my grandchildren someday of their old grandmother, and let them know she wasn't all bad."

The dream faded.

He heard one final thing. "I didn't send the Soul Devourers after you. Why would I do that to my beloved son? Farewell ..."

✱   ✱   ✱   ✱   ✱

He stood there in the yard with his hat in hand. Mother's new tombstone was there, odd and big. He was wearing his HRN coat and his mask, which he still could not take off—Mother's spell holding even in death. Lyra stood next to him.

He'd been all through the manor. Mother's bed was fresh and made—Mother wasn't there. He'd been to the dining room where Mother held court for all those years, and the sitting rooms and the libraries she once haunted—no Mother.

Here she was, out in the yard under her gravestone. She would never again sleep in her bed and terrorize his sisters in the dining room, and she would tell no more gossip in the sitting rooms.

Mother was dead.

Crushed, unable to face the moment, he dropped his hat and fell to his knees in the new dirt of her grave.

He felt like he did when he was a child: he wanted his mother. He wanted to claw his way into the dirt and pull her out and shake her awake.

Lady Jubilee could not be dead. Death could be no match for her.

Mother, wake up! Wake up!

"Did you see her, Lyra, at the end?" he asked.

"Yes."

"Did she wonder where I was?"

"She wanted me to tell you it was all right. She understood. She wanted me to tell you that she was proud of you—of the man you've become."

He glanced down at his coat and felt the fabric of his mask, suddenly feeling very silly. "Yes. And just look at me ... What am I?"

Lyra embraced her brother. "You are who you are, Bel. I think if Mother had given you every freedom, if she hadn't plunged the knife into your chest, you still would have ended up with a coat and a mask. Perhaps the fabric might have been a different shade, perhaps the mask less prominent, but they still would have been there. Mother was very proud of the man you became. She loved her son."

Lyra joined him in the dirt. "Look at me and the costume I wear—this gown . . . Is my costume so different from yours? You followed your heart, didn't let your dreams die, and ended up in the stars like you always wanted. Coat and mask—you are what you wanted to be."

Stenstrom smiled and wiped his face. "Virginia's wedding. The planning is not finished, I'm told."

"I'm going to help her plan it, and so will Lucile. Though, a wedding at this time just seems…"

"It seems perfect to me," Stenstrom said. "Life goes on at our household—just as Mother would have wanted it. Her children's lives go on. I think I'm going to stay for awhile, until I ship out again. I'd like to help plan my sister's wedding."

"She'll be very glad to hear that. I'm glad too, Bel—maybe it will be like old times. Perhaps later, we can go to the sand pit and wrestle like we used to."

He laughed. "Sure—I'll beat you down now just like I did back then."

"That's not how I remember it, sandface."

He looked around: the hills, the manor, the Merian ruins—home, yet no longer familiar, no longer what it was without Mother's presence. He raised his hand and shook it, producing three MARZABLEs.

"Here's to our mother, and the richness she left to us," he said.

Lyra shook her hand, producing the same. "Here's to Lady Jubilee, the woman who watched over us. The woman who loved us," she said.

They embraced, the shadows of the afternoon growing long.

Three months later, he became the Paymaster of the *New Faith*.

Part 3

The Demon That Came For His Soul

1

─Missing─

The *Seeker* limped through open space, its progress painfully slow. They had managed, just barely, to get the *Seeker* going fast enough to break Kana's orbit, leaving the inviting blue ball with all its safety and comfort behind. They were flying the ship backwards, as the improvised engine of the *Westminster* was located in a forward-facing bay. Stenstrom, A-Ram, and Taara stayed mostly on the bridge. That's where they had lights and a bit of fresh portable air—the Macon setup, powered on, and happily spewed condensed oxygen. In such a condition, the bridge was halfway livable.

They had completed several burns, using nothing but dead reckoning as their AM/PM compasses were off-line.

Taara's MOLLY'ed smarts were a godsend, and, if not for her and A-Ram's MOLLY, they'd still be plummeting into Kana's atmosphere.

She was still at it, putting her soul more at risk with every use. "We'll keep Kana in the window for a few more hours, then, at the Mersy ice swarm, we'll bank to 2:30PM, do a long burn with the *Westminster,* and make a bee-line for Onaris, riding Druries Belt the whole way. We'll course correct again once we're there, use its gravity to pick up some speed, and then it's on to Bazz for the final push."

Taara patted the golden chain at her neck, she gazed with wonder at the pages of pages of calculations she'd made on scavenged paper. "This thing is great, A-Ram! You're going to have to fight me to get this back. I love this!"

"What about the hoard of demons you're going to have after you? You've generated quite a bill that your soul shall have to pay."

"Screw `em!"

Stenstrom was unsure. "Taara, you're positive you know where we're headed?"

"Well, come see for yourself."

They went in his office and looked out the windows. Taara had constructed a crude sextant-like device out of metal struts. She picked it up, aimed, and pointed to a large, whitish star hanging just starboard beyond the silhouette of the *Seeker*'s cranked wing. "That big whitish-blue star is Nu Torriander, *Ole Scrub,* as we call it—that's Onaris' and Bazz's star. Now, that smaller white star hanging off Ole Scrub's ear, that's *Lil Whiteface,* Nu Torriander's dwarf companion star—that's what freakin' gives us scorching hot summers on Bazz. Damn thing."

Stenstrom looked at Ole Scrub bright in the window. "Doesn't even look like it's moving, does it?"

"Nope," she said still staring through her sextant, "but it is, slowly but surely. Soon, we'll be seeing Druries Belt. It's just a big, long cloud of glowing gas they use to use as a navigational aid back in the day."

Taara laid the sextant down, stretched and gave a long yawn. "Wow, I'm bushed. It's been a busy two days."

"I'm feeling pretty used up myself. Here, you can have my office, Taara. Stretch out and get some sleep."

He went back out onto the bridge, Taara following him. "I'm fine. I don't need a separate room—I never had one in the Marines, so I really don't need one now." She went to her favorite spot at the Missive's panel and removed her coat and her boots. She balled her coat up into a pillow and plunked down into the chair, feet up. "Ahh, this isn't bad."

Feeling dead himself, Stenstrom flopped down into his chair. "A-Ram, why don't you lock the helm and get a little sleep as well. We're on-course, right?"

"Yes, according to the last dead reckoning Taara made, we're on course. We shouldn't need a course correction for another twenty hours. I've got the helm's alarm set. According to the charts, we're heading into the wastelands between the stars. The chart has a bunch of vague references to artifacts coming up."

"What are those?" Stenstrom asked.

Taara chimed in, her voice groggy. "Ice, dust, gas . . . just 'stuff' floating around. Our next burn, that's an important one," she mumbled, settling into sleep. "Nice long five minute burn, we miss it, we'll go off into the Wildlands on the other side of Druries Belt. Bad things happen off in the Wildlands. That's what we say on Bazz."

"Oh please. We won't miss it," A-Ram replied. "I've got the alarm set."

He locked the helm and stepped down into the bridge, finding a comfortable spot near the navigator's missing seat. A-Ram recited a short prayer and curled up on the floor. "Night, Bel," he said wiggling around.

Nearby, Taara was already out, her little chest rising and falling, accompanied by a bit of snoring.

"Good dreams," Stenstrom replied. As he watched the two of them sleep, he drew his NTHs and laid them on his lap. He felt like he'd known these two his entire life and he wasn't going to allow anything to happen to them.

Taara snored a little more, and A-Ram twitched. The Macon blew fresh air, and every so often, a light blinked on the various consoles; other than that the ship was quiet. Stenstrom got out of his seat and set up his various bits of arcane protections: his silver candlesticks, pans, and various Holystones scattered about meant to warn him of danger. They were silent.

After a time he allowed his mind to wander and his eyes to grow heavy. He was tired too. Soon, he slept.

✳   ✳   ✳   ✳   ✳

He was pulled out of his sleep by an alarm ticking steadily. He looked around. The alarm was coming from the helm.

"A-Ram, I think your alarm's going off," he said, trying to clear the sleep out of his eyes. He stretched and settled back into sleep.

The alarm dug a galling trench in his thoughts and woke him up.

"Didn't you say the alarm was set for twenty hours hence?" He opened his eyes. "There's no way we slept for that long. Right?"

No answer. The alarm continued to blare.

Stenstrom stood and stretched.

"A-Ram, kill that thing, would you please?"

A-Ram wasn't where he was when Stenstrom had fallen asleep. The floor by the Navigator's position was empty.

The Missive's chair was also empty. Taara was missing too. Her Marine coat and her boots were there—but no Taara.

He was alone on the bridge.

"A-Ram! Taara!" he shouted.

No answer.

He went into his office, seeing the diorama of stars against the gigantic, blackened silhouette and cranked wings of the *Seeker*.

Nobody was there.

He saw a light snap on far away in the rear section of the ship near the wing, then it went out.

2

—Haunted—

Anger and frustration surged through him as he stood alone on the bridge. What had happened? Had A-Ram's "demon" come for Taara at last, and taken A-Ram in the process, somewhere in the middle of twenty hours of sleep? And what of the bridge, the Astral Plane? Perhaps whoever had trapped the bridge had returned.

Blast! He was supposed to protect them. They trusted him and look what he'd done—fallen asleep, and not just for a few hours, but for nearly a day! And, furthermore, they needed to do a course correction and burn, change the angle of the ship; otherwise, they'd soar off course: rudderless into the Wildlands Taara had called it, an empty, lonely stretch of space best left far behind.

Space? What a poor captain he was. Space was a term for scholars and astronomers. Fleet captains called the open stretches between the stars "The Sea." As Captain Davage would have put it, the Wilderness was a patch of "bad sea," small, insignificant, passed over in the blink of an eye.

Of course, stuck in his dead ship flying backwards, this patch of 'bad sea" was an unending ocean. He turned back and stared at the lonely helm wheel locked in place. Without A-Ram standing there, or without Captain Davage, the helm seemed to him an alien and incomprehensible thing.

The alarm blared.

It was time to alter course and burn the *Westminster's* engines. He had no idea how to accomplish either task.

He checked the arcane detectors he'd set up. They were still in place. Whatever had entered the bridge and taken them had overcome several layers of arcane protection: his Holystones and bolabungs and his silver talismans.

He went to the lift and cranked open the doors. Darkness from the empty shaft filtered into the lit-up comfort of the bridge. As usual, he heard strange noises and a general feeling of dread bubble up from the bowels of the ship.

And, somewhere out there, in all of that, were Taara and A-Ram, his friends. He couldn't delay; he had to rescue them.

Forget the ship, forget the burn, their safe return was all that mattered.

He should have never brought them here.

He waved his hands and produced a small silver chest. Opening it, inside he found three oily Holystones with a shimmering, chromatic surface. These Chromatic Holystones were adept at locking onto specific people and zeroing in on them, the fun he and his sisters Lyra and Virginia used to have with them, hiding in the Manor grounds and then being discovered, the excitement, the laughter in the afternoon sun.

The Chromatics were difficult to make and expensive and they only worked for a short time, but they should help him locate Taara and A-Ram. He grabbed Taara's left boot and dropped one of the Chromatic Holystones down into it. The Holystone needed a few minutes, to "soak up" Taara's essence. He took advantage of the time. He checked his NTHs, replaced the cinabarr strikers, and gave them the general onceover. The strikers were locked into place and sound, the hammers oiled and smooth, they should be ready to fire. He cocked the hammers and put two shots through the near wall of the bridge. The shots were nice and bright, emerald green just like they should be. So beautiful to look at and so dangerous as well. They passed through the wall without damaging it and continued on unseen until they dissipated.

He sashed them. He checked his HRN:

MARZABLES: ready.

Holystones: fully kitted out, greens, reds, blues, the works. He was ready to go.

He shook his hands and there, gleaming, was his locket with Lilly's face hiding within; the demure smile, the hopeful blue eyes. He'd fantasized about bringing her aboard someday, giving her the grand tour of his amazing ship, arm-in-arm—*his scuttled, haunted, and contaminated ship.*

He'd give anything to see her again, to give him courage.

He placed the locket back in his HRN and moved Taara's boot around, hearing the Chromatic Holystone rattle around inside like a marble. Enough time should have passed, and he dumped it out onto the floor. The oily surface of the Chromatic had dried up turning into a dirty-looking brown. Now, the Chromatic should point the way toward Taara for the next hour or so.

It lay there on the floor next to her boot doing nothing. It had to work. It just had to. He leaned down over it. "Don't mess this up," he said and gave it a slight tap. The Holystone began rolling, picking up speed. It headed toward the lift at a quickening pace. He picked it up and allowed it to settle into his palm.

Time to go.

He steeled himself and plunged into the low-grav dark beginning the perilous climb down the groaning, sound-filled lift shaft.

The shaft was rotten and noisy; groans, creaks, unidentifiable titterings and, other, softer sounds lurked behind the louder noises.

So far, the *Seeker* had been, except for the bridge, a groaning mess haunted with shadows and twisting movements of the night that they'd rather avoid if they could. Stenstrom had tried to ignore it at first, but the sounds he heard coming from the bowels of the ship couldn't be explained as simply the aches and pains of an old, silent ship torquing through space. His old ship, the *Sandwich,* was also a noisy, groaning vessel ready to sink in open space, but it never made eerie sounds like what the *Seeker* was doing. The *Sandwich* never formed words and made dire sentences.

As he made the climb down the shaft, Stenstrom tried not to listen, but he could hear, plain as day: "....beeeeeeellllllmontttt.... wheeeeere's yooourrrrrrmooooooothherrrrrr beeeeeeeellmmontttttt...."

He looked up at the open door to the bridge with its yellow cone of light pooling out into the shaft—it was a comforting sight.

He had to concentrate; he had a job to do. He checked the Holystone. He felt it tugging. A few more levels down.

He continued on, trying to ignore the sounds.

"... *Belmont!* ... *Your mother died alone* ..." a voice whispered in his ear with startling clarity.

The things haunting the ship were getting personal. He closed his eyes. "My mother died surrounded by her husband and her children, all except one."

His mother's death, and his not being at her side, haunted him to the present. It was a place in his thoughts he tried to avoid—the guilt and recriminations. The voices brought her loss back to him fully, and the evil lurking in the shaft seemed to know that.

"Where was her son?"

"Doing what she asked me to do. My mother is at peace."

He had to say it to himself several times.

"My mother is at peace. My mother is at peace."

The insufferable noises dogged him all the way down to Deck 7. The Holystone "knocked," indicating he was approximately level with Taara's position. He pried the door open, and plunged into the dark. The shadows and noises were even more pronounced in the corridor than they had been in the lift shaft. The air was cold and stale.

The thought of Lilly, bright and pink and full of light, flashed across his mind. This dark abyss was certainly no place she belonged.

He shook open a yellow Holystone for light and instantly dropped it in shock.

Four towering figures lit up in the Holystone's glow standing not three feet away. Four pairs of dark eyes boring into him. He drew his NTHs.

When he looked back up, the four figures were gone; just the great darkened cavern of the deck lay ahead stretching out into the gloom. He panned around with his NTHs at the ready. He thought for a moment that he just imagined seeing the figures, but no—they had been right there. He had seen them standing there thin and tall wearing white course-spun robes stained yellow in the Holystone's light. He didn't recall seeing their faces, for there hadn't been time: only their eyes. Shaken from the phantom encounter, Stenstrom set the Chromatic on the metal floor. He gave it a shove, and it started rolling, slowly at first and then quickening down the corridor. He followed, NTHs ready.

The corridor was like a witch's dance, echoing with disturbing sounds and hidden noise. The previous captain, Captain Gona of St. Paris, had retired, it was said, because he thought the *Seeker* was haunted, and with a cacophony like this, who could blame him? Stenstrom concentrated on his friends: on Captain Davage, on dear Lt. Kilos, and the beautiful Countess Sygillis. This was once their ship; they walked these very corridors. They are still here in the dark somewhere; he tried to remember their goodness and their light.

The Holystone continued on into the dank reaches of the ship, rolling fast with a fuss.

He was moving through the long neck of the vessel. It was quite a walk to its rear section. Wait! Ahead, he saw a figure moving in the dark. "Who's there? Answer me, who's there?"

A chiding laugh came back in return.

He lifted his NTH and cocked the hammer.

"Where is Taara?" he asked, not expecting an answer.

One came: *"We have her. We have your little girl."*

"Return her at once!"

Laughter in response.

"Return her to me!"

"HHHAHAAHAHAAHHAHAAA!!"

There was a momentary respite of silence, then: *"She belongs to us, as do you."*

"Who are you?"

"You know us ..." a voice whispered.

"Show yourself." He whirled around, dropping the yellow Holystone and drawing his second NTH.

"You want her back?" the voice asked.

"Show yourself!"

"Very well..." In the dark a figure emerged, thin and tall, leering and dreadful.

Stenstrom covered it with his pistols.

"If you've come for Taara's soul, you cannot have it," he said.

The figure giggled. *"We are here for a soul, but it's not hers."* It paused. *"We're here for yours."*

It revealed its face: a huge, smiling mouth all over the disk of its face. A great tongue sticking out.

Soul Devourer!!

It cringed and wrung its hands. He raised his NTHs, ready to fire.

"No, no, wait ..." it said. *"We've your friends. I'll let my companions kill them, eat their souls, consigning them to oblivion."*

"Where are they?"

"Not far."

"Show me."

The Soul Devourer led Stenstrom down the corridor. It danced around him, savoring his smell, wringing its clawed hands. It was just barely containing itself.

"Why didn't you just take me on the bridge while I slept and been done with it?"

"Safe on the bridge, couldn't get to you . . . But your friends . . . ahh . . ."

"How do I know they're still alive?"

"Their souls are tiny and bland, hardly worth the trouble, but yours . . . ah, yours shall make fine eating."

It tittered and reached with its hands, opening and closing its fists. *"Took us on a merry run, did you? Think you could get away from us forever?"*

"My mother is gone, and her spells are finished. You ought to go back to where you came from and leave me in peace. You can have my soul once I'm done with it."

"We'll have your soul now! Understand? We'll have it now!!" The Soul Devourer pushed him up against a bulkhead and put its clawed hands at his throat. It lost whatever patience it had and pawed at him. *"They promised us your soul; it belongs to us! Give me your soul!! Give it to me!! GIVE IT TO ME NOW!!"*

Stenstrom pushed his NTHs into its chest and fired. Green light emerged from the Soul Devourer's groaning mouth, and it fell, collapsing into smoking ash.

Panting, feeling the familiar tug in his chest caused by the infernal grasp of the Soul Devourer, he took a moment to compose himself.

Footsteps came running down the corridor!! A tooth-filled, smiling face and reaching hands. *"YOUR SOUL!!"*

He aimed and fired. Its body fell in the dark.

Behind him!

Fire! Two green globes surged out. Did he hit? He wasn't sure. He cocked his hammers and waited.

Laughter came from down the corridor. *"We have your friends. You cannot kill us all. We are ready for you. Keep us waiting and we'll savor their souls in your place."*

"Leave my friends out of this!" he shouted. "My soul for theirs!"

"Then come, come to us . . ."

Mother's demons had finally caught up to him, and now they had his friends. He searched for the Chromatic Holystone, finding it down the corridor, still rolling slowly. Steeling himself and determined to save Taara and A-Ram, he continued on.

3

—LILLY??—

Down the corridor was the Sisters' Priory, a cloistered set of small rooms where the Sisterhood of Light stayed when aboard a Fleet vessel. They often came and went from the Priory and often times disappeared into it, vanishing even when the ship was out far away in the deep sea. Many times, new and unfamiliar faces emerged from the Priory only to vanish back into it just as quickly. Stenstrom thought it was a mystical gateway of some sort. His sorcerous training told him such things could exist.

The Chromatic veered in the direction of the Priory entrance and stopped.

Taara was somewhere inside, A-Ram as well probably, along with who knows how many Soul Devourers.

Within was a small abandoned anti-chamber with an innocent door leading into the interior. All that lay beyond the door was forbidden to any but the Sisters—even the captain of the ship was not allowed past it. Stenstrom himself certainly had never set foot in one. NTHs at the ready, he opened the door; it swung open with a mild squeak.

Musty darkness lay ahead. He entered.

Inside were a confusion of modest rooms and chambers littered with overturned chairs, beds, dressers, and other forgotten bits of furniture once used by the Sisters, all rather sparse and unassuming, now dark and abandoned.

His arcane protections and warning devices were all sounding off at a steady rate, the interior of his HRN vibrated and squirmed as though it were infested with mice. There was danger all around.

"YOUR SOUL!" came a Soul Devourer out of the dark at a run. He shot it down.

Another came, and then another, his NTH shots sending them away one trigger pull at a time. They came at him with no fear, faster than he could cock and fire his NTHs.

One reached out of the dark. He aimed and fired.

Pfft!

Misfire! His cinnabar striker cracked and the NTH didn't fire. He was tackled in the mid-riff by the tittering Soul Devourer. They struggled for a moment as the monster wrangled to get at his soul. He plunged one

MARZABLE after the next into its wiry body, burying the silver daggers up to the hilt, doing nothing. The monster wore a headdress of his daggers as it got its hands to his throat. He felt the tepid beginnings of his soul being siphoned away.

A fast, whirling cone of gritty wind plowed into the both of them. The Soul Devourer was lifted up and pulled away in a roar into the dark where it disappeared.

Stenstrom stood and readied himself for the next wave of them to attack.

Silence. It became very quiet in the corridor of the Priory. No groans, no moans or other hidden sounds, just blessed silence.

His waiting NTHs shook. He sashed the one with the bad striker and waved up three MARZABLES ready to go.

"Bel!" he heard from ahead. He saw a point of light emerge, strong and clear, threatening to blind him. He didn't wait. He fired his NTH and let fly with his MARZABLE. The corridor lit up in emerald green as the deadly globes shot out into the dark. He cocked his hammer and conjured up more daggers.

"Bel, how could you?" he heard a hurt-sounding voice reply. He squinted to see.

The point of light grew to a blinding beam Someone approached in the dark. "Bel, it's me."

"Who are you?" he asked shielding his eyes.

"It's Lilly."

"Lies," Stenstrom said, trying to keep his head. He took aim.

All around him came the hissing of grit rubbing together, like course sand whipped up into a whirling storm. He blinked and covered his eyes with his sleeve.

A lilting form emerged from the gloom ahead holding a lantern. Tall and regal, inviting pink gown, and blonde hair done up in pins and curls, a little parasol resting on her shoulder. It looked for all the world like Lilly, his love.

Lillian of Gamboa.

He stepped back, weapons at the ready.

"Bel . . . it's me. It's Lilly," she said smiling. His danger detectors rattled. His heart pounded.

He struggled to maintain his bearing. "You are not Lilly," he said. "You cannot be Lilly."

"But why?" Her eyes glittered in the lantern light.

"Why? Because I am in the middle of open space on a dead, abandoned ship. Lilly is thousands of Stellar miles away, home on Kana in Esther."

She blushed a bit and raised the lantern. Her blue eyes sparkled. "But, Bel, don't I always arrive when you need me most? Am I not always there to help you?"

She took a step forward. "Stay back!" he cried.

She set the lantern down, reached out, and placed her delicate hands on the barrel of his NTH. "Perhaps you should fire your gun then. Perhaps you should just kill me."

LADY LILLIAN OF GAMBOA???

He struggled. This apparition was a Soul Devourer—it had to be.

"Remember our first meeting in the Chalk House? Remember me drawing my MARTIN on you? Seems so long ago, doesn't it?" she said.

"You are a Soul Devourer come to deceive me."

"How could I know about the Chalk House if I were a Soul Devourer?"

"You could have read my thoughts, peered into my memories, and regurgitated them back to me."

Lilly puzzled a moment. "I don't think Soul Devourers can do such things, always so hungry and driven, they are. They really aren't much into planning things; they just eat."

"How do you know about such creatures? They are spirits of the arcane and not generally known outside of Tyrol."

Lilly gave a small smile. "I know lots of things, Bel. Remember me giving you the idea to become a Fleet Paymaster? Remember me talking you into bribing people and doing questionable things in Calvert? Remember shopping for your coat with me? How happy I was. . .how happy. I remember all those things, because I was there with you. Do you remember the afternoon I gave you the locket with my portrait? How hard I worked on it, it had to be perfect. Remember me offering you five years to explore your heart? Remember that? I sat there and had to watch you fall into the arms of one woman after the next; your 'puppy dogs' I called them. How jealous I was."

"You wanted the five years, Lilly."

"Did I? Did I really, or did someone else make me say that?"

"Who? Who made you?"

Lilly smiled and held her hand out for him to take. "I'll show you."

Mesmerized by her beauty and used to submitting to Lilly's wishes as a matter of habit, he nearly took it. He shook his head, remembered where he was, and stepped back. "I have to save Taara and A-Ram."

"Your friends? No harm shall come to them. I promise."

"How can you make such a promise?"

Lilly came in close; he could feel her heat and smell her perfume—the same scent she always favored wearing. The Soul Devourer wearing her image certainly left nothing to chance.

"Come now, Bel, when have you ever known me not to keep a promise?"

She held her hand out, lit up in the yellowish light of the lantern, impatient for him to take it. He sashed his pistol and shook his hands, producing his various kit of protective Holystones, prisms, and his Astral Plane detector. "Do you mind?" he asked showing them to her.

"Of course not." She gestured to a nearby side room. "May I sit?"

"Of course."

Lilly picked up the lantern and walked into the room. She waited for Stenstrom to offer her a chair. He picked one up, dusted in off, and set it down. She then placed the lantern on the table and properly seated herself, sitting with the same grace and shape Lilly always sat with. She looked up at him, waiting for him to begin the examination.

He hoisted his prism to his right eye and carefully looked her over. If Lilly was a Soul Devourer wearing a disguise, she should appear fuzzy and indistinct, possibly tinged with red. He saw none of that. He switched prisms; again she appeared normal.

He set the prisms down and picked up his silver pyramid, moving it up her arm past the wrist. "What is this one?" she asked.

"Astral Plane detector. If you've been to the Astral Plane, it will react."

"I see. Are you expecting such a thing?"

"Possibly. I've encountered it before."

His detector remained inert. He put it away and ran his crimson Holystone down her arm, rolling it along her skin. "This one should detect the presence of Soul Devourers."

"Oh my. Is it reacting?"

Stenstrom took the crimson Holystone and held it close to his face, examining it for damage. "No. It's not."

"Well then," Lilly said happily, tapping her fingers on the table. "It's settled, per your instrumentality. I'm no Soul Devourer."

He held the crimson Holystone to the lantern lens, dousing it in the strong yellow light, further inspecting it. This apparition had to be a Soul Devourer; she had to be.

He noticed the lantern. It wasn't just an ordinary lantern one might see anywhere, it was exquisite. It was made of beaten copper, molded and inlaid with lapis, gold, silver and garnets. Its lens was some sort of flawless crystal, and the light coming from it wasn't produced by a conventional power source, like a battery pack and a filament or nano tech; nor was it a candle and mere flame; it was some sort of arcane glow.

"What is this?" he asked in wonder.

Lilly stood and put her arms around him. "I borrowed the lantern from home. I'll need to have it back soon. I think it's called *Paramel*. It illuminates much."

He moved his olive Holystone along the lantern's copper face. It rattled steadily.

"What is that?" Lilly asked.

"This Holystone detects the presence of the arcane. See . . ." the Holystone created steady noise next to the lantern. He took it and moved the olive stone along Lilly's arm. It continued to rattle.

"Ah," he said, "look here!"

"It seems to be making quite a bit of noise," Lilly remarked.

"Yes, it does. That means you are of the arcane as well."

He expected her to protest or make some plausible argument against her being of the arcane.

"But of course I'm of the arcane, Bel," she replied, smiling.

"Lilly, *my Lilly*, is not of the arcane. She is a sweet, wholesome girl of Esther. She is rooted in the mundane."

She laughed. "Oh Bel, can it be you have never put things in the proper perspective all this time? It's really rather shocking considering your training.

I should think you'd have an eye for such things." She rolled her eyes back in fond remembrance. "I remember seeing you as a little boy as you walked down Tyrol Lane, running away from home. Remember that? I fell in love with you right there and then, I think."

Stenstrom froze. He remembered that event from his childhood. The terror it still inspired in him, how alone he felt. "That . . . was just a dream."

"No, no it wasn't, Bel, and you know it."

"Then that means you're the Lady in Gray, the woman in the hat who tried to kill me."

"I've never worn gray in my life, Bel. And I would never try to kill you. If I would have stayed and witnessed what transpired that night in the park, I would have helped you. There would be no Lady in Gray today, for I'd have killed her."

"Are you a killer, Lilly?"

She seemed stung a bit. "No! No . . . but . . ." Lilly took a moment and composed herself. She moved onto another topic. "And then ... and then there was that time during your training in the culvert under your manor grounds when you walked away from your mother ... I was there with you, Bel."

"I didn't know you then."

"But I knew you. And then there was that time at the university . . ."

He stood there staring at her. "What are you, Lilly?"

She held out her hand. "Come, let me show you. Come see."

He went to take her hand, and then stopped himself. "But, Taara, A-Ram?"

"They're safe, I swear it."

He stood there, wondering if he could actually trust her or not.

"Bel, I swear your friends are safe."

Finally, Stenstrom took Lilly's hand. With her free hand, she picked up the lantern, and they went deep into the Priory following the penetrating yellow beam of the lantern. Very quickly, he no longer felt like he was on the *Seeker*. He felt the temperature change from the cold staleness of the ship to the cool humid of early night. Leaves crunched under his boots; overhead, he saw familiar evening stars in a clear azure sky.

"Is this Kana?" he asked.

"Where else?"

"How can we be on Kana?"

Lilly didn't answer. She skipped along and hummed, swinging the lantern with its eternal beam panning back and forth. They seemed to be moving through a dense, needle tree forest. The lantern cut a clear path through the murky trees. Lilly was invigorated and child-like. The Lilly he knew was reserved and composed.

"Ah, home. Home!" she cried. "It feels so good!"

"This landscape doesn't look like Gamboa," Stenstrom said.

"I'm not from Gamboa, Bel. I went there once out of curiosity and didn't like it much. So stony and closed-in. Too overcast." Lilly twirled around, enjoying the cool, damp air, the lantern rattling in her hand. "This is where I'm from."

She beamed. "Oh ... you must have so many question for me, and, at long last, I'm going to answer. I'm going to properly introduce myself to you, Bel, all of me, and nothing will be left to chance."

They crossed a shallow creek flowing with cold water and came into a clearing. Far off to the north was a tumbled barricade of massive gray mountains frosted in snow. Only one place possessed a mountain range like that on Kana: Vithland, the lands of his friend and mentor, Captain Davage.

"Are we in Vithland, Lilly?"

She laughed. "Come on, just a bit farther."

Continuing through the clearing, Lilly became more and more excited. She giggled and bounced on the balls of her feet. "You don't know how long I've wanted to share this with you!"

"Why didn't you?"

"Because they make me tell you lies. I don't like lying. It doesn't seem right."

"Who? Who makes you tell lies?"

Again, Lilly didn't respond. They entered into a small glade. The ruins of some ancient Vith structure sat in the center of it. It was mostly down to the foundations, sunken into the ground and mirror-like with a coating of cold shallow water. The ruins continued on to the west and were apparently quite extensive.

"This is an old Chapter House where the people used to meet. There's still a little left of them here in this water. This is where I come to find things out when they won't tell me what I want to know. This is where I've watched you from."

Watched him? Lilly's been watching him from afar? The thought gave him a rather uncomfortable feeling. He was square with the notion of looking in on other people, but not being looked in on himself.

"I do not like the idea of you spying on me, Lilly," he said.

"I'm sorry," she replied, rather perfunctorily.

Lilly approached a protruding buttress and placed the lantern on top of it. She then pulled off her shoes and waded into the shallow water, savoring the feeling. "Come on in, Bel. The water feels so good."

"Lilly, I've not the time."

She wouldn't give in. "Come in, Bel. There are things I want to show you."

He sighed and removed his HRN, folding it up and placing it next to the chapter house foundation. Without removing his boots, he waded in. The water was shallow, barely covering his shins. Lilly giggled.

"All right, Lilly. I'm in the water with you. What did you want to show me?"

She splashed to the lantern and pointed the lens at him, engulfing him in the yellow beam. "Does that hurt?" she asked.

"Of course not."

"Good, that means you're not evil then," she said with a wink. Lilly opened a small door near the lens. Inside there was a yellowish, facetted crystal mounted on its points so that it could rotate on its axis, and she gave it a fast spin. Globes of multi-colored light came drifting out of the lantern, racing through the water in rapid, circular pools.

"I wanted to show you these things that I've seen, Bel. I can help you. I want to help you."

A blue circle of light moved through the water. In it, an image formed. It was that of a small Fleet vessel, white with a central saucer and three curved tubes arranged around the saucer. It looked like a Fleet scouting ship. The ship was studded with the barrels of run-out guns.

"I've seen this ship quite a bit lately. I think the lady captaining it is hoping to bring you in so she can gloat."

In the pool of blue light, the stern, unsmiling face of Captain Gwendolyn came into focus: tall, her brown hair pulled back into her hat, given a wide berth by her crew.

Her rapier was drawn and held fast in a strong hand.

"She's a Zenon woman," Lilly added. "I think Zenon women are very snobby, don't you? Not your type at all. She's coming to kill you, Bel. Look at her sword, look at the guns ready to fire. Her ship is small, compared to yours, but it functions, and she has a crew and she's armed. I can . . . I can take care of her for you, if you like, Bel. Would you like that?"

"Take care of her? How so? There's no Priory on a scouting ship, so you have no way to get aboard."

Lilly blushed. "I have my ways."

Stenstrom watched the image of the ship as it glided through space, hot on his trail and studded with guns and a captain with a drawn sword. "No, Lilly. I'll deal with it myself when the times comes."

"Are you certain?"

"Of course."

Lilly splashed up to him and stood on the tops of his submerged boots. "Oh, you are so quaint, Bel; that's why I love you so. You have such resources available to you, and you choose to forego them and accomplish things the hard way. What if this Zenon woman aboard the scouting ship shoots her way aboard your ship? You'll lose your chair, will certainly be sent back to the Fleet, and possibly Barred into trial. You could face censure or worse."

"Let me deal with her. I've a good ship, even unpowered, unarmed and unlit, and my crew is the best."

"All two of them?"

"They are all I require."

Lilly laughed. "All right, Bel, have it your way. When I'm rescuing you from prison as I'm certain I shall soon be doing, don't ever forget that I offered to spare you such an inconvenience."

He struggled to make sense of all this. Though Lilly was speaking plainly, she was never more cryptic. How was she doing this? How was she doing any of it??

Lilly adjusted the lantern. "Let me show you a few more things." As the blue pool of light containing the image of Captain Gwendolyn went out, it was replaced by a green one, moving across the water. In the light, Stenstrom saw an odd lumpy shape, green in color, like a great bean sprout. He looked closer, there were two heads sticking out of the sprout. One had blonde hair.

A-Ram?

Yes, it was A-Ram, and Stenstrom thought, at first, that A-Ram had been devoured by a gigantic plant with only his head sticking out. On second glance, he saw that A-Ram was actually sitting on the ground huddled up next to a second person whom Stenstrom didn't know. It was a female with pinned-up black hair. She was wearing a vast green cloak and had it draped around A-Ram, sharing it with him. It looked like a comfortable place to be.

The green circle of light faded and was replaced by a red one. "Look at this, Bel. I've also been seeing this . . ."

In the red light, he saw a mass of chaotic movement, like looking into a beehive. He appeared to be seeing a multitude of tiny bits of machinery, squared-off, finely crafted and etched, moving in an orderly confusion. There were four distinct colors to the tiny machines: yellow, blue, green and red. Stenstrom and Lilly watched as the tiny machines separated themselves into their respective colors and then began forming roughly man-shaped masses.

"Do you know what these are?" Lilly asked.

"No. Looks like robotistry or nano tech. That's not my area."

Lilly gazed at the tiny machines buzzing with movement. "Whatever they are, they mean you no good, Bel, of that I'm certain. Look …"

In the red light, a man was on his knees, surrounded, hacked to pieces, moments away from death.

"I'm worried for you, Bel."

"I can handle myself."

"Did you not see that? I think that man on his knees was you."

Lilly gazed at the circle of light. "I've been searching for these men or machines or whatever they are. So far they've eluded me, but when I find them, I am going to finish them for no one will put my Bel on his knees. No one." There was a hard edge to Lilly's voice.

The image faded. The last thing Stenstrom saw was a great yellow circle swirling in the water.

"I see this circle a lot when I look in on you. Circles and circles."

Stenstrom observed the circle. He could see faces locked within its boundaries. He saw himself and Taara and A-Ram. Odd, he saw the squared-off yet pretty face of his pursuer, Lt. Gwendolyn. He also saw four tall figures swaying in the background. Surrounding the circle was a fifth figure clad in gray rapidly approaching.

Clad in gray? The woman from his fox park nightmare. The Astral Traveler? He looked away. When he looked back the images in the circle were gone.

Lilly rose up and kissed him, and for a moment he forgot about his situation and his crew and that this creature, with apparently vast arcane capabilities, couldn't possibly be Lilly.

The kiss felt like Lilly. It had her warmth and feeling.

What could she be? What was she? He should be impassive and calculating as his mother taught him when faced with the arcane, collecting data, demanding answers, sorting out truth from conjecture. But, come to think of it, Mother had hand-picked Lilly herself. She picked her not merely for her grace and beauty, but for her normalcy, her seemingly entrenched hold on the mundane and the well-trodden. Mother hadn't wanted a sorceress for her son, another Tyrol graduate of the black schools, a brewer of poisons and caster of spells. She wanted a quiet, unremarkable woman, someone stately and of society to sit in the parlor and love her son as a proper lady should, balancing his forays into the dark woods of sorcery with the more well-lit paths of the mundane world.

And, she'd picked Lilly. Nothing odd about Lilly, nothing supernatural about Lilly.

But look: Lilly appearing from nowhere, Lilly possessing some sort of vast power with access to arcane devices like the Paramel, Lilly triggering his arcane detectors, Lilly fooling his mother into thinking she was from unremarkable Gamboa, when she was, in fact, from the wilds of Vithland in an area simply crawling with the arcane.

Lilly was some sort of monster.

But, all that mattered little at the moment. Her embrace was comforting, her kiss sweet and familiar, bringing back all those memories of the woman he loved.

She leaned against him. He could feel the ovular shape of the locket in his breast pocket pressing against his heart.

He put his arms around her, savoring her feel.

"I take back my false words, Bel," she said between kisses, "I don't want five years, I never did. I want you now, with me forever. Make me yours."

"I've always been yours, Lilly. As before, I extend you my hand."

"And I accept. I accept, I accept." She leaned back and shouted into the cool air: "I ACCEPT!" She screamed it into the air, as if to make her voice heard to those listening from a far. "And now, it's time that I told you exactly what I am, so that you'll understand. I ..."

A horn sounded in the distance, filling the clearing and chapter house ruins with a melancholy note. Lilly's demeanor instantly changed. She cut herself off in mid-sentence, cringed and scowled. She stomped through the shallow water and kicked "No!" she screamed. "It's not fair! Not fair! I'm not ready!"

"What?" Stenstrom asked.

"They're calling me! I thought I'd have more time!"

"Who are?"

"Them!" Lilly pointed.

Through the trees, Stenstrom thought he could see a domed structure made of gray stone. A door slid open. Sitting inside were four indistinct figures.

The horn sounded again, and the wooded setting became cloudy. Stenstrom felt himself being pulled back into the dank confines of the *Seeker*, leaving Vithland and Lilly behind.

"They did it, Bel!" Lilly shouted as he was pulled away. "They did it all . . ."

The next moment, Stenstrom was back aboard the *Seeker*, the yellow light of the lantern fading.

"Remember, Bel . . ." came the ghost of Lilly's voice. *"You just extended me your hand, and I'm not giving it back."*

He was standing in the darkened rooms of the Priory. What had he just seen? Was that apparition really Lilly? He hadn't felt threatened. It seemed like Lilly, smelled like Lilly . . . felt like her.

The olive Holystone had determined Lilly was of an arcane nature. Lilly had always seemed so grounded to him, so steady and sure, painting her pictures in Gamboa. She was a rock of sanity and sure footing in an occasional turbid shoreline of mysticism and fog-shrouded places his mother took him to.

And now it's proved she is of the arcane.

"I'm not from Gamboa, Bel."

He pressed on into the depths of the Priory, finding nothing but overturned chairs and unmade beds, the Sisters long gone and all the magic sucked out of the place.

"A-Ram!" he cried. "Taara!"

No answer.

His mind spun. Lilly not from Gamboa. Lilly something other than just a beautiful woman. He reached a locked door. He took a moment to replace the bad striker in his NTH, discarding the cracked one.

Lilly couldn't have been a Soul Devourer in disguise, or she would have attacked. Soul Devourers were driven by their lust and hunger for souls; even the one that was supposed to lead him to Taara and A-Ram couldn't resist and attacked him en route.

Lilly didn't attack him. God's, what did Lady Alitrix say?

"I don't know what she is, but she's not a woman."

And Kaly that time at the dock:

"I saw you walking down the street with a mannequin."

He pulled on the door harder and it wouldn't budge.

Locked tight.

What did Kaly see? What was Alitrix sensing?

What was Lilly? She had been on the verge of telling him but had been summoned by her masters. Whatever she was, he had just offered her his hand. That, given the circumstances, probably wasn't wise. He had just committed himself to some sort of monster.

He sashed his NTHs and had his lock picks ready with a wave of the hand. He stuck his probe in and tested the lock. Though the door appeared old and simple, its lock was complex, very sophisticated and trapped—he could feel a coiled needle hidden in the lock's working ready to spring.

"They did it. They did it all!" Lilly said.

Who was "they?" Stenstrom shuddered to find out.

He selected his picks and skillfully worked the lock, disarming the needle in the process. Soon, the lock was picked clean. He put his picks back into his HRN and drew his NTHs.

He pulled the door open. Something fell out to the floor with a limp thud. A thin, sinewy arm lay there. It was a slender arm, like a lady's, smooth and delicate, only the hand at the end of the arm gave it away that it was something more sinister: the fingers curled, gnarled, and studded with claws. Stenstrom swung the door open wide and aimed down, ready to fire.

A Soul Devourer lie there, its gigantic mouth and elongated tongue lolled on the floor. It appeared to be dead. It smoked slightly. He knelt down into the grit and inspected the body. Its neck appeared to be broken, and only recently so. It was still warm. Taking no chances, he put two NTH shots into its chest. It collapsed into ash.

Beyond the door was a long corridor. Continuing on, he found another Soul Devourer lying on the floor, and then another, both dead.

More bodies waited for him further down. Look at them: piled up in heaps, hanging from the ceiling, curled up on the ground, more than he cared to count; all dead. Some were arranged in fanciful, post-mortem positions. Some were lying there holding hands, and some were propped up against each other chest to chest, fingers inter-laced like they were dancing. Several were seated at a small table as if they were having a tea party. All dead, dead bodies pushed into seated positions around the table in the illusion of merriment, their tongues all tied together in the center, knotted.

What had happened here? Could Lilly have done all this, killed all these supernatural creatures by herself.

How?

The corridor ended in a transparent dome that jutted out the underbelly of the ship, lit up in stars and some sort of bright yellowish cloud that seethed with energy. He wondered what it was for a moment—oh, it's Druries Belt. He remembered.

The Sisters' dome was some sort of meeting place lined with consoles that rolled and sputtered with hazy life. Wooden benches lined the dome, like a courtroom. This must be the heart of the Priory, a place only the Sisters had previously seen.

More Soul Devourers, everywhere. Dead, mangled, pushed against the dome, slumped over the railing, one dangling by its tongue from a light fixture.

In the center of the dome was a wooden dais. Two figures were slumped atop it.

Taara and A-Ram!

He made his way to the top of the dais. Taara and A-Ram appeared to both be submerged in a deep sleep. They were warm, and their pulses were good. Taara was sitting there in her white untucked shirt and woolen socks. A-Ram's MOLLY gleamed around her neck. As before, she snored slightly.

A pink slip of paper was stuffed into A-Ram's coat pocket. It read:

I told you they would be fine
—Lilly

"Taara!" he said, trying to wake her up. "Taara!" He tapped her twice on the cheek. She didn't awake. It was the same with A-Ram, deep in sleep.

He hoisted the two of them over his shoulder and carried them out. They were both so light, like carrying children.

He went down the long corridor, passing all the carnage along the way. He was glad they weren't awake to see any of it.

All the bodies. The charnel house of Soul Devourers, all killed and posed by Lilly.

Recent events sorted themselves out in his mind.

Lilly, no longer a stately girl from Gamboa.

Lilly, an arcane being of great strength.

"*I accept.*"

Lilly, a killer.

"*I accept. . .*"

Lilly, his betrothed.

"*I ACCEPT!!*"

He made his way out of the Priory and back down the long corridor to the bridge, the ship serenading them the entire way. Up the lift shaft and back into the bridge they went, like nothing ever happened, save for the troubling thoughts rolling through Stenstrom's head.

Soul Devourers . . .

Lilly in the dark . . .

"*I ACCEPT!*"

4

—Druries Belt—

Stenstrom laid them out on the floor of the bridge. "Taara! Taara, wake up!"

She stirred. "Hey, Bel . . . how about a few more minutes? I was having a nice dream. Okay?"

"Taara, you've been asleep for twenty hours; we all have. We're missing our burn!"

That news opened her eyes. She sat up. "What? Twenty hours? Bel, we can't miss that burn, or we'll be headed out into the Wildlands." She wobbled to her feet and grabbed her boots.

They turned to A-Ram and shook him awake. Eventually he stirred and awoke, holding his head. "Gods, I feel like I've slept for days," he said.

"You have."

"I seem to recall dreaming of . . . monsters."

Quite appropriate, Stenstrom thought.

A-Ram made his way to the helm and was shocked. "For the love of Creation, we've slept through our burn!"

Taara pulled on her boots and ran into his office. She checked her sextant, pointing it toward the window. The great yellowish rope of Druries Belt stretched off into the distance.

She cursed as she worked.

"Taara, what's our bearing?" A-Ram asked.

She stared out the window, gazing through the sextant.

"Taara!"

"Give me a minute, will you! Gods, we are well off course!"

Stenstrom watched her work. "What's that going to do to us, Taara? Can we get back on course?"

"We're way out of the shipping lanes, that's for sure." She ran back into the bridge and flopped into the Missive's chair. She brought up a screen and punched in a series of numbers.

Feeling drained, Stenstrom plunged into his chair and closed his eyes.

His leaden thoughts spun.

Captain Gwendolyn coming in her scout ship to board and possible kill him.

Lilly killed over a hundred Soul Devourers. He, with just his two pistols, would probably have been overwhelmed.

"A-Ram, hard to port three turns, Z minus 15 degrees," Taara said.

He heard the helm groan as A-Ram turned the pegs.

"They did it!" Lilly said.

Who are "they?"

Taara again, her little voice confident and full of authority. "I'm burning the *Westminster* for five minutes, in three, two, one . . ."

The ship shuddered.

"I accept," Lilly said again in his mind. *"I accept."*

"Bel, Bel, wake up."

He opened his eyes. Taara and A-Ram stood over him. "Did I sleep?"

"Sure did. Just a few minutes."

He stood up, seeing the now familiar environs of the bridge laid out with the clunky machinery of their threadbare existence on the ship: the stolen generators and dangling wires, the hiss of the Macon, and the bundle of insta-meals.

"Are we back on course?"

"Yep!" Taara said. "All fixed."

"A-Ram, how's the helm?"

"Locked and marked. We shouldn't need another burn until we get to Onaris, about four days hence."

Stenstrom thought about it. Taara and A-Ram could have been killed. Look at all of this: the dead ship, the jury-rigged parts, the vast gulf between here and their destination, a ship full of demons and a possible confrontation looming with Captain Gwendolyn. Had he the right to endanger Taara and A-Ram any further?

"I'm thinking . . ."

"Thinking what, Bel?" Taara asked.

"I think we should turn around and head back to Kana, and I should give myself up. I can't endanger you two any further. Creation knows if this scuttled tub is up to making the journey to Bazz. It'll probably break down right in the middle of nowhere. And then there's Captain Gwendolyn and her scouting ship. You two don't need that sort of trouble."

"What's brought this on, Bel?" A-Ram asked. "Did something happen while we were asleep?"

Stenstrom considered his answer. "You, and Taara were abducted and taken into the rear section of the ship, Deck 7, deep in the Sister's Priory."

"Who abducted us?"

"Demons, and, no, they weren't after Taara's soul, they were after mine. They abducted you to get to me."

A-Ram turned a slight shade of white. "And, what happened? You rescued us?"

Stenstrom shook his head. "No. No I didn't."

"Then who did?"

"The apparition of the woman I love; Lillian of Gamboa."

Taara was stumped. "You mean the blonde-headed lady in your locket?"

"The very one."

"What was she doing here?"

Stenstrom sighed. "Apparently, she's a monster too. She was waiting for me down there in the dark, dressed in pink. Pink is such a lovely color on her. And she killed every one of the demons holding you two. She stacked their bodies up and arranged them in fanciful poses—always the artist, Lilly. And then she demanded I offer her my hand, and I gave it to her. I really couldn't help myself."

Taara and A-Ram stood there listening.

"And so, I want to come about, head back to Kana as best we can and pray the ship holds together. There's some deviltry here. I don't think you two will get into trouble. They just want me."

He closed his eyes and thought about all that awaited him. When he opened them, Taara was leaning over him.

"Well heck Bel, if you're worried about your lady, I'll date you."

He chuckled, despite himself. "I'll keep that in mind, Taara. Come on, let's get this ship turned around."

"Now look, Bel," Taara said. "If you think you're doing us some sort of favor by returning to Kana, you're wrong. I don't want to go back, and I don't need you to fret over me like I'm some stupid kid. I want to be here. I want to go to Bazz, and when we get there we can say we did it all on our own, just the three of us. Look what we accomplished. Sending me back to Kana so I can guard the statue again and be despised by my entire company because I'm a screw-up isn't doing me any particular favors." She turned to A-Ram. "What about you?"

A-Ram held onto the pegs of the helm. "Well, I certainly don't want to see any monsters, that's for certain, and I also don't want to get into a shootout with a Fleet vessel. Bel, you don't strike me as an unreasonable fellow, I'm certain things won't come to that. Piloting a Fleet ship at sea is what I've always dreamed of doing, and, after this experience, after laying my hands on the wheel, I don't think I could go back to the Admiral's office again. I. . . ." He gave a sheepish laugh. "This has been exhilarating, quite frankly, and everything I'd hoped it might be. I have faith in you and in Taara that we'll all be just fine."

Taara beamed. "This is a great ship, Bel, don't let her current condition fool you. The Admiralty has taken away almost everything, but not her heart. And she, through us, is going to prove to them back there at the Fleet that she is not done, even if she has to go to Bazz crawling, on her knees. If she breaks along the way, she breaks. So what? We'll fix her. We've already done the hard part, the rest is easy. So, enough talk of quitting, Bel. We've got a job to do, so let's get to it. We've got some brandy to deliver. What do you say?"

"Lilly's apparition also shared with me a few visions of the future, and some of the items I saw appeared rather disturbing."

"Oh, no, no," Taara said. "The future sucks, that's what we say on Bazz. All those damn prophetesses, don't listen to any of them. They'll scare you to death if you let them. The future always looks a lot scarier than it actually is. You'll give yourself an ulcer, trust me."

Stenstrom peered into his office and saw the carpet of stars bisected by the glowing line of Druries Belt with Ole' Scrub, their destination, hanging in the distance. Taara's homemade sextant lay on his desk.

"All right," he said with new vigor. "If you two are game, let's do this. Taara, man your post."

She cheered and plopped back down into the Missive's chair.

"A-Ram, how's the helm?" he asked.

"A little heavy, but otherwise wonderful."

"Well then. We've a slow few days ahead of us. Things will probably be quite dull until they're not, then we'll deal with 'whatever' accordingly."

They settled into their positions and listened to the Macon clank.

On to Bazz.

What more could possibly happen?

Appendix I

THE HOUSE OF BELMONT–SOUTH TYROL

STENSTROM, 8ᵀᴴ LORD HOUSE OF BELMONT

JUBILEE, 3ᴿᴰ LADY, HOUSE OF TYROL

(KEY: B: BLACK, P: PEWTERLOCK, H/P: HALF-PEWTERLOCK)

Name	Number	Type	Name	Number	Type
Beryla	03117AX	B	Deneba	03158AX	P
Wisteria	03119AX	B	Jonnia	03160AX	B
Antonia	03122AX	P	Kormandia	03162AX	P
Celesta	03125AX	P	Deserae	03164AX	B
Munni	03127AX	B	Elma	03167AX	B
Solona	03130AX	P	Nathalie	03169AX	B
Sabra	03133AX	H/P	Embeth	03172AX	B
Andromeda	03135AX	P	Constance	03174AX	P
Phaedra	03139AX	B	Willia	03176AX	P
Ione	03141AX	Bl	Nylar	03179AX	H/P
Io	03144AX	B	Xantrope	03182AX	H/P
Miranda	03147AX	P	Lucile	03184AX	H/P
Calami	03149AX	P	Virginia	03187AX	H/P
Persephone	03152AX	B	Lyra	03189AX	B
Lenta	03154AX	P	Stenstrom (M)	03192AX	B

A Note From Author Chantal Boudreau

I'm glad that Ren Garcia is friendly and persistent; otherwise I may have never gotten around to reading his wonderful books. I resisted at first. To begin with, I have a preference for horror and fantasy, and I'm picky about what I read in the way of science fiction and steampunk. Ren's series had a sci-fi/steampunk vibe, which made me wary about trying it out. Secondly, his world-building seemed pretty elaborate from the outside looking in, and my experience with that type of writing is that authors are often so proud of what they have created, they wedge unnecessary details into their stories in encyclopaedic segments just to show-off the end results of their developmental efforts. Those sorts of superfluous descriptions bore the stuffing out of me. Lastly, from what I could see, Ren's characters struck me as larger-than-life and I'm partial to realistic and flawed characters. At a glance I didn't think his stories were for me—but I was wrong.

Fortunately, once I had befriended Ren as a fellow writer who could share advice and ideas, he started playing little excerpt war games with me. He would toss one out from one of his books, or I would present something from my Masters & Renegades series, to start things off. The other was expected to counter with an excerpt of a similar vein, competing to see if one of us could trump the other. The more I read of his excerpts, the more intrigued I was, and the more I questioned my original assumptions. Yes, there was a fair amount of steampunk and science fiction elements to his books, but he had that refreshing cross-genre approach that also included a good deal of horror and fantasy. Yes, his world-building was extremely elaborate, but from the excerpts he shared, the many details he included were well-integrated into his stories. And finally, yes, his characters were somewhat larger-than-life, but they were also both flawed and incredibly interesting.

So he triggered my curiosity and I bought the first book. I was anything but disappointed with his delightful work and I've been hungry to purchase and read everything else he has put out since. Ren had created a series that was spectacularly original, a new form of space fantasy that in some ways harkened back to the cliff-hanger series of old, full of action and adventure, and in other ways presented a visionary new approach to speculative fiction, filled with quirky wonder and great passion, but also riddled with the sort of darkness you might expect from Lovecraft.

I have definitely added this series to my list of favourites when anyone asks. I've fallen in love with his multi-layered and extremely heroic characters (especially Carahil and Ki.) I encourage everyone I can to read his books, because it is an experience that few regret, and I'd like to think that this book, as well as those that preceded it, might live on as classics someday.

Kudos to you, Ren.

-Chantal Boudreau, Nova Scotia, Canada
Author of the Fervor dystopian series and the Masters & Renegades fantasy series

--WHAT UNSPEAKABLE HORROR LURKS IN THE
BOWELS OF THE SEEKER?

FIND OUT IN THE EXCITING CONCLUSION:

Against the Druries

FROM: LOCONEAL PUBLISHING

Author Information

Ren Garcia is a Science Fiction/Fantasy author and Texas native who grew up in western Ohio. He has been writing since before he could write, often scribbling alien lingo on any available wall or floor with assorted crayons. He attended The Ohio State University and majored in English Literature. Ren has been an avid lover of anything surreal since childhood. He also has a passion for caving, urban archaeology and architecture. He currently lives in Columbus, Ohio with his wife, and their four dogs.

PUBLISHER INFORMATION

VISIT THE LOCONEAL BLOG AT

www.loconeal.com

Breaking News
Forthcoming Releases
Links to Author Sites
Loconeal Events